Y041054

M. A. Hu[illegible] s since a young age and always fancied the idea of trying to write one. That dream became a reality when One More Chapter signed The Missing Children Case Files.

Born in Darlington in the north-east of England, Hunter grew up in West London, and moved to Southampton to study law at university. It's here that Hunter fell in love and has been married for fifteen years. They are now raising their two children on the border of The New Forest where they enjoy going for walks amongst the wildlife. They regularly holiday across England, but have a particular affinity for the south coast, which formed the setting for the series, spanning from Devon to Brighton, and with a particular focus on Weymouth, one of their favourite towns.

When not writing, Hunter can be found binge-watching favourite shows or buried in the latest story from Angela Marsons, Simon Kernick, or Ann Cleeves.

twitter.com/Writer_MAHunter

D1420157

Also by M. A. Hunter

The Missing Children Case Files

Ransomed

Isolated

Trafficked

Repressed

Exposed

DISCARDED

The Missing Children Case Files

M. A. HUNTER

One More Chapter
a division of HarperCollins*Publishers*
1 London Bridge Street
London SE1 9GF
www.harpercollins.co.uk

HarperCollins*Publishers*
1st Floor, Watermarque Building, Ringsend Road
Dublin 4, Ireland

1
This paperback edition 2021
First published in Great Britain in ebook format
by HarperCollins*Publishers* 2021

Copyright © M. A. Hunter 2021
M. A. Hunter asserts the moral right to be identified as the author of this work

A catalogue record of this book is available from the British Library

ISBN: 978-0-00-844335-1

This novel is entirely a work of fiction. The names, characters and incidents portrayed in it are the work of the author's imagination. Any resemblance to actual persons, living or dead, events or localities is entirely coincidental.

Printed and bound in Great Britain by
CPI Group (UK) Ltd, Croydon CR0 4YY

All rights reserved. No part of this publication may be reproduced, stored in a retrieval system, or transmitted, in any form or by any means, electronic, mechanical, photocopying, recording or otherwise, without the prior permission of the publishers.

Content notices: domestic violence, paedophilia, sexual assault, drug abuse, child abuse.

Dedicated to 'Little' David Knowles
who passed away in December 2020.
Thank you for 27 years of great memories.

The road was jagged
Over sharp stones:
Your body's too ragged
To cover your bones.

The wind scatters
Tears upon dust;
Your soul's in tatters
Where the spears thrust.

– *Fire and Sleet and Candlelight*, Elinor Wylie

Chapter One

THEN

Portland, Dorset

Incandescent with rage, Joanna strode on, only once daring to sneak a glance back over her shoulder to where her sister watched on.

'Stupid baby toy,' she muttered under her breath, the salty breeze cooling the small blot of tears that had started forming around her eyes. 'I don't need it, and I don't need *them*.'

Everyone always said Joanna was very mature for her age, and maybe that was part of the problem: they could see she was mature, but still treated her as a child. It wasn't fair. She was practically ten anyway, and clearly her parents considered her old enough to watch over her kid sister while they *talked*, so they couldn't complain that she'd decided to walk to the shop to buy herself some sweets; she'd probably be home before they even realised anyway.

The cause of this latest outburst – one in a long line of recent disagreements blown over the top – was the seeming lack of reward for this term's school report. Joanna had worked hard to earn her high grades in English, Maths, and Science, but just because her younger sister had received a special mention in the end of term newsletter, she'd been given a new skateboard. How was that fair? Where was Joanna's own skateboard, or age-appropriate gift, for doing so well? Were strong grades in English, Maths, and Science really worth less than the piece of music her sister had learned to play on that damned recorder?

And she'd missed a note when she'd played it!

But there was no mention of that slip-up in the newsletter that was now stuck to the front of the fridge, with copies sent out to family members far and wide.

'We've high hopes for you,' their father had said at breakfast, still beaming. 'Today, the school assembly, but tomorrow, maybe the Philharmonic Orchestra!'

Yeah, sure, Dad, they have recorder players in the Philharmonic Orchestra!

Joanna had only asked for one turn on the bloody skateboard, to show her sister how to do it right, but would she listen? No! Always thought she knew better, that one. Well, Joanna would show her. She'd take the pound coin she'd earned for tidying her bedroom, and she'd buy chocolate, and casually walk home, eating it. Then her sister would know who the big fish in the family was!

But as she now looked up to get her bearings, she realised she'd missed the usual cut way that led up to the local shop. In fact, she'd missed it by quite some distance, and she wasn't totally certain she knew where she was. The sea gulls cawed nearby, but she couldn't get a sense of which end of the island she'd been walking towards. There was something vaguely familiar about the boarded-up fish and chip shop on the corner, the picture of the navy-blue fish on the orange backdrop looking ghastly. If she kept walking straight she would eventually come to one side of the shoreline or the other, or she'd see the signs for Weymouth and realise she'd walked far too far.

Stopping for a moment, and sweeping the hazelnut fringe out of her eyes, she took in the full horizon, looking for any indication of just how far she'd come. Wasn't this the way their mum drove them to the dentist? Their dentist was on the way to Weymouth town centre, and so they made the six-monthly visit by car. Most of the time, Joanna had her head buried in a book of poetry or literature, and she didn't bother to take in the scenery around her.

Not wanting to retrace her steps, she continued onwards, turning down past the fish and chip shop. If she was right, and this was the road to the dentist, then there should be a…

The smile broke across her face as she spotted the small newsagent's shop with the giant plastic ice-cream cone standing outside of it. Joanna remembered *this* shop, because every time they went to the dentist, her sister would whine and crave an ice cream that big, even though she'd have no chance of holding something so large, let alone eating it. That didn't stop her droning on about it though. And if anyone ever did invent an ice cream that big, she'd bet her parents would somehow find the money to buy it for her sister. That meant Joanna must have walked further than she'd expected, though she couldn't spot the coastline in any direction.

Thrusting her hands into her pockets, she playfully ran her fingertips around the rough edges of the pound coin. One day, when she was older and she had children of her own, she would make sure they were treated equally; no special measures for the younger child. And both children would be allowed to choose whether they wanted to buy sweets or not. Joanna knew all about healthy diets, and very rarely asked for chocolate or sweets, but every once in a while couldn't hurt, and that was why she was now determined to buy herself a treat. She wouldn't use the entire pound right now. She'd use some of it, and keep some for the next time her sister got on her nerves. After all, she'd managed to find the newsagent's shop this time without too much fuss, and so a return trip one day wouldn't be out of the question.

Entering the shop, she was immediately hit by the wave of warm air that hung at head-height. It actually felt warmer in the shop than it had outside, where the sea breeze was pushing the few clouds in the otherwise crystal-blue sky. Clearly, the owner didn't believe in the merits of air conditioning. The shop was about the size of her bedroom, but it was crammed full. Colourful magazines – like the ones her grandma read – lined the shelves, and above those were the magazines her dad would occasionally buy when Mum wasn't around. The opposite wall, by comparison, was a thing of beauty. The shelves were chockful of colourful wrappers; could it be that every sweet ever produced resided here? So much choice; too much choice! And then, above the chocolate bars, was a shelf containing tall plastic cartons of sweets, including sherbet lemons, cola bottles, and her favourites: rhubarb and custards.

Maybe she wouldn't bother saving any of her pound today; she could always earn another pound for tidying her room, or offering to dry the washed crockery after dinner. In fact, this Aladdin's cave could become her secret place – somewhere she could sneak off to on the way home from school or when she was supposed to be walking to Grandma's house. Her parents would never come in here, so it wasn't like they'd ever catch her.

She was still deliberating over which chocolate bar to buy when she felt the dryness in her throat, and spied the tall fridge of ice-cold drinks cans and bottles. How hadn't she realised just how thirsty she was? Walking to the refrigerator door, she looked in at the selection of Coke, Sprite, Fanta, and Lilt cans, but the sticker on the front of the door said all bottles were 80p, so she wouldn't have enough money to buy a drink *and* a chocolate bar. If only she'd realised she would make this trip out today, she would have raided her piggy bank for another pound. Opening the fridge door, she pulled out the bottle of Fanta.

Returning to the wall of sweets, she ran her eyes over the selection again. If only she had another twenty pence, she'd be able to buy a Twirl *and* a bottle of Fanta. Picking up the Twirl, she turned the purple packet over in her hands. If only the shopkeeper would allow her to buy half the Twirl now, she'd have the drink and a taste of chocolate to keep her going. Or maybe, if she asked him really nicely, he'd let her have both if she promised to return and pay the extra twenty pence on another day. It was worth a try.

'Hello,' a deep voice said from behind her. 'What's going on here then?'

'I wasn't stealing it,' she said, fear instantly gripping her heart, as she turned to see the tall man in the light-grey suit and tie, hovering over her. 'I have money.' She pulled out the pound coin to show him for good measure.

His eyes didn't leave hers. 'I know you, don't I?' he asked, his accent not local to the area. 'You go to St Margaret's with my daughter.'

Joanna thought there was something vaguely familiar about his face, but she couldn't place him as one of the dads of her close friends. But why would he lie? And how else would he know she went to St Margaret's?

'What's your daughter's name?' she asked.

He smiled harmlessly. 'Kim. She's in Year 4.'

She knew of a Kim in one of the other classes: a quiet girl with whom she'd had little engagement.

'I think I know who you mean,' Joanna replied forthrightly, 'but we're not in the same class.'

'Ah, I see,' he replied, looking down at the items she was gripping so tightly. 'Well now, oh, it looks like you don't have enough money to buy the drink and the chocolate.'

She looked down at the two items, deciding her thirst was greater than her hunger, and begrudgingly returned the Twirl to the shelf. She could feel his eyes watching her, but she willed her cheeks not to show her embarrassment.

'I tell you what,' the man said softly. 'Twirls are my daughter's favourite too, and look here, it says you can buy three for the price of two. How about I buy the three, and you can have the free one. That way, I can have one, Kim can have one, and you can have one; we all win.'

He reached out and picked up two Twirls, and opened his free hand, waiting for her to place the third in it. She knew better than to accept sweets from strangers – that had been drilled in long ago – but this guy wasn't exactly a stranger; he was Kim's dad, and he wasn't asking her to go with him, merely giving her a free chocolate bar. Where was the harm?

She picked up the bar and placed it in his hand, before

following him up to the counter where she paid for her drink, and then waited for him by the door.

'There you go,' he said, offering the Twirl once they were both outside. 'I'd better be on my way or Kim's mum will have my guts for garters. Do you need a lift home?'

She quickly shook her head. 'No, I'm fine, thank you.'

The man pulled up the sleeve of his grey suit jacket and looked at his watch. 'Are you sure? It is getting late. You live near St Margaret's, don't you? I could drop you off there if you want? It's on my way home.'

'Thank you, but I'm not allowed to go in cars with people I don't know.'

He smiled, and held up his hands as if surrendering. 'That is very sensible! I hadn't thought about it like that. You're quite right to be wary, and I only hope Kim is as sensible as you if a man ever offers her a lift home. Well, so long, and it was nice meeting you... Wait, I didn't catch your name?'

'Joanna,' she said, thinking nothing of it.

'I'll tell Kim you said hi, Joanna,' he replied with another smile.

He opened the door of the long BMW and climbed in, starting the engine but not pulling away.

Joanna lingered, waiting to see which direction he would go in, but the car remained stationary. She looked down at her own watch and her eyes widened with panic. She hadn't realised just how late it was. Her mum and dad would surely have noticed she wasn't home and would be starting to worry. If she ever wanted to make a sneaky trip back to the newsagent's shop again, she would have to get home sharpish.

She looked back along the road, trying to remember which way she'd come, and whether there might be a more direct route home, but she couldn't even be certain which road she'd come along.

Moving to the side of the car, she could now see the man was typing something into his mobile phone, but he looked up and smiled warmly when he saw her watching. The electric window lowered, and he leaned over the seat to talk to her.

'Is everything okay, Joanna?' he asked, with just a hint of concern.

'I wondered,' she began, 'if it's not too much bother... would you be able to give me that lift to the school?'

He locked his phone, and returned it to his inside jacket pocket. 'Of course I can. Climb in the back. I think Kim's booster seat is in there.'

She heard the rear passenger's side door unlock, and clambered in, finding no sign of a booster seat. Placing the Fanta and Twirl between her legs, she fastened the seat belt and glanced at her watch again. As the car pulled away, she suddenly realised her parents would be on to her little jaunt if she returned to the house with evidence of the Twirl and Fanta, and would have to try and hide them in the den at the back of the garden before they saw her. The side gate leading to the garden was bound to be unlocked, and if she was careful, she could sneak to the den, hide the goods, and be back out the gate before either of them saw her.

Feeling pleased with herself, she pressed her head against the head rest and looked out of the window, determined to remember the route she'd come by so she wouldn't feel so lost next time. Before she realised, she saw St Margaret's approaching on the left, and beyond it the entrance to her road. Only the car didn't slow to a stop, as she expected.

'Um, excuse me, sir,' she called out timidly, not wishing to upset him, 'but you just drove past my road.'

'Oh, did I?' he called out apologetically, staring back at her from the rear-view mirror. 'My mistake. There's a roundabout a little way along from here; I'll turn around there.'

But the roundabout came and went, and still there was no return to her road. Her pulse quickened. Tears began to pool in her eyes, and she could feel his eyes watching her. 'Please, I just want to go home,' she whimpered, fear clawing at her throat.

'We'll be there soon,' his voice soothed, even though she didn't believe a word of it.

In a final act of desperation, she subtly moved her hand to the door handle, all the time checking that he was no longer watching her in the mirror. Her fingers brushed against the cool metal, coiling around the handle, but as she tugged on it, it didn't budge.

She was trapped.

Chapter Two

NOW

Winchester, Hampshire

I can't explain the nerves I'm feeling as I wait on the kerbside. There is a small wall adjacent to my knees, and I'm tempted to perch on it to rest my legs, but it is suffering the effects of erosion, and I'm not sure it would adequately support my weight. The ball of tension in the pit of my stomach is large enough without the added embarrassment of recreating Humpty Dumpty's most memorable moment.

The high wall surrounding HMP Winchester is casting a huge shadow over the area I'm waiting in, and I'm glad I opted to wear a sweater and a thick coat today, even though the weatherman had said it would be unusually mild for February. It's been close to eight months since I last saw Freddie Mitchell, as he was led away from the dock at Reading Crown Court, sentenced to ten months at her Majesty's pleasure for deliberately causing arson and criminal damage to the former Pendark Film Studios.

I'd wept for my friend as I watched from the public gallery, but he stood resolute, showing no remorse for destroying the site of so much abuse and evil. I don't agree with the action he took, but I understand why he did it; having had his abuse claims overlooked and ignored, the arson was his way of making it impossible for him to be ignored anymore, even if it had cost him his freedom.

I've begged Freddie to let me come and visit him, but he has refused visitations from anyone on the outside. He's phoned to let me know everything is okay and that he meets with the prison chaplain on a weekly basis, but I can hear the pain in his voice when he talks to me. Given the extent of the damage caused to the site, Freddie was lucky not to receive a longer sentence, and it is a reflection of his good behaviour that he is being released ahead of schedule. Ultimately, the studios had been long abandoned, and having searched the place prior to starting the blaze, he knew there was no immediate danger to life, and the judge had taken this into account. I just hope these last eight months haven't taken anything more from my friend; he was broken when I met him, and nobody deserves a happy ending as much as him.

I can see movement at the security barrier and a moment later, Freddie appears, dressed in the denim jeans and sleeveless jacket that have become his trademark. The thick beard is certainly a new addition, as is the presence of hair on his head. It reminds me of my first encounter with Freddie when he was sleeping rough on the streets of Weymouth, and I was serving food at the shelter. I hope his time inside hasn't changed him in other ways too.

Freddie doesn't notice me at first as he steps into the cool late-morning air, and inhales a deep breath of freedom. I remain where I am, giving him the space to embrace his newfound independence. Eventually, he looks up, and double-takes when he spots me.

'Emma, what are you doing here?' he asks, quickly swallowing the distance between us.

I throw my arms open and around his shoulders when he nears, and squeeze him tight. 'I know you didn't want a big fanfare, but I didn't want you to have to make the journey back to Weymouth alone.'

His head nestles in the crook of my neck and for a moment I'm certain he's weeping, but it ends as soon as it starts and he looks away as we separate. 'How are you keeping?' he asks, unobtrusively wiping his face with his arm.

I don't want to overwhelm him by telling him how much I've missed our chats, and how life just hasn't tasted as sweet without him around. I've spent more and more time at the shelter, helping out in his absence, but it hasn't made the loneliness more bearable. That's not Freddie's fault and I'm as much to blame for my isolation as anyone else. Rachel has phoned when she can, but I don't like to intrude while her romance with Daniella blossoms.

I settle for, 'I'm well, thank you. And you? How does it feel to be out in the open again, after so long?'

His head snaps round and fixes me with a hard stare. 'Please don't do that. As far as I'm concerned, these last eight months never happened. I never want to think nor speak of them again.' His shoulders soften. 'Is that okay? It was what it was, and that's where I want it left. Can we just pretend like we've both been asleep since the summer, and now that we've woken with renewed purpose we can move on with our lives?'

I've never seen Freddie beset with such shame – even when

he finally opened up to me about the abuse he'd suffered at the St Francis Home for Wayward Boys. My friend is usually so bouncy and full of verve but today he is flat; I just hope he can rediscover some of his old self once we're back home in Weymouth.

'I'm happy to pretend,' I acknowledge, smiling warmly. 'It's what I do for a living, after all.'

He loops his arm through mine and we move away from the prison, in the direction of Winchester town centre. 'How is the writing going? You were writing about that French girl the last time we spoke. Is that what you're still working on?'

It was my investigation into the sudden return of Aurélie Lebrun that inadvertently triggered Freddie's meltdown at the film studios. She was another one with a complicated past that needed unpicking. Having escaped prosecution by the British authorities, she returned to France, and the two of us have been meeting via video call to iron out the finer details of her story. It will probably be at least another four to six months until it hits the shelves, but at least that leaves plenty of time to sharpen the prose and syntax.

'I submitted the first draft of the manuscript to my agent Maddie last Friday. You remember Maddie, don't you?'

He nods. 'She handled the contract for the TV series adaptation of your first book. It's thanks to her that I had to submit my first ever tax return last year.'

'That's her. Well, she has the manuscript now, and will be running her digital red pen over it to bring it up to her very high standards before sending it on to my publisher, which means I am now at something of a loose end. So, like it or not, Freddie Mitchell, you're stuck with me for the rest of the day. And as you weren't around to help celebrate my birthday in

August, the least you can do is come out to lunch with me now.'

He slows to a stop, taking my hand in his. 'I'd rather just get home and have a shower and a shave.'

Freddie has battled with narcotics and alcohol for most of his life and as far as I'm aware he's remained clean throughout his incarceration, but my gut is telling me not to leave him alone right now.

'I insist you come to the restaurant with me, even if you just drink tap water,' I say lightheartedly. 'There's nothing as unbecoming as a writer eating alone in a restaurant on her birthday.'

'It isn't your birthday though.'

'It is my *pretend* birthday, Freddie. If the Queen can have two, so can I!' I pull him closer to me. 'On a serious note, I'm famished and if I don't eat a proper meal, I'll end up scoffing my weight in crisps and chocolate on the train back to Weymouth and we both know I can't afford to turn into any more of a heifer.'

He laughs for the first time and I finally see a glimpse of the old Freddie returning.

'That's true, I suppose,' he teases, and I playfully slap his arm. 'Come on then, let's get something to eat. And put the world to rights.'

A steak dinner for Freddie and a garlic chicken risotto for me later, and the conversation remains as stilted as it was outside the prison; maybe I'm not as good at pretending as I thought. It's proving problematic trying to keep the conversation light and engaging whilst avoiding any mention of what happened last year.

'Have you finally made a move on that detective boyfriend of yours?' Freddie asks now, as the waiter collects our plates.

Freddie knows that mention of my feelings for DS Jack Serrovitz will be enough to get a rise out of me, but I'm not going to take the bait.

'Actually, I haven't spoken to Jack in a few weeks.'

Freddie frowns, all humour dissipating from his face instantly. 'But what about the files and paperwork I dragged out of that hell's kitchen?'

Right before Freddie set the Pendark Film Studios ablaze, he extracted half a dozen filing cabinets filled with receipts and invoices tying hundreds of individuals to the place; and whilst some of those filmmakers weren't producing filth, it was Freddie's contention that some of them would have been.

'Jack is still investigating, as far as I'm aware.'

In truth, I have no idea what Jack is currently up to. Shortly after Freddie's arrest, he was seconded to join a specialist team in the National Crime Agency with the specific purpose of uncovering a network of paedophiles and traffickers operating along the south coast of the UK. The filing cabinets and their contents went with him and although he promised to keep me updated, I guess he hasn't been allowed to do so.

'But I got those files out for you, Emma. *You* were supposed to use them to track down what happened to Anna.'

Another reason I'm disappointed that Jack hasn't been in touch recently. My sister Anna has now been missing for twenty-one years, and the only evidence that she wasn't killed the day she was abducted is her face on a pornographic video when she must have been about thirteen years old. What happened to her after that is anyone's guess, and the bane of my existence. Deep down, I want to believe that she is still alive and kicking out there somewhere, but as the days wear on, that reality grows dimmer.

I recall a conversation I had with Elizabeth Hilliard when her daughter Cassie was missing. Elizabeth was adamant that she could feel deep down that Cassie was still alive, and she was proved right, but I don't have any similar sense with Anna. Not anymore. I've tried – God knows I've fought against the cynicism – but how can she have been alive all this time and not made contact?

'Jack knows that, Freddie, and I'm sure the only reason he hasn't called is he's been snowed under with work.'

Not even I'm convinced by the line.

Freddie looks forlorn and I don't need to ask what's going through his mind right now: that the last eight months of his life have been wasted.

I settle the bill, and then the two of us slowly make our way towards Winchester station, ready to board the next train back to Weymouth, but a dark cloud hovers above our heads. Maybe we're both just bad at pretending everything is normal.

My mood lightens briefly when I see that Jack is calling my phone, and I turn the screen to show Freddie; it feels as though our prayers have been answered, but then I hear Jack's morose tone and it puts me on the back foot.

'I'm at Pendark Film Studios, Emma. I need you to come over here straightaway. We've found something buried beneath the ashes.'

Chapter Three

THEN

Newbury, Berkshire

Catching the reflection of myself biting my nails tells me everything I need to know about the anxiety throbbing through me. Jack's tone wasn't warm and welcoming, but cold and pragmatic; he refused to elaborate on the phone what had been found beneath the ashes of what remained of the site, but it clearly isn't good. My mind has been racing with possibilities and the only conclusion I can draw is that they've discovered a body, and that Freddie is now likely to be facing further criminal charges.

I could barely look at him as we parted at Winchester station, certain he'd see the alarm in my eyes. He looked relieved to be travelling back to Weymouth alone, and I just hope he stays true to his sobriety without me watching over him.

There can't have been any remains in the rubble though, as a thorough search was performed of the grounds following the fire in order to rule out the prospect that the arson had taken a life. Freddie was adamant he'd checked the site before striking the match, and given the studios hadn't been in operation for several years, there is no reason to doubt his word. Yet still, what else could have put Jack so on edge?

Newbury station is a short train ride from Winchester, and as the taxi nears the entrance towards the studios, I'm reminded of the last time I was here, after Freddie had called to tell me what he'd done. He hadn't sounded ashamed at the time; if anything, he was victorious in finding the studios where he'd been so badly mistreated for so many years, and for bringing an end to its torturous past. I can't bear to think about how many other children suffered in the same way as Freddie.

Since Freddie's sentencing, I've tried to do some of my own research into the studios in an effort to shed any light on how it became such a portent of horror. Formerly a fallow piece of farmland, the site was bought by the newly formed Pendark Corporation in 1958 and developed into what became three large sound stages in 1961, set to rival the likes of Ealing Film Studios in West London, as well as Pinewood in Iver, Buckinghamshire. With the backdrop of the high turrets of Highclere Castle, the studio had some early success with a couple of well-known medieval-set pictures. However, whilst British cinema grew in the 60s and 70s, Pendark's isolated location in Berkshire proved less appealing than London, and the Pendark Corporation flirted with administration for several years until it was bought by a Dutch entrepreneur called Arend Visser. From that point the studios' output was limited to a few B-movie horror pictures which failed to set the world alight. From the fact that the Pendark Studios didn't officially close until 2017, it doesn't take a genius to work out that the business was being funded by some other means.

Arend Visser passed away in 2010, but despite owning the Corporation, he remained resident in his native Eindhoven until his death. Whether he was aware of the atrocities being carried out on his property is unclear. I did email all this information to Jack, in case it would prove beneficial to the NCA's investigation, but he emailed back thanking me and reminding me that I am no longer part of the investigation.

What was the studios is now surrounded by high wooden boarding, branded with the name of a property developer. According to the large graphical display at the entrance, the plan is to turn the site into a luxury hotel, cinema, and casino leisure park, presumably to attract those visiting nearby Newbury racecourse. Just what the world needs: another place to go and waste precious resources. Why somewhere with so much blood spilled can't be turned into something that can bring benefit is beyond me: a new hospital; a school; affordable housing.

The taxi pulls to a halt at the wire fence, and I pay the driver, before stepping out into drizzle. Pulling the hood up over my head, I move to the gate and peer through, catching Jack's attention a few metres away. He's wearing navy jeans, brown hiking boots, and a cagoule to shelter him from the rain. He never was one for high fashion, but I must admit it's odd seeing him in anything but his usual black and white uniform.

He approaches the gate and I now see there is an officer in a high-visibility vest just inside the gate. Jack speaks to him, identifying me, and the officer then proceeds to unlock the gate and beckon me in. There is no sign of any blue and white police tape as far as I can see, and the fact that they're not following standard crime scene procedures gives me a modicum of relief. Maybe I was allowing my imagination to get the better of me, and my appearance here has nothing to do with Freddie.

Time will tell.

Jack appears at my side, shielding his eyes from the dripping of his hood as the rainfall worsens. 'Thanks for coming,' he says, nodding for me to follow him. 'We've got a hut we can wait in until the rain eases.'

I'm tempted to hug him, but as I move towards him, he turns and strides back through the mud. I hurry after him, trying to avoid the puddles strewn left and right. It's difficult to picture what the studios looked like before. Little of them now remains. The stanchions that had survived the blaze are black with soot, with great steel struts bent and twisted from severe heat exposure. It resembles a giant gothic sculpture and there is little left of the corrugated plastic roofs that would once have helped produce magnificent scores. Even now – some eight months since the last of the fire was extinguished – the pungent smoke and ash still cling to the air, reminding anyone who passes of what occurred here.

One of the sound stages looks to be in the middle of demolition. Large yellow diggers wait idly to be put to work again. A tall orange crane has been erected in the middle of the site too, but glancing up I can see that the cockpit is empty. Work here has been indefinitely stopped and that doesn't bode well for the development, nor for me, as we arrive at the small wooden hut which is akin to the sort of portable bathrooms quickly erected at music festivals.

Jack stamps his feet on the mat as he takes the large step up in a single bound. I follow suit, though it is clear from the muddy footprints already scattered across the floor that the doormat is having little effect in these conditions. There is a large table in the middle of the cabin upon which lies a paper map of what is presumably the architect's site plan. Two men in yellow hard hats are studying and occasionally pointing at the map as they continue their hushed conversation.

One of them finally looks up as he catches Jack in his periphery.

'Sir, may I introduce Emma Hunter, the writer I was telling you about?' Jack says, addressing him. 'Emma, this is Detective Chief Inspector Harry Dainton.'

The man is at least six inches taller than Jack, the skin beneath his eyes aged but taut. He extends a large hand and shakes mine firmly. 'Great to meet you, Emma; my wife's a big fan of your books. She keeps on at me that I should read them, but I just never have the time. Thanks for coming down here today.'

I've actually come up, but I don't see the need to correct him. 'Happy to help in any way I can. What's going on? What was so urgent?'

Dainton looks at Jack to take over and he nods, leading me towards the back of the room, whilst Dainton restarts his whispered conversation with the other man in the hard hat. This second man is wearing a mustard and charcoal chequered shirt and a thick gilet and, given the girth of his gut, I would assume is the foreman of the site. They are back pointing at the map again.

I can see from the way Jack looks at Dainton that there is great respect there.

'He seems nice,' I say with a shrug.

'We're lucky to have him leading this investigation, that's

for sure,' Jack whispers, as if trying to spare Dainton's blushes. 'And he's going places. Plays golf with former Met Police Commissioner Sir Anthony Tomlinson as well.'

'What's all this about, Jack?' I ask quietly, when we're as far from the other two as we can be. 'I haven't heard from you in months, and then out of the blue you phone and ask me to come back here.'

He lowers his eyes. 'I'm sorry about that. Things have been manic, what with work and Chrissie being in hospital; I just feel like I've been chasing my tail. I've meant to call and see how you are, but… I'm sorry.'

Chrissie is Jack's ex, and mum to their eight-year-old daughter Mila, of whom they share custody. Born out of wedlock to two teenagers who thought nothing could separate them, Mila lives with Jack two days each week, and with her mum and stepfather the rest of the time. Given the number of horror stories I've heard about separated couples, Jack and Chrissie are on great terms.

'Wait, what? What happened to Chrissie?' I ask, picking up on the only point that mattered in his statement.

'She was rushed to hospital just before Christmas and gave birth three months premature. The poor tyke has been in the prenatal unit ever since. It's been tough on them, and on Mila, not knowing whether her new little brother will pull through or not. Sorry, I guess this is all news to you. It's been a crazy few months. I've been trying to help out with Mila as much as I can so that they're able to spend as much time at the hospital as they need.'

Overwhelming guilt swamps my mind; to think I was assuming Jack's radio silence had something to do with his unrequited (well, almost) feelings for me.

'Oh, Jack, I'm so sorry, I had no idea you had all that going on. You should have called; I'd have been happy to help in any way I could.'

'Thanks, but we're coping, just about. But when I'm not with Mila, I'm at the office in Vauxhall. And then all this blows up at the worst possible time.'

My mind snaps back to the small hut in the middle of a construction site. 'Well, what is all this? What was so urgent you needed me here now?'

He glances over his shoulder at Dainton before returning to me and keeping his voice low. 'As you may have noticed, the site is being redeveloped, but all that work has had to stop as of this morning. While they were digging to lay new foundations, a suitcase was discovered beneath the ground containing human remains. They've been taken away for examination and the dig site is being surveyed by a team of forensic specialists, though judging by the style and age of the case, it's been down there for a number of years.'

At least that puts Freddie in the clear, but what does that mean for the investigation into the nefarious activities undertaken at these studios?

'I was hoping you might share all your notes from your original interviews with Freddie Mitchell? We're trying to piece together timelines, and I also want to speak to Freddie directly to see if he recalls anything about his time here that might help us identify other individuals in addition to the people who brought him here from the boys' home.'

'I'll have to check that Freddie is happy for me to hand the notes over, but assuming that he is, sure I'm happy to send over everything I've got, so long as they're returned to me at some point.'

'That's great, Emma. Thank you. Do you happen to know when Freddie is due to be released from HMP Winchester? I don't want to go to the hassle of speaking to the visitation office, only to miss him.'

'He was released this morning. That's where I was when you phoned.'

'He's out now?' He glances out of the portacabin window. 'He's not with you now, is he?'

I shake my head. 'I left him on a train back to Weymouth. He should be there in the next hour or so.'

Jack looks at his watch. 'Perfect! Maybe I can see him today and give you a lift home in the process. Does that work for you?'

He's going at a hundred miles an hour and I'm struggling to keep up. 'Yeah, I guess, but why did you need me here to say all this? You could have asked me over the phone for my notes; what was so important I come here?'

Jack closes his eyes, and takes a moment to compose himself. 'The human remains that were found… The pathologist believes they belong to a female aged between thirteen and fifteen, based on bone development… There's a chance they belong to your sister.'

Chapter Four

THEN

Piddlehinton, Dorset

The car's brakes squeaked as the vehicle careered along the muddy track. It had been several minutes since they'd left the road, and although Joanna had tried to keep an eye on the route they'd followed since passing her school, she'd soon become disorientated. If she ever had to show anyone back to where she'd been taken to, or even tried to get back home alone, she would easily get lost. She just wished such an opportunity would present itself.

The driver hadn't spoken a word since lying about promising to turn at the roundabout and she was terrified about asking him again. He'd continued to watch her silently from the rear-view mirror. Although he hadn't spoken since, there was a sinister gleam in his eyes that held her tongue. She would argue it was fear that had kept her from challenging him, but it was more than that. She could have demanded to know where he was taking her, why he had lied, and what he wanted, but none of those questions had sprung to mind. Instead, she'd just kept thinking over and over how much trouble she'd be in with her parents when they found out she'd been stupid enough to get into a car with a stranger.

Yet he'd been so convincing, hadn't he? She hadn't questioned whether he was who he'd claimed to be, or whether he would do as he'd said he would. He'd been kind to her in the shop, not some monster with ill intentions. He was a normal guy. No, he was more than that: he was someone she'd thought she recognised, and she'd had no reason to doubt he was Kim's dad. In fact, for all her imagination was now telling her about who this man might really be, there was no reason to think he wasn't Kim's dad.

The car pulled to a halt, and the man killed the engine, keeping both hands on the steering wheel and his eyes off the mirror. She watched him via the rear-view mirror. He bowed his head lower so that she could no longer see his eyes. He looked sad. Was he now having regrets about not taking her home? Had her compliance and refusal to scream and shout shown him how wrong he was?

With the engine off, and the wipers static, the falling rain was now obscuring the view through the windscreen. She could just about make out several white caravans ahead, standing on the brown, grassless mud.

'Where are we?' she tried to ask, the words barely escaping her mouth as his eyes shot to the mirror at the sound of her voice.

He raised his head further, his reflection smiling. 'You don't need to be scared of me. I'm not going to hurt you.'

If the statement was supposed to put her at ease, it had failed. Her heart continued to thunder in her chest.

'I want to go home,' she whimpered. 'My parents will be worried about me.'

'No, they won't,' he said so calmly it frightened her. 'I've sent them a message; they know you're with me.'

She hadn't seen him send any messages on his phone since she'd climbed into the car, so he had to be lying to her. Her eyes filled instantly.

'Please,' she tried again, 'I just want to go home.'

She'd never wanted to be back home more in her life. Even though her parents could be embarrassing and her sister could be *so* annoying, at least she felt safe with them. She didn't like the way he was watching her, revelling in her sadness.

'I won't tell anyone.'

Her eyes darted back to his in the mirror. In those four words she'd implied that his behaviour was anything but normal, and she saw his jaw tighten at the silent accusation.

'All in due time,' he replied, his voice softer than she'd expected. 'I remembered I was supposed to pick something up from a friend of mine. It'll only take a few minutes and then I'll take you home. Okay?'

Had she got it wrong? Had he actually messaged her parents to let them know she was safe, and as soon as he'd collected whatever it was they'd stopped for, they'd be on their way again? As much as she wanted to believe he was telling the truth, her mind refused to take him at his word.

'How long will it take?' she checked.

He looked at his watch.

'My friend lives in one of those caravans. Can you see? He said he'll be home in a minute and then he'll give me what I came for. It's a present for my daughter Mel.'

Joanna knew Kim was an only child. Her eyes narrowed.

'I thought you said you were Kim's dad?'

He clamped his eyes shut in frustration. 'I did say Kim, didn't I? Shit, then I guess the game is up.'

Her throat burned as her nausea grew. 'Who are you?'

'I really am a friend of your dad's,' he said, looking back at her. 'Listen, we'll go in to my friend's caravan, and then I'll explain everything to you. Okay? You really don't need to be scared of me. I'm not going to hurt you, Joanna.'

She hadn't even considered the possibility that he *might* hurt her until that moment, and suddenly she could think of nothing else.

'I just want to go home,' she sobbed. 'Please? I promise I won't tell anyone that you lied to me. Just take me home now and nobody will ever know.'

The rain seemed to have stopped, and that was his cue to open his door and poke his hand out. 'Ah, look, it's dried up now. I can't leave you in the car – there are some dangerous people out there, you know? – so come with me to the caravan, I'll get you something to eat and drink, and then I'll tell you what's going on. Okay? You don't need to look so worried; there is a perfectly reasonable explanation.'

Tears spilled against her cheeks, as she shook her head. 'Take me home. Please? I won't tell anybody. I want to speak to my mum and dad.'

He didn't respond, pushing his door open further, slamming it shut once he was out, and then disappearing behind the car. She tried to swivel round to look out of the back window, but before she had the chance, he'd pulled open her door and was leaning over, fumbling for her seat belt latch.

'No,' she screamed, sensing she would be safer in the car than in his care.

But he was too strong for her and simply batted her hands away, lifting her from the seat with one arm and dragging her out of the vehicle, slamming the door behind them. Her Twirl and Fanta had fallen to the floor of the car when he pulled her out, but he'd made no effort to go back and collect them. She kicked and clawed as best she could but it did nothing to slow his stride. They soon made it to the steps leading up to the first of the white caravans. He unlocked the door and pushed her inside. Before she could even consider her next move, his finger was in her face, a silent warning.

'My friend lives in the caravan next door. You'll be safe in here until I've collected what I came for, and then I'll be back. Don't do anything to annoy me. You won't like me when I'm angry.'

It was so dark inside the caravan that she could barely make out what any of the shadows represented. Some kind of shutters covered the limited number of windows inside. It suddenly felt like Halloween, with nothing but terror lurking in the darkness.

'There are some colouring books on the table over there,' he continued, pointing to the far side of the interior. 'Why don't you colour a nice picture for your mum and dad, and I'm sure by the time you've finished, I'll be back.'

She felt his hand on her back, pushing her further inside, and then the door was slammed shut and she heard the key the other side locking it tight. She tried the light switch on the wall to her left, but no amount of flicking brightened the gloom.

He hadn't shouted or threatened her, yet she'd never felt so afraid to be in the presence of the man in the grey suit.

Her mum would be pacing the house frantically by now.

Joanna could no longer see the face of her watch but it had to be an hour since she'd set off for the shop, and she'd never been out alone for this long before. They had to know she was missing by now. They were sure to ground her for several weeks after this incident whether Kim's dad had messaged or not.

He isn't Kim's dad, she had to remind himself. And if that was true, then he probably wasn't a friend of her parents either. And if that was also true, what else had he lied to her about?

Holding out her hands to check for obstacles, she made her way to the cushioned bench and table, finding the colouring books he'd referred to along with a woollen pencil case. Sliding onto the cushion, she unzipped the pencil case and examined the collection of blunt and broken pencils and crayons inside. They reminded her of the motley collection of stationery in the dentist's reception room. Opening the top colouring book, she found that the first ten or so pages had already been scribbled over; whoever had been responsible for these colourings didn't appreciate the benefit of staying inside the lines.

She found an uncoloured picture but it was of a boring flower and didn't appeal, so she continued to flick the pages until she came to one that stopped her in her tracks and made her blood freeze. The image of the bunny rabbit on its own was harmless enough, but the three letters scrawled over the top in thick red crayon were clearly a warning:

RUN

Pushing the colouring book away, she slid off the cushion and hurried back towards the door. Although she'd heard it lock, there had to be some way to get it open from inside. The door handle didn't budge so she moved into the small kitchen area, opening and closing cupboards but finding nothing but dust and dead bugs inside.

The panic started to rise in her throat again; she had to get out, but she had no idea how to. What would her dad do? Clearly, he wouldn't allow himself to get into such a tight spot, but if he were trapped, what would he do?

She thought back to the time last year when they'd returned from a weekend away and found their front door wouldn't open. It had been bolted from inside, her father had determined, which suggested someone had broken in. He didn't let it faze him, and had used a charge and his shoulder to break through the door, finding valuables smuggled away inside a stolen pillowcase.

She wasn't as tall nor as strong as him, but she had to try.

Running as fast as she could, she slammed her body into the door, and although the whole caravan shook, the door remained firmly locked. She tried it again, but all she managed was to bruise her arm.

Slumping to the floor, she pressed her back into the door, cursing herself for being stupid enough to climb into the man's car; stupid enough to believe his act of generosity in the shop was anything but sincere; stupid enough to think she'd get away with sneaking to a shop and indulging herself.

She buried her head in her hands and wept silently.

And then she heard voices beyond the door. It was the man in grey and at least one other, making no attempt to cover their words.

'We'll lay low tonight and make a move at dawn,' the man in grey said.

'And what if she causes trouble in the meantime?' the second voice asked.

The man laughed. 'If she gives us any trouble, we'll kill her, and leave the body where nobody will ever find it. It wouldn't be the first time, and I'm certain it won't be the last.'

Chapter Five

NOW

Newbury, Berkshire

'My sister?' I clarify, my brain unable to comprehend. 'You think the bones are Anna's? No. No way. They can't be.'

We've stepped out of the hut for fresh air, but my cheeks are flushed and my body is telling me I could throw up or pass out at any minute.

Jack fixes me with a pained stare, forcing eye contact. 'We don't know for sure, but given the victim's age, the fact we know your sister was probably here when she was that old, and given the age of the suitcase the remains were discovered in… I'm not saying it's definitely her, but there is a chance. *That's* why I thought I should tell you in person.'

I stumble backwards as my knees threaten to give way. For so many years I've refused to acknowledge the likelihood that Anna is dead. She's my big sister, and I won't accept it until I know for sure. I've felt in my heart that she has to still be out there somewhere. Hearing Jack daring to even mention the possibility that I've been wrong for so long is enough to make my blood boil.

'No, Jack,' I repeat. 'You're wrong. It's not her; not my Anna.'

The poor guy doesn't know which way to look. 'Oh, well, no, of course, I'm sure you're right, but in any event, I wanted you to know what we'd found. God knows, had Freddie not torched the place last year, this victim might have remained undiscovered for many more years.'

It's such a morbid thought. I'm not sure what I believe in terms of God and afterlives, but there's something quite horrific in thinking of my remains lying unfound for eternity. Can a soul ever be at peace if not laid to rest properly? It's hard to believe in a merciful God when you've seen some of the things I have.

A fresh thought smacks me across the face. 'Is this the only suitcase you found? I mean, if there's one victim, couldn't there be more. . .?'

Jack looks away but I see him nodding. 'It's a possibility. We're going to have some specialist equipment brought over in the morning to check the rest of the grounds. Do you remember when we had to have the ground scanned at the Bovington army barracks in search of Sally Curtis?'

'Sure.'

'Well, that same team are going to work with the building crew here to systematically clear and check the land with their X-ray type machines. That's what my boss Harry Dainton was speaking to the foreman about. It's going to take time to check the whole site, but you know what they say about smoke and fire. It's easily going to set the development of the site back by months.'

I'm suddenly conscious that I could be standing over the remains of any number of victims and I desperately want to be anywhere else.

'We had the suitcase and remains moved to the local morgue for examination,' Jack says quietly. 'I was going to head over there in a bit and wait to hear the results. Ordinarily, I wouldn't invite the victim's potential family with me, but if you'd like to come, I could do with the company. I understand if you'd rather not.'

'No, I need to,' I say, my head snapping up to meet his gaze. 'I have to know one way or the other.'

The mortuary in question is at the Basingstoke and North Hampshire Hospital, thirty minutes away from the site of what was once Pendark Film Studios. The journey is made in silence, with neither of us comfortable making small talk given the enormity of what is hanging over us. It isn't just having to accept that I have lost the big sister who was my source of knowledge and experience when I was finding my way in the world; it also throws a huge question mark over everything I've done with my life since that day we lost her.

Finding Anna has been my reason for living: it's why I went into journalism to begin with – to right the wrongs that others couldn't; it's why I accepted Lord Templeton Fitzhume's offer to create the Anna Hunter Foundation; it's why I haven't had much of a social life; why I haven't felt the urge to settle down and start a family of my own. I haven't been able to rest knowing that every passing minute is another minute of me not finding my sister. The prospect that I have wasted all that time and energy doesn't sit well, and that is why I won't accept Jack's theory until I hear it confirmed by indisputable DNA evidence.

The forensic pathologist isn't ready for us when we arrive at the mortuary in the basement of the hospital. Jack suggests we grab a bite to eat as it's nearing dinnertime, but I have no appetite for food. We settle for a beaker of ice-cold water from the dispenser in the corridor, before we both sit on the squeaky plastic chairs just outside the secured doors. The air is musty and stale down here and so I focus on breathing through my mouth instead of my nose.

Jack looks over at me. 'It might not be her,' he offers in an attempt to calm me, but there's no confidence in his tone.

It makes me wonder how long he's suspected Anna might be dead. I've known Jack for nearly two years, since our paths were meshed together when I was asked to look into the disappearance of six-year-old Cassie Hilliard. It took me a while to trust him enough to spill the details of Anna's disappearance, and all this time I thought he shared in my belief that she's still alive, but now I don't think I can be certain of anything where he is concerned. And to think I actually considered we could have some kind of romantic future together.

Jack stands suddenly and, pulling a phone from his pocket, he moves along the corridor, but not far enough that I can't hear his end of the conversation.

'Thanks for calling me back, Tamara. I have a work thing that's going to keep me out until late tonight and I need you to collect Mila from school and watch her until—'

He falls silent as he's cut off by whoever he's speaking to. He's never mentioned anyone called Tamara before, and for all I know she could be a new girlfriend.

'Yes, I understand that, Tamara, but there's nothing I can—' Another pause. 'Look, I'm sorry, but a body's been found, and I can't leave my post until—' Again. 'That's not fair. You know Mila is my number-one priority…'

I feel guilty about eavesdropping and pull out my own phone, looking for any kind of distraction to block out the sound of Jack's hurt and restrained voice. He's doing his best to remain patient with this Tamara, but even I can hear how close to breaking he is.

'I wouldn't ask if I wasn't desperate. I can come and collect Mila from you when I get back… No, I don't know when that will be… Come on, Tamara, please? You're her grandmother, for pity's sake!'

Well, that answers the question about whether Tamara is his new girlfriend. I'd be shocked if he refers to his own mother by her first name, so she must be the maternal grandmother. Jack's mentioned very little about Chrissie other than that they have a good relationship despite going their separate ways. I've always thought how lucky Mila is to have two parents willing to put their differences behind them for her sake. After Anna's disappearance, my parents could barely stand to be in the same room as one another, so I've seen the effects of separation first-hand, although my parents didn't formally divorce.

'Sorry about that,' Jack says quietly, returning to the seats, the phone now back in his pocket.

'If you need to leave and fetch Mila, this can wait,' I offer. 'Assuming the pathologist won't confirm any details to me directly, I'm sure she could phone you, and then you could pass on the news.'

'No, it's okay. Tamara is Mila's grandmother and her baccarat night can be postponed until tomorrow for the sake of her granddaughter. Chrissie's always saying that she doesn't do enough babysitting. And with Chrissie still at the pre-natal unit, it's the least she can do.'

The bags beneath his eyes look so dark under the ultra-bright halogen bulbs hanging above our heads. I sensed he was under stress when we were at the Pendark site, but I don't think I appreciated just how much he's carrying alone.

'If there's anything I can do to help?' I say, knowing there's very little I could do from my poky flat in Weymouth.

'Thanks. Don't worry about it. Tamara was never my biggest fan. She never thought I was good enough for her precious Christine. When we first got together, she'd go out of her way to make me feel as though I was worth less than the dirt on her shoes. When we did eventually call it a day, she actually sent Chrissie a bottle of Moët in celebration. Thankfully, my interaction with Tamara is now limited to the occasional awkward encounter at Chrissie's house when I collect or drop off Mila, but that's about it.'

He smiles in defeat. 'I'm sure she'll give me hell for it, but she's agreed to collect Mila from school and look after her until I can get there. You'd have thought any other grandmother would be thrilled to spend extra time with their offspring, but she's one of those grandmothers by convenience. She loves to tell her sewing circle about everything Mila excels at, and is happy to show her off when it suits, but woe betide you if you expect anything more.' He pauses. 'I'm sorry, I shouldn't be dumping all of this on you.'

'It's okay,' I tell him, smiling back. 'That's what friends are for.'

He looks down at his feet, before returning his eyes to mine. 'Listen, I've been meaning to—'

We start as a woman's shrill voice echoes down the corridor. 'PC Serrovitz?'

Turning, I now see a woman in face mask and stained overalls standing just inside the secured door.

'Yes,' Jack says, standing. 'And this is my colleague Emma Hunter. She's civilian liaison but has clearance to be here.'

I don't know how true that statement is, but the pathologist doesn't bat an eyelid, holding the door open with her shoulder and beckoning us through. The air inside the secured doors instantly feels much cleaner, as if every molecule has been sanitised before being pumped in through the air-conditioning system. And the entire *place* just feels cleaner. The walls are bright white in comparison to the dreary mustard shade in the corridor, and the doors are all made from shiny stainless steel. It feels as if we've stepped onto some kind of spaceship, rather than into a place that few feel comfortable in.

The pathologist shows us to a small room with a round table at its heart and even brighter lights than those we've emerged from. Naively, I'd thought she would show us into her lab, but I suppose for hygiene reasons that won't be the case. She closes the door and dims the light before tapping buttons on the side of the round table. Lights flicker on the table top and a moment later a 3D image of a skeleton is projected just above it. I have to give it to the hospital, no expense has been spared on this equipment. Without being told, I can see we are viewing the remains discovered in the suitcase, which have been systematically catalogued and then rearranged into a kind of digital jigsaw puzzle of a skeleton.

'The victim was female,' the pathologist begins, without any introduction. Her name badge reads 'Dr V Chang', though I've no idea what the 'V' stands for. She must be in her early forties, I would guess, but her weary face adds at least a couple of years. When she speaks, there is no emotion, just fact stating.

'Aged between thirteen and fifteen, though I would estimate the latter stage of that range, based on the development of bone around the sexual organs. Cause of death was most likely a fractured neck,' she says, using a biro to point at the area of damage visible beneath the skull, 'but further examination of the decomposing flesh that we found still congealed around some of the bone tissue may highlight alternative theories. DNA will be extracted from the bone material and passed to the CSI team to trace, but given the age of the victim, unless she'd been in trouble with the police before, I'd be surprised if a match was made.'

I don't like this pragmatic description of what could be Anna, and as I stand staring at the hologram I try to imagine her face over the skull, but it's too painful and I'm forced to look away.

'Can you estimate how long the victim has been in the ground?' Jack asks quietly, conscious of my feelings, but eager to establish the facts as swiftly as possible.

'I will need to continue my examination to be certain; the case was relatively airtight, which explains why we've been able to recover as much tissue as we have. Had the body been dumped in the ground in a sack instead, there's a chance we wouldn't have found all the pieces. The case has protected her from scavengers, and has given us a better chance of discovering who she was.'

I can't listen to any more. Maybe it's easier for Dr Chang and Jack to talk so matter-of-factly about a teenager who was probably murdered before being discarded like a piece of old furniture, but it's too much for me and I hurry from the room, desperately searching for the exit button to release me from the secured doors.

Jack approaches from behind a moment later and places his hands on my shoulders. 'I hope as much as you that it's not her, and had we found any other sightings of your sister since that despicable video was made, we probably wouldn't even be considering this. But I swear to you, if that is your sister in there, I won't rest until I find who did this to her.'

I can't speak. I turn and bury my head in his shoulder, allowing the hot tears to flow from my eyes.

Chapter Six

NOW

Weymouth, Dorset

'Thanks for driving me back,' I say, as the beautiful Dorset coastline creeps into view. It's just coming up to six, and there is little light in the sky ahead. I feel emotionally drained from seeing Freddie finally released, Jack's call, and then his conclusions about my sister; all I want now is the comfort of bed, and to put this day behind me.

Jack didn't have to drive me all the way back here from Basingstoke, particularly considering he is already in Mila's grandmother's bad books, but I have to admit I'm grateful not to be left to my own thoughts on the arduous train journey home.

'To be honest, you're not the only reason I offered,' he says, keeping his eyes fixed on the road.

'No?'

He turns his head fractionally, maybe feeling my eyes trying to burrow into his mind. Despite the empathy and comfort he's offered since the hospital, it feels like this isn't the Jack I'm used to speaking to; he's withdrawn. No, it's more than that. It's as if he's put some invisible shield around himself, and even his closest friends can't get near enough to see beyond it. Or maybe I just previously imagined we were more intimate than we actually are. Thinking about the time we have spent together, it's never been socially driven; there's always been some underlying agenda – a case, my sister, Freddie – and now I'm not sure I've ever known the real Jack. Maybe this divide has always been there, and I've been naïve to think that his awkward grin is anything more than my own physical attraction.

'I want to speak to Freddie,' Jack finally says, returning his eyes to the road.

I know instinctively Jack's planned chat won't be a social call, and quite frankly Freddie doesn't need to be reminded about the time he's had to spend away – at least not on his first night out.

'What about?' I ask, as casually as I can manage.

He narrows his eyes, but doesn't respond.

'I'm not sure where Freddie will be,' I say to break the enveloping silence. 'You should have said that's what you were intending and I would have phoned Freddie to see if he's free. It's his first night out; can it not wait until tomorrow?'

'No.'

Despite my own fatigue, I'm not prepared to leave Freddie unprotected tonight. 'Okay, well, if I know Freddie, he'll be volunteering at the shelter's kitchen. I'll show you where it is.'

We don't speak again until we near the former church hall with the leaky roof. Prior to the incident at Pendark Film Studios last year, Freddie had been planning a summer fête to raise funds to fix up the crumbling premises, but that had all fallen by the wayside when he'd been sentenced. The queue at the door is already into double figures as Jack parks his car at the side of the road and studies the parking meter.

'There's no charge at this time of year,' I tell him as I get out and head towards the entrance.

'What are you doing?' he asks, hurrying after me.

'I'm coming with you. Freddie is my friend and I promised I'd check in on him tonight, so unless you're planning to arrest him and take him back to London, I'm staying.'

I don't mean to sound so off-hand, but I have a horrible sinking feeling about how this talk is going to go, and I'm not prepared to take no for an answer.

Jack opens his mouth to argue before thinking better of it and ushering me inside. I immediately spot Freddie behind the main table, ladling steaming soup into bowls cupped by grateful hands. This is so typical of Freddie; anyone else would be making the most of their freedom after so many months under lock and key, but not Freddie. He spends more time volunteering in this shelter than some of the visitors do eating meals. Judging by the clothes he's wearing, I'd guess he hasn't even been home to change since he got off the train.

His eyes brighten when he spots me, but a frown quickly follows as he spots Jack lurking behind.

'Can we have a word when you have a minute?' I ask.

He ladles another bowl of soup before looking back at me. 'I'm a bit busy at the moment. Can you come back in an hour or so?'

Jack steps past me. 'It's kind of urgent.'

Freddie isn't one who responds well to confrontation. When I first met him, I quickly learned that the best way to make him open up is with gentle coaxing; he needs to want to open up, and direct questions won't do it.

He calls over Judith, one of the other volunteers, and whispers something into her ear before handing over the ladle and moving around the table. 'We can sit over there,' he says, indicating a dark corner away from the serving tables. 'Do either of you want soup and a roll? It's winter vegetable.'

'No, we're fine,' I answer for both of us, as we take our seats.

As with all the other tables and chairs in the hall, this one has been donated and would look more fitting on someone's patio than in a dimly-lit hall on a cold February night. The white plastic is scratched and weathered, but it serves a purpose – in many ways as the three of us do. We've all seen better days, but aren't ready for the scrapheap yet.

'What can I do for you, officer?' Freddie says, adopting a faux Texan accent, like we're in some western.

'What do you remember about your time at Pendark?'

The question is so direct and abrupt that even I'm caught on the back foot. Freddie looks to me, disappointed maybe that I haven't taught Jack how to coax. 'It was a hell hole and I'm glad it's gone.'

'I want to know more about the time you spent there when you were younger.'

The look of disappointment on Freddie's face is growing, and I really wish I'd had the chance to forewarn him about the slew of questions.

'I've told you everything I remember about that time,' he growls under his breath.

I don't blame him; this is neither the time nor the place to get into specifics about that period in his life.

'I'm not interested in what they did to you,' Jack snaps back, keeping his voice low too, 'I want to know what else you saw there; *who* else you saw there.'

'Take it easy, Jack,' I warn quietly, before looking back at Freddie. 'A girl's body has been discovered buried in the ruins,' I tell him. 'I think what Jack is asking is whether you witnessed anything beyond what you've already told us, when you were there all those years ago.'

'I've told you before,' Freddie growls, 'I remember very little of that time… I must have repressed the memories, and the last thing I want to do is go digging up the past.'

'You should have thought about that before you lit the match,' Jack barks.

'Might I remind you that had Freddie not burned down Pendark, you might never have found'—I can't bring myself to say Anna's name—'*her*.'

A couple of the diners on the closest of tables have looked up and are glaring at Jack and me in support of their friend. I try to ignore their stares and soften my tone. 'I think we should all calm down, and remember where we are. Freddie is as much a victim as the girl you've found, Jack.' I sigh. 'Yes, the fire was reckless, but he's served his punishment for the crime, and now he wants to move on with his life. You know the pain he has suffered, and dredging it all up here and now isn't right.'

Jack's glare hasn't left Freddie and I'm not sure he has heard me; he certainly hasn't listened. 'Why set fire to the place?' Jack says next, no longer concerned about the rising aggression in his voice. 'If you knew where the place was, you could have phoned me, or Emma, or 999, and reported it. That way a professional team of forensics experts could have gone over that place brick by brick searching for answers about the people who were there. But no, instead, you douse the place in accelerant and destroy all the evidence that could have helped catch the bastards who did this to you and countless others.'

Freddie stands, no longer prepared to put up with Jack's bluntness, and frankly I don't blame him. But Jack isn't prepared to give up that easily and snatches at Freddie's arm, dragging him back down.

'I'm not done with you yet. You tell me what you know now, or so help me, I'll have you in the nearest nick for impeding an investigation.'

'Jack!' I gasp, shocked at just how hostile this last threat is. 'Freddie is doing his best, and this is not the right way to treat him.' I coil my fingers around Jack's and pry them off Freddie's wrist. Freddie looks ashen but I nod for him to return to the food table and continue working.

'That is no way to speak to him,' I chastise, keeping my voice low but filled with anger.

Jack pulls his fingers from mine dismissively. 'You really have no clue, do you?'

'No clue about what, Jack? I don't understand why you're being like this.'

He has pushed his tongue into his cheek and is shaking his head, holding back again.

'Are you going to tell me what's going on?' I press. 'I know you're under pressure because of what's happening with Mila's mum and because of the extra hours you're putting in, but there's something else you're not telling me. It's okay to be pissed off, Jack, but taking it out on Freddie is not the answer.'

'No?' he shouts, his head snapping round. He leans closer, his voice barely more than a pained whisper. 'He's hiding something. He knows a lot more than he's letting on, but you're too blind to see it. Maybe it's because you've allowed yourself to become too close to your subject, or maybe it's because, despite all your intuition, you are nothing more than a writer. You're not a detective, Emma, and your desperation to see the good in people all the time stops you seeing what is right in front of your face.'

I'm not prepared to become the next target of his frustration. Grabbing my satchel, I scrape my chair from the table, causing more people to look over. I can't bring myself to look at Jack, let alone speak to him. I make my way over to the table, move around it, and grab an apron from behind the door. Standing next to Freddie, I begin to ladle from the second tall pot of soup, faking a smile as I hand the bowls over to expectant hands.

I see Jack shrink away in my periphery, but I keep my gaze firmly fixed on those I'm serving.

'I'm sorry about that,' I whisper gently to Freddie when the queue has died down.

He doesn't respond, and I can't help thinking our friendship will never be the same again. Freddie trusted me with his story, and now I'm the one who invited the wolf into our little cave of trust. Jack is wrong about me though. Wanting to find the good in people isn't a flaw, it's a strength.

Chapter Seven

THEN

Piddlehinton, Dorset

Rattling of the caravan door had Joanna pulling up her knees and tucking them beneath her chin. It had to have been nearly an hour since she'd overheard the men threatening to kill her, and so she'd remained quiet as a mouse, sitting on the small bench, crying to herself and praying fervently for a solution to her problem.

It was much darker outside now, and she couldn't stop thinking about how frantic her mum would be. She'd never stayed out this late alone before, but the one bright spark she was focusing on was that her not returning home today was so out of character. Her mum and dad would know she hadn't run away and that meant they'd know there had to be another reason she wasn't home; they were probably thinking she'd been in an accident, or that the worst had happened and she'd been taken. Mum would be phoning her friends, hospitals, and probably the police, which in turn meant there were people looking for her.

Whether they'd know she'd been brought to this tiny campsite in the middle of nowhere was a question she was refusing to ask. They would find her; bad things didn't happen to people like them. Aside from the burglary, the family had never had need of the support of the police; they didn't know anyone who'd been beaten, mugged, or murdered. They were a good family who went to church most Sundays, and didn't welcome trouble into their lives.

The door rattled again and she held her breath, willing the men to go away. She'd been good; she hadn't made a fuss. Whatever they had planned, surely they wouldn't kill her as they'd threatened.

The door cracked open a moment later but the figure who stepped through wasn't the man in grey who'd brought her here, nor the man he'd been speaking to. Instead, a younger man – possibly fifteen or sixteen with tight red curls on top of his head – bounded up the steps.

'Oh, bloody hell, it's dark in here. Why are the friggin' lights not on?'

The tone of his voice was pitched much higher than she'd been anticipating. She instantly recognised the dulcet tones of his Irish upbringing, as his voice sounded similar to that of Sinead O'Donovan in her class at school. The accent wasn't as harsh as her teacher Mr Allen, who was from Belfast.

The young man bounded back out of the caravan, leaving the door swinging open, as he moved about and fiddled with something clunky outside. To have left the door so open like that meant he either hadn't seen her, or he had no idea she was in here. Was this the chance she'd been praying so ardently for?

Lowering her legs off the chair, she kept her breath held, conscious that her footsteps would echo around the cabin if she didn't place them carefully. The young man hadn't returned, and she could still hear him bashing away at something outside. She crept forwards slowly, beginning to feel lightheaded at the lack of fresh oxygen, but she swallowed down the anxiety until she found herself at the doorway, staring out into the darkness. A small security light just outside the door showed the wet mud beyond the steps, and as she peered ever further out, she could see that each of the three caravans had a similar spotlight projecting down from a pole on the roof.

There was no other sign of life outside, which meant if she could get down the steps without the younger man hearing and seeing her, she could get across the mud and back onto the track before anyone knew she was gone. What she would do when she got there, she hadn't thought through yet, but it had to be worth the chance.

'Oh, hi, there you are,' the young man's voice said, as he suddenly materialised in the doorway, the caravan rocking as he once more took the steps two at a time, making no effort to tread lightly.

Joanna scuttled back to the seat, fearing that his intentions were anything but friendly, but he made no lunge towards her. Instead, he flicked on the switch by the door and suddenly the room filled with light.

It took a moment for her eyes to adjust and to take in his full figure. He had to be close to six feet in height, but thinner than any boy she'd ever seen. He was wearing fluorescent swimming trunks and a sleeveless vest that only made him look scrawnier and limper, as his stick-thin arms and shoulders protruded out from the straps. A cluster of reddish-brown freckles covered almost every inch of his face, but there was no malice in the huge smile that was slowly spreading across it.

'I'm Chez,' he said, moving into the open kitchen area, reaching for the kettle on the stove and promptly filling it beneath the sink tap. 'I can't believe they left you sitting in here in the dark. Not to worry, I've got the generator going, so now we can see each other without squinting. Do you want a cuppa?'

She hadn't drunk any of the Fanta she'd bought at the newsagent's shop, such had been the panic when she'd realised the man wasn't taking her home, and it had fallen from her lap when he'd dragged her from the car. Only now that she thought about Chez's question did she realise just how thirsty she was.

'Yes, please,' she said cautiously.

She watched as he located two mugs in the back of one of the cupboards she hadn't been able to reach, before removing a small box of teabags and dropping one in each.

'You don't take sugar do you, 'cos I don't think we have any.'

She doubted that was the only ingredient he was missing; given the lights hadn't been working, she doubted the fridge would have been running. To her surprise, he reached into the high cupboard again, this time removing a carton of milk.

'It's long-life,' he said when he saw her frowning. 'Means we don't have to rely on the dodgy generator that's always conking out. It tastes like pish to drink, but it's okay in tea. So, have you been here long?'

She glanced at her watch, but her eyes couldn't focus on the hands, so she really had no idea how long it had been since the man had locked her in the car and brought her here. She shrugged instead.

'Well, not to worry. I'll whip us up something to eat when we've finished our tea. They say it's good for shock, and judging by how pale your face is, I think it's just what you need. In fact, actually I think it's sweet tea that's good for shock, but as we have no sugar, we'll just have to make do.'

Every time he spoke, it was like he was in a race to finish his sentences, such was the speed the words tumbling from his lips. And she couldn't tell if he was deliberately trying to sound like one of her girlfriends, but he didn't seem ashamed of the effeminate nature of his voice.

The kettle whistled on the gas stove, and she continued to watch him as he made the tea. He'd shut the door when he'd come in, but had made no effort to lock it, nor barricade her in. It wouldn't be too much effort to wait for his back to be turned, before rushing at the door. She wouldn't have the head start she would have had when he was still outside, but if she ran with all her might, was it possible she could get out of the light and to the track before he caught up?

He carried the mugs over, and the chance was gone again.

Resting one of the mugs on the table before her, he moved around the table and sat next to her. 'It will be hot, so I'd give it a couple of minutes before drinking it if I were you.' He paused. 'So where are you from?'

'Portland,' she whispered, still unsure whether he was just lulling her into a false sense of security.

'Ah, so you're local then? I'm from Donegal originally. Have you ever been to Ireland?'

She shook her head. The furthest they'd been was the Lake District. Whilst all her other friends had at least been to the Costa del Sol on holiday, she'd never left the UK; her parents didn't believe in spending money to aid foreign markets when the British tourism industry was in greater need of support.

'Well, if you ever get the chance, you *must* go. It's a lovely town, and the people there are so friendly.'

As she studied his face more closely, trying to read him, her eyes widened as she saw the long, thin scar running from the edge of his right eye down his cheek. She tried to look away, but he'd seen her shock.

'Beer bottle,' he said, running a finger over the now smooth edge. 'My stepfather was a drunk who didn't appreciate my smart mouth. I certainly don't miss *him*.'

'How long have you been here?' she dared to ask.

He didn't immediately answer but his eyes brightened a moment later. 'I tell you what, why don't we do each other's nails? Have you had your nails painted before?'

The only reason she wasn't wearing nail varnish at that moment was because the school frowned upon it, and her mum would only let her wear it during the school holidays.

He bounced from the seat, knocking into the table and causing some of her tea to slop onto the top, returning a moment later with a small zip bag. He located some kitchen roll and mopped up the spillage, before unzipping the bag. It was as if he had raided the local Boots, as bottle of polish after bottle of polish cascaded onto the table.

'What's your favourite colour?' he asked, standing up close to two dozen bottles.

She was about to reach for the violet varnish, when she thought again. Her mother never let her wear black nail varnish ('the devil's colour', she would say), and so Joanna pointed to it.

'Ooh, you're such a vixen,' Chez gushed, grabbing the bottle and shaking it vigorously. 'You know, you remind me of my wee sister Kylie, do you know that? She has brown hair like yours, and the most piercing green eyes.'

He took her left hand in his and held it gently as he began to apply the varnish to the nail. She'd always wanted to have her nails painted professionally, but her mum had called it a frivolous expense when she was just as capable of doing it herself. She imagined this must have been what it felt like. He was so gentle and delicate in the application that she knew instantly hers weren't the first nails he'd painted in this way, and suddenly the image of the word RUN, which had been scrawled in the colouring book, flashed to the front of her mind. Snatching her hand back, she eyed the caravan door once more.

'What is it?' he asked, following her gaze to the door.

'My parents will be worried,' she eventually confided. 'They don't know where I am. If I could just phone them, and—'

'Grey will have phoned them by now, to be sure,' he interrupted.

'Grey?'

'Ah, that's what I call him, the man who brought you here. He's nearly always dressed in a grey suit, so I call him Grey. I'm guessing you haven't met Mr Brown yet?'

She shook her head.

'It figures; probably best to steer clear of Mr Brown until you're settled. He has a bit of a temper if you rub him up the wrong way.'

The man who'd taken her – Grey – had said he'd messaged her parents, and she hadn't believed him, but now she wasn't so certain. The way Chez was behaving seemed so fearless, and she couldn't sense any worry or anxiety in his tone or mannerisms.

'What is this place?' she asked, moving one foot from beneath the table, ready to throw some of the bottles at Chez as she made her bolt for the door.

He screwed the top back on the bottle of polish, and patiently laid it back on the table. 'Have you ever been at home and thought, why do they always treat me like some dumb kid?'

She nodded at the question, though this afternoon's experience suggested her parents had been right to be cautious.

'Well, this here is a very special place. How old would you say I was?'

She shrugged, not wishing to offend him by guessing too old, nor too young.

'I'm fifteen, and I've been with them for four years. In all that time, they've never once treated me like some dumb kid. Here, I am free to be who I want to be, do whatever I want. It's a place where we get treated as adults.'

That still hadn't answered her question, and so she tried again. 'But *what* is this place? I didn't ask to come here.'

His smile returned. 'No, you were *chosen* to be here. That's how it works. You're going to be a model and film actress. You don't realise just how lucky we are to be here. Just relax and trust me, okay?'

She'd heard rumours at school about Misty Reynolds, two years above her, whose mum had been approached while they'd been out shopping in town. The man was a talent scout for a modelling agency, and Misty had been signed up to appear in television commercials. Was it possible that was what had happened here too? Had Grey spoken to her parents as Chez had said, and they'd agreed for her to start a modelling career?

She tucked her foot back beneath the table and passed Chez her other hand, nodding at the black polish again.

Chapter Eight

NOW

Weymouth, Dorset

I remain at the shelter until the food rush is over, but Freddie says very little during the time. As I hug him when it's time to leave, he doesn't shirk the embrace, but nor does he squeeze tightly, which is his usual way with me. It feels like I'm hugging a tree – getting nothing in return.

'Are you sure you're okay?' I ask for the umpteenth time, looking for the tiny chink in his armour.

'I told you, I'm fine.'

He's totally flat; no effervescence or 'Freddie spirit', as I like to think of it. In fairness, it's probably been quite an emotional day for him too, having been released from prison, and then learning the remains of a body were discovered on the site of the fire, but I can't help blaming myself for his current state.

'It's Sunday tomorrow,' I try brightly. 'Do you fancy going somewhere, or doing anything? A walk along the beach, or for a coffee somewhere, or just hanging out at my place? I've got a book signing in town to attend first thing, but that should be done by twelve…'

I desperately want him to shout at me, and release the tension in the room; either that or to tell me we *can* get over this hurdle. But he simply shrugs and tells me he doesn't know what his plans are for tomorrow yet, but he'll call me.

I don't push him any more but hug him again, with no response, and head out into the cool chill of the night. The sky is pitch black now, and the moon must be hidden by a cloud somewhere. The streetlights do little to brighten the slippery paving slabs, and so I eventually resort to pulling out my phone and using the torch to light my way. The shelter is only a ten-minute walk from my flat and I know the route like the back of my hand, but given everything running through my mind – Freddie, Jack, Anna – I don't think I've ever felt so vulnerable. Every rustle of a discarded carrier bag, every cat scurrying for dinner, and every gust of wind has me looking over my shoulder for some evil spirit about to strike out at me. There's nobody watching or following me, but my shoulders don't relax until I see the lamppost outside my flat.

My relief is tempered with surprise as I spot the car parked beneath the light, and then see Jack emerge from the driver's side as I near.

'Before you say anything,' he blurts out, stopping me in my tracks, 'I just wanted to apologise for my behaviour back there. It was unprofessional and insensitive.'

I cross my arms. 'It isn't me you should be apologising to.'

Jack locks the car and comes over, wearing the face of a disciplined school child. 'You're right. I owe Freddie an apology too, but I'm still convinced he's hiding something. Don't ask me what, but my sixth sense – that tiny voice in my gut that hears what I can't – is telling me that your friend is holding back. And I will find out what he's hiding and why.'

This isn't the first time Jack has met Freddie, but he hasn't spent nearly as much time with him as I have, and I just don't see this deception. It makes me wonder for how long Jack hasn't trusted Freddie.

'It's freezing out here,' Jack continues, glancing over to my front door. 'Can we go inside, so I can apologise properly?'

It's tempting to send him on his way after his performance at the shelter but I can read the sincerity in his eyes, and so I give him the benefit of the doubt. I nod for him to follow, and once we're inside I fill the kettle with water and switch it on. It feels good to be back in the warmth with the smell of this morning's burnt toast still hanging in the air.

'What's going on, Jack?' I ask bluntly, no longer prepared to beat about the bush and wait for him to open up. 'I know you said things have been stressful managing work with additional care for Mila, but Freddie isn't the only one holding back, is he?'

It's like the question has triggered a switch in Jack's head as his eyes suddenly fill and he can't bring himself to look at me. He shakes his head. I pass him a tissue and allow him space to compose himself as I make the tea. We move into the living room and sit on opposite ends of the sofa.

'I bet the last thing you expected to find on your doorstep was a sobbing bobby, right?' he says, eyes now drier, and with his gawky grin.

'I'm worried about you, Jack. I haven't heard from you in weeks, haven't seen you in months, and then today you're not the Jack I remember. Do you know what I mean? You've been a pent-up ball of tension all day, and then the way you went for

Freddie – and in a place where he feels secure – was so unlike you. What's going on? What's *really* going on?'

Jack takes a sip of his tea before placing the mug on the carpet by his feet. 'I thought I was keeping a lid on it all but the truth is I've been burying my head in the sand. Things with the investigation have all but stalled. When I started the secondment with the team at the National Crime Agency, they were all looking to me for background and context, and those first few days were spent with them interrogating me on every detail of what we – you and I – had managed to find out. I spoke to them about your history with Arthur Turgood and the St Francis Home for Wayward Boys. One or two of them had read your book, *Monsters Under the Bed*, and knew the history. I spoke about the hard drive recovered from Turgood's home, and the underage pornographic material discovered on it, and how that led us to finding Freddie's footage, that of Jemima Hooper, and of course your sister, Anna. They listened and they questioned until they understood what was required: find the other children in the videos, and use the files recovered from the Pendark Film Studios to tie culprits to the footage. In the near eight months the investigation has been in full swing, do you know how many perpetrators we've brought to justice?'

I shake my head. I certainly haven't read about any in the news.

'Zero. And do you know how many new faces we've managed to identify from the video footage? One! A lad called Billy Watson who went missing on his way home from school in Edinburgh in 1997. He's still listed as a missing person, and we've made no progress on finding out who took him, how he ended up on film, nor where he ended up. Given Jemima

Hooper's demise, I'm not holding out much hope of finding him. You and I achieved more in less time and there were only two of us. I am working as part of a team of twenty trained detectives and we've still made virtually no progress in uncovering the network of monsters responsible for all this abuse and tragedy. And it's killing me knowing that we're failing these kids. God knows how many more missing children are out there right now suffering at the hands of these evil bastards.'

I had no idea his mental health was suffering so much as a result of this race I feel responsible for starting. 'I'm sorry, Jack,' I offer sincerely, choosing my words carefully. 'I'm sure you and your team have given everything you can, and I would imagine you've chased down a lot of false leads, right?'

'Every avenue of investigation feels like it ends at a brick wall.'

'But there's a silver lining to that cloud: it means you're getting closer to finding the right avenue that won't lead to a dead end. Think about how people make it out of a maze. You have to pursue wrong routes to find the way to the treasure in the middle. What feels like little progress due to the lack of success is in fact taking you closer to the truth. You shouldn't beat yourself up over that.'

His eyes are watering again but this time he keeps the tears at bay. 'I feel like I've let you down most of all. I promised you I wouldn't stop until I found out what happened to Anna, but we're no closer to knowing who took her, nor how she ended up at Pendark. And if she is the one we found…'

I reach out and take his hand in mine. '*If* that is my sister, then you will have achieved something I never could in bringing her home to me. I've always accepted deep down the possibility that I would never learn the truth about what happened to her, so you shouldn't feel like you're failing anyone. She went missing twenty-one years ago, Jack; that's a helluva lot of history to churn through.'

His face softens for the first time all day and I catch a glimpse of the old Jack again, fighting to break through.

'I miss this, you know,' he says. 'I never appreciated just how good you are at seeing the edges of the jigsaw pieces, and how they fit together in a logical manner. I don't doubt if we had you supporting the investigation we would have made more progress, and plotted a better course out of the maze.'

I squeeze his hand. 'I've missed you too.'

Jack swivels around so he's facing me better. 'I'm glad to hear you say that. After we worked together on the Aurélie Lebrun case, it felt like… I don't know… like something had changed between us. I know you said you weren't interested in pursuing anything romantically with me with everything that was going on, but right before I joined the NCA, I got the impression you'd lost interest altogether.'

My cheeks are burning with embarrassment. When I' invited him in to apologise, I hadn't anticipated having to discuss my personal feelings. I'm not ready; I need time to prepare and think about how I feel. That's the beauty of writing: you get to sketch an idea and then edit it until it's just right. On the spot conversations are not my strong suit.

How I wish Rachel was here. My best friend would know what to say right now, but she's off in Barcelona living her best life whilst her beautiful girlfriend Daniella is modelling. Not that I begrudge Rachel any happiness; God knows, she deserves a little positivity in her life, and I am so relieved she and Daniella worked things out.

'You need to say something,' Jack says, edging closer. 'Was I imagining it?'

'To be honest, I didn't know where I stood after you slept with your former flame, DS Zoe Cavendish.'

I've never seen a frown form so quickly on anyone's brow. 'What? I never slept with Zoe!'

'It's okay, Jack, it's not like we're involved. You're free to pursue whoever you wish.'

He's shaking his head in disbelief. 'No, but I didn't. Zoe is an old acquaintance, rather than an old flame. There's never been anything between us, at least *nothing* like that! What the hell made you think I'd slept with her?'

I can't read him. In my head I know he slept with her, but he is putting up such a strong defence that my conviction is waning.

'She told me you did – or at least she implied it. And you did crash at her place for a couple of nights. Given your history…'

'She told you we slept together? Wait until I speak to her next… For the record, I have *never* slept with DS – sorry, she's a DI now – Zoe Cavendish. When we first met at police training, I was already involved with Chrissie – Mila's mum – and I'm not the sort to do the dirty on someone I'm seeing. I can't believe you actually thought I would have slept with Zoe of all people. She's hardly my type, is she?'

It's my turn to shrug. 'How would I know, Jack? I don't know what "your type" is.'

He looks down at his hands, still shaking his head. 'It's you, Emma.' He looks up and meets my stare. '*You're* my type. Someone who is smart, and funny, and doesn't realise how special and beautiful she is.'

My heart is racing so quickly it may very well fly out of my chest. God, why are my hands suddenly so clammy? I've been waiting to hear someone say those words to me, but now that they're here, I feel nauseous. Is he about to try and kiss me again? I've had no time to ready myself for this! My lips are chapped by the cold weather and I'm dressed in a plaid skirt and turtleneck jumper.

He takes my hands in his. 'I don't want you to doubt how I feel about you, Emma, but…' He pauses. 'There is so much going on right now with work and Mila that I don't think it would be fair on either of us to pursue this right now. I need to sort things out and get my head clear, but once I do, I hope we can explore *this* at some point.'

He releases my hands, and is quickly on his feet, looking at his watch. 'I need to get back for Mila.' He sighs. 'Thank you for the tea, and for not laughing at me when the floodgates opened.'

He is moving towards the door, but I'm still frozen with fear on the sofa, my mind yet to catch up with the reality that he isn't about to try and kiss me and worrying about how awkward it's going to be.

'I'll show myself out. If you see Freddie before I do, can you pass on my apology? I'll try and call him at some point.'

And suddenly I'm alone in my room and the front door is closing, and I didn't get to tell Jack that I'm happy to wait for him for as long as it takes.

Chapter Nine

NOW

Weymouth, Dorset

Dinner – if you can call it that – was a bowl of whole-wheat pasta with what remained of the open jar of pesto at the bottom of my fridge. Sometimes, there's nothing wrong with waiving the need for fresh fruit and vegetables. Technically, the large glass of Chenin Blanc that accompanied the meal was made from grapes, and so in my book that's one of my seven; I'll just have to eat double tomorrow!

With the pan and my bowl soaking in a basin of hot water, I finally catch my breath after what has been a rollercoaster of a day. If I'd known everything that would happen today, I might very well have rolled back over in bed and remained there for the rest of the day. It's not even ten o'clock, and already my warm duvet and soft pillows are calling for me. The wine probably wasn't such a well-thought-out idea considering my mental state, but it's too late to worry about that now; it's not like I need to drive anywhere tonight.

Staring at the calendar in my kitchen I can see the bold letters of the leaflet hanging from the pin board beside it. You'd think after two years of publication parties, book launches, and signing events I'd be comfortable with what awaits in the morning, but the truth is today's turmoil has served as a welcome distraction. The signing is at the Waterstones in the centre of town, and is being hosted in celebration of the paperback release of my last book, *Isolated*, which tells the story of Sally Curtis, the teenager who went missing from the nearby Bovington army barracks. Awkwardly, the book signing event my agent Maddie organised for last autumn's hardback release was at the WH Smith's a few doors away from tomorrow's venue. It will likely generate some local interest, and as Maddie always tells me, 'You can't sign books once you're dead!'

No, it doesn't make a lot of sense to me either, but that doesn't stop her using it *every* time she's trying to cajole me into attending one event or another.

'It's about giving back to your fans,' she reminds me, and I owe my readers a lot so it's only right I try and repay them in some way.

The signing doesn't start until ten, and Maddie is planning to meet me at the venue half an hour before to ensure the table is set up and there are enough copies of my other books on hand should anyone be interested in purchasing them for signing too. I don't know what I'd do without Maddie in my life. Her commercial eye means I can focus solely on creating the work, and she is worth every penny of the commission she collects from royalties earned. I'm planning to wake at eight, shower, and dress in an outfit Maddie has picked out for me, before taking a leisurely stroll into town, stopping for a cooked breakfast on the way to settle any last-minute nerves.

'The day will pass without hitch or issue,' I tell myself, breathing in deeply and exhaling as I repeat the mantra.

I'm about to switch off the kitchen light and head through to bed for a read when the phone erupts to life on the side and frightens me half to death. I shouldn't be surprised to see Maddie's name in the caller display; she's probably just checking I'm not planning to back out of the signing at the last minute.

'Hi, Maddie. You caught me on the way to bed; want to be fresh for the morning.'

'Good girl. Glad to hear it. I was just checking that you know to be there for half nine, and to bring a couple of pens in case one runs out.'

I quickly grab two pens from the mug by my writing desk and place them on the unit beside my door, silently reprimanding myself for not remembering I'd need something to sign with.

'Already sorted,' I lie confidently.

'I figured it would be, but no harm in a gentle reminder. Are you all set? No last-minute nerves?'

'No,' I lie again, though less convincingly. 'It's a couple of hours of sitting behind a table, thanking people for their interest in my work. How hard can it be, right?'

'That's the spirit! Actually, there was another reason for my call; we received an envelope for you at the office yesterday. Addressed to you, but care of the office. I was just going to bring it down tomorrow, but then I suddenly thought it might be urgent. Probably just fan mail, but I can open it if you want?'

Right after *Monsters* became the overnight success it did, I found I started receiving all sorts of letters from readers to my home address. Some were sweet messages of support, but not all, and in the end we had to hire a company to remove all traces of my home address from the web for protection. It still terrifies me that some crazed fan could find out where I live and come to my door. I still get to read any messages that are sent via Maddie, and most remain heart-warming and inspirational letters that touch my heart. There was one gentleman, who shall remain nameless, who sent me a box of his old pornographic magazines, advising that he had turned over a new leaf and put that seediness behind him because he'd seen the error of his ways having read *Monsters*. We passed the box and note onto the police, but I don't know if anything ever came of it. Maddie now acts as my filter and doesn't show me anything that might put my nerves on edge and stop me agreeing to events like tomorrow's signing.

'Yeah, go ahead,' I say, stifling a yawn, the wine slowly pickling my brain.

'Okay, one second,' she says, and I hear her lowering the phone.

I yawn again while waiting for her to come back on the line.

'Mmm,' she mumbles, 'it's a black and white photograph. No letter, just an image of a girl. There's no return address or contact details on the envelope.'

I've received crude messages on social media from men telling me how they could blow my world, or how I should agree to meet them because they feel we'd have such a great time together. And yes, there has been the occasional dick-pic as well, and it's the reason I was so keen to avoid social media in the first place. If it weren't for Maddie's insistence that authors need to have a social platform, I wouldn't be on it today. I've never received an image through the post though, let alone one of a girl.

'How old is this girl?' I ask.

'Hard to say. Adolescent, I guess. Oh, wait, there's a name scrawled on the back. Faye McKenna.'

The name doesn't ring any bells in my tired mind. 'Is there anything else?'

'Nope, just the name. It's been written in some kind of thick permanent marker, I'd hazard.'

I know I'm tired, and the only semi-logical explanation my mind can conjure is that it's a picture of a missing girl sent in by a fearful parent, or one of her family. Given the work Rachel and I are undertaking with the charitable Anna Hunter Foundation, offering emotional and financial support to the families of missing children, I suppose it's possible an applicant has sent the image to try and attract my attention.

'I can take a photo of the image and send it over via email,' Maddie offers.

'Sure,' I relent, and check my phone until my inbox pings. Switching Maddie to speaker phone, I download the image and stare at it on my phone. 'I can't say I recognise the name, or the face,' I admit. 'Pretty young thing though. I don't remember coming across the name Faye, nor McKenna, in any of my previous research, but I can check on the Foundation's database and see if her family are listed.'

I hope this doesn't become a common thing: parents trying to emotionally blackmail me into accepting their requests for financial support. Since we launched the Anna Hunter Foundation a little over a year ago, we have been inundated with requests for help, and that's the purpose of the charity, but there are also those chancers who will request support under the pretence of having a missing child. Each application is rigorously checked, and we even have a small team of private investigators on retainer to verify the authenticity of each claim.

Loading up my laptop, I log into the Foundation site and check the database of claimant names, but there is no Faye McKenna listed.

'Are you sure there was nothing else in the envelope?' I check with Maddie. 'It isn't possible a letter fell out when you pulled out the photograph? No explanation of who sent it to me, or why?'

I can hear Maddie scuttling about on her carpet, before she returns to the phone. 'No, I'm sorry. I'll bring the envelope and original picture with me in the morning, and you can see for yourself. Maybe whoever sent it forgot to include a letter of explanation. I wouldn't let it worry you tonight. Go to bed and get a good night's sleep for tomorrow. Remember, I will meet you at the shop at half nine. Okay?'

'Sure, thanks, Maddie. I'll see you in the morning.'

Switching off the laptop and locking my phone, I head to bed, but I don't settle for ages as all I can see when I close my eyes is Faye McKenna's face.

Chapter Ten

THEN

Piddlehinton, Dorset

'Do you want to wash your hands? Dinner's nearly ready,' Chez said to her, as she continued to stare lovingly at her freshly polished nails.

'It smells delicious,' she told him, sliding out from behind the table and squeezing past him into the small bathroom at the rear of the cabin.

'It ought to be! Spaghetti bolognese – my grandmother's recipe – the only thing she taught me before I left.'

Joanna used the facilities, the nerves that had gripped her bladder so tightly finally easing. For all the fear and anxiety, nothing bad had happened. And if Chez was so bright and positive about life here, who was she to question it? Deep down, she knew Grey taking her hadn't been right, but there was also something inside that told her if this was all some elaborate ruse, then her parents would use the police to find her, so why not play along until then? Grey's words were still fresh in her mind, and she didn't want to end up buried in some hole, never to be found.

After washing her hands she exited the small bathroom and returned to the kitchen area. Chez had cleared the table of the nail polishes and had placed forks and plates where they had been sitting.

'You can grate the cheese if you like,' he said over his shoulder, stirring the pan of red sauce, while steam from the pan of pasta hovered in a cloud above her head.

She spotted the block of cheese and the metal grater on the table with the plates and headed over. 'You know, my mum never lets me near the grater; she always says I'll cut myself and ruin the cheese. Are you sure you want me to do it?'

Chez looked over, his mouth pulled into a pitying grimace. 'Do *you* think you'll cut yourself doing it?'

She shook her head firmly.

'Well, then,' he replied. 'Neither do I. Go on, you'll be saving me the effort if you do it. I'll strain the pasta and start plating up.'

Taking the block of cheese in her hand, she dragged it over the metal ridges, each stroke giving a satisfying tear. Her mum never trusted her to do anything! Everyone always said how mature she was for her age, yet they still treated her like a seven-year-old. She was more than capable of grating some cheese; in fact, she was pretty sure she could learn to make spaghetti bolognese like Chez if he showed her how.

He arrived at the table and slopped the strands of spaghetti onto their plates before returning with the second pan, ladling generous helpings on top of the pasta.

'Would you teach me how to make this?' she asked nervously, not yet sure how much of an act his generosity was.

'I'll teach you anything you want to know, Ky—' He stopped himself. 'Sorry, it's just you really do remind me of my sister Kylie. For a moment it was like I was back with her.' He paused. 'In fact, do you know what, I'm going to call you Kylie from now on. Is that okay with you? You could do with a big brother around here, and it would be nice having a little sister again.'

She'd never been a fan of the name Joanna – not that her family ever used her full name anyway.

'Okay, big brother,' she gushed, her heart warming.

He looked just as pleased. 'Well, isn't this just grand? The two of us reunited over Grandma's spaghetti bolognese.'

He squashed into the seat beside her, taking the pot of grated cheese and sprinkling a handful over the steaming dinner, before repeating the action for her. She watched as he picked up his fork, drove it into the mountain of strands, twirled it into a ball shape, and pushed it between his freckled lips. At home, her mum always chopped the spaghetti into smaller strands, but she was keen to learn how to eat it like a grown-up. Stabbing the pasta, she had to use both hands to twirl the fork as Chez had, but when she extracted the fork, most of the pasta fell off. She tried again, this time managing to keep a couple of strands precariously balanced on the tip of the fork, and quickly inhaling them into her mouth. The sauce was rich and tomatoey.

'What's Grandma's secret recipe?' she asked. 'Will you tell me?'

'I will tell you anything you want to know, Kylie.' He dropped his stained fork back onto the table and squeezed back off the seat, returning to the kitchen area. She saw him rustling through the bin, before extracting an empty glass jar.

'Here we are,' he said, twirling it around in his hand. 'So, what you do is boil the pasta for ten or so minutes, pour this bad boy into a separate pan and simmer it until the pasta is ready. Dead easy, but so tasty.'

Is that it? she wanted to ask, disappointed that Grandma's so-called secret recipe could be purchased in any decent grocery shop. At least it wouldn't be too difficult to master.

'It's yummy,' she said, trying and failing to twirl her pasta again.

'Well, I'm glad you're enjoying it. It's one of my jobs here, taking care of our guests. My cookery skills are a tad limited, but you won't ever go hungry.'

She studied his pasta twirling technique once more, committing the action to memory, and determined to show him that she was mature for her age. On the third attempt, she managed to create a small ball, and quickly shovelled it into her mouth. Pleased as punch, she did it again, this time calling to him, but just as he looked over, the pasta slipped from the fork, cascading down the front of her dress.

Her cheeks instantly reddened and she grabbed handfuls of the pasta, quickly returning it to her plate and looking for something to wipe her top.

'Oh no, it's going to stain. Mum's going to kill me.' The tears filling her eyes were unexpected, but she didn't fight to restrain them.

'Hey, hey,' Chez sighed, 'there's no need to upset yourself. It's only a bit of sauce. I can get that cleaned up for you. Don't worry about it. Removing unwanted stains from clothes is something I'm particularly good at.'

He reached out and began grappling to lift the dress over her head, but she didn't feel comfortable stripping off in front of him and wrenched the material back. In that moment, she would have given anything to be back at home, even though her mum would be in the middle of reprimanding her for being so careless.

'Listen, it's okay,' he tried again, calmness personified. 'I've got some of my sister's old clothes in a case in my room. I can pick you something out to wear while I give your dress a clean.'

It didn't cross her mind to question why he would have his sister's clothes here when he'd left home three years earlier. Instead, she watched entranced as he took her hand and led her through the kitchen area, turning right at the door to the small bathroom and into a bedroom with twin beds. He encouraged her to sit on one before pulling open a wardrobe and extracting a tattered case from the darkness. Plopping it on the bed, he lifted the lid and began to rifle through until he located the prettiest black sequined number.

'This ought to fit,' he exclaimed happily as he hoisted it into the air. 'You're about the same size as Kylie. Get that one off and you can wear this while we finish dinner.'

She began to peel the dress up, before hesitating. 'Could you turn around?'

He rolled his eyes in a forgiving way. 'You don't need to be embarrassed about changing in front of me. I'm your brother, remember, and I have no interest in your naked body. Besides, if you want to be a movie star, you're going to have to get used to having strangers looking at you.'

She remained still until he turned his back, and then she quickly whipped off her stained dress and slid the black one over her head. The material felt rougher on her skin than she'd anticipated; it certainly looked nicer than it felt. But with it in place she stood and admired her reflection in the small mirror hanging from the cupboard door.

'Oh my God, you're the spitting image of Kylie now,' he gushed. 'It is scary how much you look like her.'

The garment certainly made her look older – or at least she thought so. She could probably pass for twelve now at a push, and this thought wiped away the tearful grimace, replacing it with a vibrant smile.

'Here, I'll zip you up,' Chez offered, fiddling with the catch behind her head. 'Now, shall we go and finish our dinner? I can't stand around chatting all night, or I'll be late for work...'

His eyes widened and the blood drained from his face in an instant as his arm flew up so he could check his watch. 'Oh Jesus! I'm going to be late. Feck!' He looked back at her. 'Are you all right to finish up without me? If I don't get my arse to work now, the shit's gonna hit the fan.'

She hadn't realised he would be working tonight, and had hoped he would remain with her, telling her more about the nature of his work.

'Can I come with you?' she tentatively asked, already anticipating his response. 'I'll be super quiet and I won't get in the way, I promise.'

He was only half-listening, bounding out of the room, grabbing a leather-look jacket from a peg on the wall by the main door. 'Not tonight, sorry. It's a closed set and only authorised people are allowed inside to watch.' He stopped when he saw the despondency creeping across her features. 'Listen, I'll be quick as I can and I'll be back before you know it. Why don't you finish up your dinner, and just have a rest. If you feel tired, your bed is the one I left the case on. Just put it on my bed and you can go to sleep.'

With that he pushed out of the door, locking it behind him.

Dejected, she returned to the bench behind the table and squeezed in, but her appetite had gone. It wasn't Chez's fault he had to work, and maybe he'd been telling the truth when he said he'd be back sooner than she was expecting.

The light overhead flickered for a moment before flashing out, and the cabin suddenly plunged into darkness again. Even if she'd wanted to finish her dinner, she couldn't see it. Thoughts of her mother and father flooded her mind once more, wondering whether they were out looking for her now and how much longer she'd have to wait before they found her. The tears began to flow again and once more she didn't resist. Fatigue eventually arrived, but it was so dark that she didn't dare venture out from behind the table, instead curling up on the cushioned bench and resting her head on the rolled-up remains of the dress she'd arrived in. Closing her eyes, she allowed the darkness to embrace her.

Chapter Eleven

NOW

Weymouth, Dorset

Fevered knocking at my door isn't welcome, especially as I was having the most wonderful dream – not that I can now recall what it was about. Rubbing my eyes, I'm curious to know who would be causing such a racket before eight on a Sunday, and as my mind tries to consider and rule out illogical possibilities, when I open the door I'm half-expecting to see one of Maddie, Jack, Freddie, or Rachel (even though I know she's in Barcelona). The one person that hadn't made it onto the roulette wheel in my head was the smiling Police Community Support Officer sheltering from the rain.

'Miss Hunter?' he enquires, and for the briefest of moments I'm almost convinced that I'm still dreaming, but then a gust of wind blows rain into my face, and the cool splashes are a rude awakening.

'Yes, sorry, can I help you with something?' I yawn, quickly covering my mouth.

'I'm Rick Underwood. Would you mind if I came in out of the rain for a second?'

I'm not usually willing to allow perfect strangers to enter my home uninvited, but he does appear to be wearing the requisite royal-blue polo shirt and high-visibility vest supporting his credentials. I take a single step back, keeping the door's edge gripped firmly in my hand, ready to force it closed if the need arises. He steps in, removing his hat and showing off a buzz cut more befitting an army recruit in some film about the Vietnam War.

'Thank you,' he says quickly, not forcing himself any further in. 'I'm sorry, did I wake you? I would have thought all writers would be up at the crack of dawn writing.'

Glancing over his shoulder, it doesn't look as though it's long since dawn. There is nobody on the beach, save for the odd dog walker wrapped in waterproof coats, braving the elements.

As a rule, I try not to write on the weekends. Since signing my first publishing deal, I've tried to remind myself that I am a professional writer now, and as such I need to treat my profession in the same way as any other. That's why I will write Monday to Friday, usually somewhere between the hours of nine and five. Ultimately, it doesn't matter where or when I write, but I seem to respond better to a routine, and that's mine.

'I'm between books,' I tell him, as it's easier than going into the truth.

He smiles pleasantly, tucking his thumbs into the edges of his high-visibility vest. 'Sorry, you'll have to forgive me, but I can't quite believe I'm standing here right now. I'm such a huge fan of your books, Miss Hunter. I read *Ransomed* cover-to-cover twice in a week. The way you tell the story… and leave tantalising clues at the end of each chapter, forcing the reader to just read one more chapter… and then another, and then another. I'm pinching myself right now; I can't believe it's really you.'

You'd think I'd be used to these moments by now, but as soon as anyone offers praise for my writing or one of my book babies, I clam up and will a hole to open in the ground and swallow me. It's less common to hear such positivity from within the police community, especially after the publication of *Monsters*, though there have been one or two who've spoken kindly.

'It's always nice to meet a fan,' I say, releasing the door so that I can allow my hands to fidget and twitch behind my back. 'Do you have any identification?'

His head wobbles as he realises his error and he quickly reaches into his pocket, removing a small lanyard containing a picture of his face, rank, and identification number. Satisfied that I'm not dealing with a crazed fan looking to have their wicked way with me, I beckon him inside, for no reason other than the chill wind is giving my legs goosebumps. Heading into the kitchen, I boil the kettle and fix myself a much-needed cup of strong tea.

'Would you like anything to drink?' I offer, but am not surprised when he politely declines.

I'm about to ask him exactly why he has darkened my door so early on a Sunday when my brain finally whirs to life and connects the dots. I should have seen it sooner. Given his handsome face, spontaneity, and appearance today of all days, he must be an actor Maddie has hired to escort me to the book signing at *Waterstones*. Typical of Maddie to instigate a stunt to highlight the work I've done with the police in the last couple of years that has directly contributed to the books I've produced. I shouldn't criticise, but I wish she'd warned me; I'm not going to be able to call in for that cooked breakfast on the way to the signing now either. Maybe that's why she really phoned last night, to check I'd be home when her actor arrived.

I freeze as last night's call fires fresh in my mind, and I think back to the black and white photograph of Faye McKenna she emailed to me. I checked for the name on the Anna Hunter Foundation database, but I didn't think to check on the missingpeople.org site where I host a page for my sister.

'Will you excuse me for a moment?' I say to Rick. 'I need to get dressed and check my emails before we go.'

He nods his understanding, but makes no movement towards pulling out a chair to sit on.

Tucking the laptop beneath my arm, I carry my tea back to my bedroom and drop the computer on the bed, before washing and quickly dressing in the outfit Maddie had selected. It's a cream blouse with purple flower petals, matched with a violet skirt that apparently highlights my femininity and shows off my 'fabulous legs'. I don't care what Maddie wants, I *will* be wearing tights today, based on the chill in the wintry air.

Satisfied that my hair and makeup are passable, I put on my glasses and hunker over the laptop. It's nearly eight now, so we have plenty of time before the signing is due to start. Loading up the missingpeople.org site, I type Faye McKenna's name into the search box, and view the results. There's one hit, and sure enough the picture that presents itself is of the same girl Maddie emailed over, albeit she is several years younger.

She has dark hair tied in pigtails, uneven teeth, and large square prescription glasses that do little to compliment her round face. According to the site, she was twelve when she went missing in November 1998. There is a message from her family begging her to get in touch, but little other detail. I can only assume someone in her family sent the picture to Maddie's office in a cry for help; perhaps they haven't heard about the Anna Hunter Foundation, and given the success Jack and I experienced in locating Cassie Hilliard and Sally Curtis, maybe they were just hoping to appeal to my better nature and stimulate some interest in their case.

I hear Rick approaching, but thankfully he makes no attempt at pushing open my bedroom door. He clears his throat. 'Miss Hunter? I'm sorry to hurry you, but we really should be making a move; time is of the essence.'

'Won't be a minute,' I call back, opening an internet search window and typing in Faye's name and disappearance date. There are a number of internet articles that open, mostly from local Oldham-based news agencies. The same picture as on the missingpeople.org site is used in the articles. I skim-read, conscious that Rick has remained just the other side of the door. According to one, Faye was last seen waiting for a bus home from secondary school. She'd stayed back as a result of a school detention, and although one witness recalled seeing her siting at the bus stop, she never boarded the number eighteen bus that would have taken her back to her estate.

My heart goes out to her family. There are so many similar stories of children who just disappear, with no trace of who has taken them, nor the reason why. A neighbour is quoted as saying that Faye and her mum were such a close pair but Faye's father hadn't been on the scene for a number of years.

Presumably he would have been the investigating team's first suspect, but the article doesn't allude to his identity.

Rick clears his throat again. 'I'm sorry, Miss Hunter, we really must be going now. I was tasked with bringing you to the station as a matter of urgency.

I close the laptop lid, leaving the search page open so I can do some further digging later. At the very least I feel I should reach out to Faye's mum and tell her how the Foundation might be able to provide some guidance or support.

Standing, I double-check my appearance in the mirror; it certainly isn't the outfit I would have selected for today but I promised Maddie I would follow her instructions. When I pull open the door, Rick stands there, his mouth open.

'Wow! I never realised just how beautiful you'd be in real life.'

I should have powdered my cheeks because I can feel how much they're glowing right now. 'What do you mean, you were tasked with bringing me to the station?' I say, ignoring the compliment. 'Surely you meant bookstore, right?'

He frowns. 'No, I meant the police station in Portland.'

I mirror his frown. 'Why would you need to take me there? I thought you'd been sent to escort me to my book signing.'

He shakes his head. 'Oh, I'm well aware of your book signing today, Miss Hunter – I've asked my sister to queue and get my books signed for me – but that's not the reason I'm here.'

I fold my arms, embarrassed by my own mistake and suddenly conscious that I haven't a clue who Rick really is, nor whether he is the PCSO his lanyard suggested. 'Then exactly why are you here?'

'I'm not allowed to say; I just need to take you to the station. Please?'

I make no effort to move, making my stance clear.

'Okay.' He relents with a small sigh. 'All I can tell you is a nine-year-old girl went missing from her home in Portland yesterday afternoon and the parents have insisted you be brought in to assist the investigation.'

Chapter Twelve

NOW

Portland, Dorset

Coming back to Portland after so many years away feels so odd, but even more so since Rick explained the reason my presence has been requested. Most people of my age probably associate the small island with the popular children's show from the 80s, but for me it harbours such painful memories that have driven and shaped my future. Almost twenty-one years after my sister went missing from the island, the same fate has befallen another family. I can imagine exactly what they're going through.

The island itself hasn't changed a lot in the years since it was home. The prison where my father worked still dominates the landscape, cut into the hill as it is, and references to the prison can be found on virtually every street sign, as if nobody would come here for any other reason. Away from that though, there is still a real sense of community amongst residents, and whilst it isn't an island accessible only by water, the feeling of 'us versus the world' remains. This isn't my first time coming back here, but it's the first time in two decades that I've been summoned.

The police station at Portland brings back too many unwanted memories as well. It still carries that tired mustiness in the air that instantly transports me back to that time: the smell of the unwashed criminals dragged through these very doors as the men and women in blue try to make charges stick; the smell of terrified victims being gently coaxed to reveal the truth of what happened to them; the smell of families alert to the possibility that they're about to receive the most heart-breaking news.

The entrance and reception area have both been given a makeover since I was last here, but it does little to prevent the memories resurfacing. I still recall the social worker taking my hand and leading me to a tiny room filled with children's toys and games. She'd encouraged me to play as I would at home, but they weren't my toys, so how could I play with them as I would at home? I wanted to be with my mum and dad, but they were being interviewed in another room somewhere; out of sight, out of mind, the social worker had probably thought, when the opposite was true.

I'd wanted to know what all the fuss was about. I'd heard Anna's name being screamed by my frantic parents; I'd been in the blue and yellow police car that turned up at home and drove us here; I needed my big sister with me to explain what was going on, as she always did. Since that day, Anna has never been out-of-sight-out-of-mind; if anything, I've spent more of my life thinking about her and that day than if nothing had happened. I wonder whether we would still be close now had she not disappeared twenty-one years ago.

Back then, the parents of the missing child were always the preliminary suspects, but at least the world has moved on somewhat now. It's a hard enough time for parents to experience without feeling the need to be so defensive all the time.

PCSO Rick Underwood asks me to sit in the waiting room while he fetches one of the team to speak to me, but I'm too on edge to rest. In this day and age it appals me that the horror that tore my family apart can still continue unchecked. In a world of digital surveillance and curtain twitchers taking to social media to spread rumours and gossip, how is it possible for such heinous acts to continue? Although it's anti-Orwell, maybe the idea of 100 per cent surveillance isn't so bad if it can prevent tragedies like this unfolding; how many other crimes could have been discovered and prevented if we were all under the eye of Big Brother?

I'm grateful when Rick returns and distracts me from the dark place my mind was headed. 'DS Robyn Meyers will be out in a moment,' he informs me. 'She's the Family Liaison Officer and should be able to give a bit more detail about what's going on and why you're here. The SIO is actively rallying the troops; as I'm sure you know, the first twenty-four hours are key to finding out what happened to Jo-Jo.'

The hairs on the back of my arms stand involuntarily. 'Jo-Jo? Is that the name of the girl?'

He nods grimly with what looks like a fraction of regret in his eyes. Was he not supposed to give me her name?

'DS Meyers will fill you in on the rest. In the meantime, is there anything I can get you? Cup of tea or coffee?'

'No, I'm fine,' I say, not wanting the bitter taste of the tea to take my mind back to that time again.

'Are you sure? You're as pale as a sheet.'

I force my face into a smile of reassurance. 'I'll be fine, but thank you.'

He remains standing beside me until a black woman in her early forties is buzzed through the security door. She is wearing impossibly high heels, but doesn't wobble once as she approaches. The suit jacket tied at the middle looks ready to burst and the tight skirt looks mercilessly uncomfortable, and yet there is something that tells me she welcomes the discomfort the outfit causes, as if it reminds her there are others suffering more than her. Her hair has been chemically straightened and catches the overhead light as she approaches and extends her hand. I shake it, and there is a suitably efficient motion before her fingers begin dancing over the tablet screen resting on her left forearm.

'Emma Hunter?' she asks, eyes only rising from the screen for a moment to register my acknowledgement.

'Yes,' I say, still on edge.

'I'm DS Meyers, but you can call me Robyn. I don't know how much Rick has told you, but a nine-year-old girl has gone missing from the area and we've launched an immediate emergency response. She was last seen yesterday afternoon by her younger step-sister, and we believe that was around three. We are canvassing the area, looking for witnesses who may have seen where she went, whether she met up with anybody, and whether we can pinpoint a more exact time. I'm sure I don't have to tell you that our number-one priority is getting Jo-Jo home.'

Succinct, efficient, and pragmatic, DS Robyn Meyers, I can see, would be a vital cog in any investigative operation.

'Jo-Jo isn't the sort to run away, according to her parents, and they are well known in the local community. The SIO is treating the investigation as an abduction until we know more, which means Jo-Jo's face has been circulated amongst all neighbouring forces, a social media campaign has been launched, and there will be a press conference before the end of the day. Jo-Jo had use of a mobile phone, but that was found at the family home. There is family living nearby, and we are working with them to pinpoint anywhere Jo-Jo might have gone had she chosen to run away.'

'I'm happy to do whatever I can to help,' I say, cringing at how lame it sounds; what can I do anyway?

'Jo-Jo's parents – Mr and Mrs Neville – are here at the station now and are bereft with worry. They specifically asked you to come in. Can I ask how you know the Neville family?'

My brow furrows at the mention of the name. 'I don't know them – at least, I don't think I do.'

Robyn's eyes narrow. 'As soon as they arrived here today, they specifically requested you be brought in. Can you think of any reason why?'

My instinctive response is no, I have no clue as to why anyone would reach out to me in their hour of need, but then I think about the photograph of Faye McKenna that was sent to Maddie's office and my heart sinks.

'I'm a writer and investigative journalist,' I concede, feeling the heat beginning to fire in my cheeks. 'I've been able to help a couple of families to locate missing family members, and'—I pause, unable to believe I'm about to make such an arrogant-sounding statement—'and I believe people now have this impression that I'm able to find missing children. I've been incredibly lucky with how events have played out in the last couple of years, and I wouldn't presume to think that I can do anything more than the police.'

The words are getting twisted in my mouth when all I want to tell Robyn and Rick is that they are the experts and I'm merely an amateur armchair detective. Judging by Robyn's blank expression, I'm guessing I've missed the mark.

'You shouldn't be so modest,' Rick chimes in, but a cheerleader is the last thing I need to convince the FLO.

Robyn's eyes are back on her tablet. 'Regardless, the family have asked to meet with you, and it's my job to work with them to garner as much information as possible. If you'd like to follow me…' She turns effortlessly on those heels, clicks her fingers at the white-haired man behind the desk, and he buzzes the security door open again.

Following her through the door, with PCSO Rick close behind, it's clear the makeover the entrance and reception area received didn't extend further into the station. The corridors bear the same dreary grey paint I remember from childhood, and the carpet is, impossibly, even more threadbare than I remember.

I'm playing the name Neville over in my mind but I'm definitely sure I don't know any family by that name so I can't think of any other reason they would summon me here. I suppose desperate people do desperate things, and they're willing to do anything to get their daughter back. Wouldn't I do the same if I thought there was some quicker route to finding her?

We reach the end of the narrow corridor and Robyn punches a code into the panel on the wall before pushing open the door. The room is larger than I'm anticipating, roughly the size of my kitchen, with a round table in the centre, cupboards on the wall, and a kettle standing atop a small fridge unit in one of the corners.

A man and woman are slumped at the table, and when the woman raises her head, her eyes are red raw from crying. The skin hangs from her cheeks and her coloured hair is tied in a messy bun, but there are no roots showing. Her husband draws my eye next; he's dressed in a navy gilet and Manchester United football shirt, and I can picture him knocking back pint after pint in the pub with his mates – the life and soul of the party – but the droop of his mouth and the tear-filled eyes tell me all I need to know.

'Mr and Mrs Neville,' Robyn begins, 'this is Emma Hunter.'

The woman immediately releases her husband's hand and is around the table before I can move. She throws her arms around my shoulders and I feel compelled to catch her.

'Thank God you're here,' she says loudly into my ear. 'You've got to help us find our poor Jo-Jo.'

'I'm happy to do whatever I can,' I offer meekly.

Robyn pulls out one of the chairs to sit on but nods for Rick to leave the room. He closes the door behind him, and Tina Neville finally releases me and reclaims her seat. I take the remaining vacant chair, sliding the satchel from my shoulder and resting it beside my feet.

'I can't believe it's really you,' Tina says next, once again picking up her husband's hand and squeezing it tightly. 'That Rick said you'd come but I didn't want to believe it. Do you think you can help us find our Jo-Jo?'

I don't know how to answer. I can see from the way they're both trying to meet my stare that they have pinned all of their hopes on me performing some kind of miracle, but they really would be better placing their faith in the police officers who are already working the case. I don't want to tell them that they've got the wrong idea about me because I know from personal experience how important it is for parents in their position to keep hope alive.

'I'm sure the police are already doing everything they can,' I try.

'It must feel like history repeating itself for you though, right?' she asks, and the question catches me on the back foot.

'Excuse me?'

'Well, your sister went missing when she was that age too, didn't she? This all must be a bit weird for you.'

I've made no effort to hide details about my sister's disappearance so I suppose I shouldn't be surprised that they've made such a connection.

'What can you tell me about Jo-Jo?' I ask in an effort to steer the conversation back to the present. 'Did she know not to get into cars with strangers?'

Tina looks to her husband for reassurance.

I can only assume the picture he is clutching so firmly is Jo-Jo. She's very pretty, with chestnut-brown hair, presumably more akin to her father than to her mother's bleached locks. In the picture she's sitting on a neon-pink bicycle, proudly smiling and holding up a pair of stabilisers in her hands.

'She's a good girl, you know,' he says, his voice less polished than his wife. 'Kicked up a right fuss when me and her mum first got together, but things have been better these last six months. We've become a proper little unit, us and my Lola.'

'Lola?' I question.

'Trey's daughter from his first marriage,' Tina clarifies. 'Jo-Jo wasn't happy when me and her dad got divorced last year, and she was a bit of trouble when we moved in with Trey, but things have improved a lot since then. Her grades have improved in school too. It actually felt like things were going our way for a change.'

There's a knock at the door and Robyn stands to answer it, but I can't see who's there through the crack. She closes the door and leans over to whisper in my ear. 'The SIO is outside and wants a word.'

Giving the Nevilles a reassuring smile, I stand and follow Robyn to the door. Stepping out into the corridor, my mouth drops when I see who's called me outside.

'The world really is too small a place,' DI Zoe Cavendish says.

Chapter Thirteen

THEN

Piddlehinton, Dorset

Joanna was shivering when she woke up. She ran trembling fingers over the small bumps lining the skin of her arms. It was only as she forced herself to sit up that she saw the plates of pasta and sauce on the table, and the grim realisation of her current dilemma hit directly behind her eyes. It hadn't been a nightmare, and she really was still inside this bitterly cold caravan. She scratched the tickle at the back of her neck, realising she was still dressed in the black sequin dress Chez had found for her. She'd felt every part a model when she'd pulled it over her head, but now she realised she was nothing but a cheap imitation.

Her mouth felt so dry, and as she skimmed the immediate horizon of the kitchen counters for anything resembling a drink, she was left disappointed. The mug of tea she'd all but finished on the table stared up at her, but she wasn't desperate enough to down the ice-cold congealed contents. She was about to pick it up and attempt to fill it with water from the tap when she heard the key rattling in the door. Tucking her knees beneath her chin, she couldn't tell if she was relieved or not when Chez crept inside.

'Oh, you're up,' he muttered, closing the door behind him but not locking it. 'Did you sleep okay?'

His eyes wandered across the table and settled on her pinhole eyes and squashed hair, realising exactly where she'd slept. He flashed her a pitying look, and it was all that was needed for the floodgates to open. She buried her eyes behind her kneecaps.

'Hey, hey,' Chez cooed, as he came over and squeezed himself behind the table, wrapping a warm and comforting arm around her shoulders, 'there's no need for tears. Your big brother is here now, Kylie, and you know I'll look after you, don't you?'

The truth was she knew nothing about him, and although she'd been willing to play along last night – her nails, eating pasta like grown-ups – she was suddenly only too aware of the grimness of their situation and she couldn't pretend any longer. When sleep had finally come last night, it had been focused on the belief that she would be woken to the kind eyes of a police officer with her parents nearby, waiting to be reunited. She'd hoped if she wished for it hard enough that she could make it happen, but nobody had been listening.

'W-w-where were you?' she asked, her sob stuttering the words.

He rested his cheek on the top of her head and gently kissed it, in the same way her father did. 'I was working.'

He'd said he would be back quickly, but judging by the

amount of light that had penetrated the gloom when he'd opened the door, it had to be morning.

'All night?' she asked.

'We were doing a night shoot... It overran. I'm sorry. I thought I'd be back sooner.' His head suddenly snapped up. 'Speaking of which, what time is it?'

He checked his watch and she saw his eyes widen with something close to fear. 'Oh shit! We need to get this place cleaned up. Mr Brown doesn't like messy quarters.' He pushed himself away from her, lifting her plate, ready to stack it on his own. 'You didn't finish your dinner.'

The spaghetti had hardened during the night and some of the tomato sauce had stained the edge of the plate. It had felt so mature and fun to be eating last night, but now all it did was remind her of what she was missing out on.

'I wasn't hungry,' she lied, as her stomach grumbled in disapproval.

He carried both plates to the kitchen countertop and she watched as he scraped the remnants of dinner into a polythene bag, tied the ends and carried it outside. He didn't close the door, and a voice in the back of her head told her to stand and move to the exit. She obeyed, despite her terror at Grey's words the night before.

A carpet of mist hung half a metre off the ground, giving the impression that they'd somehow been transported into the clouds. Beyond the immediate field, she could now see a barbed-wire fence, leading to a second field, on which cows were grazing and braying their woeful tune. Had they been there last night when she'd arrived? She couldn't recall hearing any animal noises, but now she could hear nothing but their moos and detected the unmistakeable pong.

There was no sign of life in either of the other two caravans but, daring to move down to the next step, she could just make out a tall building beyond the third caravan. A barn of some sort, she would guess, though it wasn't obvious how the cows would access it, as a small stream bisected the land near to it. As she stepped down again, the barn came into clearer view and it appeared to only be accessible from their current field. If there were fields and cows and a barn, they had to be pitched up on a farm of some sort, which had to mean there would be a farmer or farmhouse nearby. If only she could find it, perhaps she could signal for help.

'Whoa, whoa, whoa,' Chez said, reappearing from behind the caravan and ushering her back inside. 'If Mr Brown saw you out in the open, he wouldn't be happy. Come on, you can dry up while I wash.'

Stepping back inside, she made a promise that she wouldn't spend so much time thinking about escape when the opportunity next presented itself. Instead, she would just run. To hell with the consequences; it sure beat the alternative.

Chez filled the sink and deposited the plates and cutlery inside, then wiped the table down with a wet cloth and straightened the cushions. He was surprisingly domesticated for one so young, but then he had commented how they were all treated as grown-ups in this place. It triggered a fresh thought in her head.

'Are there others? Like you and me, I mean.'

He fixed her with a cautious stare. 'You mean models and actors?'

She nodded.

'Of course there are.'

'Where are they now?'

'Ah, well, we don't all spend time in the same places all the time. You'll get to meet them soon enough. I'm here now to oversee your arrival, you see.'

He handed her a bubble-covered plate, and she wrapped it in the towel he'd handed her, wiping the suds from the surface, before standing it back on the table, uncertain where the plate had come from originally.

'How many others are there?' she tried again.

He passed her a second soap-streaked plate. 'It varies. People come and go, but on average there's between seven and a dozen at a time. They're all a friendly bunch if that's what you're worried about.'

'Oh no,' she replied defensively, 'I was just curious to understand how all of this works.'

'It's best not to ask too many questions, and just go with the flow; easier that way.'

She dried the plate and stood it atop the first. 'What happens to the videos you appear in? What I mean is, would I have seen you in something at the cinema?'

She didn't know why she'd asked the question in that way, but something was chattering in the back of her mind.

'They're a special type of movie,' he said. 'Let's just leave it at that. Okay?'

It would have been better had he just lied, but she wasn't as slow on the uptake as he'd wrongly assumed. 'Do the others act in these movies too?'

Chaz drove his hands into the water, sending a mountain of bubbles to plash up onto the draining board, and she heard him sigh in frustration. She hadn't meant to anger him and took an uncertain step backwards.

She could see from the movement of his jawline that he was

grinding his teeth, and she continued to move backwards like a naïve zoo keeper who had wandered into the wrong cage. 'I'm sorry,' she said quickly. 'I'll stop asking questions. It's just… there's so much I don't know, and I thought it would be better to ask you than one of the others. I'm sorry.'

He looked up and the anger immediately left his expression, but it was as if he was seeing someone else when he spoke. 'I know, and I was wrong to get cross with you. If you can't ask your big brother, who can you ask, right? It's okay. Come on, let's get the cleaning up finished and then we'll get you changed into something more appropriate for travelling.'

She dropped the towel on the table beside the plates. 'Travelling?'

He withdrew the cutlery from the plastic bowl, rinsed the suds from them with the tap, and placed them on the drainer. 'Of course. We have to go and meet up with the others. You do want to meet them, don't you?'

Her eyes flew to the door. He hadn't locked it, but he was taller and quicker than her, so she'd never get away without distracting him. Unless…

Hurrying over, she gently wrapped her fingers around his upper arm. 'Chez, can I ask you one more question?'

He emptied the bowl of water, dried his hands on his trousers, and faced her. 'Go on then, but then we must get changed. I need a shower before we leave.'

Leading him to the cushioned bench, she pulled out the stool and sat. 'I want to go home,' she said, as her lip began to tremble. 'I didn't ask for any of this, and I really don't want to be a model or an actress. I want to help people, not perform. Will you help me get home?'

He frowned at the suggestion, looking as though she'd just asked him to voluntarily lop off one of his limbs. 'I understand your worry,' he said quietly. 'I was the same at first; terrified about what life would be like, but then I gave it a chance and it really isn't all that bad. You'll see.'

'But I don't want to see, Chez. Please, tell me what I have to do to get home.'

She dropped her eyes in what she believed was her most pitiful puppy-dog routine. She half-expected him to shout or grab her, but instead he pressed a warm and clammy hand to her cheek and just held it there until she met his stare.

'Don't be silly, Kylie. You are home.'

He wasn't listening, and this was how she'd feared he would react. But sitting on the cushioned bench, he now had the table between him and her, which could buy her valuable seconds. There was no time to think about it, and she slipped off the stool, and charged towards the unlocked door, bursting through it and leaping off the three steps without even thinking. But impatience wasn't her friend this time, and she landed in the surprised arms of Grey, whose surprise quickly darkened and he forced her back inside the caravan.

'What the fuck, Chez?' he glowered, as the boy fiddled to close and lock the door, with a hundred apologies spilling from his lips.

She rocked and squirmed, determined not to give in, fighting for her freedom with all her might, summoning the rage that had been building in her gut since the argument with her sister. But just as she seemed to be breaking free of Grey's grip, Chez was at her feet, hoisting up her legs, and leading them through to the back bedroom.

'Hold her still,' Grey ordered with a growl, as they forced her onto the bed.

Still she continued to struggle, even more so as Grey placed his forearm across the top of her ribcage, so that he could reach for something inside the pocket of his suit jacket. His hand emerged a moment later and at first she couldn't tell what he was holding, but then she saw him squeeze off the top of the syringe with his teeth, and before she could resist, the point of the cold needle was in her neck, and she couldn't keep her eyes from closing as the cool liquid entered her system.

Chapter Fourteen

NOW

Portland, Dorset

Jack's denials about sleeping with this woman are all that fill my mind from the moment I lay eyes on her, and it's all I can do to choke the words.

'Wait, how come you're here?' is the best I can manage to mask the burning rage in the pit of my stomach. 'Are you based in Portland now, instead of Poole?'

She smirks at the preposterousness of the suggestion. 'They've drafted in detectives from neighbouring stations to join the hunt. Given my own extensive experience in this area, they've asked me to head up the investigation.'

I'm certain there's an edge of excitement to her voice, like this is just a game to her, but I'm also sure that isn't the case, and it's just my feelings of resentment towards her that are colouring this whole experience. And I hope the 'extensive experience' she's referring to has nothing to do with our last encounter; although she was SIO into the sudden emergence of

Aurélie Lebrun, it was Rachel and I who stumbled upon the den where she'd been held, and it was my interviews with Aurélie that revealed the true extent of the abuse she'd suffered at the hands of her captor, Jasper Derwent. I'm not usually one to blow my own trumpet but I resent anyone taking credit for my work, especially someone who tried to drive a wedge between me and Jack, and lived to tell the tale.

She stands, feet apart and shoulders as fixed as ever, and despite her small frame, she edges me by an inch or two. Her hair is shorter than I remember, but although it has been shaved at the back, her fringe hangs low over one eye. I hate how self-assured she seems when all I want to do is pull the rug from beneath her feet.

'Is Jack around here too?' she says casually, studying my face for any sign of reaction.

I do my best to hide my annoyance. 'Jack's working with the National Crime Agency now. In fact, they've taken over the project he and I were working on so that they can give it the necessary resource and support.'

I hate myself for stooping to her level of cockiness.

'That's a shame; it would have been good to catch up with him again.' The smug look remains plastered over her face, and I wonder now whether she is revelling in the knowledge that she directly undermined my relationship with him. 'Anyway, I was going to ask you what *you're* doing here. Unless I'm very much mistaken, this is still an *active* investigation, and I certainly haven't called upon the services of "Super" Emma Hunter.'

The air quotes feel like another personal attack.

'Mr and Mrs Neville asked her to come in,' the FLO chips in, and I'm grateful she's picked my side over Cavendish's in this embarrassing entanglement. Her interruption also serves as a valuable reminder that I shouldn't be allowing personal feelings to intrude on the gravity of the situation we find ourselves in. Jo-Jo is still missing, and the two of us bickering like adolescents is not what she needs.

'You know the Nevilles well, do you?' Cavendish asks, each syllable painted with scorn and mocking doubt.

I take a moment to compose myself before snapping back an answer that will give her the upper hand. 'As it happens, no, no, I don't know the Nevilles. I'm at something of a loss to understand why they felt the need to request my help, when they have such an experienced detective at the reins.'

Okay, I know it's a cheap shot and I should be taking the moral high ground, but it feels good to temporarily wipe the smugness from her face and drag her down a peg or two. Ultimately, we both know I can't be anywhere near an active investigation without the express permission of the SIO, and even then there are Non-Disclosure Agreements and the Official Secrets Act to be signed. I don't think either of us is naïve enough to think Cavendish will be reaching out for my help any time soon.

'And you're sure it was the Nevilles who asked for Emma here, and not the other way around?' The question is directed at Robyn, even though Cavendish's glower doesn't leave me.

'Yes, Ma'am,' she replies without flicking an eye. 'They're in there now, and asking for an update on the case.'

Cavendish nods, and it's the reminder she needs to get things back on track. Pushing between Robyn and myself, she thrusts the door open and enters the room, immediately dropping to her knees at the table's edge, taking Tina's hands in hers. 'Mr and Mrs Neville, we've not been formally introduced yet. I'm Detective Inspector Zoe Cavendish, and I'm the Senior Investigating Officer.'

I'm sure the emphasis on the words *detective* and *senior* were for my benefit.

'I am at your service,' she continues, and for once I don't think the dutiful tone is fake. It serves as a reminder that before my rude awakening with her last year, she was a highly respected officer and must be well regarded to have earned her promotion to Inspector.

'Is DS Meyers taking good care of you? If there's anything you need, then you just need to ask her. She's one of our most experienced Family Liaison Officers and it's her responsibility to keep you informed of any updates from my team, and progress on us bringing Joanna back.'

'She prefers Jo-Jo,' Tina clarifies, but looks grateful for Cavendish's personal assurance.

'Of course, my mistake. Bringing *Jo-Jo* back is my number one priority. Okay? I have officers being drafted in from all corners of Dorset, and am in constant contact with neighbouring forces in Devon, Hampshire, Somerset, and Wiltshire. We will close the net on whoever took your daughter, and do everything within our power to bring her back to you safe and sound.'

I lower my eyes, unable to shake the sensation that I wish we'd had someone as determined as Cavendish when Anna had gone missing. How can I despise and respect someone in such equal measure? Does that make me a hypocrite? I feel so confused right now.

The room feels stuffy with the five of us in here. Although there is a large window at one side, it faces out into the secure courtyard and there is no opening mechanism. There is an air-conditioning unit secured to the ceiling above the table; it's not making any noise, suggesting it isn't on, but it really should be. The blouse Maddie chose for me is now sticking to my lower back.

My eyes widen as I suddenly realise exactly where I'm supposed to be right now. Glancing at my watch, I know there's no chance of me getting to the bookstore in the next five minutes, but it would be ill-mannered to whip out my phone and offer apologies to Maddie. I'll have to message her as soon as I'm out. I'm sure when I explain what's happened she'll be understanding – at least, I hope she will.

'That team of officers are securing surveillance camera footage from the properties and shops near your home,' Cavendish continues, still crouched by their feet, 'and that should help us understand exactly how Jo-Jo left the scene, and hopefully give us a valuable lead into where she went and if someone took her.'

The Nevilles tense at this last statement, but nod their understanding. I know better than most exactly what they're going through, and it becomes clear to me that my being here will only serve as an unwelcome distraction to Cavendish and her team. As much as I want to help the Nevilles recover their daughter, I don't want to be a hindrance.

'I know you've expressed a desire to undertake a press conference today, and I have a public relations team sorting that as we speak,' Cavendish continues, 'but we have to tread carefully. Smothering the news and social media with Jo-Jo's face is the best way to get the public looking for her too, but it could equally tip any abductor into acting rashly. We've already commenced the social media campaign so she's in the public eye, but it would be my suggestion to wait a day or so before proceeding with the press conference—'

'No, we want the press conference straightaway,' Tina interrupts, searching her husband's face for reassurance. 'We just want her home as soon as possible.'

'As do we, Mrs Neville,' Cavendish placates, 'but I don't want to induce any unnecessary harm.'

'But children not located in the first twenty-four hours rarely return home, isn't that right, Detective Cavendish?' Tina challenges, before catching my eye. 'I read that in one of your books, Emma. It's true, isn't it? Shouldn't we do everything we can to get her back today?'

I don't think the question is aimed at me, but Tina's hopeful stare is fixed on me, and I don't know how to respond.

There is a hint of irritation in Cavendish's voice when she answers. 'I don't believe in statistics when it comes to missing-person cases, Mrs Neville. Every investigation is different and just because one set of circumstances occurred once, it certainly doesn't mean they will occur again.'

'She's been missing since three o'clock,' Trey Neville grunts, 'and there's only five and a bit hours left until we hit twenty-four. We do the press conference as soon as possible, and get our Jo-Jo back.'

Cavendish is smart enough not to argue and nods as she stands. 'Very well, I'll have our media team draw up a script that you can use to make a personal plea for her safe return.'

'We want Emma to read it,' Tina says matter-of-factly.

'What?' Cavendish and I say in unison.

'Well, she's a well-known figure in the area, and because there are similarities in how her own sister disappeared, we thought it could help the case. Maybe if the kidnappers know she is on the case, they'll have a change of heart and return Jo-Jo.'

Grief and desperation can make anyone act out of character, but this is a new one even on me. I'm trying to think of a gracious way to explain that my involvement in the press conference would just muddy the waters, when Cavendish beats me to it.

'No way! I'm sorry, but the last thing your daughter needs is the media circus that follows Emma Hunter around town.'

I'd have phrased it differently but at least we're on the same page for once.

'And nobody has drawn any link between what happened to her sister and what has happened to Jo-Jo. There's no reason to think the cases are connected. It's purely coincidental that they went missing from this area. I think the press conference needs to be personal and heartfelt.'

The Nevilles both look to me, like they're expecting me to argue with Cavendish, but I offer a meek shrug of my shoulders. 'I think DI Cavendish is right,' I mumble.

Cavendish claps her hands together as a judge would bang his gravel to indicate the end of court proceedings. 'Good. That's settled then. Emma, can I have a word with you outside, please?'

I'm grateful to be exiting the stuffiness of the room, but Cavendish closing the door and leaving Robyn inside puts me on edge.

'How is your book with Aurélie progressing? When can I expect to see it on the shelves of the local supermarket?'

I don't rise to the bait.

'We're putting the finishing touches to it now. It's been a

rough few months for her, but I think she's finally able to see some light at the end of the tunnel.'

Cavendish presses a finger to her lips, as if she's deep in thought, trying to unravel some great mystery akin to the eminent Sherlock Holmes. 'Mmm, good. I still think she should have stood trial in this country for her complicity in some of those activities, but it wasn't my decision.' She pauses, the finger still pressed to her lips. 'I've been thinking… I don't want my real name used in your book.'

Of all the things I thought she might say when we were alone, this was the last. 'You don't want me to use your name?'

'That's right. If anyone wants to know who the SIO was, they can look it up online. I'd rather any lasting memory of me not be consigned to some second-rate book bought by those seeking titillation and conspiracy.'

I bite down hard on my tongue so as not to react to the slight on my writing career. 'You're barely a footnote in the manuscript anyway,' I offer disingenuously.

She lowers her finger, and fixes me with a hard stare. 'Even so, I'd rather not see my name in print.'

I can't believe I'm even considering her request. 'What do you propose I do instead?'

'I don't know, make something up. You're good at that, aren't you?'

I bite harder on my tongue. 'Okay. I suppose I can give you a different identifier if that's what you want.'

She smiles, but it is clearly forced and lacks sincerity. 'Good. And I'd appreciate you not speaking to the Nevilles again while we continue to search for little Jo-Jo. I don't want you using yet another family's misfortune to further your career.'

My mouth drops in astonishment. 'I wouldn't! I want to see Jo-Jo's safe return as much as you.'

'Good, then we have an understanding. I'll stay out of your way, and you stay the hell away from this case.'

I had naively hoped that after the support Rachel and I provided with figuring out the truth about Aurélie's abduction she would understand my writing takes second place to finding justice for the victims and their families. I have never put my writing career ahead of that virtue. Do other people think that too?

Shrinking back into my shell, I follow Cavendish back along the corridor, and I'm relieved when she doesn't follow me through the security door. She's about to pull it closed when a troublesome thought pops out of my mouth before I can stop it.

'You're certain Jo-Jo hasn't just run away? Tina Neville, she said something about Jo-Jo giving them a bit of trouble when she and Trey got together.'

Cavendish considers me for a moment. 'Okay, I'll bite, Emma, what is it you're suggesting?'

I'm genuinely not trying to trip her up this time. 'I just meant, if there's a history of trouble in the family, I'm surprised you've automatically jumped to the conclusion that somebody abducted Jo-Jo rather than she's packed some things and is camping out at friend's house or some hideaway somewhere.'

Cavendish folds her arms. 'You mean aside from the fact that both parents, her step-sister, her grandparents, and *her teachers* have assured us she isn't the sort to run away? Of course we're keeping that possibility in mind, and all uniform units in the area and bordering towns are checking the homeless shelters and parks for anyone matching her description, but I'm not going to waste valuable time searching for an unlikely runaway when her potential kidnappers could be putting distance between themselves and here.' She lowers her voice again. 'Given your own history, I would have thought you'd encourage such proactive decision-making, rather than criticise.'

'I wasn't criticising...' I begin to say, but she's allowed the door to close in my face, and I know I'm wasting my breath.

Pulling out my phone, I see I've missed several calls from Maddie. She's panicking because it's quarter to ten and I've yet to arrive at the book signing to set up. She probably thinks I've chickened out.

'Hey there,' I hear a familiar voice call from behind me.

Turning, I'm pleased to see the friendly face of PCSO Rick Underwood.

'Can I give you a lift home?' he asks jovially. 'It's the least I can do after dragging you from bed this morning.'

I can feel eyes burning into the back of my neck from within the station, but I don't turn to check they belong to Cavendish. 'A lift into town would be great,' I say, returning Rick's smile.

Chapter Fifteen

NOW

Weymouth, Dorset

My first reaction to the enormous line of people is that some major incident has occurred and all the shops on the high street have had to evacuate their customers. It's only when we reach the end of the queue that I can see where it originates. Surely all these people can't be here to see me?

Although Waterstones has two entrances, only the rear one faces the road we've travelled along, and so I'm forced to walk past the queue of people to the front door, where I can see Maddie inside pacing relentlessly and practically wearing a hole in the carpet. She is chewing the end of a biro (a habit she developed to counter stress when she quit smoking), and it wouldn't surprise me if that's the second one she's got through while she's been waiting.

'Where have you been?' she hisses under her breath as she has the security guard unlock the door.

'Sorry,' I offer, nodding at Rick, who has escorted me to the door like I'm some kind of pop star and he's my bodyguard.

Maddie eyes him with confusion, not quite able to connect the dots, but then her face lifts and the worry lines dissipate. 'Oh, this I *like*,' she declares broadly. 'Being escorted to the store by an officer of the law is a *great* publicity stunt. I wish I'd thought of it myself.'

I wince, but don't correct her. 'I really am sorry I'm late. Something came up that required my attention.'

Maddie's anxiety has been totally washed away by Rick's chiselled features and her eyes haven't left him since I drew her attention. 'Don't worry about any of that,' she says. 'You're here now, and that's what matters.' Then it's as if I'm not even there. She thrusts her hand towards Rick. 'We haven't been introduced. I'm Maddie Travers, Emma's agent. And you are?'

He blushes slightly at her directness, but shakes the hand. 'Rick Underwood. I'm the reason Emma is late, so please don't take it out on her. It's entirely my fault.' He glances over at me, and his smile grows. 'Thanks for this morning. If you need anything else, don't hesitate to call.'

He allows the grumpy security guard to lock the door and Maddie's focus finally returns to the job at hand. 'They've set you up a table just over here so that the event doesn't clog up the main entrance. Did you bring a drink with you?'

Brightly coloured posters are taped all over and around the table, each one produced by my publisher to promote the launch of the books. It looks a bit tacky to me, but who am I to criticise Maddie's efforts? At least she arrived on time. I had meant to buy refreshments on my slow meander into town after the fry-up I never got, and so I can only shake my head meekly.

'Never mind, I'll buy you a bottle of water once the tills are open. We have a huge crowd of people to get through. I had planned that you would have pre-signed some copies, but we haven't time for that now, so you'll just have to go one at a time. I'll stick by for as long as I can to keep things moving. Okay? Are you ready for this?'

Am I ready to smile non-stop for the next two hours, listening to praise for my books when all I want to do is hide in a cave and let Maddie handle all forms of criticism? Of course I'm not, but I know that isn't what she wants to hear. Cavendish's words are still stinging in my mind, and I hate the thought that there are others out there who think that the books I have written were done with the intention of profiting from the tragedies that befell my subjects. I only wrote *Monsters Under the Bed* to cast much-needed light on the abuses at the St Francis Home for Wayward Boys. I never would have described the events surrounding Cassie Hilliard's abduction in *Ransomed* had my publisher not insisted on it. I am here today as much because of circumstance and Maddie's insistence that I contribute to the publicity machine. If I had my way, I would write at home and only venture out for food and drink. I envy those who write under a pseudonym. Anonymity is not my shield.

I nod in response to Maddie's question and try to make myself comfortable on the hardened plastic chair behind the table.

'There are three boxes of hardback copies of *Isolated* under the table to your left,' Maddie points out. 'And a box each of the paperback versions of *Monsters* and *Ransomed*. If someone wants to purchase all three then fab, otherwise focus on pushing the new book, as we have more copies of that. They have two more boxes in the storeroom if we run out, and judging by the length of the queue already, there's a real possibility of that.'

I take out the two pens I packed in my satchel and hold them up so Maddie knows I'm as ready as I'll ever be.

'I'll take you for a nice spot of lunch when we're done here,' she says excitedly. 'I'll put it on company expenses.'

With that, the security guard unlocks the automated doors, and signals for the first of the queue to enter. The woman practically bounces up to the desk, the leopard-print spectacles sliding down her nose.

'Can I just say, I am your *biggest* fan, Emma? I've been queueing here since five o'clock this morning just so I could guarantee getting a copy of your new book signed.'

At first I assume she is joking, but she is smiling so much that even my face begins to ache. 'Wow, really? 5am? That's dedication for you.'

Her expression suddenly becomes graver. 'I am dedicated. I was the first to buy *Ransomed* when it came out in hardback, and now I'll be the first to get my hands on *Isolated*.'

I don't mention that copies of the book have been on sale in airports since Friday.

'Who should I make it out to?' I ask, reaching for one of the copies lying flat on the table.

'Can you put, "To my number one fan, Ruby"?'

I begin to write the inscription. 'Do you want any other personalised message?'

The question has thrown her. 'Oh, I don't know, just put whatever you think is good.'

I cringe inwardly at this response, as I do *every* time I hear it at this sort of event. Is it not enough that I poured my heart and soul into producing the finished article without being expected to come up with some meaningful and heartfelt dedication for a person I've never met before? I remember raising this challenge when Maddie forced me into a signing of *Monsters* and her response was: *just put something like, I hope you enjoy reading this as much as I enjoyed writing it.*

I say the words aloud as I write them in the book, before scrawling my author's signature beneath them. That was another thing I didn't learn until after that first book signing; the need to develop a signature different to the one I would use for writing cheques, and signing contracts. How easy would it be for a forger to get hold of one of my autographed books and learn how to imitate my hand? And so I now use a flowing E and H as my sign-off, which looks nothing like what's scrawled on the back of my debit card.

Ruby snatches up the book and admires the message but makes no effort to move away from the table and allow the next person to come forward. 'What's it like being able to see the clues to a mystery that us normal folk miss?'

I look to Maddie for support but she's gone off to buy me that bottle of water, which means I'm stranded and won't be able to move Ruby on without offending her. I don't have an answer to her question, because I've never really looked at myself in that way.

'I... um... I just do my best to assess the facts.'

I'm cringing on the inside, but she isn't done yet.

'Did you know instinctively that Cassie Hilliard was still alive when her grandfather approached you that morning?'

I puff out my cheeks, stalling for time. 'Well, um, so much has happened since that day that I...' Why am I trying to actually think of an answer to this question? If Rachel were here (God, I miss her!) she'd give the response of least resistance and move excitable Ruby on. 'I had no idea,' I say. 'I just followed the evidence as you read in the book, and everything slotted into place.'

Maddie returns and plants the bottle of water beside my writing hand, frowning at Ruby. 'Oh you don't pay for the book here. You need to take it to the till first,' she says, and as soon as Ruby looks over to where she has indicated, Maddie is calling for the next fan to step forward.

The young woman who approaches next must be sixteen or seventeen at most, in ripped jeans and a crop top, despite the cold temperature outside. Her face is buried in her phone and her jaw is bouncing rhythmically with the gum in her mouth. I'd bet she hasn't been standing in the queue as long as Ruby. In fact, she doesn't even look up as she reaches the table. It's only when I see Rick bouncing up and down outside the door that I realise who she is.

'You must be Rick's sister?' I ask, as I reach into the box for a fresh copy of the book. I wave him over, as I know the dedication is for his benefit and the grumpy security guard steps aside to allow him entrance.

'What should I put?' I ask him, and is face is almost as giddy as Ruby's was.

'That's okay, you only need to sign your name,' he says stoically. 'Would you mind if I got my sister to take a picture of us to go with it?'

How can I refuse when he gave me the lift here?

'Sure,' I say, cringing inwardly again, and he crouches down beside me at the table while his sister – who finally looks up from her phone – snaps the picture on his phone.

Outside the door there is a sudden surge of excitement as

those at the front extract their phones, and I now realise the error of my ways. This event is going to last all day at this rate.

'It really has been a pleasure meeting you,' he says when I hand him the book, 'and I was wondering whether it would be possible for me to see you again some time? Maybe we could go for a drink in town? You live locally, and I'm just up the road in Dorchester… what do you say?'

In my periphery Maddie is tapping the watch on her wrist. I need to choose the path of least resistance.

'Um, yeah, okay, a drink in town sounds great,' I respond, scribbling my number on the back of a promotional bookmark that is set into a fan-shape on one corner of the table.

He presses the bookmark into the inside cover of the book, and peels away with his sister in search of the nearest till. When he calls later, I'll just have to tell him that I'm not officially on the market as I'm waiting for Jack, but then who knows if that wait will ever end? I don't have time to think about it because the next reader approaches carrying copies of *Ransomed* and *Isolated,* waiting to be signed. When she tells me she's flown in from Canada just to be here today, my head feels ready to explode.

Chapter Sixteen

THEN

Hayling Island, Hampshire

The rumble and bouncing had stopped, and as Joanna struggled to separate her eyelids it was impossible to hazard whether it was night or day. Her head ached like never before, but it wasn't just her brain that was out of sorts; her entire body ached, like it had just been put through the most rigorous physical activity and then tossed onto the scrapheap.

Blurred shapes drifted in and out of one another as she forced her head up off the mattress, and desperately tried to make sense of what had happened. The memories that she could just about cling to didn't make any sense, and she urgently needed the warm hands of her mother and the reassuring voice of her father to let her know that everything would be okay.

The ache wasn't restricted to the area just behind her eyes. In fact, as she finally managed to lift her torso from the firm mattress, it felt as though kilogram weights had been attached to both ears and it was all she could do to stop her head lolling from one side to another. Was this what a hangover felt like? She'd heard her parents discussing the after-effects of drinking too much alcohol, but if this was the effect then she couldn't understand why anyone would put themselves through it. If someone had emerged and offered to end her life there and then, she would have been hard-pressed not to consider it.

Fragments of memory returned: getting in Grey's car; them driving past her road; the death threat of the men outside; the caravan; Chez making the pasta. None of it had been real, had it? Surely this wasn't now her reality? Sitting upright on the mattress, she compelled her eyelids to open wider, despite the agony of additional exposure to light. She couldn't remain in this half-functioning state. The blurred shapes before her sharpened fractionally and she realised she was inside the back bedroom of the caravan. Immediately in front of her was the small chest of drawers attached to the paper-thin wall that enclosed the small toilet and shower. To her left was the single bed that Chez had said she should sleep on last night before she'd curled up on the bench in the main room.

She couldn't bear to acknowledge that this was in fact her new reality, and so instead she focused on the one thing that offered a modicum of hope: escape. Sitting on the edge of the bed wouldn't help, and she had no idea when someone might return to check on her. Pressing her cold hands into the mattress beside her bottom, she launched herself up, not realising the message hadn't reached her legs. She crashed forwards into the chest of drawers, narrowly avoiding cracking her temple on the sharp corner.

Her right knee hit the unforgiving floor, but she managed to steady herself long enough to thrust her hands to the thin carpet and stop full-on collapse. A fresh memory fizzed: Grey thrusting her back into the caravan, and Chez lifting her legs. They'd carried her into this room and pinned her to the mattress. Her hand shot up to her neck where she now recalled the prick of the needle as it entered her skin. There was no pain there now, only numbness.

What had they injected her with? Was that why she felt so crooked now? Would she ever feel herself again, or was this the new normal? Had they meant to kill her, and she'd clung onto life, or had the intention just been incapacitation?

Chez's betrayal had hurt more than the needle. What kind of brother would allow his sister to be drugged? And not only that, he had participated in the pinning down. Had she been naïve to think he was on her side? Had all that big brother stuff just been an act to keep her from thinking about running?

Too many questions, and nowhere near enough answers. Would they know she'd be due to come round about now? If so, that limited her opportunity to get out – not that she was in any state to go anywhere.

Planting her fingers into the carpet tiles, she crawled on hands and knees along the narrow corridor and into the kitchen area. It was much brighter here than it had been in the bedroom and she had to keep her chin pressed into her chest to shield her exposed eyes. It smelt less musty in here than she remembered; there was something different now hanging in the air, something familiar that her broken brain just couldn't quite get at. Continuing across the strip of linoleum, she felt the rough graze of the carpet tiles again, and beyond it the door to freedom.

'It's locked,' a voice called to her from somewhere to her right.

She froze, not having considered the prospect that they wouldn't leave her alone in the caravan.

The voice was gruff, and lacked the Celtic lilt of Chez. 'There's no point in trying to leave. Your parents know you're with us, and they aren't out there looking for you. You're ours now, and the sooner you accept that, the easier it will be.'

She didn't move, willing her body to wake up so that she could throw herself at the door, in case Grey was lying about it being locked. There was no sign of a key in the lock, so it was possible he was tricking her. After the collapse in the bedroom, she had to be sure the messages would pass to every muscle and nerve of her body.

She could barely get the words out of her mouth without slurring. 'I want to go home.'

She heard Grey's movement, but before she could steel herself for an attack, his hands were clasped around her middle and he lifted her effortlessly into the air, her legs and arms unable to hold their fixed position. She was powerless to prevent him carrying her over to the cushioned bench where he now laid her down, flat on her back, but facing him as he retook his place on the stool.

'That's better,' he said, reaching into a small tin and extracting a pinch of tobacco, which he proceeded to sprinkle onto a square of white paper folded between the fingers of his left hand. She could now see just how rough and yellow his fingertips were, though she couldn't recall seeing them that way when they'd met in the newsagents, and now she remembered he'd been wearing driving gloves.

'What do you want?' she tried, closing her eyes to allow her lips to focus on pronouncing the words.

'That's entirely up to you,' he said, as the crinkle of paper confirmed he was now rolling his cigarette. 'What did Chez tell you about this place?'

She couldn't exactly recall his words, but he'd spoken about modelling and acting. She shrugged instead.

'We do very important work here. Chez told me you want to help people, is that right?'

She couldn't remember telling him that, but as she nodded she felt something warm and wet on her cheek, but couldn't understand what had sparked the tear.

'Well, we try to help people here. You have a very unique gift, Joanna – or is it Kylie now? Maybe it's better if you think of yourself as Kylie instead; it'll make things easier in the long run.'

He paused, and she heard the flick of a cigarette lighter, followed by a sudden violation of tobacco smoke.

'Anyway,' he continued, inhaling deeply, 'I have a special job for you, if you want it, that is. It pays well. Here, take a look.'

Prying her eyes open, she saw he was holding out a fan of crisp notes. 'This is what Chez earned for his work last night. Not bad, right? Do you like money?'

She was nine years old, did he really think a flash of cash would entice her? Realising the error, he quickly lowered the money and reached into his pocket, withdrawing something small she couldn't immediately focus on.

He thrust his hand towards her. 'Go on, take it. Call it an advance on your wages.'

She focused her stare on his scabbed fingertips, and saw the glint of a gem attached to the metal band he was holding out. Reaching her own hand out, it took several swings until she finally took hold of the gem, and brought it closer to her eyes.

It really was a pretty ring, even though the band was too large for her fingers.

'There's plenty more of those where that came from. If you want to keep it, all I need from you is a few photographs. You've had your picture taken before, right?'

She briefly thought about all the silly poses she'd pulled whenever Mum and Dad were trying to take a 'nice' family picture. She nodded.

'And it didn't hurt having your picture taken, did it?'

She looked at the sparkling gem as the ache behind her eyes slowly diminished. It was so pretty, and she could see the colours of the rainbow reflected in it when it caught the small glimmers of light coming through the shuttered windows.

'You keep hold of that for now,' he said, pushing himself off the stool, the caravan shaking as he suddenly straightened. 'I have a few bits and pieces to sort out. I'll send Chez over in a bit, and you can ask him anything you like, and then I'll return for your decision later.'

He moved towards the door, inserted a key and unlocked it, thrusting it open. She expected to hear the cows groaning in the neighbouring field, but was shocked to see the field gone, now replaced by crashing waves, and the salt in the air assaulted her nostrils again. They weren't at the campsite anymore, and now she had no clue where they were.

'What happens if I don't want my picture taken?' she called after him, and he stopped, half in the door and half out.

He didn't meet her gaze. 'I've been kind to you so far, Kylie, but it won't take much for my patience to wear thin.' That was the moment he chose to meet her stare, and it was her turn to look away. 'You'll do what we want whether you're willing or not.'

'And if I want to leave, and go home?'

She felt his hand on her jaw before she'd even heard his movement. 'There's only one way out of here, and you wouldn't be the first to suffer from big ideas.'

She tried to break free of his grasp, but he pulled her so close that she could smell the stale stench of tobacco on his breath. And then she felt the rough edges of his tongue as he ran it across her cheek.

Chapter Seventeen

NOW

Weymouth, Dorset

The waiter has barely left our drinks on the bright tablecloth before I'm reaching for the chilled glass of Chenin Blanc and knocking it back in one. I'm not usually one for downing wine, but I need something to settle the relentless activity in my head. Maddie watches with something resembling admiration at my sudden enthusiasm.

'That's the spirit,' she comments, signalling to the waiter to bring another over.

'Sorry,' I say, breathlessly, suddenly remembering we're in one of Weymouth's more salubrious restaurants, and any of the other well-dressed patrons could report my excessive drinking via social media. Casually allowing my eyes to wander around the room, I'm relieved that nobody appears to have noticed, nor is anyone pointing a phone in our direction.

'Don't apologise,' Maddie coos. 'If I'd known you wanted

to hit it hard I'd have ordered a bottle for the table and a room for the night.'

I reach for the glass filled with water and take a long drink to wash down the sharp aftertaste of the wine, which is definitely made for sipping.

'You look exhausted,' Maddie continues. 'Is everything okay with you? It feels like forever since we had a proper girly catch-up. You okay?'

To be honest, I don't know where to begin. Maddie is my agent and one of my closer confidantes, but I've never been able to overcome the fact that as an agent she is in my employ. Is it fair to burden her with the fact that I am waiting to hear whether my sister's remains have been discovered? I've been deliberately resisting the urge to think about the prospect and have spent all day keeping my mind preoccupied with missing Jo-Jo and the book signing, but now that I've finally stopped and am attempting to relax, all I can see is the suitcase, and the sympathetic look offered by the forensic pathologist. Jack said he would follow up with Dr Chang and her team this morning, but I haven't heard from him. I'm hoping no news is good news, and trying not to worry that Jack just doesn't know how to break the news to me.

Maddie raises her eyebrows expectantly, still awaiting my response.

'I'm fine,' I lie, lowering my arm when I realise I'm chewing on the cuff of my blouse; it's been a nervous habit for as long as I can remember, but Maddie is aware of it too.

The waiter collects my empty glass and replaces it with an identical but full version. I leave it where it is, already feeling lightheaded after the last glass.

'Are you going to tell me the real reason you were late this morning?' Maddie asks, opening her menu and scanning the lunch options. 'I'm not cross if it was because you hooked up with that Rick last night – if anything I'd rather that be the truth – but just let me know next time.'

I can't recall many catch-ups with Maddie that haven't included invasive questions about my love life (or lack of it), so it isn't a surprise that this is where her imagination has gone.

'Why don't you let me stick with making stuff up,' I tease. 'If you want to know the truth…' I lean closer and raise my menu to block out potential eavesdropping, 'I was asked to attend Portland police station at the request of a couple whose daughter has gone missing.'

Maddie's eyes widen, and I can't tell if it's concern at Jo-Jo's safety or because subconsciously she's already seeing the prospect for a new story.

'Do you know them then?' she asks, also leaning closer to the menu.

I shake my head. 'Never met them before, but I think they were hoping I could use my unwanted fame to help promote a police-instigated media campaign. Their daughter's only nine, and was last seen around three yesterday afternoon.'

Maddie's expression softens to that of any parent who wouldn't wish such a circumstance on even their greatest enemy. 'And the police think she's been abducted, rather than just run away?'

'I guess so,' I say, shrugging. 'I didn't get to ask many questions, as the investigation is being headed up by Zoe Cavendish.'

Maddie sits back, curling her top lip over the bottom one, and nodding sagely. I've told her all about Cavendish's obtuse reaction to my involvement in the Aurélie Lebrun investigation. She took an instant dislike to me when Aurélie's father insisted I be included in any investigative decisions, and my offers of olive branches were thrown back in my face time and again. Her implying she'd slept with Jack to spite me was the final straw.

'I want to help the Nevilles in any way I can,' I say now, 'but Cavendish won't want me anywhere near them, and I'm not going to beg her. Hopefully they can find Jo-Jo and put this behind them swiftly.'

'You said she was nine?'

I nod, lowering my menu and taking another sip of water.

'Like your Anna then.'

'Yeah, I suppose there are similarities, but given the twenty-one-year gap since Anna was snatched, I'd be surprised if the same perpetrator was involved.'

Maddie frowns. 'Why? Isn't it possible that the person who snatched Anna all those years ago has been away – prison, abroad, or whatever – and has now returned?'

I smirk. 'What, like some cheesy, straight-to-video Hollywood flop? Besides, I'm now convinced that Anna was taken by someone with links to the paedophile network Jack is investigating.'

She doesn't miss a beat. 'And has he made any progress in finding out what happened to Anna?'

I picture the suitcase again but shake my head. 'Not yet.'

The waiter returns and we place our orders. Despite Maddie reminding me that I can choose whatever I want to eat, and that company expenses will foot the bill, I still opt for the least expensive starter and main I can find. I'm the same whenever I eat out, regardless of who is paying the bill. I'm sure it's partly my need to please mixed in with my upbringing, when my parents would encourage us to eat within our means.

'All I'm saying,' Maddie adds, waving her hands in a pacifying gesture, 'is I wouldn't put all my eggs in one basket. It's been, what? Six months?'

'Eight,' I correct.

'Well, there you go, eight months and he's not found anything even though he's now working with a team of qualified and experienced detectives. You'd be better off chasing leads on your own. I bet you'd do a better job of finding out what really happened.'

Is Maddie saying what I think she is? It's always been a bone of contention – my wanting to investigate and write about Anna's disappearance – but Maddie has always discouraged me. Is this a change of heart?

'You think my next book should be about Anna?' I ask to clarify, but my heart sinks when she shakes her head.

'No, I've told you before, Emma, your publisher and your readers want something more up to date. No, what I'm saying is you should do some private digging on the side. You don't have to turn it into a book, and if anything I'd have thought you'd want to keep that side of your life more private anyway.'

'I do,' I acknowledge, even though I don't agree that there would be no reader interest in my sister's backstory.

Maddie suddenly snaps her fingers. 'That reminds me.' She reaches down into her enormous handbag and rifles through it, before withdrawing an envelope and sliding it across the table. 'This is that picture that was sent for you care of the office.'

I'd almost forgotten about the black and white still of Faye McKenna and can't resist slipping the image out of the envelope to look at it closer.

'Did you manage to find out any more about her?' Maddie asks.

'Not much,' I admit. 'She's listed on the missingpeople.org site, and I found a couple of stories from local newspapers from when she disappeared in November 1998, but it doesn't seem her family have made an application for financial support to the foundation, so I'm really not sure why they would send the picture to the office.'

'Well, I wouldn't worry too much about it then. You've got enough on your plate already, which also reminds me, I was contacted by Reflex Media – the production company who adapted *Monsters* for television – and they'd like to option your account of Aurélie's return.'

I can't say this news is a surprise given the media interest generated in Aurélie's return last year after fifteen years away. It feels almost inevitable that someone would request the rights to televise or trivialise the story. Since she returned to France late last year she's been in isolation, avoiding the public eye, but I think part of that is because her father – the great politician Remy Lebrun – is coaching her on how to court the media.

'My advice would be to hold out for more money,' Maddie says, sliding on her tortoiseshell bifocals and studying the offer letter before handing it to me. 'Any option money will have to be split with the Lebruns, so you have to think of the figure on the table as half of what is quoted there.

My mouth drops at the printed figure. Even a fifty per cent cut is more than was offered for *Monsters*.

'I'm pretty sure they won't be the only company interested either, so I should be able to play a couple of them off each other to get the price up. Leave it with me. Okay?'

I pass her the letter back and nod. 'Thank you, Maddie. I don't know what I'd do without you managing all these affairs for me.'

She beams at me. 'That's what I'm here to do. I just wish you'd let me handle your romantic affairs too.'

I return her chuckle, and await the inevitable interrogation about Jack and Rick.

Chapter Eighteen

NOW

Weymouth, Dorset

Whenever I feel lost, or uncertain which direction to take, I know there's somewhere I can always go to find some context, and ultimately prioritise the important stuff against the anxieties that I just can't control. They also say mums give the best hugs. Watching my mum's deterioration as a result of Alzheimer's is something I don't think I'll ever get over. I've said before that it really is one of the cruellest diseases a person can be subjected to, and the effect isn't just on the sufferer, but also on their loved ones too. I never wanted to see my mum end up in a nursing home before her sixty-fifth birthday (that's not even an age, is it?) but it was what her physician recommended, and at least I know she won't come to any harm.

Tragically, her condition has gradually worsened, and these days I'm lucky if I manage to time it when she's having what the nurses refer to as 'a good day', which essentially means her memory is in better working order and she won't mistake me for one of the nurses or – worse still – a total stranger. We've both learned to adapt to the situation, and when it isn't one of the good days, I tell myself that next time might be better and play along with her view of who I am. I still get to talk to her about my life and immediate worries, and I think it helps that any judgement she confers she won't remember anyway. I suppose that makes it easier for me to be honest with her about my feelings because the slate is wiped clean each time.

Approaching the wrought-iron gates that add a Gothic air to the listed building, I already know I can't bring myself to tell her what was discovered at the Pendark site yesterday. At best, it isn't Anna's remains, and it would be cruel to worry Mum unnecessarily; and if the worst is confirmed, I will need to psych myself into breaking that news. I'm not ready for that today, but I have so many thoughts whizzing around my head that I just crave the chance to see Mum and reflect on a time when life just didn't seem as complicated.

I usually pet the overweight ginger cat at the door before entering, and once I'm through I mention Ginger to the girl behind the desk, but she grimly shakes her head.

'Got run over she did,' she tells me. 'Between you and me, some kid found her sprawled in the road just outside the entrance, squashed flat; all very messy.'

I grimace as I sign the visitor book. I don't recognise the girl, so she must be new here, but I'm sure the Home Manager, Pam Ratchett, wouldn't appreciate such candour with visitors. The girl is smartly dressed but can't be long graduated from college, and by the look of boredom on her face, and the half-completed Sudoku puzzle on the page before her, I don't think she's found her vocation just yet.

'I'm here to see Winnie Hunter,' I announce, waiting to hear if she'll give me an update on whether it's a good day or not, but she simply nods, and points towards the corridor of private rooms.

'Do you know where you're going?' she asks, her eyes reverting to the puzzle.

Luckily for her I do, and I'm in no mood to launch into an argument about manners and her not checking in what capacity I'm here to see one of the residents. Making my way along the corridor, I take my time, allowing my nostrils to acclimatise to the pungent aroma that clings to every surface here. It's yet another reason why the staff here must be angels; I don't think I could stomach the smell for eight hours a day as they do.

Knocking at Mum's door, I'm surprised when she yanks it open and glowers at me. 'Oh, it's you – that's all I need!'

I can't remember the last time I saw Mum up and out of her hard-backed chair or bed, but she leaves the door to close by itself as she turns and stomps back inside. I wasn't expecting her to roll out the red carpet, but this lack of welcome is unusually cold. Catching the door before it closes, I head in, immediately seeing the shards of broken glass on the carpet on the far side of the room, the fragments mingled with dead flowers.

'Oh no, Mum, what happened to your favourite vase?' I ask, moving across and looking for something I can use to safely pick up the pieces.

'Bloody flowers give me hay fever, you know that! It doesn't seem to matter how many times I tell these bloody nurses I hate flowers, they still put the bloody things in here!'

She is pacing backwards and forwards on the carpet

between the television set and the door, and this aggression is making me nervous. I suppose it could be that she's frustrated with herself for dropping the vase and her deteriorating mind is lashing out, but she hasn't seemed this agitated in I don't know how long.

In that moment, I'm suddenly back in our old house and I can see her pacing in a similar way – head bent forward, hands twisted behind her back – as she stares at a map of Dorset, trying to determine where they might have been holding Anna. The memory fades as quickly as it arrived, and I have to accept that although she's recognised me, today is not a good day.

'I didn't know you suffer with hay fever, Mum,' I admit, conscious that I'm the one who'd brought the flowers in last Tuesday.

'What do you mean? Of course you know! I've suffered with it all my bleeding life.'

The pacing continues at quite a rate and I'm eager to calm her down and bring some tranquillity back to the room. 'I tell you what,' I try calmly, hoping she'll reflect my pitch, 'why don't I get this tidied up and then maybe you and I could go for a walk somewhere?'

'I don't want a bloody walk,' she snaps back, without looking up.

In fairness, our walking options would be relatively limited anyway. Whilst I'm allowed to sign her out for day trips and exercise, the home isn't particularly close to any sites of beauty or parkland, and having taken her on a walk around the local housing estates shortly after she first arrived here, I don't blame her for not wanting to go out. It's also drizzling, and my coat is soaked through following the walk from the restaurant.

Finding an old magazine in the wastepaper basket, I fish it out, separate the pages from the staples, and tentatively drop each piece of glass into the makeshift parcel before placing it back in the carrier bag inside the basket.

'I'll need to get someone to dispose of that carefully,' I tell her, standing and brushing loose hair and dust from my skirt where I've been kneeling.

'Do what you like. You always do anyway.'

This really isn't like Mum at all. Clearly she's got a bee in her bonnet about something and unless I can get to the bottom of it, neither of us is going to appreciate my visit. Moving across to her, I stop her relentless marching and take her hands in mine.

'Can you tell me what's upset you so much?' She tries to snatch her hands away, but I hold them firm. 'Please, Mum, I can't help unless you tell me what's happened. Is it just the vase breaking that's upset you? If so, I can buy you a replacement vase. Accidents happen, and—'

'It wasn't a bloody accident,' she growls. 'I threw the bloody thing at the wall so they can't bring any more flowers in here when I'm not looking!'

'Mum, I brought you those flowers on Tuesday, remember? I didn't realise you suffered with hay fever, otherwise I wouldn't have got them for you. I was only trying to brighten the room. There really wasn't any need to break the vase.'

'Don't treat me like a child! If I want to break a bloody vase then I bloody will.'

She is trying to pry her hands away again, and I've never felt so out of my depth. I don't think I've ever seen her looking so angry, and my efforts to pacify her aren't working.

'I don't know why you're so worried anyway,' she

continues. 'I'm sure I'll be the last thing on your mind when you leave anyway. It's so easy for you, isn't it? Able to just get on with your own life without having the burden of me on your shoulders too.'

I can feel the sting of tears in my eyes. 'Mum, how can you say that? I work so hard to afford this place for you, and I come and visit whenever I can—'

'Why don't you just go on your bloody way then? You've done your civic duty and now you can wash your hands of me once more.'

It's all I can do to keep the tears at bay. There is such venom in her eyes that I can't process what to do for the best.

'You know I never bloody wanted to come here in the first place, but you couldn't wait to get rid of me. You forced me in here and then you abandoned me, just like you abandoned your sister!'

I release her hands and allow her to pace again, unsure how else to react. Slumping down on the bed, I can't look at her for fear of the floodgates opening.

'It was your fault she ran off that day, into the arms of some pervert or whatnot. I bet she wouldn't have shoved me in somewhere like this at the first sign of trouble neither.'

There is a knock at the door and I'm grateful when I see Pam Ratchett's round face appear in the gap. 'Everything okay in here, Winnie?'

'No, it bloody isn't. Your bloody nurses keep bringing in flowers and it's doing something rotten to my hay fever. You're in charge of this bloody place – make them stop, will you?'

'Of course I will, Winnie,' she says, even adding an empathetic smile, before turning to face me. 'Would it be okay if we had a little word in my office, Emma?'

I nod and feel the splash of warmth on my cheek but quickly wipe it away before Pam sees. She leads me from the room and along to her office. She hands me a box of tissues as she squeezes into her chair, and I sit across from her.

'Don't blame yourself,' she begins. 'I overheard the end of your mum's tirade. I had meant to call and advise you it might not be best to come in today, but what with one thing and another… I'm sorry. Today isn't the first time your mum has become aggressive towards the staff and other residents. I've spoken to the doctor overseeing her Alzheimer's and this level of hostility isn't uncommon in the later stages of the disease. Unfortunately, there is a chance that we will see more outbursts of this nature as the disease continues to eat away at the synapses in her brain. The good news is we can manage some of it with medication, and from your point of view, you can phone us on the morning when you're planning to come in and see her, and we can give you an idea of whether you should or not.'

I wipe my eyes with the tissue and blow my nose. 'I've never known her be like that before. It felt like there was nothing I could say or do to help.'

The compassion is radiating off her in waves, and I doubt I'm the first relative she's had to have this conversation with down the years. 'I know you want to see your mum, and to help her, but on days like this your being here could actually do more harm than good. I'm sorry, I appreciate that's not easy to hear.'

'I genuinely had no idea she suffered with hay fever.'

Pam sits back in her chair and opens a large drawer in her desk, withdrawing a small photo album and sliding it across the desk towards me.

'What's this?' I ask, but she merely indicates for me to look for myself.

Opening the album, I see it is filled with photos from a much brighter and evidently warmer day than today. The nurses are wearing short-sleeved versions of their uniforms, some of the older residents are wearing shorts and summer dresses, and the pictures appear to have been taken outdoors somewhere. I continue flipping through the photographs enclosed in transparent sleeves.

'We had a summer party eighteen months ago. We took most of our residents on a coach trip down to Swanage for a look around the shops and concluded the day with a picnic in a farmer's field we'd managed to hire. The weather was superb, and you could see how much everyone enjoyed the day out from the smiles and laughter we all shared.'

I arrive at a picture of Mum with the biggest smile on her face. Her mouth is open as if caught laughing raucously. She is holding a stick with pink candy floss and I think it may be the happiest I've ever seen her.

'When we were on our way home,' Pam continues, watching me carefully, 'a number of our residents were complaining of itchy eyes, sore throats, and runny noses, and we had to make an emergency stop at a supermarket to buy some antihistamines. That picture of your mum with the candy floss, look at where she's sitting.'

I look at the picture again, allowing my eyes to blur out her face and just focus on the background, which is filled with pretty flowers in rainbow colours.

'She was one of the few who didn't need any medication, and she probably spent more time smelling and touching those flowers than anyone else. I don't think your mum suffers with hay fever, Emma. You really don't need to blame yourself for today.'

I appreciate Pam's efforts to ease my guilt, but not remembering whether Mum suffered with hay fever isn't what is breaking my heart. It is what she said to me last: *it was your fault she ran off that day.*

Chapter Nineteen

THEN

Hayling Island, Hampshire

She'd been determined not to cry again; didn't want to give them the satisfaction, nor any reason to carry out their threat. Her new plan was simple: play along until an opportunity to get away presented itself. Clearly, Chez had earned the trust of Grey if he had a key to the caravan and seemed to be able to come and go as he pleased. If she could earn that level of trust, then maybe she'd find a way to escape and never look back. Whilst she didn't know where she was, she was pretty sure she was still in the UK and so she'd be able to find someone to take her to the police. It was all about waiting.

When Grey had said to expect Chez back she'd assumed he would be back quickly, but it had to have been at least an hour, and with her stomach grumbling she made her way into the kitchen area and searched for any sign of food. Dragging over the stool that Grey had been perched on, she clambered up, having to stand on tiptoes to see into the cupboard above the small gas hob. She found more dried pasta and jars of tomato sauce, but nothing she felt confident about cooking alone.

Clambering down, she moved across to the tallest cupboard and opened it. She was surprised when the internal light came on, and realised it was in fact a hidden fridge. Not a cold fridge – clearly the generator wasn't working again – but a fridge nevertheless. She found a block of cheddar, a jar of melting butter, and a carton of orange juice – not exactly a feast, but it would do to start. She carried the items to the table, returned, and continued her examination of the kitchen, using the stool to reach the cupboards she otherwise wouldn't be able to look in. Finally returning to the table, she was pleased with her finds. In addition to the cheese and juice, she'd managed to find a bag of prawn crackers, a packet of digestives, and a bottle of ketchup.

She was halfway through the feast when she heard the key rattling in the door, but this time she held her breath and didn't immediately shrivel up in fear. Chez entered, quickly locking the door behind him. He turned and quietly observed her before his eyes lit up. She'd wondered whether he would be angry that she'd raided the provisions, but if he was he was hiding it well.

'What's all this?' he asked, coming over, picking up one of the prawn crackers and dipping it into the splodge of ketchup on her plate.

'I was hungry,' she replied, slowly releasing the breath.

Chez smiled affectionately at her. 'Looks like I've got myself a rival in the kitchen then. You've got all my favourites here.'

She could barely bring her eyes to meet his, the flashes of

him pinning her feet while Grey injected her still fresh in her mind. It didn't look as though he was carrying any guilt as he sliced off a corner of cheddar and threw it into his mouth. Maybe he didn't think that what he'd done was wrong, or maybe he was hoping she'd already forgotten about it.

Think about escape, she reminded herself, finding the strength to offer a smile in return.

'I'm famished too,' he said, sliding onto the bench and taking a handful of the prawn crackers and shovelling them into his mouth like a hamster.

'Is there any bread?' she asked. 'I could make you a sandwich?'

His bright eyes dipped momentarily. 'Ah, no bread left, I'm afraid, but we should get some more supplies now that we've reached our destination.'

She desperately wanted to ask him exactly where they were and how long they would remain here, but she needed to keep him onside and lulled into a false sense of security. Too many questions now might make him suspicious.

She reached for the knife and tried to slice the cheddar without success. Chez seemed to take pity on her, and hacked off several slices and handed them over. Key to her success would be playing up to his thinking of her as a younger sister. Ironically, if he hadn't helped Grey to drug her earlier, she might have still seen him as just as much a victim as her, but clearly Chez was working with them, and that meant he couldn't be trusted.

'I don't think there's any electricity,' she said casually. 'The fridge doesn't seem to have any power.'

His eyes widened in panic, and he squeezed out from

behind the table. 'Oh shit, I forgot to start the generator when we pitched up.'

He hurried to the door, not noticing her slip the small cheese knife into the pocket of the dress he'd given her last night. She watched him unlock the door, leaving it swinging as he hurried down the steps and disappeared from view. She knew better than to run now, but quietly got down from the stool and walked to the door, quickly slipping out and down to the last step, but didn't move any further. This was her way of showing him she could be trusted to go outside and not try to run.

Wherever they were now, she could hear seagulls cawing to one another; a tall wood blocked out the horizon immediately in front of her, but she couldn't see what was behind the caravan. The grass between them and the trees stretched several hundred metres ahead, and apart from the other two caravans to their left, she couldn't see anything else; no farm animals this time.

She could hear Chez huffing and puffing off to the left as he pulled on the generator's starter cord, and finally the motor whirred to life and he reappeared from beside the caravan. She closed her eyes, and tilted her head back, breathing in the fresh air.

'Oh no, you shouldn't be outside,' he said, trying to usher her back inside. 'Grey would kill me if he found out.'

'Please, Chez, just a few seconds of fresh air. The cabin is so stale and stuffy. I have such a headache.'

'That's probably the after-effects of what Grey gave you,' he said glumly, before quickly changing the subject. 'The others will be back soon, and then we'll have supplies and can cook up a big feast.'

She remained where she was on the step. 'Would you take me for a walk?'

Chez looked around uneasily as if he could feel unwanted eyes on them. 'No, sorry, out of the question. I'm to keep an eye on you here.'

'Oh, but please, Chez. My head is pounding and I'm sure that some fresh air is all I need. We wouldn't have to go far. Maybe just to the trees and back. Please? I won't be any trouble, I promise.'

Chez looked over his shoulders at the wood and she sensed he was starting to wane.

'You can hold onto me if that would make you feel better. What's the worst that can happen?'

He looked back at the woods again, behind his eyes calculating the distance and time required to go there and back.

'Please, Chez. Maybe then you can tell me a bit more about the photoshoots Grey told me about. He told me my parents know where I am, and how lucky I am to have been chosen. I know I was acting immature before but I understand now, I think. Please, just a five-minute walk, and then we can be back.'

'Ah, okay,' he grumbled reluctantly, 'but we come back as soon as I say. Yeah?'

She raised herself onto her toes and pecked his cheek. 'One other question: can I have some trainers to put on?'

He ushered her back into the caravan and this time she obliged, sitting patiently on the stool as he moved to the back bedroom and rummaged inside a carrier bag, emerging a few seconds later with the trainers she'd been wearing when Grey had picked her up at the newsagent's.

'Put these on, but we'd better be quick.'

She took the trainers and slipped her feet in, tightened the Velcro straps, and leapt up excitedly. Chez gripped her hand tightly and led her back out of the door, closing it behind him and pocketing the key. Leaving the steps, they moved across the damp grass, Joanna nearly losing her footing at one point when it was more slippery than she'd anticipated. He certainly was keen to get to the trees and back in a hurry and she struggled to keep up with his large strides, having to take two quick steps to his one.

She hadn't lied about the headache, although she'd exaggerated just how much her head was spinning. The fresh air was certainly helping to sharpen things in her mind, and she prayed he couldn't feel just how fast her pulse was racing. He'd trusted her to come this far, and she felt pleased with how she'd managed to manipulate him into doing what she wanted.

The world around them darkened as they neared the edge of the wood, the tree branches blocking out the sky. She'd half-expected to see a trail or path through the wood, but as they neared, it appeared to stretch on for ever and she had no way of knowing what lay beyond it.

'Right, time to head back,' he said, yanking on her arm as he turned around on the spot.

But she pulled her arm back and managed to break free of his grasp. Reaching into the pocket of the dress, she coiled her fingers around the handle of the cheese knife, and quickly yanked it out and pointed it at him menacingly.

'You're going to show me a way out,' she said, trying to keep the sheer terror from her voice. 'Right now.'

'W-w-what?' he asked, but then his face screwed into a ball

as realisation hit him. He glowered in frustration. 'You lied to me.'

She shook her head. 'No, but come on, Chez, this is our chance to go. You could come with me. If we can get to a town, or village, we can have someone ring for help, and then you can return to that little town you told me about and I can get back to my home too.'

She was waiting for the moment he would slap the blade from her hand and drag her back to the caravan, but he didn't make any move towards her. 'You don't realise what you're asking. It isn't that easy, Kylie.'

'It can be, Chez. The two of us together is all it will take. You know this place better than me; we can get away now before anyone realises we've gone. Please? I'm asking as your sister.'

His eyes shone in the dimming light of the day, but he still made no effort to take the knife from her. 'Just go,' he eventually whispered. 'I can't go with you, but if you really want to take your chances, then just go. I'll give you ten minutes before I raise the alarm.'

She held the knife firm, unable to read whether it was him who was now trying to manipulate her.

'Go through the woods and keep going straight until you come to a stream. Turn right and follow the stream until you get to a footbridge, which will take you past a golf course and into the town centre. You need to move quickly though.'

She hadn't expected him to be so obliging, but the thought of heading into the dark woods alone was almost as terrifying as remaining with him. Threatening him with the knife was a line she couldn't cross back from, and if she didn't make her move now she'd never get another chance.

Stepping slowly backwards, she kept her eyes fixed on him, waiting for any sudden movement or lunge that would indicate he'd been stringing her along but he remained where he was, the tears now dripping from his eyes.

'Come with me, Chez,' she tried again, still delicately stepping backwards.

'I told you I can't. Go now, before I change my mind.' With that he turned and started making his way back across the grass towards the caravans.

Taking a deep breath, Joanna slipped between the trees and prayed he'd told her the truth about the stream and footbridge.

Chapter Twenty

NOW

Weymouth, Dorset

The taxi journey home from Mum's has done little to ease the throbbing headache that developed as I was leaving Pam Ratchett's office. To think, I'd gone to see Mum to gain some much-needed perspective and help me put my thoughts in order, and now I feel even more lost. Mum blames me for Anna's leaving that day, and whilst I've always carried some guilt for the argument we had before she said she was going to Grandma's house, I thought it was just me who blamed events on the argument. How many years has Mum been holding those thoughts in? Was it to protect me, and so that I wouldn't experience the brunt of her anger as happened today?

It's all very well Pam telling me not to pay too much attention to Mum's outburst – given the absence of hay fever – but she didn't hear how Mum phrased her statement: *it was your fault she ran off that day.*

There was real venom in her tone, as if years of bottling it up had turned it into pure hatred once uncorked. And if she secretly blamed me, did Dad too? I can't ask him, and looking back on it now, I recognised we were spending less and less time together after Anna disappeared and before his sudden death at HMP Portland. I'd put that down to him ploughing his free time into work and his spare time into drinking away his sorrows; both roads were meant to serve as a distraction for him, but I'm not sure either ever did. Maybe it was less to distract him from the daughter he'd lost and more to distract him from the one who remained.

I wish Rachel were here. She'd probably tell me I need to pull myself together, and whilst I wouldn't believe her words of warmth and sympathy, I'd appreciate her efforts. Right now, I have nobody to offer me a shoulder to cry on. I could phone Maddie, but I've never liked discussing family dynamics with her; it just doesn't feel right. She's been like a mother to me in the publishing world, and to mention my personal family would be like cheating on our relationship.

Part of me wants to phone Jack, not to pour out all my problems but so that we could talk about something to distract me for a few minutes, but he said he's got the day off with Mila today and he probably needs that time as much as she does. I'm not prepared to disrupt that. Besides, Jack has enough on his plate without me adding my woes.

Closing the front door behind me, I'm glad to be home, even if the silence is overwhelming. I've always been so adamant that I'm happy with my ordered life; I haven't wanted ties and commitment, allowing me to focus my time on searching for Anna and helping the families of missing children when the opportunity presents itself. If I want to stay up until the early hours writing and then sleep until midday

I'm free to do so, and that's where I've wanted to be. But right now, I would give anything for a warm, non-judgemental hug from a partner.

As if he can read my mind, my phone beeps with a message from PCSO Rick Underwood.

> *This is my number, so you have it. I'm really looking forward to seeing you later for that drink. Any preference where we should go? Would you like me to pick you up on the way? Rick x*

I had forgotten about agreeing to meet him for a drink, and to be honest, I don't think I'll be very good company tonight. I'm about to type a response to that effect when my doorbell sounds, startling me as I'm still leaning against it.

'Oh, are you off out?' Freddie asks when I open the door and he spots I am still wearing my coat.

The rain seems to have eased off and I suddenly don't want to be surrounded by all the silence of my flat. 'Just for a walk,' I tell him, closing the door behind me as I step out and join him. 'Come with me?'

Freddie presses knuckles to his hips, allowing me to link my arm with his, and he leads me away from the doorstep. After the way we left things last night, after Jack's aggressive outburst, I thought it would be days or weeks until I saw Freddie again. Resting my head on his shoulder, I don't know how to tell him just how pleased I am to see him.

'You know you have no chance of scoring with me tonight, right?' he jokes, and my laugh comes out as part cry, part chuckle, and I press my head more firmly into the sleeveless denim jacket he's rarely without.

We walk along the front, bypassing the town centre. At this

time of year, there are no donkey rides on offer, no fairground attractions, and a distinct lack of beach-dwellers. Over the winter months, dogs are allowed to be walked on the beach, and right now a large German Shepherd tears past us towards the water's edge, sending a flurry of sand into our faces. Neither of us breaks stride and we brush the sand from our faces and continue as if nothing has happened. I wish it was as easy to do the same with life's challenges.

'You're very quiet,' Freddie eventually says, breaking the comfortable silence. 'Penny for them?'

'Jack thinks he might have found Anna's remains,' I say gravely. It's the first time I've allowed myself to say the words out loud, and I'm not surprised by how much they sting.

Freddie immediately stops and pulls me into a hug. 'Oh gosh, Emma, I'm so sorry.'

It feels good to just be held. 'We should know for certain in the next few days. I gave him a few hairs from one of her brushes so a DNA comparison can be run.'

'Wow! How many years has it been since… since she disappeared?'

I rest my temple on his chest. 'Twenty-one years of not knowing where she is, nor what happened. At least the first question will now be answered, and I can lay her to rest.'

I'm not just being pragmatic either. For the first time, I see that DNA confirmation will mean I can stop looking for Anna, and there's some heart-breaking relief in that. It's possible I will never know who took her, nor why she was chosen, but that doesn't mean I'll stop trying.

'Is there anything I can do to help?' Freddie asks.

I look up into his eyes and release a sigh that's been building for I don't know how long. 'Thank you. We need to wait first, but yes, I may need an occasional shoulder to cry on from time to time. Are you qualified to be my wingman?'

He suddenly straightens his body, as if standing to attention, and salutes me, adopting a fake posh voice. 'Wing Commander Freddie Mitchell reporting for duty, ma'am. I won't let you down.'

He always has this ability to make me smile even in the face of adversity. I'm so blessed to have him in my life; in many ways, he's the big brother I never had.

'And how are you after last night?' I try, fixing him with an open stare.

He breaks eye contact and stares out at the sea behind me, sighing heavily. 'Your friend Jack was right about me, what he said last night – about me holding back… he was right. I didn't think about that period in my life for a long time, but seeing that place has brought so much back. I keep having flashes of memories – fragments really – in dreams and when my mind is elsewhere. It started when I was inside, and I thought it would stop once I got home and was amongst familiar surroundings, but last night was the worst one yet. I was back at that place, cameras pointing at me, being forced to remove my clothes, and then… It isn't right. There's a reason sex at that age is illegal; the adolescent brain isn't able to process the emotion and confusion of all of that… I wasn't ready and I didn't know what to do, or how to escape.'

His eyes are watering but he continues to stare out at the horizon, the wind whipping sand around us.

'I knew what they were doing was wrong… I knew I wasn't the only one suffering… But… It sounds so lame, but I was too scared to speak out. At night at St Francis, I would imagine myself killing Arthur Turgood and the others, but as soon as one of them approached I'd become a terrified schoolchild, weak and pathetic.

'When I was inside I read a book on the tools abusers use to psychologically manipulate their victims, and for the first time I could understand why Turgood and the others acted as they did. For them, the thrill is exerting power over the helpless; probably more so than any sexual gratification they received. But they were just the tip of the iceberg, right? There are plenty more predators still out there and so many children suffering as I did, and I've had enough.

'There was a police press conference on the television news just after lunch. Did you hear about the nine-year-old girl who's gone missing from the area, Jo-Jo?'

I nod. 'I met her parents this morning.'

'I watched and listened to the whole thing, but my eyes never left the picture of Jo-Jo hanging behind their heads. I've known children like that; I was a child like that. I wasn't abducted, but I was left at the hands of merciless monsters who were allowed to get away with what they wanted for too long. Enough is enough, Emma. I can't sit idly by and allow this kind of thing to continue. I need to do something. I need to stop these bastards.'

I've never known Freddie be so open about his feelings without copious coaxing efforts on my part. I know it can't have been easy for him to come to my flat and to pour his heart and soul out like this, but I'm grateful he felt able to trust me.

'We don't know that Jo-Jo has been taken by the same sort of people that took Anna,' I counter.

'They're *all* those sorts of people. They may have different names and faces but they represent the darkest element of society, and someone needs to stop them whatever the cost.

That's why I burned down that cursed film studio. It might have been closed now, but I knew some of the things that happened there. When you and Jack told me remains had been found at the site, I wasn't at all surprised. In fact, I'd put money on there being more undiscovered victims there too.'

I don't know how to respond, so I leave the statement hanging.

'Jo-Jo's parents asked me to help bring their daughter home,' I tell him. 'The lead detective isn't my biggest fan and doesn't want me anywhere near her investigation, but I don't want Jo-Jo to follow in my sister's footsteps and become just another statistic either.'

Freddie lowers his gaze to meet mine. 'Then we're agreed? We do something about this.'

My thoughts have been so muddled since I woke this morning, and for the first time I feel I have a purpose and reason to keep going. 'Yes, Freddie, we'll do whatever it takes to find Jo-Jo and the monsters haunting all our dreams.'

Chapter Twenty-One

NOW

Portland, Dorset

It feels strange walking the streets I did as a child. A simple internet search confirmed the address of the Nevilles, and we're now rapidly approaching our destination on foot.

I smile as I spot a large oak tree at the edge of the modernised playground we're nearing. 'I used to climb that tree with my sister,' I muse.

It looks smaller than I remember, but then I suppose I've grown since I last saw it. A much simpler time then.

Freddie looks up from the pavement for the first time. 'Which one?'

'The big oak one there with the shaded bark that resembles the face of a growling bear. I was always jealous of how high Anna would climb; she was always so fearless. I'd just about make it onto the first branch that still hangs out today, but then I'd feel queasy and need to clamber down. Not Anna though; she'd climb maybe ten feet up before wrapping her legs around the branch and hanging upside down like a bat. I always used to panic she'd slip and fall and that I'd be the one to get it in the ear from Mum and Dad, but she never fell.'

My tears begin to well and I can almost picture her hanging bat-like from that branch now, but it's momentary, and then I see it is just an old tree standing guard at the playground's edge. Given the bitter chill of the wind and the rapid ascendency of the moon, I'm not surprised there are no children inside the playground railings now. Back when Anna and I were kids, there was no fence, and where there is now a climbing frame in the shape of a pirate ship was a see-saw and set of swings. The children these days don't know how lucky they are!

We turn left onto the Nevilles's road once we're past the playground, and it isn't difficult to see which their house is as there are two police patrol cars parked across the drive, keeping the handful of journalists back. When Freddie had suggested we go to their house, I hadn't even considered the prospect of reporters being camped outside trying to hook an exclusive interview for whichever journal they represent.

I cringe when I hear my name being shouted by an eagle-eyed reporter who is dressed in faded jeans and a jumper, though his overhanging gut has slipped through the gap between the two. 'Emma, Emma, are you here to help find little Jo-Jo?'

I ignore the question, doing my best to pretend I haven't heard, and approach one of the two uniformed officers standing guard at the perimeter. I introduce myself and ask whether DS Robyn Meyers is inside with the family. He sends his colleague to check my credentials at the house, meanwhile the remaining journalists and two photographers are pushing in behind Freddie and me. Given we're here to offer our support, it feels more like I'm a student again and trapped in a mosh pit with no obvious means of escape.

The second officer returns and whispers something into his colleague's ear, and the perimeter tape is raised for Freddie and me to duck beneath. We follow the second officer past the parked cars and up the patio drive to the front door where Robyn is waiting, arms folded, and looking less than impressed by my arrival.

'I want to do whatever I can to help Mr and Mrs Neville to find Jo-Jo,' I say with steely determination.

She has every right to refuse me entrance to the property and to slam the door in my face, something I'm sure the photographers are poised to capture, but she doesn't. Instead, she takes a step back and opens the doorway wider, allowing me to enter, but pausing when her eyes fall on Freddie.

'He's a colleague,' I lie quickly. 'He's here to help too.'

She considers Freddie for a moment, as if she recognises him, but can't quite place why or from where. She finally relents and allows him to hustle in behind me before explaining that the family are gathered in the back room, away from flashing cameras and shouted questions. What she doesn't explain is just how many people are gathered there; it's standing room only, and it takes a moment for my eyes to locate them.

Tina is the first on her feet, wiping her eyes with the sleeve of her cardigan as she takes my hands in hers. 'Emma, I can't believe you've come here in our hour of need,' she says, as if formally introducing me as part of a ceremony.

She proceeds to drag me across the room, urging her relatives to shuffle up and allow me to squash onto the sofa beside her. Once we're seated, she pulls me into a cringeworthy embrace – I'm not a hugger – and I find myself awkwardly patting her on the back, as if we've been best friends for years.

'Did you see the press conference earlier?' she asks eagerly – I sense she's craving my approval – and I have to shrug guiltily.

'I was out when it was on,' I admit, 'but Freddie here saw it, and was so moved that he insisted we come and lend any support we can.'

Tina looks at the stranger in her house, and in fairness he does stand out with his heavy metal T-shirt and sleeveless jacket, amid the cast of tracksuit bottoms and sports tops currently lining the room.

Freddie drops to his knees at her feet and takes one of her hands from mine. 'I'm so sorry for your loss. I've been in Jo-Jo's situation and I feel it is my duty to try and help get her back by any means, Mrs Neville.'

This seems to ease her concern. 'Please, you should both call me Tina. When I hear someone say Mrs Neville, it has me looking over my shoulder for my mother-in-law. God rest her soul.'

I see Trey Neville nodding in my periphery. 'I just pray she's looking down and keeping an eye on our Jo-Jo for us.'

Murmurs of agreement echo around the room.

Trey then stands and forcefully claps his hands together. 'Right, let's set about our manhunt,' he declares and the rest of the room – all but Tina, Freddie, and me – are on their feet, ploughing towards the door through which we entered only moments earlier.

'They're going to walk all the nearby streets calling out Jo-

Jo's name,' Tina explains, 'and showing her picture to whoever they find. Someone must have seen what happened to her.'

Robin appears at the door and offers to make tea, which we all agree to, and then there are only the three of us left in the room.

'I'm so glad you're here,' Tina says, squeezing my hand. 'It means a lot that you've taken time out of your own busy life to be here and support us at such a difficult time.'

I don't know how to respond. I don't know that there is a lot I can do to help, other than offer words of encouragement. I'm reluctant to tell her about the people Jack and I have been hunting, as I don't want to worry her any further. If she's lucky, then whoever snatched Jo-Jo has nothing to do with the sorts of men who still haunt my and Freddie's dreams. For now, we just need to keep her spirits up.

Robyn returns to the room with the tea and a plate of Jaffa Cakes, taking a seat across the room, her eyes never leaving me, nor Freddie; I imagine she's already reported our arrival to Cavendish and has been told to keep a close watch on us.

'You certainly have a lot of friends and family here offering support,' I say, as I sip the tea.

'They have been a godsend too,' Tina tells me, reaching for a Jaffa Cake and placing the whole thing in her mouth. 'We're a pretty large but close family; the lot who've just gone out with Trey are all this side of Dorchester, but we have other family in Wiltshire, Hampshire, and Sussex too. Everyone's ready to drop everything to get our Jo-Jo back.' She stops and looks skyward, blinking back the urge to cry.

'She's lucky to have so many people who care for her,' I reply, thinking back to how isolated my parents felt when Anna went missing. We didn't have a large support network to rely on, and maybe if we had, the cracks in my parents' marriage wouldn't have become unrepairable. 'Trey is Jo-Jo's step-father, right?' I ask, keen to better understand the family dynamics. 'Is Jo-Jo's birth father still in the picture?'

Tina fires a troubled look towards Robyn before meeting my gaze. 'He's not on the scene anymore. Trey's her dad now, and that's all I have to say on that.'

Heat rises to my cheeks as I realise I've overstepped the mark, and quickly try to change the subject. 'Has Detective Cavendish said how many potential leads the press conference generated?'

'I have cautioned Mrs Neville from discussing any operational matters of the investigation with the press,' Robyn warns from her perch.

I resist the temptation to challenge that I'm not here in a media capacity, but I don't see the point.

'What can I do to help?' I ask Tina instead. 'I'm happy to retweet and share any posts on social media that you think will help.'

She squeezes my hand again. 'Just having you here and knowing that you're on our side is enough.'

Freddie moves to the cushion beside her and I can see he's keen to speak but is reluctant to do so without invitation.

'Freddie here knows the streets of Weymouth better than anyone, and he has contacts with our homeless community. I'm sure he'd be happy to hang some pictures of Jo-Jo at the shelter where he works and get more eyes out there looking for her.'

She looks at Freddie and he nods eagerly. 'I've already put the word out, and will report back anything and everything I hear.'

She smiles thankfully. 'You're both being so kind. I just wish…' She can't finish the sentence, as her eyes shine with tears.

Robyn's phone beeps loudly and she quickly reads the screen before standing and moving over to the three of us. 'Freddie Mitchell, right?'

Freddie stands, concern gripping every feature. 'Yes, why?'

'You're out on early release; you shouldn't be anywhere near here. I'm going to have to ask you to leave now.'

He doesn't argue, just lowers his cup to the coffee table beside the plate of Jaffa Cakes. I stand too, not willing to see him evicted alone. Passing Tina my business card, I tell her to contact me if there's anything specific she needs, and then I follow Robyn and Freddie to the door.

Chapter Twenty-Two

THEN

Hayling Island, Hampshire

She had to hurry, but it was so difficult to do so when every attempt at finding a path resulted in stumps and bark sticking out at acute angles. She was sure Chez had said something about a path leading to the stream, but if such a path existed she'd yet to find it. Of course that could be because she'd become disorientated and could no longer be certain she was walking in a straight line. She'd had to take so many sidesteps that for all she knew she was completing circular laps of the inside of the woods. It felt like she'd been walking for at least ten minutes by now, which would mean Chez would have sent the alarm out to Grey and Mr Brown, and they would soon be on her trail. If they had a better idea of the layout of the wood then it wouldn't be long until they were close behind her.

They'd probably be armed with torches and equipment for chopping down some of the lower-hanging branches that clawed at her face as she failed to push them aside. The cheese knife she was still gripping tightly in her right hand would offer little resistance if the two of them jumped her.

A twig snapping somewhere to her left instantly froze her movement while she tried to determine where it had come from and what could have caused it. She tried to hold her breath, but she could barely manage it for more than a few seconds, and then her lungs would burn and she'd have to inhale again. Surely they'd be able to hear the sound of her hot breath, or even see the plumes of it as the condensation rose in the rapidly cooling air. She closed her eyes, straining to hear any sound that wasn't the thunder of her heart against her ribcage or her breathlessness.

Silence returned to the forest and she pictured her pursuers paused in their pursuit, listening for the sound of her movement. If neither of them moved, would they remain frozen like statues all night? Deciding that every second counted, Joanna took flight once more, charging into the darkness, her arms crossed in front of her face to offer what little protection they could.

Nettles and thorns scratched at her bare legs, and in hindsight making a break for it in the sequined party dress hadn't been a good idea either. Why had she been so impatient? She had convinced Chez to take her outside for a walk, and had she not made her move and simply returned to the caravan, maybe a better chance would have presented itself tomorrow when she was better prepared.

Her right trainer struck a stump protruding from the black floor, and she lurched forwards, stretching out her arms and somehow managing to break her fall with only grazed hands. She could hardly breathe, the air unable to enter her lungs quickly enough to dilute the lactic acid building in her calves and thighs. She curled into a ball on the floor, hoping anyone passing would mistake her for a frightened animal or bush. She could barely see her hand in front of her face down here, so what chance would Grey and Mr Brown have?

She remained tucked up on the rough ground, composing herself, and all the time listening out for the sound of snapping twigs and voices. It had to have been ten minutes by now, hadn't it?

Get up, she willed. Staying still wouldn't help her get home. Chez had offered a head start, and resting here was throwing away that chance a second at a time. Grey and Mr Brown were much taller and would probably swallow the distance between them in half the time it had taken her, so there was no more time she could waste. If she could just make it to the stream, she felt confident she'd be closer and able to up her speed.

Driving her palms into the rough terrain, she took five deep breaths, and then forced herself up, careful not to grunt with the exertion. But the ground before her was already darker and it wouldn't be long before the still blue sky over her head darkened, and then it would be impossible to see anything.

Suddenly she spotted a gap in the trees ahead, and was that…? Yes, the ground seemed to shimmer and flow through the clearing. Upping her speed and diving through the space, she found herself on a stony path, a fast-flowing stream beside it. With no time to lose, she immediately turned right and tried to find an even pace without breaking into a noisy run.

It was slightly lighter here where the trees on either side of the water separated at the top, rather than entwining, and the sky reflected off the murky water. The pathway was barely half a metre wide, and large bushes of nettles formed a barrier to the trees to her right, but there was no safety barrier stopping her from falling into the stream to her left either. Twisted tree roots protruded from the ground in web-like fashion; chipped stones in charcoal, silver, orange, and brown crunched beneath her trainers as she moved as swiftly as her dwindling energy would allow; bare branches, like skeleton fingers, hung down, waiting to snatch her up. Thick green reeds danced in the flow of the stream, and the occasional fish plopped and splashed as it battled against the current; the stream stank of damp and decaying matter. As she looked ahead of her for any sign of a bridge, it became clear just how precarious a situation she now found herself in.

She'd turned right onto the path, but was that what Chez had said? Or had he said to head left? She genuinely couldn't remember, which meant there was every chance she wasn't heading towards the town like he'd said – assuming he'd told her the truth in the first place. Maybe the directions he'd actually given would lead her straight back to the camp. And if that was the case, then he definitely wouldn't have waited for ten minutes before informing his companions that she'd bolted for it, which meant they were probably circling nearby somewhere, waiting to strike. Maybe that had been their plan all along: lead her to the stream, where they'd throw her in, never to be found again.

Then suddenly, from out of nowhere, she spotted a wooden bridge up ahead. No longer caring about the sound of footfalls, she broke into a jog, willing her legs to move quicker, allowing her brain to finally believe that things would be okay. If she could get over the bridge and find the road into the town, she would simply stop the first person she spotted and explain who she was; she didn't know her home phone number, but she could tell the person her name and address, and he or she could then phone the police and have her taken home. If she told her parents how sorry she was about going to the newsagent's shop alone, and that she really did want to stay at home, then maybe they wouldn't return her to Grey and Mr Brown.

The curved bridge had metal netting across its base, giving her added grip as she tore up and over it, only stopping momentarily once she was on the opposite bank to look for any sign of Grey or Mr Brown. She could no longer see the break in the trees she'd come through, and the light was rapidly fading, but their absence gave her renewed belief. She didn't like to think what kind of punishment Chez would receive for aiding her escape; she wished he'd come with her, but he'd made his choice for whatever reason, and now it was up to her to make the most of the opportunity. If she could show the police where she'd been held, then maybe they could rescue Chez and he'd be safe too.

Continuing along the narrow pathway, which was so overgrown she couldn't be sure anyone had stepped foot on it in the last ten years, she eventually spotted a tall, thin post, with an arrow sign indicating the town centre was 500 metres further along. Checking back the way she'd come, she could no longer see the footbridge in the darkness slowly enveloping the entire landscape and she certainly couldn't hear the sound of anyone giving chase.

The pathway beside the stream ended at a rusted wire fence, beyond which the pathway quickly disappeared into the stream. Bending to the left, she followed the even narrower cutaway out to a quiet road. More dark forest stretched out across the road, suggesting the strip of concrete had been built to bisect the trees. The road sign here indicated parking and the town centre to the right, and although her legs didn't want to move any further, she swallowed the pain and placed one foot in front of another. Chez hadn't mentioned a police station in the town centre, and since she had no idea what time it was, she couldn't be certain she'd find any open shops along the way.

The road lit up as a car approached from behind, and in sudden panic that Grey and Mr Brown would know where the stream pathway came out and might have pursued her in Grey's car rather than on foot, she looked for anywhere she could hide out of sight until the vehicle had passed. Darting back into the trees that lined the pavement closest to her, she ducked her head and squashed her body into the ground, desperately hoping they hadn't seen her last-minute decision, and breathed out a huge sigh of relief when the car continued without stopping.

That was close, she told herself. She couldn't risk being seen again, and so would have to find a way off the road. Waiting for a second car to pass in the opposite direction, she once more forced herself to her feet, now limping, such was the fatigue in her legs. It felt as though her prayers had been answered when she spotted a small chapel a few hundred yards ahead. She hurried towards it, ducking in through the arched entrance and hammering her fists against the small door of the property at the rear of the building. She was now out of sight of the road so she didn't care how much noise she made, but at first it didn't appear anybody was home. She hammered the door again, this time daring to call out.

A light flashed on inside, and a moment later she heard the door being unbolted. She practically fell into the arms of a kindly, old man with hair as white and fluffy as clouds. The dog collar around his neck was a sign of salvation, and she hurried to get the words out of her throat: who she was, where she'd come from, the fact that men were chasing her.

The kindly old man, Reverend Peter Saltzing, listened attentively, even jotting notes on a piece of paper so that he'd be able to accurately relay the message to the police.

'You look exhausted,' he told her. 'And I bet you're hungry too.' He smiled. 'I was just heating up a can of tomato soup, but I'm afraid it's too big for me to eat alone. Would you like some?'

She didn't need asking twice, following him through to a small kitchen at the rear of the property where she saw steam rising from a pan on the stove and a place setting for one at the rickety old table in the corner. He encouraged her to sit at the only chair, pouring a generous quantity of soup into the bowl before her, and inviting her to tear off a chunk of bread from the freshly baked loaf in the centre of the table. The bread was still warm to the touch and the butter instantly melted when spread.

'Why don't you eat while I phone the police and let them know you're safe?'

She nodded, dunking the chunk of bread into the red soup and savouring the mouthful as she placed it onto her tongue. Bread and soup had never tasted so good, and she vowed she would never again complain when her mum insisted on making it for lunch. She was halfway through the bowl, and feeling so much more relaxed, when the kindly old man returned to the room and topped up her bowl.

'Good to see some colour back in your cheeks,' he said, leaning against the counter and urging her to keep eating.

'They're on their way, and shouldn't be too much longer. They sounded very worried on the phone, but they've said they'll get a message to your family and let them know you're safe.'

She looked at him and wanted to say thank you, but her eyes quickly filled and the sob trapped the words in her throat. Reverend Peter put a gentle arm around her shoulders and held her while she gave in to the relief.

Chapter Twenty-Three

NOW

Weymouth, Dorset

The wind has whipped up since we've been inside and the sun is now nowhere in sight; what little glow emanates from the lampposts is barely enough to light the path back to the main road towards Weymouth town centre.

'It's so dark around here,' I comment, as we once more pass the playground, but it is impossible to even see the play equipment unless an occasional car's headlights catch the railings as it passes.

It's almost Gothic, and certainly reminds me of horror stories Anna would tell me about the monsters lurking beneath my bed when she wanted to give me a fright; if only she knew they were more than just stories. There's no sign of the group that went out from the Nevilles's house to search for Joanna; I suppose maybe they've already been along this way, or are headed further into Portland. I can't imagine that Jo-Jo is hiding out here in the dark on her own. It's interesting that Cavendish was adamant in her thinking that Jo-Jo had been abducted, and yet the family seem to think a search of the neighbourhood will prove more successful. Something doesn't add up, but I can't quite put my finger on what.

'You look troubled,' Freddie comments beside me. 'You're pulling that face that makes you look like a squirrel sucking on a lemon. What's wrong?'

I don't know whether I should be a tad offended at the squirrel comparison, but I let it slide as Freddie isn't the sort to take such a cheap shot.

'I don't know,' I admit with a deep sigh. 'I guess I was just wondering what could lead a normal person to do something so cruel as to abduct a child from her family.'

'You've answered your own question there, Em,' he replies. 'Those people aren't *normal*. I read once that the majority of physical and mental abusers were once abused themselves, and so it becomes this never-ending cycle of depravity. I think the world's been broken for a long time, it's just many years ago it was all taboo. Kids were warned not to talk to strangers but they weren't told why. Then you have operations like Yewtree, and my own story becoming an international bestseller, and suddenly the world is enlightened about just how evil some bastards are. Throw social media into the mix and there aren't many places left to hide.'

'And yet they somehow manage to,' I say grimly. 'With surveillance as advanced as it is, how can a person seemingly abduct a child and nobody *see* it?'

Freddie can only shrug. 'The world sees what it wants to see. How many homeless people do you think really get *seen* by those walking past? If you're lucky, and you get just the right pitch near a shop or the train station, then you might get a couple of dozen noticing you over the course of the day, but most *choose* not to see what's right in front of them.'

I link my arm through his. 'Well, *I* see you, Freddie Mitchell, and I am so proud of the man you've become today. Weaker men would have given up, but you're resilient, and there's a lot to be said for that.'

'Does that mean I can convince you to come and help me with my shift at the shelter tonight? I imagine we'll be pretty busy with how cold it is right now. We've got an enormous batch of vegan chicken soup on the go.'

I cock my eyebrow. '*Vegan* chicken soup? How does that even work?'

He snorts with laughter. 'Don't ask me; I'm not in charge. If they can make sausage rolls that look and taste like meat but aren't, who's to say what they can do with chicken? I mean, it has such a nondescript taste anyway, so it's probably pretty easy. Is that a yes then?'

I fold my face into an apologetic grimace. 'Sorry, but I can't. I have a date. Well, no, not a date as such, but I'm meeting someone for a drink in town.'

Freddie's eyes widen in gleeful surprise. 'A date?' He adopts a sarcastic flourish. '*The* Emma Hunter – Weymouth's answer to Bridget Jones – is going on an *actual* date? Someone pinch me; I must be dreaming.'

My cheeks shade with embarrassment. 'Just a drink.'

'Who with? Don't tell me Jack has *finally* stepped up to the plate and offered to make an honest woman of you. God knows I was starting to wonder whether I should buy you your first cat.'

'No, not Jack,' I say with more than an edge of remorse. 'I'm meeting Rick for a drink.'

He rolls his eyes. 'Boy, can you pick them! When things don't work out with Jack and Rick, who's next? Dick? Vic? Mac?'

I playfully slap Freddie's arm but I know he's only teasing me. The name similarity is unfortunate, but given this will probably be our first and only non-date, it shouldn't matter anyway.

We arrive at the pub and, although I'm ten minutes early, I can see Rick is already inside, sitting at a table with a single-stemmed rose in a small vase. He appears to be talking to himself, occasionally pausing and laughing at whatever imagined conversation he's heard. It's sweet, and I feel bad for watching, but I can't help it. He's wearing navy jeans and a formal shirt with the top two buttons unfastened. He suddenly looks up to the window and smiles broadly when he sees me there.

'You'd better go in,' Freddie says, flouncing my hair before giving me the thumbs-up.

I take a deep breath and am about to follow Freddie's instruction when Rick appears at the door, pulling on his jacket.

'Emma, I'm so sorry, but do you think we can take a raincheck?'

I won't deny that the possibility of a postponement is a relief.

'Of course,' I tell him quickly. 'Is everything okay?'

He looks at the phone in his hand before shaking his head.

'Yes and no. Detective Cavendish has called everyone back to the station. Rumour is there's been a reported sighting of Jo-

Jo.' He turns to leave before pausing. 'I don't suppose you want to tag along, do you?'

Freddie nudges me towards him.

I can already picture Cavendish's face, but it's time to put the animosity between us to one side. A girl's life is in danger.

Chapter Twenty-Four

NOW

Weymouth, Dorset

The air at the police station is electric with anticipation. It only took Rick and me ten minutes to get here, but in that time it looks like half the South Coast's officers have been called in. I know Cavendish is a fan of the dramatic, but I don't think she'd have called on this effort if she didn't truly believe in the intelligence she'd received.

Rick approaches one of the uniformed officers who is smoking just outside the station.

'I'm hearing there's been a sighting of Jo-Jo,' Rick starts, pushing his hands together and blowing warm air into them.

The guy nods as he inhales, watching me, but not questioning who I am or what I'm doing here. 'There was a call about twenty minutes ago. The DI is getting everyone together to scour the area.'

I don't know the child, and I've only met her parents twice, but I feel ready to punch the air with delight and relief. Having been in their shoes – on tenterhooks for information – I know better than anyone how relieved they must be. A sighting means that Jo-Jo is still alive and that the net on her whereabouts has narrowed significantly. All things being equal, it should only be a matter of time until she's safe and home.

Reported missing just before three on Saturday, and relocated less than thirty hours later – maybe I really did do Cavendish a disservice when I questioned why she'd been drafted in from Poole to run the investigation. I may not agree with her approach to an investigation – nor her personal morals – but credit where it's due: she's found Jo-Jo.

The officer drops his cigarette to the ground and squashes it underfoot before picking up the stub and depositing it in the small metal bin attached to the wall of the police station.

'You coming in?' he asks Rick, who looks at me as if trying to decide whether to head in through the staff-only entrance or wait with me.

I make the decision for him.

'I'll wait around the front,' I tell him. 'You'd better get in and find out what your orders are.'

He leans across and kisses me on the cheek in gratitude, before following his colleague through, while I make my way around to the front.

Some of the family members I observed at the Nevilles's house are camped outside – some smoking, others puffing warm air into brittle hands. But the group seems to have swollen in size, with more than thirty people awaiting the news that will bring a happy end to a terrifying weekend. I've no idea how they all could have heard about the possible sighting so quickly, especially as there are still officers arriving and heading in through the back.

There's no obvious sign of Trey or Tina or the FLO, so I squeeze my way through the crowd and wait just outside the front door. The station has been officially closed to the public since 5pm, but I don't imagine anyone anticipated such a turnout for this evening's news. I promised Freddie I would give him an update as soon as I know more, but I could see the joy in his eyes as Rick and I left. For all the victims of such evil and abuse, Jo-Jo being found really will be welcome news.

I turn to look at the front desk and am not surprised to find it unmanned. Something just doesn't add up in my head. I still don't understand what the gathered group are expecting to be told by waiting here. From what I've learned from Rick and the other officer, Jo-Jo hasn't actually been found yet, only sighted. It could be many more hours before something concrete is confirmed, unless the truth is actually being withheld from the public at the moment. Cavendish was already under enough pressure to locate Jo-Jo without having her every move under scrutiny. Wouldn't it be just like her to hold back, only to suddenly present Jo-Jo for the UK media to observe and celebrate the fine job she's undertaken? Maybe I'm being cynical, but I can't help thinking that Jo-Jo might already be inside with Tina and Trey for some carefully orchestrated presentation.

That is, until I spot DS Robin Myers escorting Tina across the road and round to the rear of the station. Forcing my way back through the crowd, I hurry after the pair of them.

'Tina, I heard the news, is there anything I can do?' I ask as Robin presses her pass up to the sensor securing the door.

Myers looks at me and frowns, gently shaking her head, but it's already too late.

'News? What is the news, Emma?' Tina says hurriedly, quickly embracing me. 'All I've been told is to come to the station. Have they… have they found Jo-Jo?'

I look to Robin again but she is still shaking her head. Something feels very wrong about this.

I've never been good at thinking on my feet and as my brain tries to think of a way out of this Freudian slip, I flounder.

'Um… I don't know,' I say shrugging. 'I only heard that there was a gathering here. I assumed it meant good news. No?'

It's lame, but Tina doesn't seem to notice. 'You think? Do you think they've found her?'

I'm looking for Robin to step in here and either tell me to pipe down or offer some better explanation, but she remains tight-lipped, eventually settling for 'We should head in.'

The door buzzes, but as Robin pulls on the handle someone is pushing it from the other side, and suddenly Detective Cavendish is in the doorway, staring daggers at me. She doesn't speak, instead pushing past me, as she leads out her team of officers in high-visibility vests, who quickly gather in a circle around her.

'What is all this?' Tina asks quietly, her eyes widening at the sheer volume of officers who've been tasked with an appearance tonight.

'Mrs Neville,' Cavendish says, taking her arm and deliberately leading her away from me, 'we believe we know where Jo-Jo is, and I've tasked my team with securing the area so we can catch the people responsible for her abduction and false imprisonment. Now, she is some way away, and so I'd ask that you wait with Robin here until we've got her in our safe custody, and then we'll be able to provide you with more of—'

'No,' Tina interrupts. 'I want to know where she is. Who has her? I want my daughter back. Emma?'

She thrusts out a hand and her fingers twitch, beckoning me over. I rush across and take her hand, ready to do whatever I can to keep her calm whilst Cavendish and her team complete their work.

'Why am I not surprised to see you here?' Cavendish snaps. 'I suppose I have you to thank for the camera crews setting up at the front of the police station too?'

I frown. 'What cameras? No, I don't know what you're talking about.'

She rolls her eyes. 'Of course not. Why would a publicity-hungry writer want a media circus gathered as she attempts to promote yet more of her drivel?'

My mouth drops at the barb, but she speaks again before I have chance to think of something to defend myself.

'And how exactly did you catch wind of what was going on this evening?'

She must catch me glance in Rick's direction.

'Ah, I see,' she says. 'Seems you'll do anyone as well as anything for a story then.'

Rick takes an unnecessary step forward, but I stop him with my raised hand.

'I asked her to meet me here,' Tina says loudly. 'She's become a real friend these last couple of days, and if anyone can help me understand all this madness, it's her.'

It feels like such a false statement to make, but I'm relieved when Cavendish finally takes her glare from me.

'Whatever,' Cavendish says. 'Your *friend* can wait here with you then. As soon as we have news, we'll phone—'

'No,' Tina interjects. 'Jo-Jo is my little girl, and I want to be there the second you find her. She needs her mum, so like it or not, I'm coming with you.'

I can feel the heat of Cavendish's fury emanating from her, but Tina isn't done yet.

'And Emma is coming with me to make sure that you lot don't miss any obvious clues. She's good at stuff like that.'

She squeezes my hand and nods at me, as if expecting me to echo her thoughts when nothing is further from my mind.

Cavendish opens her mouth to argue but then surveys the perimeter and can see her team in their cars itching to get going.

She sighs audibly. 'Do what you like. Robin will make sure the two of you aren't in the way.' She turns to Myers. 'Hitch a ride with Rick Underwood, seeing as he and Emma seem to be such a close couple.'

With that, Cavendish stomps away and climbs into the back of the lead vehicle which tears out of the walled area a moment later, its blue lights flashing silently.

Chapter Twenty-Five

THEN

Hayling Island, Hampshire

Joanna dropped her spoon into the bowl and used the last lump of bread to soak up the final dregs of the tomato soup from the edge, before depositing it in her mouth with a satisfied smile. Tucking a lock of her thick brown hair behind her ear, she looked up at the kindly Reverend Peter Saltzing, who was smiling warmly at her as he watched her chewing the bread.

'How long did the police say they would be?' she asked, surprised that she'd managed to finish the soup without them arriving.

'Shouldn't be much longer,' he said, glancing at his wrist watch nervously before collecting her bowl and plate. 'Would you like anything else to eat? Or perhaps a cup of tea to calm your shock?'

'Tea would be great, thanks,' she said, so relieved that the first house she'd called upon belonged to a man of the cloth, and not some kind of pervert.

'Well, why don't you go and wait in the living room next door while I fix us both a drink? I've got the fire on in there. There's no television, I'm afraid, but the wireless is playing.'

Her brow ruffled.

'Sorry, I meant the radio is on,' he said, chuckling at himself for the outdated terminology.

Joanna wiped her lips with the scrap of kitchen roll he'd left on the side for her, and headed back into the corridor, following it until she could feel the air warming as she approached the main room. Twice the size of the kitchen, it had a two-seat sofa with an old-fashioned pattern of oranges, yellows, and browns, like the sort of furniture she'd seen in old pictures her mum would show her of what life was like back in the 70s. There was an unpleasant smell too – like rotting fruit – so she focused on breathing through her mouth, rather than her nose.

She could hear actors reading lines on the radio but it wasn't of much interest to her, and so she sat down on the sofa and curled her legs up.

'It's okay to have a nap if you're feeling tired,' the vicar said, draping a small blanket over her legs, nodding towards the mug of tea he'd placed on the small table to the left of the sofa. 'It sounds as though you've been through quite the ordeal.'

'I just want to go home,' she said, and he nodded his understanding.

'I'm sure you do, my dear. One cannot underestimate the support of family and loved ones in these scary times.'

She smiled at him; it was nice that he wasn't talking down

to her like a child, as some of her teachers occasionally did, and her parents did all the time.

'Do you have any family?' she asked.

He moved across to a framed photograph on the wall and carried it back to her. 'This is my younger sister, and her three children. It's a few years old now, so the children are all probably teenagers by now.' He paused, lifting his glasses and moving the image closer to his eyes, studying it intensely. 'The oldest one here is Billy, then there's his brother Kieran – he's two years younger than Billy – and then last but by no means least, our precious Vanessa.' He lowered the frame and a deep sadness overcame him. 'I do so miss them; they moved to Australia a number of years ago, and I haven't seen them since.'

'I'm sorry,' she offered, meaning every word. 'Do you speak to them on the phone ever?'

He returned the frame to the wall. 'Alas, not as much as I would like. Their mum and I... we had something of a falling out before she left, and... now it's just me rattling around in the old vicarage.'

'I know how that feels,' she admitted, thinking back to the reason she'd gone to the newsagent's shop in the first place.

Watching him fiddling with the frame, she realised now that the entire wall was covered in framed photographs – some were cuttings from newspapers, including pictures of a younger-looking Reverend Peter.

'What were you in the newspaper for?' she asked as he stepped back from the wall.

It took him a moment to realise where she was looking, but then he moved over and studied the framed article. 'Ah, yes, this was a local piece written about the work we do here to support orphanages in the county. You see, I was fortunate enough to have something of a privileged upbringing, and I feel it is my duty to do what I can to support efforts to improve the lives of less fortunate children. On this particular occasion, we held a church fête with all proceeds being shared between a number of orphanages and charities supporting the less fortunate. That day we raised over ten thousand pounds through a variety of raffles and donations from local businesses. I didn't particularly want my picture in the newspaper, but they insisted as it was a celebration of community spirit. I don't suppose you know what I mean by that?'

She considered the question. 'Yeah, I kind of do, I think.'

The sound of knocking at the front door had him back on his feet and heading out of the room. 'I imagine this will be for you,' he called out over his shoulder, though she wasn't convinced as she hadn't seen any flashing lights pass the window behind the sofa.

Standing, she tiptoed towards the newspaper article, and read the story about the monies raised from the fête. Her eyes then wandered to the next framed article, this one without a picture of Reverend Peter, but equally admiring of his contribution to fundraising in the local area.

The next headline caught her attention. She couldn't see mention of Reverend Peter's name, but it spoke about the closure of a boys' home somewhere further north, despite the fundraising efforts of a local vicar and a number of former residents at the home. The story was cut short by a fold in the page, and with Reverend Peter yet to return, she took down the frame and removed the fastening holding the glass in place. Lifting the back plate from the frame, she could see the story continued on the folded page, and learned that the St Francis Home for Wayward Boys had been closed pending an enquiry into the treatment of some of its former residents. The article was adjacent to a picture of a much younger-looking Reverend Peter standing stern-faced beside a taller young man in a dark suit, whose face looked vaguely familiar, but she couldn't place it.

And then she realised exactly who she was staring at, and her blood ran cold. At the same moment Reverend Peter returned to the living room, but it wasn't a uniformed police officer he was leading into the overly warm room.

The picture frame slipped from Joanna's fingers and her mouth dried instantly as she saw the man in the grey suit hovering over her. She looked to the vicar, who was only half in the room, but no longer able to bring his gaze to meet hers.

Joanna shuffled backwards, until the curtained window stopped her escape.

Grey reached into his pocket and removed a pair of leather gloves, sliding his hands inside and interlocking his fingers to ensure a proper fit. '

'You've caused us a great deal of trouble, young lady,' Grey said. 'I warned you what would happen if you tried to run away.'

Joanna couldn't stop the wee trickling down her leg as she stood frozen with terror. She was tempted to beg for her life, but didn't want to give him the satisfaction of seeing just how terrified she was.

Reaching into the pocket of her dress, she whipped out the small cheese knife, and held it out with as straight an arm as she could muster.

Grey erupted into a deep and sickening laugh. 'You got a

lot of heart, kid, you know that? You think you can kill me? You think you have what it takes?'

The vicar mumbled something behind them, but Joanna could no longer see him as Grey towered over her.

'I tell you what I'm gonna do,' Grey mocked, sliding the grey blazer from his shoulders and draping it over the old-fashioned sofa. 'I'm going to give you one shot. Okay? One chance to see whether you have what it takes to kill me.'

Joanna could barely hear the words, the boom-boom-boom of her heart echoing in her ears.

Grey knelt down and smoothed the creases from his white shirt with his gloved hands, thrusting his chest out towards her. 'Here it is, kid: this is your one chance to kill me and make your escape. Are you ready for it? Are you ready to do what is necessary?'

The tiny blade looked so insignificant against his huge chest, and as the edge skirted across the edge of his shirt, she knew she wouldn't have the strength. Not that it mattered, as his arm swung out and cracked into her wrist, the small knife flying across the room and disappearing somewhere behind the sofa as it crashed into the wall. Without missing a beat, he wrapped his single gloved hand around both her wrists and dragged her towards him, as he stood.

'You won't get another chance like that, kid,' he whispered loudly, again running his rough tongue the length of her cheek, savouring the taste of her tears.

Scooping up his jacket with his free hand, he pulled her across the room, past the cowering vicar who still refused to look at them, and back out into the dark night to his waiting car. Pulling open the door, he flung her into the back in a single motion, making no effort to buckle her in, slamming the door and turning his attention back to the vicar.

'Go inside, and wipe the place clean,' Grey glowered, handing him a small wad of folded notes. 'And consider this a donation to the church for services rendered.'

'What will happen to her?' the vicar asked quietly.

'Don't worry about it. I'll take care of it.'

'You never should have allowed her to get away in the first place!'

Grey stepped forwards, forcing the vicar to move backwards. 'Let he who is without sin cast the first stone. Isn't that how the saying goes?'

Reverend Peter scowled. 'Mr Brown will hear of this. You mark my words.'

'You'll keep your mouth shut, old man. You're not the influence on me you once were, and you'll keep your gob shut for once if you know what's good for you.'

The vicar took a further step back, lifting his arms in surrender and protection of his upper body. 'Okay, okay… I just need assurances that *this* will be taken care of. She knows who I am… She can identify me.'

Grey turned back and looked at the car. 'You really have nothing to worry about. I'll do what's necessary.'

Sliding the jacket back over his shoulders, Grey made his way around the front of the car and looked both ways before climbing in and starting the engine. Joanna was stretched out on the rear seat quietly sobbing, regretting that she hadn't continued into the town centre in search of a police station.

The car bounced and buffeted along for at least ten minutes, with Grey chain-smoking until the thin light through the windows disappeared and Joanna could no longer see where they were going. She finally sat up when the car came to a sudden halt, but she wished she hadn't when she saw they were surrounded by dark and foreboding trees on either side.

Grey exited the car, pulled open the rear door, and dragged her from the seat by the ankles. Joanna bashed her head on the cushion and frame of the car, before hitting the rough leaves and twigs that scattered the ground. She kicked out and screamed as he dragged her from the car, further into the wood where she could no longer see the sky above the entwining branches.

They eventually stopped when she could hear the sound of water trickling nearby, but by the time he released her foot, she was too cold and sore to make any effort to get back to her feet and run.

Grey took a deep breath before lighting a fresh cigarette and inhaling it deeply into his lungs.

'It didn't have to be this way,' he said quietly. 'You could have learned to follow the rules… You could have seen that things really aren't as bad as you feared.'

He turned until he was facing her. The only light she could see was the orange tip of the cigarette as he sucked on the end.

'Such a pity that you had to keep fighting. Hope will kill you, you know that, right? It isn't your fault; they drill it into kids in school. They brainwash you into believing that the world is a good place and that if you love thy neighbour, you'll wind up in paradise. What you realise when you get older is just how much of a crock all of that is. In reality it's every man for himself, and no amount of good deeds will see you end up anywhere but in a furnace or as worm food. There is no better place after all of this, as you're about to find out.'

She couldn't move. Frozen to the ground, her bladder

having emptied twice since he'd shown up, she accepted that she would never see her family again. She prayed her end would be quick and painless.

'I remember being your age – maybe a little older – and feeling like I wanted to die. But then I was given a second chance. And so I'm going to do you that same kindness, kid. I'm going to give you the choice about how the rest of this night goes.' He bent over so she could just about see his lips as he spoke. 'Beg for your life and I'll let you live.'

She squirmed as some of the ash dropped from the tip of his cigarette and floated down to her face like a snowflake.

'P-p-please,' her lips stammered, her breath escaping as a cloud in the cold night air.

He straightened. 'You've got to do better than that, kid. I said *beg*.'

He took a step back, allowing her to shift the weight onto her side so she could then move onto her knees, biting down as the sharp twigs scratched at her skin and bone.

'P-p-please d-d-don't kill me.'

She heard him laughing, even though she could no longer see him as he flicked the cigarette away in a shower of sparks. And then suddenly he was down on the ground beside her, whispering into her ear.

'That's better, kid. Now, you'll do what I say going forwards, won't you? And you won't be any more trouble, will you?'

'N-n-no,' she stammered breathlessly.

'Good,' he sneered, his breath hot and smelly against her neck. 'Just remember, kid, I've helped you tonight. From now on, you owe me.'

Chapter Twenty-Six

NOW

Weymouth, Dorset

The journey from Weymouth to Bridport along the A35 takes forty minutes, and there hasn't even been a murmur from Robin in the back. Tina, on the other hand, hasn't stopped talking, asking my opinion on matters but not leaving any space to respond. I shouldn't be surprised; I'm sure if the shoe was on the other foot I'd be full of nervous energy too.

When we finally pull up at the campsite on the outskirts of Bridport, it feels like we've arrived on the set of some elaborate crime drama series. The entire road leading from the site is packed with marked and unmarked police cars, and my eyes widen when I spot an armed response unit receiving instructions from their commander.

Cavendish is already out of her car engaging with the senior-looking official at the perimeter, and a small crowd has gathered near the entrance to the site. It's the first time Tina has been silent since we got in the car, and as I now look at her, I can see she is as pale as a sheet.

Rick parks as close as he can but it is still a short walk back to the throng of people. Cavendish rolls her eyes when she spots the four of us, but comes over to instruct Robin to keep us back and out of the way.

The whole scene feels so over the top. In my limited experience, this amount of manpower wouldn't be necessary for a couple of small-time hoods. There has to be a reason Cavendish has brought the cavalry with her, and second-guessing her motives has my head in a spin. The only conclusion I can draw is that there is far more going on here than any of us anticipated.

What if there really is some connection between what happened to Anna and the men responsible for abducting Jo-Jo?

I was adamant that no such connection could exist because of the twenty-one-year gap between the cases, but have I blinded myself to the truth? What if the ring of traffickers Jack and I have been searching for are holed up inside this campsite, and Cavendish is about to blow the investigation sky-high? Shouldn't I phone Jack and warn him?

The armed response unit, dressed head-to-toe in black and donning night-vision goggles, prime their weapons and head into the campsite, dispersing into the shadowy darkness, before Cavendish leads the rest of her large team in through the security barrier. Anyone from the outside would be forgiven for thinking the police are taking control of some kind of terrorist incident, such is the level of activity unfolding before our eyes. The first high-vis officers arrive at the nearest bank of caravans, knock at the doors, immediately ask the residents to follow them out, and congregate them at the fire evacuation point behind the reception building and pool.

Tina has started pacing behind us, and Robin now goes to her to check she's okay. I can just about make out Rick helping an elderly couple to the muster point, but the scene is bringing back unwanted memories. It was at a site not dissimilar to this one that Jack and I discovered Cassie Hilliard being held. We were fortunate that Hank Amos bore her no ill-will, but what if the predators who took Jo-Jo aren't so forgiving?

'Teens?' a male voice calls from the distance. 'Teens? Where are you?'

A moment later Trey Neville emerges from the darkness and immediately hugs his wife.

'I came as soon as I heard. Is this the place? Is this where they think little Jo-Jo is?'

Tina doesn't respond, breaking free of his embrace and continuing her pacing. Trey spots me and comes over.

'Do you think she's in there?' he asks quietly.

I'm not sure how to respond. Of course I want to say she is and that they'll all be reunited any moment, but if this level of armed response is required to subdue her abductors, then I desperately pray she is a million miles away.

'We'll find out soon enough,' I tell him, offering my most reassuring smile.

A sudden commotion on the other side of the security barrier has us studying the darkness for the source of the noise, but I'm not sure any of us are expecting to see the armed response unit returning so soon. There are scowls and angry rants as they remove their masks and discharge their weapons, clambering back into the van from where they emerged only minutes earlier. I can also see that the small crowd of residents at the muster point are being told they can return to their homes.

Just what is going on? A false alarm? Or were they too late?

Robin's radio crackles and she moves away from Tina to receive the message. I can't see Rick to ask for an update.

'Mr and Mrs Neville,' Robin says, returning to the group, 'if you'd like to follow me, please? Miss Hunter, you too.'

I don't like the sharpness of her tone, but I don't argue as she leads us to the barrier and shows her identification to the officer standing guard, who allows us entry. It feels as though we're going against the tide as the stream of officers in their high-visibility vests heads in the opposite direction, down the hill we're now climbing. I spot Rick, but his eyes don't meet mine as he continues at a pace. An ambulance speeds past us, and when we eventually arrive at a single caravan at the far side of the site, the ambulance is already parked up and two paramedics are tending to somebody inside.

Cavendish appears at the entrance of the caravan and surveys the four of us before stepping out and coming over to Robin, whispering something into her ear. Robin nods and takes the Nevilles over to the ambulance. I'm about to follow them when Cavendish places her hand on my forearm and leads me in the opposite direction.

'Did you know?' she says quietly.

I frown. 'I don't follow.'

She makes a show of cracking her knuckles. 'I'm only going to ask you once more, and I'm only giving you the benefit of the doubt because Jack rates you highly.' She pauses. 'Did you know?'

I'm still at a loss as to what she's implying, but a troubled gasp from behind us has me turning to see Tina inside the ambulance with a pair of tiny arms wrapped around her shoulders.

'Jo-Jo's safe?' I ask rhetorically.

'Of course she is… But then she always was going to be, wasn't she, Emma?'

My confused gaze returns to her expectant eyes.

'I'm really not following, Zoe. What are you saying?'

She grunts, shaking her head slightly.

'Let me paint you a picture, and stop me when any of this sounds familiar. An author with an element of notoriety has a new book hitting the shelves, and in her vain attempt to get it onto this or that bestseller list hatches upon a plan. A means of getting her name in the headlines once again. A missing child reunited with her terrified parents courtesy of said author's expertise and diligence. It would sell one helluva lot of papers, and probably have that author's book on everyone's wish lists. But the only stumbling block is that having a child go missing isn't something that can just be organised. Or is it…?'

My mouth drops at the insinuation. 'You're kidding me, right?' is the only retort I can manage. 'You think I somehow arranged for Jo-Jo to be abducted to sell more books? You're unbelievable!'

'Am I? It isn't so ridiculous when the parents of the missing child *insist* that the writer become involved in the hunt for the child.'

'Listen, Zoe, I know you don't like me, but to accuse me of something so sordid with no evidence is bang out of order.'

She grunts mockingly. 'No evidence? Okay, I'll tell you what I *do* know, and then we'll see what you have to say for yourself. The anonymous phone call that alerted us to the fact that Jo-Jo had been spotted in Bridport was traced back to an unregistered mobile phone. But triangulation tells us that the call was placed in Portland this afternoon. So, either our witness spotted Jo-Jo in Bridport but waited until he or she returned to the area before placing the call, or…'

She deliberately leaves the sentence hanging.

'You think I placed the call?'

'Not necessarily you, no, and I certainly can't prove that one way or another, but that isn't the part that I find so strange. Less than an hour after the anonymous tip-off, a crowd gathers at the Portland police station where I happen to be briefing my team about the call. And what shows up next but a local news station van with cameras primed to roll. Somebody wanted the story to make the news.'

I feel sick as I slowly play the theory around in my own mind. Something has felt off about this whole thing from the beginning, and I don't like the ring of truth to what Cavendish is suggesting. It sounds so preposterous, and yet I find myself turning and looking at Tina and Trey and questioning everything they've said to me to this point.

'It troubled me when I learned that Tina Neville had insisted on having you tag along on the investigation, and how disappointed she looked when I said I didn't want you anywhere near the public appeal for information. I was surprised that you didn't insist on being involved, but then when the FLO told me you and your ex-con friend Freddie Mitchell had arrived at the residence, I figured you were playing the long game.'

I pivot round as my anger reaches boiling point, but she holds up her hand before I can speak. She isn't finished yet.

'Imagine my surprise when a check of family holdings revealed that Tina's ex-husband owns a caravan in Bridport.

Well, he doesn't own it exclusively – it's in his sister's name – but he is listed on the servicing contract here at the campsite. And when we arrive, who do we find inside with little Jo-Jo but Tina Neville's former sister-in-law. And little Jo-Jo? She's perfectly well and eating spaghetti on toast.'

'I swear on my life, I had no idea about any of this,' I say earnestly, though I get the impression she doesn't believe me.

She holds her hands up. 'Well, I gave you the courtesy for Jack's sake. I swear to you, though, *Emma,* if I find any reason to doubt the truth of your answer, I will drag your name through the mud until I get to the truth.'

She moves to walk away but it's my turn to reach for her arm. 'I don't know what I ever did to offend you, but I'm going to repeat the statement to remove any ambiguity between us: I had nothing to do with any of this! How you could think that I'd be so willing to go along with any scheme which might threaten the welfare of a child is beyond me. For Jack's sake, I'll do you the courtesy of not raising a complaint with your superior officer, Zoe. Your attitude towards me on the Aurélie Lebrun case and now stinks, but despite that, I respect you for the way you have recovered Jo-Jo unharmed.'

She moves away without further comment. I doubt there's anything I could say or do to mend the bridge between us.

I watch as she next approaches Tina and Trey, and their reactions to whatever she says paint a picture of how involved they may or may not be. Whilst Tina throws her arms up in apparent anger and unleashes a verbal assault at Cavendish, Trey looks like a broken man. His head dips with the realisation that the wife he has trusted with his own daughter's care could be capable of such scheming.

Beyond them, Jo-Jo laughs happily with the paramedics

who are checking for any injury or trauma, oblivious to what is unfolding outside of the ambulance. I feel sick to my stomach at the prospect that at least one of her guardians could treat her safety with such disdain. And for what purpose? Fame? Is the cost really worth it?

It reminds me of a case up in Yorkshire where the mum was going to leave her abusive partner but lost the bottle, and then concocted a story about her daughter going missing. I remember the controversy that followed in the trial. I hate that my recent brush with fame could have encouraged someone to repeat the mistake.

Did Tina and her former sister-in-law fabricate the story about Jo-Jo wandering off so that I'd make them the subject of my next book? If their motive was money and five minutes of fame, the cost is likely to be jail time now.

I can't look at either of them any longer and begin the slow descent down the hill, with my own indirect involvement weighing heavy on my mind.

Chapter Twenty-Seven

NOW

Weymouth, Dorset

Monday mornings are made for gallons of coffee, and hoping for the best outcome to all endeavours in the forthcoming week. At least, I think I read that in someone's motivational tweets once. And then I think back to Jack and the suitcase discovered at Pendark, and the urge to pull the duvet back over my head and remain where I am grows. He's not messaged to say the DNA comparison has been completed, but I'm reluctant to chase him for the news I'm dreading. Until he tells me otherwise, I can cling to the hope that those weren't Anna's remains we found.

Pushing the bedding from me with a groan, I am annoyed at my own inability just to relax and take a duvet day. Instead, I sit up, rub the remaining sleep from my eyes, and head to the shower. I feel more alive when I step out and brush my teeth, before combing my hair and tying it into a messy ponytail that will keep it out of my way.

The black and white image of Faye McKenna stares up at me from the kitchen table where I left it after my meeting with Maddie at the restaurant. Her hair is much longer in the photograph than the image I found of her aged twelve on the missingpeople.org site. It's only just occurred to me how much older she looks in the photograph on my table. Lifting and moving it closer to my eyes, I inspect the image for any other differences. Her hair was tied in bunches in the picture on the site, whereas it is hanging looser here; gone are the square-shaped prescription glasses, and even her teeth look less crooked. The essence of her is the same, but I would estimate the picture I've been sent is Faye at least two, if not three, years older than when she disappeared in November 1998.

My pulse quickens as my mind reaches the only possible conclusion: whoever sent this picture knew Faye years *after* she disappeared. That could mean it has been sent by one of the kidnappers (though that feels unlikely); by another victim being held by the same people (assuming a ring is involved, like the one Jack is hunting); or by Faye herself. Who's to say she didn't escape her captors and continue her life under an assumed identity? If she was twelve in 1998 that would make her thirty-four now.

The information I managed to dig up about her disappearance was limited – last seen waiting for a bus home from secondary school, a bus she didn't catch – but this photograph emerging could be something tangible for the police to follow up. Loading up the site again, I search for the name of the force overseeing her case, and am directed to a phone number for Greater Manchester police.

Dialling the number, I am connected with a generic answerphone advising me to phone 999 if I have an emergency, or to leave a message if my query relates to anything else and they will arrange for someone to call me back. I leave my name and number, and explain I have information relating to Faye McKenna.

No sooner have I hung up than I'm hurrying to the knocking at my door. Rick stands there smiling in the same clothes as last night, and looks more handsome than I remember.

'Morning,' he says jovially. 'I was about to grab some breakfast before heading home, and wondered if you fancied coming for a cup of tea and a muffin?'

We didn't speak much when he dropped me home last night. Although Cavendish had told him he wasn't required at the station, he told me he was keen to return and lend a hand regardless.

'Or we could get coffee and a waffle, if muffins aren't your thing,' he adds, maybe sensing my reluctance. 'Please don't make me beg,' he says, that friendly smile breaking through, a small dimple forming in his cheek. 'I'm not one for big scenes, but if getting on my knees is what it's going to take…'

I stop him as he starts to bend and stoop. 'Okay, okay, I'll get a drink and some breakfast with you,' I say, grabbing my purse, phone, and keys from the side table and pulling the door closed.

We walk into the town centre and conversation is stilted, neither of us really knowing what to say that avoids the topic of Jo-Jo; he's not at liberty to discuss the case with me, and I don't want to put him in an awkward position by asking.

'You weren't really going to get down on your hands and knees, were you?' I ask.

His cheeks redden a fraction. 'To be honest, it wouldn't

have been the first time I begged a girl to go on a date with me.'

I frown cynically. He's tall, handsome, and confident; I find it hard to believe he's ever had difficulty picking up women.

'I was a late bloomer,' he confides. 'At sixteen, I was still carrying baby weight, had a mouth full of metal, and acne that could be used as Braille. At my secondary school, the girls outnumbered the boys, so there wasn't an option to go stag at our senior prom. I was seventeen and desperate, and I ended up *begging* Veronica Gibson-Dahl to be my date. She was just grateful to have been asked by anyone.

'And then it was like I woke on my nineteenth birthday and had grown a foot overnight, slimmed down, and the face is pretty much as you see it today. After four lean years of no relationships, things started to improve. I imagine you've not been short of admirers down the years either, especially since your books' success.'

If only he knew just how far back my lean spell stretched! I'm not about to share any of that though.

We arrive at a café where I actually wrote part of *Monsters*, and when Rick suggests we stop here, I'm more than happy with the suggestion.

'Did you always want to write?' he asks when we've ordered and are seated near the counter.

'I used to write a lot of stories as a child. Back before... before my sister went missing, we used to sit in the garden making up stories and telling them to each other. When she disappeared, it felt easier getting lost in those stories and the world I could create in my imagination where such evil didn't exist. It probably sounds lame to say it, but I think those stories are what got me through my formative years. My parents would argue a lot, and sometimes it was just easier burying my head in a book or scribbling down ideas than actually confronting them. I don't think I necessarily considered just how tough it was for them too – tougher probably, because they'd lost a child.'

I'm grateful when the coffee arrives, and am suddenly conscious that I've shared far more than I'd intended. I don't know why but it just felt so natural to tell him.

'Mum is so thrilled with her signed copy of the book, but she's now requested I buy a second copy of it for her to read so that she can keep the signed edition in pristine condition.'

'Oh, that really isn't necessary. My scrawled name on the book doesn't add any value—'

'On the contrary, she's already put it in pride of place on the mantelpiece; she even moved one of my old chess trophies to make space for it.'

I raise my eyebrows. 'Chess trophy?'

He blushes. 'Yep, I probably should have warned you: I was a bit of a nerd at school. Head of the chess club. I represented my school at several national tournaments.'

I decide not to tell him about my own brushes with a chess club. 'I probably have an old proof copy lying about the house if she's just looking to read the text and isn't worried about keeping it.'

'Thanks, but she'd never forgive me if she thought you weren't getting paid your royalties. I'm a fan of your writing, but she's like a super fan! I think your stories help her forget about the MS.'

I bite my lip, unable to resist the urge to please. 'Tell me if I'm overstepping, but what if I came by to visit your mum at some point? I could sign her other books at the same time, and thank her for such loyal support.'

Rick's eyes are practically on stalks. 'Really? I mean, she'd be blown away by that. You wouldn't mind?'

'It would be my honour.'

'Then I'm going to hold you to that then. Thanks, Emma, that's very kind. You'll have to give me a couple of days to make sure the place is spick and span, but that will be amazing.'

My phone is ringing, and as I look at the screen I see Maddie's name. 'Do you mind if I take this? It's my agent.'

Rick shakes his head as he tucks in to the blueberry muffin that has just been delivered to our table.

'Hi Maddie, everything okay?' I ask, as I move away from the table.

'There's another large envelope here for you. Just like last time. Your name on the envelope, care of this office. I'm sure the envelope is a match to the one that came last week. Do you want me to open it?'

I gulp, but curiosity gets the better of me. 'Sure.'

Maddie lowers the phone and then I hear her ripping into the envelope. 'It's a picture of a lad this time. Curly hair and freckles. I'll take a picture of it and email across again.'

'You think he's a local lad?' Rick asks, as he walks me back to my flat.

'The other picture wasn't of a local girl.'

'*Other* picture?'

I fill him in on the photograph of Faye McKenna, but omit

the answerphone message I left with Greater Manchester Police.

'Who do you think is sending you these pictures?' he asks as we reach my front door.

'I... I'm not sure,' I reply honestly. 'One of the online articles made reference to Faye's mum, so I automatically assumed it was from her.'

'First rule of policing: assume nothing.'

I know he's right, and I will my cheeks not to burn with the embarrassment I'm feeling. 'Okay, smarty-pants,' I retort, 'who do *you* think sent the photographs?'

He opens his mouth to speak, before thinking better of it. 'Can I see the picture of the girl?'

I invite him inside and take him to the image still resting on top of the kitchen table.

He stoops over it, studying every pixel. 'Can you flip it over for me?' he asks, tucking his hands beneath his armpits, keen to avoid touching the picture.

'My agent and I have both held the image, and I couldn't see any obvious fingerprints when I held it up to the light,' I point out, guessing that he's thinking there might still be trace evidence to collect. I turn it over regardless, resting it face-down, and indicating the date of birth in the top corner.

'Do we know if there's a date of birth on the second photograph?' he asks next, his jaw stiffening.

'Maddie has only scanned one side of the image. I'll ask her to send the reverse too,' I say, typing the message. 'I take it you don't recognise him as missing from this area?'

Rick considers the image again before shaking his head. 'Sorry.'

Opening my laptop I load my emails so I can look at the

picture of the young man on a bigger screen. He has a face full of freckles and his auburn hair curls naturally, from fringe to the crown. I'd guess he's fifteen or sixteen at most, but there is a seriousness to the half-smile he's holding, and it reminds me of the picture of Faye. She too had this semi-serious pose, and when I load the two images beside each other on the screen, I'm suddenly struck with a thought.

'What do these look like to you?' I ask Rick, turning the screen so he can see it better.

'School photographs?' he shrugs.

'No uniform,' I counter, 'besides, school photographs are usually head, shoulders, and upper torso. These are headshots, like you'd see in a modelling portfolio, or—'

He clicks his fingers. 'Actors.'

I shrug in acceptance. 'Maybe. If I'm a casting director auditioning for roles, this is what I'd expect to see alongside a résumé…'

My mind continues to process the theory as nausea bubbles in the back of my throat. An image of the Pendark Film Studios sign flashes behind my eyes. Given Freddie's and Anna's faces both appeared on footage discovered on the late Arthur Turgood's hard drive, is it possible Faye and this young man also did? I will have to raise the question with Jack when I next speak to him. In the meantime, there isn't a lot to go on.

My phone pings and I see Maddie's next email appear in my inbox on the laptop screen.

'My agent has sent the reverse now,' I tell Rick, opening the attached image. 'It's not easy to read… Does that say Chesney Byrne?'

Rick leans so close I catch the scent of his eau de toilette again. 'I think so. That name mean anything to you?'

I shake my head but log in to the Foundation database just in case, once again drawing a blank. I open a search window and type his name and the date of birth scrawled beneath it, but there are no hits. That's odd. When I searched for Faye's name, I immediately found news articles relating to her disappearance, but Chesney Byrne is drawing a blank. Opening the missingpeople.org site, I search for his name, but the results are either for "Chesney" or "Byrne", but no "Chesney Byrne", and no picture that matches the face before us.

Rick sighs in defeat. 'Not all children who go missing are abducted by evil monsters; some just run away.'

I shake my head. 'I'm still not buying it. If Faye and Chesney were both actors, then searching for them online would reveal more about them as actors – films or shows they've appeared in, websites. The only references to Faye's name are those relating to her disappearance.'

Rick moves away but he isn't cross; watching him as he stares into the distance, I know exactly what is on his mind – it happens to the best of us. He's caught in the mystery, wanting to figure out exactly what's going on. He suddenly spins on his heel and points at the laptop screen.

'Search for Chesney online,' he says.

'I tried that, but there was no trace.'

'No,' he corrects, 'you searched for his name and date of birth. Search with his face. You can upload the image and the search engine will look for similar matches. If this particular image has appeared anywhere online, the search engine should be able to find it.'

I slide the laptop to the edge of the table and watch as he performs the search. 'No exact matches,' he tells me. He expands the search and then a satisfied look creeps across his face and he slides the laptop back to me. 'There you go.'

The image on the screen isn't the headshot Maddie has scanned and emailed, but the young face I'm now looking at definitely has an abundance of freckles and the curliest auburn hair I've ever seen. Younger here, the *Star & Crescent's* image of missing eleven-year-old Cormack Fitzpatrick is a very good likeness.

'What do you think?' Rick says. 'I reckon they're one and the same. Why don't you check that missing people site for Cormack Fitzpatrick?'

I do as instructed, and also search for the name on the Foundation database without success. He is listed on the missing people site, along with a phone number for Hampshire Police.

'Cormack was eleven when he was last seen. Left for school on Friday 1st April 1996, but never arrived. He was known for being a practical joker, and at first his parents thought his disappearance was part of some elaborate prank, but when they still hadn't heard from him by ten o'clock that night, they phoned the police. He withdrew all his savings the night before his disappearance, and although the police searched local hostels, they couldn't locate him. The image that's been sent must be three or four years older, right?'

Rick compares the images again before nodding. 'Give or take, yeah.'

'Then who sent the picture to my agent's office?'

It's a question neither of us can answer. Rick is hunched over the screen again, studying something intently.

'And why send them to me? Aside from Faye and Cormack both being missing children, what else connects them? She was from Oldham and disappeared in November 1998, and he was from Gosport and vanished two years earlier. He was on his way to school, and she was on her way home, but I can't see anything else, other than both their headshots have been sent to me via my agent's office. And what's with this particular date? The first image has Faye McKenna's date of birth on it, but this date isn't Chesney's date of birth.'

I clamp my eyes shut as the early embers of a headache smoulder in my temple.

'Can you see that?' he whispers after a moment.

I prise my eyes apart and look over to him, where he's pointing at something on the screen. Stepping closer, I follow his finger to the screen but I can't focus. 'What is it?'

He pulls out his phone and types something in. 'Unless I'm very much mistaken, it looks like the imprint of a postcode. Can you see? Like someone wrote the postcode on a different piece of paper, but it pressed through to the photograph. It's very faint, but I'm sure that's a P, and an O, and possibly the number 11.'

He's typing the digits into his phone, but I can barely register them on the screen.

'Maybe whoever sent the picture to you lives at this address,' Rick suggests. 'Or maybe whoever lives there might be able to shed some light on who sent the picture of Cormack to you. There's only really one way to find out,' he adds, checking his watch.

'Are you suggesting I go to Portsmouth?' I clarify.

'No, I'm suggesting *we* go to Portsmouth – well, Hayling Island actually, as that's where the postcode is located.'

Chapter Twenty-Eight

THEN

Hayling Island, Hampshire

The smell of fresh toast woke Joanna, and as the craving grew and her stomach grumbled its discontent, she prised her eyes open and grimaced as soon as she saw the pale green curtains hanging in front of the bolted plastic window. Grey's arrival at Reverend Peter's cottage flashed through her mind and the sheer panic that he was going to kill her.

But why hadn't he killed her? He'd been so open about what he would do to her if she stepped out of line, and she'd gone beyond the brink in making a break for it, so why was she back in the caravan and still alive? Was all his talk of killing before just bravado in front of his friends, or did he have a more severe punishment in mind for her?

Focusing on the smell of the toasting bread, she pushed back the thin blanket and allowed her nose to guide her along the narrow corridor to the main cabin where she found two plates on the table, along with a tub of butter and a small knife.

The door to the small bathroom opened and a girl stepped out. Her thick, dark hair was spiked up and over her head, her eyes were as black as coal, and the silver dress she was squeezed into was practically ripping at the seams, despite her thin frame.

'I'm Precious,' she said, moving through to the kitchen and lifting the two slices from the toaster. 'You must be Kylie, right? You want some toast?'

Precious dropped a slice onto each plate, immediately reaching for the knife and spreading a generous portion of butter over each.

Joanna tucked into the toast but could feel Precious watching her. With the first slice gone, she wiped greasy crumbs from her lips.

'Someone was hungry,' Precious commented, standing and moving back into the kitchen, dropping two more slices of bread into the toaster. 'Cat got your tongue?'

Joanna slowly raised her eyes and simply shrugged. The girl before her had to be at least four or five years older, but wasn't nearly as tall as Chez, making it difficult to place her exact age. She carried herself with confidence, and didn't seem fazed by Joanna's appearance in the caravan. Her accent was from up north somewhere, but Joanna couldn't begin to guess exactly where.

Precious rolled her eyes. 'Figures. We should get you cleaned up after breakfast; wash some of that mud from your arms and face.'

Joanna immediately looked down at her forearms, suddenly aware of the brown streaks and blotches of red where Grey had dragged her through the woods. She was still wearing the dress Chez had given her on the first night, and as she trained her nose to ignore the smell of the toasting bread, she became acutely aware of the pong emanating from the lower half of the dress.

Precious carried over the new slices, again depositing one on each plate, before moving to the fridge-freezer and withdrawing a bag of what looked like frozen peas, which she applied to a swelling beneath her right eye.

'Ar-ar-are you okay?' Joanna stammered.

Precious narrowed her eyes as if determining whether it was a trick question. 'I'm fine,' she said, turning away, but keeping the peas pressed to her face. 'Walked into a door,' she said eventually, with more than a hint of sarcasm. 'You know how it is.'

'How long have you been here?' Joanna asked, mesmerised.

Precious took a bite of her toast. 'Best not to think about time while you're here, or it'll really drag. Trust me!'

'Do you miss your home though? Your mum and dad?'

Precious dropped the toast on the plates, growling. 'I don't want to talk about any of that. Right? I'm here now, and so are you, and the sooner you put all of that out of yer mind, the better, yeah? I promise it's easier just to forget yer previous life. Focus on the here and now.'

Joanna ignored the burn of the tears behind her eyes. 'Where's Chez? I want to see him.'

Precious narrowed her eyes. 'He's gone; that's all you need to know.'

'But why? He said he would be like my big brother here. I want to see him.'

'Well you can't!' Precious snapped back. 'That's the price to pay for running off like ya did. Chez got in trouble for your antics, and now they've dumped you on me instead. Don't go giving me no trouble, ya hear me? The first sign of trouble and I'll stick you myself.'

Joanna couldn't tell whether Precious had meant to pick up the small chopping knife, or whether it had been subconscious, but the threat was clear.

'I-I-I won't give you any trouble,' she said, pulling her knees up to her chest. 'I-I-I promise.'

Precious seemed to accept her submission and quickly dropped the knife on the table. She reached for a packet of cigarettes on the side and lit one, inhaling and exhaling like a locomotive.

'You want one?' she asked when she caught Joanna watching her.

'I don't smoke.'

Precious located an empty cup and flicked ash into it, carrying it over to the table and reclaiming her seat. 'Have you ever tried smoking?'

Joanna shook her head; she'd had enough warnings at school and from her parents about the dangers of smoking and cancer. She coughed as Precious's smoke drifted across the table.

'How do ya know whether you like something unless you try it though?' she said, proffering the cigarette. 'Go ahead. Give it a puff, and then make yer mind up.'

Joanna didn't need to put the cigarette between her lips to know she wouldn't enjoy it. The stench already clinging to her clothes and irritating her throat were enough signs.

'Put the cigarette in your mouth and suck in,' Precious demanded, pushing it closer to her.

Joanna thought about the way Precious had held the small knife so tightly and relented, her hand trembling as she took the cigarette between her thumb and index finger. The paper felt damp as it touched her lips, and she took a deep breath, instantly reeling and coughing the smoke back up, relieved when Precious snatched the cigarette back.

'First inhale's the worst,' she said, patting Joanna on the back. 'It gets easier, I promise. One day yer gonna be grateful to have things like this to distract ya.'

Joanna continued to cough and retch, certain she might bring up the toast, until her breathing returned to a more regular rhythm.

'Let me know when you want another puff.' Precious laughed mockingly as she squashed the stub into the cup, and wafted away the remaining cloud of smoke. 'We should celebrate. My girl Kylie here has just had her first fag.'

She hurried back to the fridge-freezer, tossing the bag of peas inside and removing a half-full bottle of wine from the door. She opened one of the cupboards and withdrew two mugs, placing one in front of Joanna and pouring some of the straw-coloured liquid into it. She repeated the gesture with her own mug, filling it to the top before lifting the mug into the air.

'A toast. To my new friend Kylie. I'm gonna teach you everything you need to know. Go on, have a drink; it'll help soothe yer throat after the cigarette.'

Thinking about that chopping knife again, Joanna lifted the mug and clinked it against the other mug as she'd seen her father do countless times, and then held her breath as she sipped the beverage. It was sweeter than she expected.

'Can I tell you something?' Joanna tentatively asked.

Precious nodded with a long swig.

'My name's not really Kylie; that's just what Chez decided to call me. My real name is—'

Precious slammed her mug down, wine splashing out on the table. 'We don't do real names here, sweetheart. You're Kylie now, and I'm Precious, and that's all you need to remember. Right! Now drink your drink, there's a good girl.'

The room spun as Joanna swished and swayed in time to the music blaring from the radio while Precious did her best to sing along. It wasn't a song Joanna knew the words to, but she recognised it as an older song, the sort her dad would play on the radio when driving at night when she and her sister should be asleep in the back of the car.

Precious, on the other hand, was managing to get most of the notes right, but the music was too loud for her to be able to hear whether she was actually in tune or not. Not that Joanna cared, as she reached and drained her second mug of the wine and scrambled for the bottle, disappointed to find it now empty.

'Out of wine,' she slurred, and then roared with laughter at how difficult it had been to mouth the vowel sounds. 'I think… Am I a bit drunk? Is this what being drunk feels like?'

Precious reached the crescendo, putting her heart and soul into the final rendition of the chorus and then taking a theatrical bow as Joanna clapped and whooped for her. Precious then collapsed onto the cushioned chair behind the table, panting, and her forehead cloaked in a fine sheen that reflected the overhead light.

'Your turn next,' Precious wheezed. 'We can search for other radio stations until we find a song you know. Okay? Like karaoke.'

'I can't sing,' Joanna said now, putting the empty mug to her lips a second time.

'Of course you can,' Precious said, her breathing now returning to a regular rhythm. 'You can do whatever you put your mind to; this place teaches you that. Things I never thought I'd be able to do, I now can. It's all about perspective. I'll get us some more wine.'

Precious didn't appear to be slurring her words, but Joanna couldn't ignore the feelings of envy starting to bubble up. Precious was so cool and confident, and nothing seemed to faze her. Fresh wine sloshed onto the table once more as Precious continued to dance, pouring more into Joanna's mug, and then her own.

'A toast,' she declared, raising her mug into the air. 'To my new best friend, Kylie.'

'Can we go and see Chez?' Joanna asked.

Precious shook her head. 'I told you, he's gone now. Best you put him out of your mind, yeah?'

'But it wasn't his fault. I ran off and he shouldn't be blamed. I had a knife, so there wasn't anything he could do to stop me.'

'He was left in charge of you, and he screwed up. I don't want to talk about him anymore. Let's change the subject.'

Even through her lightheadedness, Joanna could hear irritation in Precious's tone.

'Have you ever kissed a boy?' Precious asked next.

Joanna dropped her gaze to her lap, where her fingers were fidgeting with nervous energy. She imagined Precious had probably had lots of experience kissing boys, and that was probably what gave her such confidence. Would admitting her lack of experience make Joanna appear immature? She didn't want to lie to her new friend.

'It's okay if you haven't,' Precious said, lifting Joanna's chin with her finger. 'I'd never kissed a boy before I came here either, and you're what, ten or eleven, right?'

Joanna's heart warmed at the thought that she appeared older than her nine years, and made no effort to correct her.

'I was twelve when I first had to kiss a boy. I was really nervous and didn't know if I was doing it right, but then someone showed me how to do it, and then I wasn't so nervous the next time I had to do it.'

Joanna blew air up to her fringe, trying to cool down as the spinning room picked up speed, and suddenly felt unbearably warm.

'I could show you what to do,' Precious offered, sliding closer. 'It's how girls learn what to do; they practise with friends they can trust.'

Joanna's frown deepened. 'You want to kiss *me*?'

'No, I want to show you how to do it properly, so that when you have to do it you won't mess it up.'

'But I don't want to kiss boys. It's disgusting.'

Precious laughed quietly. 'I used to think that too, but when you do it right… it can be nice.'

Joanna leaned back, widening the gap between them. 'Are there other boys here? I mean, I met Chez, but I don't want to kiss *him*.'

'There are others who come and go from time to time.'

'But is there anyone else who lives *here*, on this site?'

'Right now it's just the two of us – and Grey of course, but you've met him, haven't you?'

Joanna shuddered at the memory of his tongue on her cheek. 'He scares me.'

'It's Mr Brown who you want to be really scared of. Grey is a pussycat most of the time; you just have to do what he says and he'll leave you alone. I'll protect you from him if you want me to?'

Joanna nodded.

Precious lifted Joanna's mug and passed it to her. 'Very well, I will do that for you, but in return I need you to do this for me. Kissing is just a way people show affection towards one another. Right? Why do you think grown-ups do it so much? Because of how it makes them feel. You might not want to do it, but you're going to have to at some point. I told Grey I'd help you be ready for that.' Precious sighed deeply. 'It's up to you. Learn with an expert, or go it alone. It's your choice.'

Joanna pressed the rim of the mug to her lips, and swallowed the chilled liquid, hoping it would cool her now sweltering head. 'Okay,' she said, lowering the mug. 'I'm ready.'

Precious shuffled closer. 'Good, now first of all I want you to relax. Your shoulders are too tense, and you need to remember this is a perfectly natural situation. Take a deep breath and slowly exhale, feeling your shoulders lower.'

Joanna did as instructed, but her shoulders and neck remained rigid.

'Kylie, you need to relax. Okay? I'm not making you do anything you don't want to.' She took Joanna's hand in her own. 'We're friends now, and you need to trust me and listen to what I'm saying.'

Joanna tried again, breathing deeper and exhaling for longer, allowing her body to yield.

'Good, now I want you to close your eyes. Not tightly, but just enough that your eyelids join together, as you would when you are going to sleep.'

Joanna allowed her eyes to close, and jerked as she realised she was falling back onto the cushion. She felt Precious moving closer, and her shoulders tensed again as she waited for the impact.

'Just wet your lips with your tongue, and purse them a bit. This won't hurt.'

Joanna's toes wouldn't stop making fists on the carpet tiles, and her stilted breaths weren't helping her rapidly rising heartbeat, and as she smelled Precious closing in she retched, only just managing to avoid throwing up all over Precious, but the floor didn't escape unscathed.

'Ooh, gross!' Precious exclaimed, sliding away and then heading into the kitchen to collect a roll of kitchen paper.

'I-I-I'm so sorry,' Joanna slurred, a claw-like ache digging its sharp nails into every crevice of her brain. 'I-I don't feel very well,' she concluded, tears rushing to escape her eyes.

'All you need is some fresh air,' Precious said, hoisting Joanna off the cushion, draping an arm over her shoulders and half-dragging her to the caravan door. 'I swear to God if this is some elaborate escape plan, you'd better rethink it; I'm not so easy to fool as Chez. If it comes down to a choice between saving you or myself, I'm looking after number one. You get me?'

Joanna welcomed the breeze and drizzle on her face as they made it down the steps and onto the wet grass. 'Please tell me where they've taken Chez. He shouldn't be punished for what I did.'

'Oh my God! Will you stop banging on about Chez? He's gone; you won't see him again. Forget about him.'

'No, we need to speak to Grey. You can explain that it was my fault, and if someone should be sent away, it's me and not him.'

'Oh my God! Why can't you get this through yer thick head? Chez is gone. He's gone. He's not coming back. They killed him cos of what you did last night. Don't you get it yet? These are *bad* men here. You want to survive, then you do as they say. You screw up and they put you in the ground and find the next one to take your place.'

Joanna crashed to the floor as Precious released her arm in disgust, and the claw in her head dug deeper. They'd killed Chez because of her, and she would never forgive herself.

Chapter Twenty-Nine

NOW

M27, Hampshire

'Are you sure this is the place?' I ask, staring up the narrow, tree-lined lane.

'This is the postcode I jotted down,' Rick replies. 'Let me see the image on your phone again. Maybe if I zoom in I can check it.'

I pass him the phone, double-checking the satnav system hasn't made a huge error, but it is definitely indicating we've reached our destination. We've pulled into a small car park linked to a tiny church and adjacent vicarage.

'I've checked online and the postcode covers more than just this road. I think this just happens to be the start of the postcode. Maybe there are more residential streets further along. I think I saw a sign for a campsite pointing this way, so maybe this Chesney's or Cormack's family lived there.'

I shake my head. 'No, the article I read said his family were from Gosport, not Hayling Island.'

He is studying the imprinted postcode again. 'Well, maybe I misinterpreted these digits. It's definitely a PO11 at the start, but after that maybe what I thought was a 0RT is in fact a 0PT; it's so hard to tell without seeing the original. You said your agent copied the image and emailed it, right? Does that mean she has the original that we could look at?'

'Yes, she'll still have it, but she's working in London, and having come this far I really don't want to wait for her to post it down.'

He passes me the phone back. 'What do you think: is it an R or a P?'

I squint at the screen, squeezing my fingers out to enlarge the picture as much as the phone screen will allow, but it's just blurred pixels at this range. 'If I had to guess, I'd say it's an R, but I wouldn't rule out the possibility it is a P. I just don't know.'

'Could we phone your agent and see if she can maybe zoom in on the impression? Or maybe we could ask her to take a rubbing using tracing paper or something. Then we'd know for sure whether it's an R or a P.'

It's better than just sitting here wondering. If it is a P then we're in the wrong place. Locating Maddie's office number I dial it, and am relieved when she answers on the third ring. I put it on speakerphone so Rick will be able to hear directly.

'Maddie, hi, it's Emma, how are you?'

'Up to my neck at the moment, Emma. Is it urgent or can I call you back later?'

'Have you still got that photograph of Chesney Byrne?' I say quickly. 'It's just I need to check something.'

'Sure, hold on,' she says, and I hear her fumbling on her desk, before coming back on the line. 'Okay, yes, I've got it. Do you want me to send it down to you? I'm not sure I can get to the post office today, but tomorrow looks—'

'No, it's not about that,' I interrupt. 'I mean, yes, please do send it down when you get a minute, but can you check something on the original for me? On the back of the photograph near where the date is written, we think there is something that looks like a postcode imprinted. Can you see it?'

'Hold on, I'll have to put on my glasses… Oh, yes, there it is. Ha! I wouldn't have known that was there unless you'd pointed it out. How on earth did you find that?'

I look up to Rick, but don't acknowledge the question. 'Can you read what you think it says? I've got the PO11 bit, but trying to figure out the rest.'

Maddie is making an unusual array of noises as she tries to find an answer for us, and I can picture her taking it in turns to put her nose on the page, before turning it towards the light coming through her small office window, and then back again. 'I think it's 0RT, but it really is very faint. Perhaps even the T could be a P. I'm sorry, Emma, but it's so difficult to tell for certain. If you pushed me, I'd agree with 0RT, but I'm no expert.'

'Okay, thanks, Maddie, I appreciate you taking a look.'

'Can't you just Google his name and date of birth?'

'I've done that already and found him, but the date written isn't his date of birth.'

'Oh, I see. Well, I'll send the original down first thing anyway. What's the significance of this postcode business? Do you think that's where he's being held?'

'I honestly don't know, Maddie. There's not many properties here, but you never know.'

'Okay, well, don't do anything dangerous. You still haven't sent me the copyedits of *Trafficked* yet, so I don't want any harm coming to my favourite client.'

'I'm quite certain I'm safe here, but I appreciate your concern, Maddie.'

'Have you figured out who's sending you these pictures yet?'

'Not yet, but I'm working on it. Thanks again, Maddie. Speak soon.'

I disconnect the call and look sceptically at Rick. 'What do you think then?'

He sits back in his chair, pressing his hair into the headrest but keeping his eyes on me. He's about to respond when my phone rings again with a number I don't recognise.

'Can I speak to… Emma Hunter, please?' a woman's voice says.

'Speaking.'

'Hi, I'm Detective Constable Caroline Knox, calling from Greater Manchester Police. You left a message saying you had information about the disappearance of Faye McKenna?'

'Oh, um… Yeah, that's right… Well, not exactly new information… Um…'

Her voice is soft but I instantly sense an element of frustration in her tone. 'Well, you either do or you don't.'

I wish Rick wasn't next to me right now, able to overhear every word. 'Sorry, let me explain. I'm a writer, um, and I specialise in missing children cases. On Friday I was sent a picture of Faye McKenna out of the blue, and I guess I thought I should inform someone about it.'

'I see. What can you tell me about the photograph? How do you know it's of Faye McKenna?'

'Her name and date of birth were written on the back of the image. I looked her up online and that's how I got your number. I can forward you a copy of the image if that would help?'

'Sure, it can't hurt.'

'Would you mind if I asked you a couple of questions about the case? I looked online, but couldn't see much other than she went missing on her return from school.'

'I'm sorry, Emma, I can't share details of an open investigation with members of the public.'

'Absolutely, I understand that, and I've signed numerous Non-Disclosure Agreements with the Met Police in London when I've helped them with open investigations. Perhaps you've heard of me?' I cringe at the line but I want to stress that I'm not just looking for sordid details; I want to help.

'Sorry, I can't say I have.'

At least she can't see my cheeks burning.

'I'm trying to figure out who might have sent me the picture. I'd say Faye looks older than she does in the images used on her missingpeople.org page, so I wondered whether her mum might have had her aged using software, and it was her way of reaching out and asking for my help.'

'Unlikely. Mrs McKenna died two and a bit years ago.'

'Oh, I see. Is it possible that someone else in the immediate family could have sent it instead then? I read that Faye didn't have any brothers or sisters, and that her dad wasn't on the scene, but are you in touch with him, or maybe any uncles or aunts of Faye?'

DC Knox sighs. 'Faye's case remains open, but after Mrs McKenna passed, nobody has been in touch with us to ask about Faye – until you, that is. We will continue to review the case every couple of years, as we do with all our cold cases, but unless new evidence comes to light, there's little chance of us ever finding out what happened to Faye.'

I picture Faye's face in my mind. 'Do you know if Faye ever did any acting at school or in her spare time?'

'I'm not sure. Why?'

'The picture I was sent – it's going to sound silly, but – it resembles a headshot like actors would use when requesting auditions for parts, and I wondered whether… I don't know what I wondered really.'

'Listen, Emma, I wasn't involved in the case originally, so I don't know all the ins and outs of it. Send me the image and I will add it to the file along with your number, and when it next comes up for review, someone can contact you and provide an update.'

I know the drill, I don't say.

'Is there anything else you'd like to tell me about Faye or the picture you were sent?' DC Knox asks, bringing the call to an end.

'No, I don't think so. Is there an email address I can forward the image to?'

She dictates one to me and then hangs up.

'Any luck?' Rick asks quizzically.

'No,' I reply, sighing heavily. 'Faye doesn't have any next of kin who would have been likely to send the picture, which puts us back to square one on who and why it was sent to me.'

Frustrated, I push open the door and clamber out. My legs are grateful for the movement, and I welcome the rush of fresh air as the branches sway overhead. The car park is barely large enough to fit more than half a dozen cars, and is probably here primarily for the use of those visiting the adjacent cemetery.

'Why don't we go for a wander,' Rick suggests, climbing out and stretching his aching muscles. 'Maybe we'll run into someone who can tell us more about Chesney whatever his name is.'

There's that positivity again, but in fairness a stretch of our legs is probably a good idea after the two-hour car journey. I certainly could do with burning off the calories we filled up on from the crisps and biscuits we both consumed on the way here. Locking the car, Rick leads us back to the main road, and I can immediately see there is a smattering of properties nearby, which were obscured by tall bushes and our low centre of gravity in Rick's car.

'Which way do you want to go?' he asks.

The thought of knocking on all of the doors and asking whether the residents have heard of Chesney Byrne doesn't feel like a good use of our time, but the road is empty of passers-by and very well may remain that way for the foreseeable future.

'We could do with a list of names of everyone who lives within the postcode,' I say aloud, though not sure where the thought is headed. 'Maybe we'd then see a name that somehow links to Chesney.'

I know I'm clutching at straws, and I now regret us making this journey on such a whim. It was Rick's idea, but I should have known better than just to go along with it. We could have researched the area, or reached out to the local police and explained who I was and what I'd received, as I did with DC Knox in Manchester.

'I don't think they make a phone directory by postcode, but we could always ask at the church and see if there is a list of local parishioners. It's a start.'

I exhale loudly, but nod my head and follow Rick as he leads me out of the car park and in through the wooden gate. It really is a pretty church, set close to the road, and surrounded by a small collection of evergreen trees. I imagine on a sunny day it would be so picturesque – ideal for a wedding for those inclined to celebrate in a church.

'It's all closed up,' I observe.

'Yeah, but there's a small house adjoining at the back. You see?' He points around the side of the brick building. 'Let's try there and see if the name rings any bells inside.'

Rick leads the way and rings the rusty bell hanging from the wall outside the paint-chipped wooden door. It is opened a minute or so later by a woman in a black collared shirt with glasses perched on the end of her nose. She considers Rick and me before closing the small book she's carrying. The salt-and-pepper streaks in her otherwise dark bob put her older than me, but younger than my mother.

'Hello, can I help you?' she asks.

'Hi,' I say, 'we've travelled from Weymouth because we're looking for someone who might know a man called Chesney Byrne, or a Cormack Fitzpatrick. He went missing when he was an adolescent several years ago, but we have reason to believe he has links to this postal code. I don't suppose you recognise the name?'

Her blank expression doesn't change. 'I'm sorry, no, I don't recognise the name.'

Pulling out my phone, I share the image that Maddie sent down. 'Does his face seem familiar in any way? I'd estimate he would look older than this now.'

She accepts my phone and studies the screen. 'I'm ever so sorry, but no, I can't say it rings any bells. I've been the reverend here for three years and I certainly don't recognise him. Could he be the relative of one of the parishioners perhaps? Is there anything else you can tell me about him? What does he do for a living, for example?'

I don't doubt that she is keen to help us, but coming here is another dead end.

'I don't suppose you can tell me the name of your predecessor, can you?' I ask next.

'I replaced the late Reverend Peter Saltzing, and he was the vicar here for'—she puffs out her cheeks—'at least twenty years before he retired. It's possible he might have heard of this… sorry, what was his name again?'

'Chesney Byrne, but he may also have been known as Cormack Fitzpatrick.'

'Yes, I'm sorry, but that name certainly doesn't remind me of anyone specific within the parish.'

We thank her, and step away from the door as she closes it.

'I guess we can go door-to-door next then,' Rick suggests, leading us back along the path and through the cemetery back to the car.

'Hold on,' I say to him. 'What if we're looking at this all wrong, and the reason the postcode was etched into the image is because this was his final resting place? What if there's a Chesney Byrne buried in the cemetery?'

Rick shrugs. 'Well, as we're here, there's no harm in checking the gravestones. The cemetery isn't very big, so it shouldn't take too long.'

We split up, moving systematically from one gravestone to the next, reading the names, but there isn't a plaque to a Chesney or anyone with the surname Byrne anywhere. We meet again in the middle, but it does seem this trip to Hayling Island has been a waste of our time.

But then a thought fires in the back of the mind, and I quickly begin scanning gravestones again, with Rick following clueless behind me.

'What are you looking for?' he exclaims. 'I've checked all of these, and there is no Chesney Byrne.'

I can't explain it, but when I find what I'm looking for, the breath catches in my throat. Even more so when I see the fresh bunch of flowers that has been laid on the grass beside the eroded stone.

'What's so special about this one?' Rick asks, unable to read the weathered name on the tombstone.

I don't respond at first, taking tentative steps towards the flowers, and instantly recoiling as I read the inscription on the card.

'What is it?' Rick asks, dumbfounded.

'We need to call the local police immediately,' I whisper. 'I believe we may have found Chesney Byrne's final resting place.'

I point at the date on the tombstone, which is a match to the one on the back of the photograph, and then I show Rick the card attached to the flowers, which reads:

Rest in peace, Chez.

Chapter Thirty

NOW

Hayling Island, Hampshire

My mind is working overtime as I bang my hand against the door of the vicarage. Whoever left those flowers at the graveside could very well be the same person who sent me the image of Chesney/Cormack. Whether they intended to leave the postcode imprinted on the image remains unclear, but if their plan was to steer me towards this particular grave, why not write the postcode in ink like the name and date?

'Hello again,' the vicar says as she opens the door and recognises Rick and me from a few minutes earlier. 'Was there something else I can help you with?'

'Does the cemetery have any CCTV cameras that we could take a look at?'

She eyes the two of us suspiciously and grips the door tighter.

'Some flowers have been left beside one of the gravestones,'

I continue, attempting to put her at ease, 'and I really need to know who left them.'

Her eyes don't leave Rick's as she responds, 'There isn't any CCTV on the cemetery; we like to allow mourners their privacy.'

'Would you have records of who is buried in a particular plot?' I persevere. 'Or when they were put there?'

She shelters behind the door. 'What is this all about really? Who are the two of you?'

'I'm a writer and investigative journalist,' I tell her. 'I have reason to believe that the young man we are looking for may have been buried in that grave, so that's why I want to know when it was dug.'

The vicar narrows her eyes, studying my face. 'Would you mind waiting for one moment?' she asks, closing the door.

I look over to Rick who is moving from one foot to the other. 'Am I being crazy?' I ask. 'The date on the gravestone is the same as the date on the image sent to me, and the flowers reference "Chez", but could this just as easily be someone's idea of a practical joke?'

He frowns. 'A pretty twisted joke if it is.'

'But I just keep thinking back to Tina Neville, and how we were all so willing to buy her story that Jo-Jo had been snatched, when all along she was just pretending. What if this is all someone else's elaborate ruse to have me trekking across the country looking for false clues?'

'There's only really one way to know for certain.'

I'm grateful when the vicar returns and her nervous energy is gone. The smell of burnt incense hangs like a cloud above our heads, and reminds me of the vigils held in honour of Anna for those first few months after she left. I can't even remember the last time I stepped inside a church. Maybe prayer is the one remaining avenue I've yet to explore.

The vicarage isn't as I would have expected. Where I would have imagined seeing rickety old furniture and a home in desperate need of modernisation, instead I recognise several pieces from the IKEA catalogue. The walls have been recently painted, and are covered in framed artistic impressions of flowers and beaches.

'I'm Victoria,' she says after a moment, 'and am known as Vicar Victoria locally.' The grey streaks in her short bob glisten in the light flooding in through the large bay window in the main room. 'So, back to your problem then: you believe that this young man you're looking for could be buried in our cemetery here?'

'Maybe,' I reply. 'He went missing from Gosport in 1996 having withdrawn all his savings, and was never seen nor heard of thereafter. Today I received the picture I showed you of him, but in that image he's older than eleven – his age when he disappeared – which suggests he wasn't killed back in 1996. On the back of the photo, whoever sent it wrote the date 19th January 2000. Looking through the cemetery, we came across a grave with that date of death, where someone has left a bunch of flowers with a card reading "RIP Chez".'

'I see,' she says. 'Well, I can tell you nobody has been buried in our cemetery since 2010, as it's now full, but give me a moment and I will go and dig out the grave records, no pun intended.'

By the time Vicar Victoria returns, carrying a cardboard box on top of which sits a large leather-bound book, I'm convinced we've made a mistake in coming here, and that someone is using my obsession with Anna's loss to lead me on a wild goose chase. And the most irritating part is that I allowed myself to succumb.

'I've found the register of plots and graves,' she says, lifting the large green leather-bound book and flicking it open. 'It's ordered by plot, by date of burial, and by name,' she explains. 'When they say we have to fill it in in triplicate, they really mean it.' She chuckles to herself, and adjusts her glasses, beginning to flick through. 'You said the date of death was January 2000?'

'Yes, the 19th.'

She flicks through several pages. 'Okay, I have a Jean-Claude Ribery who was interred the week after on Tuesday 25th January, which would probably tie in with the date of death. The next burial after that wasn't until May of the same year.'

'Does it say who oversaw the service?' I ask.

'Yes, hold on… Looks like it was my predecessor, the Reverend Peter Saltzing.'

'Is there any further information about who attended, or who paid for the burial?'

'No, I'm sorry. It was dealt with by one of the three funeral directors on the island. Grady's is a family-run business. If you contact them they may be able to confirm more details for you. I have a business card of theirs around here somewhere that I can let you have.'

'Thank you. Is your predecessor still around? You said he retired when you took over?'

Her face drops. 'He passed away not long after he retired, I'm afraid. Left under a bit of a cloud, by all accounts.'

My spidey-senses are tingling again.

'In what way?' I ask as casually as my growing excitement will allow.

'Well, rumour had it that he had been involved with that boys' home in the Midlands; you know, the one where there was all that business about abuse? There was a court case about it a couple of years ago.'

My blood runs cold, and I struggle to get the words out of my mouth. 'You mean the St Francis Home for Wayward Boys?'

'Yes, that's the one. He was working there briefly as a pastor, providing spiritual guidance to the boys. I don't think he was ever accused of being involved in what went on, but the fact that he was there at all and *didn't* pick up on what was happening… Mud sticks, doesn't it?'

Why does everything keep looping back to *that* place? Freddie's comments about Pendark also echo in my head: *I'd put money on there being more victims undiscovered there too.*

'After he died and I was having a proper clear-out, I found this box in the small loft above the kitchen. Some of Peter's old things, I believe. It didn't feel right to just throw them away, but I didn't know what else to do with them.'

Part of me doesn't want to look through the box, but I can't stop myself reaching for it and sliding it across the carpet. When I lift the lid a musty bubble of damp seems to escape, and as I sift through, I see they are mainly framed pictures and newspaper articles. I pull one out when I read the name St Francis in the headline. I recognise Arthur Turgood standing beside a man in a dog collar and a younger man, the three of them beaming. I'm not sure how much longer I can keep my nausea at bay.

'Would you mind if I borrowed these?' I ask, determined to

ask Freddie if he recognises Saltzing or the man laughing beside him.

'You're welcome to them,' Victoria says, standing. 'I'll go and find you that business card for Grady's.'

St Francis, Pendark, and Chesney / Cormack – it's all related somehow, but I've never felt so out of my depth. There's only one person who will understand the significance of what I'm holding, but as I unlock my phone, I see Jack is already calling me.

Moving to the bay window, turning my back on Rick, I press the phone to my ear. 'Jack, you're never going to believe—'

'Emma, there's something I need to tell you,' he interrupts. 'The remains in the suitcase aren't Anna's.'

It's nearly four o'clock by the time we see Jack's car drive past the bay window of the vicarage and park up. He is in a state of confusion as he rings the bell and is shown through to the front room. As soon as he sees me standing by the window, he crosses the room and pulls me into a platonic hug, squeezing just tightly enough to take my weight should my knees fail again.

'I'm so sorry I didn't phone sooner,' he whispers into my ear. 'I only found out this morning, but we had to try and tell the victim's family before I could confirm to you, and it took longer than expected to find a next of kin.'

He smells like strawberries and cream, but I can't tell if that's because he's been eating sweets on the drive down or if he's been using his daughter's shampoo. I don't care either way; I'm just glad to have someone here who understands the pain coursing through my veins right now.

'Are you going to be okay?' he whispers next, and I find myself nodding, as if his strength is pulling me back out of the hole.

'I will be,' my muffled whispers say, with my head buried in his shoulder.

'Do you want me to take you home?'

Usually there's no place I'd rather be than home, but the thought of the silence of my flat leaving me to wallow doesn't appeal. I need distraction, rather than self-pity. They may not be my sister's remains, but they still belong to someone, and I am duty-bound to help that victim's family understand how she ended up in a suitcase, discarded for all time.

'Who was she?' I ask, breaking from Jack's grasp and perching against the window frame.

Jack is about to respond when he suddenly notices Rick sitting in the tall armchair, and his face tightens with concern.

'Um, this is Rick,' I say quickly, 'he's a Community Support Officer from Weymouth who drove me up here. Rick, this is PC Jack Serrovitz, who, of course, you'll recognise from my books.

Rick stands and strides across the room, thrusting out an arm and shaking Jack's hand firmly. 'Good to meet you, Jack.'

Rick is a good six-to-eight inches taller than Jack, who has to crane his neck to meet his gaze. 'And you. How do the two of you know each other?'

Rick's brow furrows and he looks to me for confirmation, but I don't know where to begin explaining why he is here with me.

'Um, well, I'm…' he begins, breaking off while searching for the right noun to describe our relationship.

'Rick has been helping me with a new investigation,' I say, choosing not to share details of the Tina Neville debacle. 'That's what brought us to Hayling Island today. Rick very kindly drove us here.'

They're still shaking hands, sizing up one another.

'You were about to tell us whose remains were in the suitcase,' I try. 'Jack? The remains?' I press.

They both release their grips and Jack turns back to me, still giving Rick an uneasy look.

'I suppose it will be in the newspapers by morning anyway… The remains belong to a missing girl who disappeared from Oldham in 1998.'

It's like a sucker punch to the gut, and I have to grip the window ledge tighter as the wind is knocked from me. 'Faye McKenna,' I gasp.

Jack starts. 'How the hell did you guess that?'

I stagger towards the sofa where my satchel sits open. Reaching for my phone, I unlock the screen and load up the image Maddie emailed to me on Saturday, handing it to Jack.

'Yes, that's her,' he says, 'at least it looks like her. Where did you get this from?'

I take a deep breath, before telling Jack about the photographs sent to me via Maddie's office; how they led us here to Hayling Island; and how we now believe that Cormack/Chesney is buried in the cemetery beyond the bay window.

'Holy shit!' Jack exclaims under his breath, quickly blushing apologetically. 'Do you know who's sending you these photographs?'

I shrug. 'I assumed at first a family member, but then I spoke to a DC Caroline Knox with Greater Manchester Police this morning and she said Faye's mum passed a couple of years ago, and she didn't have any brothers or sisters.'

Jack is nodding along. 'She told me the same thing a couple of hours ago. Funny thing is, she said I was the second person to be asking questions about Faye, but wouldn't reveal who else she'd spoken to. I was guessing that was you. Unbelievable – we've been looking at the same problem from different ends.'

'Faye's picture arrived at the office on Friday, and Cormack's this morning. They have to be connected, but I just don't know how.' The image of Reverend Peter Saltzing flashes before my eyes, and has me reaching for the cutting in the box, which I pass to Jack. 'And to top it off, the vicar who used to live here had dealings with the St Francis Home. See here? We know that Turgood and the Home have connections to the Pendark Film Studios, so it's not a huge leap to suppose that Saltzing did too. What if…?' But I stop myself, because my next thought is too ridiculous to say aloud.

'What if what?' Jack questions.

'I don't know,' I say, the blood finally returning to my face. 'What if those associated with Pendark forced Saltzing to help them hide Cormack's body? Where better to hide a body than in another man's grave? Nobody would ever be any the wiser unless Jean-Claude Ribery was exhumed. Loose end tied up. The current vicar said that Saltzing retired under something of a cloud when the truth started to emerge about the St Francis Home. What do you think?'

'I think we need to exhume the coffin and check,' Rick pipes up affirmatively. 'It will prove the theory and tie this Saltzing to the mess.'

Jack is shaking his head incredulously, but I speak first. 'We can't just dig up a coffin and look inside. There's an impact on the family of the deceased, an impact on the local community, and we'd need a court order, I would imagine.'

'Yes, yes, and yes,' Jack echoes. 'There isn't any concrete evidence to suggest that Cormack Fitzpatrick is buried there. The flowers and the date on the photograph aren't enough. I will ask my boss at the NCA what we'd need, but unless we find something tangible, that grave remains undisturbed.'

Chapter Thirty-One

THEN

Basingstoke, Hampshire

'Stop worrying about it; you'll be fine,' Precious told her, squeezing her hand reassuringly. 'And relax. On the first night you won't have to… to do anything; you're just there for show.'

Joanna exhaled slowly and tightened her jaw into a smile of encouragement that she wasn't feeling.

'Remember how nervous you were before your first photoshoot, and I told you it would all be fine, didn't I? Wasn't yer Auntie Precious, right?' She chuckled to herself, as if tonight's party was perfectly normal, and nothing to be feared. 'This won't be much different, other than Grey won't be popping about with his telescopic lens.'

Joanna could still recall the pure terror she'd felt the first time Precious had taken her to the film studio. The barn had stunk of animal faeces, and the tiled floor of the sectioned-off studio had been cold to walk on. Precious had promised she'd hang around in the barn and escort Joanna back to the caravan when the shoot was over. Joanna had naively begged her not to go, but it had been too much and Precious had let her mask of empathy slip. The wide-eyed angry glare had revealed the beast that lay dormant beneath the surface, and although it had peered out several times in the eighteen months that had passed, Joanna now knew the signs, and how to tame the beast.

'I don't want no more talk about nerves,' Precious continued, standing and heading into the kitchen area, removing a bottle of wine from the shopping bag on the table and carrying it back to the table. 'Now, I want you to pour us both a large glass of this to settle any remaining anxiety while I go and find us something pretty and sparkly to wear.' She paused, running her fingers through Joanna's hair. 'Yer so lucky to have such long, smooth hair. It takes me hours to comb mine into anything nearly as straight as this. Hey, I know, why don't we both wear wigs tonight? I can be blonde for once, and you can be…'

'Violet,' Joanna blurted, picturing the exact hairpiece she'd seen in Precious's room when she'd been rifling through the drawers last week.

The excited grin and bounce in Precious's step as she headed towards the bedroom confirmed she concurred with the selection. 'We should dress first,' she called back over her shoulder, 'and fit the hair right before Grey comes calling for us.'

Joanna shuddered at mention of his name. Although he'd never laid a hand on her, she now recognised that lustful look in his eyes when he lowered the camera when he didn't think she was looking. The fact that she was only eleven didn't seem to matter to him.

'You've no idea how beautiful you are, Kylie,' he said yesterday, running his index finger the length of her arm.

They both knew he wasn't allowed to do anything about his lust – Mr Brown would be livid – but Grey had made his intentions clear. If she was prepared to keep quiet, he was ready to make his move. He enjoyed reminding her that she still owed him for sparing her life that night in the woods.

She shuddered again, and brushed his imagined finger from her shoulder, like a scurrying spider. She'd never asked what happened to all the photographs he took – where they ended up; who'd requested them in the first place – and she knew better than to ask Precious and wake the beast within. But the question remained near the surface of her mind. She knew they weren't just for Grey's own gratification, though she was certain he enjoyed the experience more than he was probably supposed to.

Tonight's party had been Precious's idea too.

'Parties are where the big money's at, Kylie,' she'd told her two nights ago. 'You want to earn some serious cash? That's how.'

That was the only reason Joanna had agreed to tag along tonight. All she knew was that Grey would collect them from the caravan at seven and drive them to wherever the party was being held. The exact location was only known to Grey, as far as Joanna knew, but what did it matter where it was? They wouldn't be left alone long enough to disappear, so it could be in the far reaches of Timbuktu and it wouldn't matter.

Precious hadn't said how much she would earn for just

attending, but if it was more than the ten pounds she earned per photoshoot then it would help supplement the secret stash she'd been building for close to a year. A pound here, two pounds there – not a lot, but small enough amounts that Precious wouldn't notice. She hadn't discussed her plan with Precious – the beast wouldn't like it – but if she could squirrel away enough cash, she would be able to make a break for it, and maybe get far enough away that Grey and Mr Brown would simply give up looking for her. The night she tried to escape before had been flawed from the start because she had involved Chez, and he'd suffered as a result of her actions. She wouldn't allow Precious to fall to the same fate.

Opening the bottle of wine, she filled two glasses, grimacing as she sipped the tepid liquid. 'The wine's warm,' she called out.

'Just drop some ice in it,' Precious called back, her head popping out from behind the bedroom door. 'It'll chill quickly enough.'

Joanna nodded as the head disappeared again and she opened the fridge-freezer, plopped two cubes in each glass, and turned on the radio.

'Oh, I love this song,' Precious called from the bedroom, singing along to it and dancing out of the bedroom, clutching two dresses in her hands and holding them out for Joanna's approval.

Joanna didn't like the short red dress as it barely covered her bottom and had a tendency to ride up, which made it one of Grey's favourites to photograph her in.

She scrunched up her nose. 'The red one? Really?'

Precious wasn't listening, draping the garment over the arm of the chair, the message clear: the choice wasn't up for debate. She continued to dance, twirling in the spotlight overhead. It made Joanna suddenly self-conscious about her own lack of breast development. The bra Precious was wearing could barely contain her, but Joanna at eleven was as flat-chested as when she'd first arrived.

Precious caught her looking and Joanna quickly averted her eyes, but it was too late. Dropping onto the seat beside her, Precious said, 'Don't worry, we'll give you a bit of extra padding for tonight; make you feel like a proper lady.'

It wasn't what Joanna had been hoping for, but she didn't disagree.

'What will the party be like?' she asked, gnawing at one of her fingernails.

Precious rolled her eyes in frustration, sensing the nervous energy radiating from her roommate. 'Listen, it'll be in some fancy house, right? We'll be asked to wait in some room where there'll be wine to drink, and when the time is right, Grey will open the doors and we'll be invited into some boardroom or whatever and we'll meet the clients. Some will be overweight, some balding, but their eyes won't leave us for a moment. They'll ask us to sit and talk, and the one thing you need to remember – I can't stress this enough – *be nice*. Compliment them on what they're wearing, or how handsome they look, or whatever. Our job is to make them feel special by any means. Okay?'

Joanna tried to ignore the wave of nausea bubbling nearby. 'And then what happens?'

Precious sighed loudly – a sign that she was losing patience. 'And then if the client yer paired with wants to talk privately, he'll invite you to his room. But you don't need to worry about that. Like I said, you won't have to do anything you don't want because it's your first time. Grey knows yer not ready for that yet, and you coming along tonight is just so that you see what it's like.'

Joanna didn't want to upset her friend further, but she couldn't stop herself blurting it out. 'W-w-what happens in the bedroom?'

Precious turned her head and glared. 'What do you think happens in the bedroom, Kylie? It's a *sex* party! You know how Grey makes you pose and play with things in the studio? Well, that's what'll happen in the bedroom, only it won't be toys you're holding.'

Tears burned behind Joanna's eyes but she knew better than to let them out.

Precious reached for the packet of cigarettes on the table top and lit one, blowing the smoke at Joanna in frustration. 'That's what we're doing here, Kylie. Don't you understand that yet? We're paid to provide a service that these men can't get elsewhere. Mr Brown runs a club that relies on the discretion of its clients and the willingness of its employees, the likes of you and me. You can hate it, but that's what this is.'

Joanna nodded frantically, breathing in deeply and exhaling to control her emotions and repress the need to shout and scream and cry.

'I-I-I'm sorry,' she whispered, barely audible over the sound of the radio.

Precious folded her arms before offering the cigarette like an olive branch. Joanna accepted it gratefully, and put the butt between her lips, allowing the smoke to fill her mouth, before drawing it down into her lungs as Precious had taught her, and then exhaling through her mouth and nose simultaneously. She passed the cigarette back, her panic slowly settling; the beast was back in its cage for now.

A knock at the door was followed by Grey entering, tottering slightly, the smell of whisky on his breath overcoming the cigarette smoke hanging overhead. 'How are my two favourite young ladies tonight?'

'Half-dressed,' Precious snapped back, infuriated by the interruption.

'Oh, don't mind me,' Grey replied, holding his hands out in some kind of surrender. 'Why don't you run along and finish getting ready while I keep Kylie company?'

He tottered over to where she was sitting, the lust in his eyes more determined tonight.

Joanna couldn't bear to look at him when he leered in that way, and was relieved when she felt Precious tugging at her hand.

'We *both* need to get ready,' she growled, pulling Joanna out of his clutches and towards the bedroom, dragging the dresses with her. 'Don't worry about him,' she said quietly when the door was closed. 'He knows his place.'

Joanna allowed her friend to pull the T-shirt up and over her head and raised her arms when instructed to do so, as Precious fastened the loose bra at the back, before shoving in soft fillers. With the red dress then pulled over her head, Joanna fixed her makeup as she'd been shown, applying the eyeliner, mascara, and bright red lip gloss, before Precious tied her hair and fitted the violet-toned hairpiece. Ten minutes had passed, and it was like she was watching someone else now in control of her body, and Joanna merely a casual observer.

With Precious also dressed, and the platinum-blonde wig secured over her tight black knots, they admired the results in the mirror. 'Grey will probably spunk himself when he sees you walk out,' Precious said, as if that was a perfectly normal reaction to a child dressed to look older than her eleven years.

Exiting the room, Precious wolf-whistled as she presented the new Kylie, but froze when she saw Mr Brown glaring back from the table.

'Change of plans,' he barked. 'Tonight we're going to the studios. And take that ridiculous-looking thing off your head. When the client orders a coloured girl, he doesn't expect half-measures.'

Precious pulled the wig from her head, without even removing the pins, and allowed it to drop to the floor. Lowering her eyes, she walked quietly to the door, Joanna cowering behind her, and then both climbed into the back of Mr Brown's waiting 4x4.

Chapter Thirty-Two

NOW

Hayling Island, Hampshire

Poor Victoria doesn't seem to know what to do with herself as we continue to use the vicarage as a makeshift base of operations. Jack has taken his phone call with his boss at the NCA outside, and I don't blame him for desiring a bit of privacy; I too wish I could go for some air and try and get out of my own headspace.

Rick is still sitting in the tall-backed armchair, but judging by the way he keeps glancing at his watch when he thinks I'm not looking, I sense there is somewhere else he needs to be. However, when I meet his gaze – inviting him to say something – he just smiles empathetically, before breaking the eye contact.

'Do you need to go?' I venture when I can't take the suspense any longer.

He checks his watch again, even though it's only ten

seconds since he last looked. His jaw tautens into a grimace as if he's just pulled a muscle at the gym. 'I do kind of need to head back in a bit. I'm on an early shift tomorrow, and want to grab a few hours' sleep beforehand. I can wait with you a bit longer. Hopefully your… I mean, Jack will get an answer on next steps soon.' Another check of the watch. 'I'd have said if it was my relative's grave where a body was suspected of being hidden, I think I'd be comfortable with the coffin being exhumed to check. Don't you think?'

I don't blame him for his naivety because he hasn't lost anyone dear to him, so can't imagine the heart-wrenching pain that such a request could cause to Jean-Claude Ribery's family. That said, I share his frustration that, without an exhumation, we'll never know for certain whether Cormack/Chesney is buried there. If the suspicion was that Anna was buried in the grave, would I be so considerate of the Ribery family? In truth, probably not.

'We'll just have to wait and see what Jack can sort,' I say diplomatically. 'But listen, if you need to get back, I don't want to be the reason that you stay out. I can probably get a taxi and a train back home, which I'm absolutely fine with.'

There's a momentary widening of his eyes – excitement maybe? 'Are you sure? I feel responsible for you, as it was my idea that we come here and I was the one who drove you.'

If only all men were so considerate!

'Listen, seriously, you've already done enough for me, Rick. I really appreciate you being here today, and if it weren't for your eagle eyes, I probably wouldn't have spotted that postcode, and I'd still be at home scratching my head about why the two pictures had been sent to me.'

'Pretty incredible that Jack was the one who found Faye

McKenna's remains so soon after you were sent the picture too.'

I don't correct him on the fact that the remains were discovered on Thursday *before* Maddie received the image, but there's no doubt that the timing feels a little too coincidental. So much so that I can't accept it as merely coincidence. Whoever sent Faye's picture to me must have known that we'd discovered remains, or that we were about to. It still feels like there's someone taunting me. It also has me terrified at the prospect another photograph might turn up tomorrow or in the days to come.

'At least her family will be able to lay her to rest at last,' I agree, not adding how envious that makes me feel.

Rick sits forward in his seat. 'Listen, it's fine for me to wait around for a bit longer. I'm sure traffic on the way home won't be too heavy, and I don't mind dropping you in Weymouth before heading back to Dorchester.'

I actually look at my watch as I don't know how late it is. 'Thank you, Rick, but I really can't ask you for anything else. You go on and get some rest. The last thing I want is for you to be tired when you're on duty tomorrow.' I stand, offering a mock salute, and putting on a fake drawl. 'The good people of Weymouth need you, son.'

He frowns, and I cringe inwardly at the lame impression, but he stands and comes towards me, taking my hands in his. 'I'm sorry we didn't manage to solve the mystery of who is sending you those photos, but I don't doubt you'll crack it as you always do.'

This is not a good moment for my hands to become clammy.

'And in case I haven't made it clear to you yet, Emma, I

want you to know how much I dig you.' His cheeks redden as he half-smiles. 'I understand if you're already spoken for, or if whatever you have with Jack is where your head's at, but if not, I'd love to ask you out on a proper date.'

What I would give for the chance to live in Jane Austen's England, where such courting was only ever undertaken in letter form. I know Rick is a good guy – his devotion to his mother is proof of that – and in any other situation I'd kick myself for not swooning at his suggestion, but there is just too much going on in my head to really know what I want in my future. I want my sister back, and until that happens, any thoughts about romance or relationships or even dating have to remain on hold.

I can't keep him waiting much longer. A good ten seconds has elapsed and I'm yet to speak. I want him to know that I appreciate the offer, *and* the courage he has shown to cross that bridge.

Fifteen seconds.

I want to be honest about my feelings, but I don't want to see that hurt expression he's desperately trying to keep hidden.

Twenty seconds. If only I had a pen and paper.

'You don't have to answer straightaway,' he says, cutting through my thoughts. 'I just wanted to float the idea and see what you think about it. With everything that's going on today, I'm sure your mind is probably everywhere but here, and it's unfair of me to put you on the spot like this.' He releases my hands. 'I'm gonna go and head back to Dorset, and give you the space to think about what I've said, and when you're ready, you have my number and can let me know. Yeah?'

I nod, as I still can't find the words I want to say.

'Are you sure you *don't* want me to stick around and give you a lift?'

'You should go,' I manage to say. 'I will speak to you soon.'

He smiles once more before disappearing out of the room, and as I hear the front door close, I finally exhale the breath that has been trapped in my throat.

'Can I fix you a cup of peppermint tea?' Victoria asks, apparently alerted by the closing of the front door and surprised to find me still camped out in her living room.

'That's very kind, but no, thank you. And I promise we will be out of your hair as soon as possible.'

She smiles warmly. 'Please don't rush off on my account. The Lord clearly has brought you to our little island for a reason, and who am I to question his motives?'

Come to think of it, with Rick now gone, and Jack already outside, there really isn't any need for me to remain inside the vicarage. Jack has already packed the box of Peter Saltzing's belongings in his boot, so I thank Victoria for her help again, and leave a donation in the small charity box hanging by the front door as I take my leave.

The air is so fresh against my cheeks and I'm grateful for a few minutes on my own when I don't have to pretend that everything is okay. I'm not sure I share Victoria's sentiment that I was brought to Hayling Island for any particular purpose; it certainly doesn't feel like I've achieved anything in the few hours I've been here. If anything, I have more questions than answers, and the one question I'm trying to avoid is who is sending these photographs? I'm not a riddle solver, I don't like crosswords, and I'm even less keen on puzzles.

'The boss was on the fifteenth hole with the ex-Met Commissioner when I called, and not pleased by the interruption,' Jack explains glumly, turning the corner and finding me leaning against the door to the vicarage. 'He says we don't have enough for exhumation.'

'Figured as much,' I reply, hoping he can't see just how close to tears I am. 'Where do we go from here?'

He doesn't answer, looking at me for too long. 'Are you okay? I didn't want to say too much when we were inside, but the news about your sister must have been a shock to hear. I'm sorry I wasn't able to deliver it in person.'

'What are you talking about?' I blag, invoking a positive expression that I'm not feeling. 'It's good news, right? The remains in the case *aren't* my sister, which means she could still be alive somewhere. Why would you think that would make me sad?' I barely get the final word out before the tears are streaming down my face, and I have never been more grateful to feel a pair of arms wrapping around my shoulders, and just holding me.

'We *will* find her,' Jack whispers into my windswept hair. 'This is merely a pothole in the road to the truth.'

Stupidly, I think the thing that is upsetting me most is the fact that I had accepted she was buried at Pendark. I hate myself for giving up on her so easily.

'The pathologist told me that the DNA sample on file for Faye McKenna wasn't ideal, and they needed to locate a separate comparison sample to confirm her identity. It was her dental records that confirmed the truth. She'd had extensive work undertaken by an orthodontist, and in the end that proved conclusive. Then there was this morning's delay in being able to find a family member to break the news to. I finally got hold of some distant cousin of Faye's who said she would share the news with remaining members of the family. I'm just gutted her mum didn't live long enough to bury her only child.'

'Who's doing this to me?' I manage to blurt.

'Sending the photographs? I wish I knew. Clearly someone with an inner knowledge of what became of Cormack Fitzpatrick and Faye McKenna, but who that person is is beyond me.'

'Do you think it's the person who killed and buried them?'

'I wouldn't rule out any theory at the moment.' He rests his cheek on the top of my head. 'I saw your PCSO friend leaving... Does that mean you're in need of a lift back to Weymouth?'

I break free of his embrace, and look into those coal-like eyes. 'I'll catch a train home.'

'Are you sure? I mean, Weymouth is kind of on the way home.' His goofy grin appears and I find myself reflecting it.

'On your way back to West London, is it? From Hampshire?'

'Well, I've got to make a detour via Weymouth on the way home anyway, as I was planning on calling in on your friend Freddie and asking whether he recognises the late Reverend Peter Saltzing. If truth be told, I could do with the company if you wouldn't mind forgoing the train and riding shotgun with me.'

'What about Mila? Don't you need to get back for her?'

He shakes his head but the goofy grin remains. 'Her mum was released from the hospital at ten this morning, and her new baby brother will be out first thing so Chrissie wants a Mummy–daughter night for the last time.'

I'm not one to look a gift horse in the mouth. 'Okay, Jack, then for your benefit – and only because I worry about you driving for so long on your own – I accept your offer.'

Chapter Thirty-Three

NOW

Weymouth, Dorset

We drive straight to the shelter where the queue outside is starting to grow as hungry guests await the opening of the doors. I nod and say hi to a few of the regulars I've served here before, but most keep their distance from Jack. Even though he's dressed in jeans and a winter coat, I guess he still has that police-vibe that so many find intimidating.

Bypassing the queue, I lead Jack around the side of the former church hall and in through the rear entrance and into the kitchen, where we're greeted by the sweet smell of garlic, warmed winter vegetables, and just a hint of chilli. Barbara briefly stops stirring her pot to glance at me before smiling welcomingly and confirming Freddie is setting up the tables out front. I thank her and we continue through to the main hall, finding Freddie setting out chairs around the tables in the centre of the room.

I don't speak, but nod for Jack to help. Freddie pauses when he sees movement and looks at the two of us, but doesn't say anything.

'Jack's come to apologise,' I say to cut the tension, and Freddie's eyes switch to Jack, whose arms are in mid-flight, reaching for the next chair in the stack. He freezes and nods.

'What do you want this time?' Freddie croaks.

There is hurt in his tone, and he has a point; it does seem these days that I only come to him when I need something. I make a promise to myself that I'll pick up some shifts at the shelter next week with no ulterior motive.

'I take it you heard the news about Tina Neville?' I try, hoping to build bridges rather than leaping into the real reason we're there.

He grunts and straightens the cutlery on the table he's standing next to. 'People like that deserve everything that's coming to them. I think next time I look to help someone, I'll think twice about it.'

'I'm sorry I didn't see what she was up to sooner; it's my fault you got dragged into the search. I think we've all learned a lesson there.'

Freddie moves to the stack of chairs, which Jack has continued to lower to the floor, and begins to position them around the tables. 'Look, you've got ten minutes to ask me whatever you're here to ask, and then it's doors open and my attention will be on those who are in genuine need.'

'Thank you,' Jack whispers, looking back to me to take the lead, which is probably the smart move given their last encounter in this room. Not ideal for me, however, given what I'm about to ask Freddie to relive.

Reaching into my satchel, I extract the cutting of Peter Saltzing, Arthur Turgood, and the younger man. I rest it on the table cloth, and study Freddie's face for any kind of reaction.

'Where did you get this from?' he asks, as the breath catches in his throat.

'Do you recognise the two men in the photograph with Turgood, Freddie?'

His head snaps up to meet my gaze and the shine in his eyes tells me everything I need to know.

'You've never mentioned Reverend Peter Saltzing to me in any of the conversations we've had, but you recognise his face, don't you?'

Freddie holds my gaze but I don't know how long he'll keep the tears at bay. 'That was their answer when the first rumblings about mistreatment surfaced – the local authority, or the governing body, whoever they were. A couple of the boys complained about beatings, and the solution was to send a local vicar in to provide *pastoral care.*' He snorts with derision. 'He wasn't violent, but his motivation for being there was the same as Turgood and the others.'

He's stopped positioning the chairs, as if his body is frozen by the memories now playing out behind his eyes.

'He didn't meet with me specifically – I guess by that time I was a bit too old for his tastes – but Mike will remember him. He used to run these group prayer sessions, where the boys in his care were supposed to pray for the Holy Spirit to help set them back on the path to enlightenment.' He pauses, but maintains the ice-cold stare. 'But then he'd keep one behind afterwards for *additional spiritual guidance*. He'd say, "Down on your knees, boy, and show the Lord how willing you are to receive his spiritual direction." I never knew his full name, and when you and I discussed my time at that shithole, I didn't even remember him.'

My heart is breaking for Freddie but I have to continue. 'And do you know who this other man is with them?'

'Graham Meacham, or "Grey" to his friends, former resident at St Francis. He was a few years older than me, so we didn't tend to hang out in the same circles. He didn't complain like some of the others and he didn't seem to wear the same scars and bruises as the rest of us. One of Turgood's favourites, it was rumoured, but then he left and I used to hope it meant he'd managed to get away and start afresh somewhere.'

A tear escapes and is blotted by the dry skin of Freddie's cheek. 'I used him as a kind of inspiration, figuring if he could get out and move on, then one day maybe I could too. But then I saw him again a bit later on, and it sickened me to think that I'd wanted to be just like him. I told you about the film studios, and what we'd been *paid* to do, but I never told you about the parties. That's where I saw him. He hadn't escaped the life… Instead, he'd become one of them – a ringleader of sorts.

'It was like a private members club, where old, rich white men would come and smoke cigars and drink brandy and pass social commentary on the failings of the world, before selecting a victim to go and sodomise in a private suite. The members, you see, were asked to pre-order whatever it was they were after: young or old; black or white; boy or girl; experienced or… untouched. Graham Meacham and this guy called Terry Brown would bring two to three examples to the parties, and then the member would make his choice. I was older by then, and I guess my spotty face and hairy chin didn't appeal. I was never invited back.'

I move to hug Freddie but he holds his hands up and stops me. 'Don't pity me, Emma. Please? You must have suspected deep down that there was more I hadn't told you about that period in my life. Jack here spotted it straightaway, and you're a smarter cookie than he is, so don't pretend like this is news to you.'

He grabs hold of the back of the chair closest to him and I know already that us being here tonight has forced him to cross a line from which there may be no return.

'I am sorry, Freddie,' I mouth, but the words stick in my throat. Unlocking my phone, I open the gallery to show him the images of Faye and Cormack. 'Do you recognise either of these children, Freddie? We have reason to believe that one or both of them may have been known to Peter Saltzing.'

He stares at the phone for a long time before his breathing intensifies and the tears do break free. I look to Jack for guidance, and he nods for me to continue. I wish we hadn't come here tonight, and I know if I ask any more there really will be no way back for my and Freddie's friendship; I know how much it took for him to admit the truth to me the first time, and I am systematically pulling down all the walls he has put up around that pain in his life.

Barbara appears at the entrance to the hall and looks from Freddie to us, and then says she'll let the queue know there's going to be a slight delay.

Freddie takes a deep breath and exhales it loudly, his eyes widening and fixed on the phone. 'That night at the party,' he says quietly. 'There was a fight, um, an argument of some kind between Brown and the girl here. Her name was... um... Jewel, or Gem, or...'

'Faye?' I offer, but he shakes his head.

'No, more elemental than that… Patience? No, *Precious*, that was it. I only remember her because… well, she was the only black girl there. She kind of stood out, but she had this confidence – so self-assured for one so young. Her and Brown had this coming together, and I saw her being dragged out of the place. I didn't see exactly what happened next, but I went outside for a cigarette sometime after. The perverts were off with their selections and the rest of us were being rounded up to be shipped off back to where we'd come from. I was near these trees and I could see that castle – um, Highclere Castle – in the distance. The moon was full and it was like a giant spotlight on the place. I saw Meacham and some other fair-haired bloke with shovels and they'd already dug pretty deep. When you came here the other night and told me a body had been found… I figured it was probably her. May she rest in peace, at last. I'm sorry I didn't tell you then but I hope you understand why. And I have nothing else to say to either of you right now. I have a queue of people who need my help, and who won't judge me for a life I tried to leave behind a long time ago.'

I try to move closer to Freddie again but he turns his back on me.

'You know your way out.'

The car ride back to my flat is made in silence. Jack doesn't gloat once at the fact that he's been vindicated – not that I'd blame him if he did. How much more is there that Freddie has kept hidden from me? I thought my gentle coaxing had uncovered everything, but now it feels like we've barely scratched the surface, and yet I have a horrible feeling he won't welcome me back anytime soon.

'We should probably take a raincheck on dinner,' Jack says, as he parks up in the space outside my building. 'I don't have much of an appetite anymore.'

I nod my agreement. 'What will you do from here?'

Jack sighs. 'Terry Brown and Graham Meacham are new names to the investigation, so I guess finding them would be a good start. I don't think there was much by way of forensic evidence uncovered at the site or in the suitcase, so proving this Brown or Meacham were responsible for burying Faye is going to be a challenge. There probably isn't much evidential value in what Freddie told us either, given the passage of time, so I don't see any benefit in formalising his statement.'

'What about the photographs sent to me?'

'I'll call by your agent's office and see if she's still got the envelopes and request forensic examination of them; if we're lucky there could be a clue there somewhere. Otherwise, I don't know what else to tell you.' He stifles a yawn but I can see how much today has taken out of him too.

'It's getting late, Jack, and it's pitch black outside. Why don't you come in and crash on my sofa? You look exhausted, and driving in that condition isn't safe for you.'

'I'll be all right,' he says, yawning again. 'I'll grab an energy drink from the first petrol station I pass.'

I lift the keys out of the central tray and press the off button to kill the engine. 'I'm not taking no for an answer. Come in, get some sleep, and then you can drive back first thing. If you're lucky I might even throw in a bacon sandwich before you go.'

I'm relieved when he nods in acknowledgement and

doesn't argue. 'I meant to tell you the other day, I got stopped by one of the parents in the playground when I was dropping Mila at school and she asked for my autograph.' He chuckles gently, and the tension in the air eases fractionally. 'Turns out she's been reading your books and knows all about me apparently.'

I know how awkward those situations are and I'm inwardly cringing just thinking about it. 'What did you do?'

'What else could I do? I signed her book. Seems she'd brought it with her on the off-chance I'd be dropping Mila in, and I didn't want to disappoint. Came as a bit of a shock, to be honest, and I think I have a better understanding of why you dislike that recognition thing so much.'

'You ought to try sitting behind a table and having fan after fan approach asking for autographs and selfies, and telling me how wonderful a writer I am. If I believed half of what I'm told, my head wouldn't fit in this car.'

'And now you have a new fan in Rick... Sorry if I made things a bit awkward turning up like I did. He seems nice.'

I'm grateful it's so dark that he won't be able to see the Belisha beacon my face has transformed into. 'There's nothing going on between me and Rick; it was strictly professional.'

'Yeah, but I think he probably wants it to be a bit more than that. Honestly, I think you should give him a chance.' He pauses. 'I know you and I have this chemistry, but I don't want you putting your life on hold for me. Okay? If you like this Rick, then I think you should go for it. I only want to see you happy.'

If only he could read my mind, he'd know what would make me happy. Instead, we exit the car and head inside, and I fetch blankets and a spare towel from the airing cupboard, finding him already passed out on the sofa when I return.

Chapter Thirty-Four

THEN

Newbury, Berkshire

The leather seats in the back of Mr Brown's car were cold to the touch, and even though they'd been travelling for some time, the material still felt cool against Joanna's bare legs. She'd tried to whisper to Precious to check she was okay, but had been summarily dismissed with a finger jabbed at her lips and a sullen shake of the head. Mr Brown had always given off an uneasy vibe, but Precious's submissiveness to him alarmed Joanna more than she wanted to admit. The thump-thump-thump in her chest was all she could hear as they continued through the darkness. Thick trees lined both sides of the narrow road so even if she dared to look out of the window, she wouldn't see much beyond her reflection in the glass.

Aside from the occasional glance up at the rear-view mirror, Mr Brown did little to acknowledge their presence. By contrast, Grey hadn't stopped jabbering since they'd left the campsite, and judging from the nervous energy laced in every sentence they had to be nearing their final destination.

A large spotlight pointed at the gated entrance caught the corner of the sign as they pulled past, but Joanna didn't recognise the name Pendark. Driving past one large building after another, they finally stopped at what looked, from the outside, like a modern estate but on closer inspection was merely a fascia stuck to the front of a brick box.

'When we get inside, keep your head down and don't speak,' Precious whispered, as her door was thrust open by Grey and he helped her out. Mr Brown made no effort to open Joanna's door, so she slid along the leather and slipped through the open door.

There was no sign of Mr Brown when Joanna emerged, but she soon fell into line behind Precious and Grey as he led them not through the entrance but around the back of the building, where two men dressed head to toe in black were smoking cigarettes and talking about football. They hushed the moment they saw Grey, who nodded at each of them as he passed and went into the property.

'Ladies,' one of the doormen acknowledged as Precious and Joanna entered, but neither responded.

Grey led them to a door, unlocked it, and ushered them inside. 'Make yourselves comfortable. Precious, explain to Kylie what happens from here, and give her something to drink. The deer-in-the-headlights look isn't attractive.'

'Remember our deal, Grey,' Precious whispered back.

'Yeah, yeah, I know,' he said, closing and locking the door behind him.

The room looked more extravagant than Joanna had expected, with a rich ruby-coloured thick-pile carpet, gold-patterned wallpaper covering every wall, and a large chandelier dangling from the centre of the ceiling. A large leather chaise-longue was positioned in front of the small curtained window. The drapes too were golden, adding a sense of luxury. Beside the chaise-longue – which wasn't dissimilar to one in her grandma's house – stood a small drinks trolley with maybe a dozen flutes half-filled with a straw-coloured liquid.

Precious immediately made her way to the trolley, lifted two flutes, and passed one to Joanna. 'Drink this,' she instructed, downing hers in one.

Joanna copied her, grimacing at the bite of the bubbles on the back of her throat. It was different to the sweet wines Precious usually brought back with her from the shopping trips she would undertake while Joanna was at the studio with Grey.

'I need you to listen very carefully,' Precious said, taking the flute from Joanna's grip and replacing it with a fresh glass. 'There will be others brought in here with us soon but you and me need to stick together. When everyone's arrived, we'll be taken in to meet Mr Brown's guests. As I told you before, they'll be told that you're off-limits for tonight, but that doesn't mean they won't want to speak to you. That's fine. A bit of a chat counts for nothing. Think about it like you're speaking to a distant relative – an uncle or a grandfather – yeah?' She sighed. 'Then after a few minutes of talking, some of the others will go off with the guests, leaving us behind. I have an agreement with Grey that I'm off-limits tonight too, so I can keep an eye on you. Okay? So, when everyone else is gone, Grey will drive us back to the campsite and we can go to bed.'

Joanna tried to smile through the terror and had never been

so grateful to have Precious by her side. They didn't always get along perfectly, but Precious had sort of adopted her as a sister, and Joanna appreciated the lengths that she must have gone to in order to strike that deal with Grey.

'Thank you,' Joanna said, 'for whatever you arranged with Grey. Thank you.'

'That's what friends are for, right?' She gave her a reassuring smile. 'It's Faye, by the way.'

Joanna frowned.

'My name,' Precious continued. 'You asked me once what my real name was, and it was Faye.'

'That's a pretty name,' Joanna commented.

'Yeah, well, I'm not that girl anymore; she's long gone. It's funny, I don't remember hardly anything of my life before all this. Better that way, I think. I'd advise you to forget about any previous life too. Focus on making the most of what we've got here and now. The past is for the history books and the future is for dreamers.'

The key turned in the lock and Grey led four others in; this time, there were two lads there too. One had to be in his late teens or early twenties, head shaved so short that he looked like an army recruit. He nodded at the two of them before moving across and helping himself to two of the flutes, tipping one into the other. The other members of his party steered clear of the trolley, but squashed up on the chaise-longue.

'Who are they?' Joanna dared to whisper to Precious, not brave enough to look specifically at any of them.

Precious turned her back on the group so they wouldn't hear their conversation. 'They're like us; they work for Mr Brown's friends, but they're located elsewhere. I recognise one of the girls from a previous night, but not the other three. Best not to talk to them; Grey's instructions.'

Joanna kept her head down and her thoughts to herself as more girls were led into the room, some choosing to indulge in the Dutch courage, and others looking as terrified as Joanna felt. And before she knew it, the closed double doors were opened, and they were shown through to a much larger and even more decadent room with a roaring fire and marbled hearth at one end, half a dozen grandfather-type figures holding tumblers of brandy, and the ceiling thick with cigar smoke.

Joanna huddled close to Precious, coiling her fingers around her friend's elbow as the first of the men approached and scrutinised them like a consumer comparing fruit, before selecting one of the other girls, and leading her by the hand to his chair in one corner of the room. The next figure approached, this one with a thick, bushy beard who wouldn't have looked out of place at a Santa's grotto. He perused them all once, a sickening twinkle in his eye, eventually offering his hand to Precious, who accepted and prised Joanna's fingers from her arm in the process.

'Just talk,' Precious growled under her breath at Joanna before moving away with the man.

The next man's eyes didn't leave Joanna's as he made a beeline for her. In her periphery, Joanna saw Grey step forward, arm stretched out as if he was going to shoo the man away, but he stopped still as Mr Brown moved forward.

'Whatever the client wants,' Mr Brown sneered, before turning and smiling at the other man, beckoning him to continue with his selection. The last thing Joanna wanted was to place her hand in the man's enormous palm, but as she looked over and saw Precious nodding encouragingly, she reluctantly gave it to him and he moved her gently towards his chair.

Joanna couldn't hear what Grey and Mr Brown were arguing about because they had left the room, but through the gap in the door she could see Mr Brown was the one giving the orders, and Grey looked far from happy with what he was being told.

Chapter Thirty-Five

NOW

Weymouth, Dorset

I'm up and drinking coffee when Jack surfaces and walks into the kitchen, his shirt creased from sleep and his hair looking as though he has been dragged backwards through a bush.

'The kettle's just boiled if you want a tea or coffee?' I say, nodding towards the kettle on the side and the pots of tea and coffee beside it.

He's squinting as he rubs the sleep from his eyes, and for a moment I can't be sure if he's awake or I've caught him sleepwalking.

'Would it be all right if I take a shower?' he finally asks, stifling his yawn.

'Of course,' I say with a smile. 'I left a towel on the chair beside you. You go shower, and I'll have a coffee out here waiting for you.'

He thanks me, collects the towel, and continues through to

the small bathroom. With the door closed and locked, I slide out the postcard I'd hidden as soon as I'd heard him surface. The image of two parasols on golden sand and a tropical ocean on the horizon has me cringing with jealousy. It's been too long since I've been abroad, or on any kind of holiday really.

The postcard was on the doormat when we returned last night, and I'm touched that Rachel thought to write to me; she's always been anti-postcards, which makes this arrival all the more surprising. I remember one of our many drunken conversations when we were at university when she started on her 'postcards are a waste of time and money' rant.

'Most people only go on holiday for a week – two at most – so what's the need to write back and tell your friends how wonderful a time you're having?' she questioned. 'Holidaymakers spend ages trying to find the *perfect* card to send to that friend or relative – that's assuming they've remembered to bring everyone's addresses with them – and then have to think of something to say that is more original than *wish you were here*. Then there's the mission to find somewhere speaking English where international stamps can be purchased at extortionate prices.'

'I think it's a nice thing to do,' I argued. 'Receiving a postcard from someone you've maybe not heard from in a while is a reminder that you're still in their thoughts.'

'Send them a text message or a WhatsApp instead.'

'It's also a nice way to see parts of the world you may never have visited.'

'But most of the time the person arrives home before the damned postcard does anyway!'

Turning the card over in my hand, I laugh when I see Rachel has stuck with the usual postcard tropes. She and

Daniella are having a wonderful time; the weather is warmer than the UK; she's been pigging out on paella, and she's missing me. It's the final line in the postcard that had me hiding it beneath a pile of papers on the kitchen table when Jack stumbled through.

Have you shagged Jack yet?

I know she's only teasing, but I can't believe she had the audacity to write that on the back of a postcard – a postcard that will have been handled by at least four or five people as it moved from Spain to England, and then arrived on my doormat. I'm not saying that every person working in the postal service reads other people's postcards, but they *could* have. I dread the next time I come face-to-face with my postman, knowing he may be looking at me and wondering the same thing.

Turning the card back over to stare at the beach scene, it really could have been snapped anywhere with a warmer climate than the UK. There's nothing distinctively Spanish about it, aside from the stencilled letters advising me it is from España. What I'd give for a few days by a pool, putting everything out of my mind.

A vigorous knocking at my door snaps me back to my kitchen. Standing and straightening my dressing gown, I have a panic that the postman will be on the other side, snickering, even though I know he's already been.

Rick's face pops out from behind the bunch of flowers as I open the door. 'Morning,' he says. 'I wanted to apologise for taking off yesterday. As soon as I was back on the motorway, I hated myself for not sticking around. I was actually worried this morning that you wouldn't be here and I'd never forgive myself if I didn't get to see you again. Here, these are for you,' he adds, thrusting the flowers towards me.

They are white lilies – my favourites. 'You have nothing to be sorry for,' I say, hiding my red cheeks behind the cellophane. 'I told you to go, and I shouldn't have kept you for as long as I did. These really weren't necessary, but they are beautiful, so thank you.'

'I also felt bad about how we left things. It wasn't right for me to put that kind of pressure on you. You barely know me, but through your writing I feel like I do know you, and I'm in no position to be making demands. Of course I should expect there to be competition for you; you're the great Emma Hunter. I'm only surprised there isn't a queue of suitors ahead of me here today.'

If any more blood rushes to my face, it may explode. I'm trying to find the words to respond when Rick touches my arm and saves me the effort.

'There was another reason I stopped by: I thought you might like to hear the latest about the Neville family.'

Despite my involvement with the Nevilles still being so recent, it feels like days since I've thought about them. 'There's news?'

He nods, with a look of sadness that I don't expect from someone who always seems to be smiling. 'They interviewed Jo-Jo yesterday and asked her about how she ended up at her auntie's house, and she told the specialists that her mummy drove her there and told her she'd be staying with her aunt for a few days, and that when the holiday was over, she'd have to pretend she hadn't been there so that her aunt didn't get in trouble. When confronted with Jo-Jo's admission, Tina admitted the whole thing, and was charged late last night.

She's been bailed pending a court appearance, and Jo-Jo will remain in the care of social services until a decision can be made about her long-term wellbeing.'

I now understand the melancholy in Rick's expression. That poor girl. It isn't her fault that her mother saw an opportunity to use her for ill means, and yet her family home – and life as she knows it – will probably never be the same again. Even if Tina avoids jail time and manages to retain custody of Jo-Jo, I'd be surprised if Trey and his own daughter will stand by them.

'Oh, I see. That poor girl.'

'Tina's shown genuine remorse by all accounts, but it's the world we live in now. This obsession with celebrities, and the money offered for scandal, has the world out of shape.'

Given his own desire to have my signature on his book, his statement seems at odds with his own actions, but before I can challenge him on it, something over my shoulder has caught his attention, and as I turn it is all I can do to avert my gaze. Standing in the doorway of the kitchen is Jack, towel wrapped tightly around his waist, drinking from my mug of tea. His hair is wet from the shower and the light catches on his perfectly formed abs. He doesn't look ashamed to have stepped out at the most inconvenient time.

He moves through to the living room with a casual nod towards Rick, and a cheerful 'Morning.'

'It isn't what you think,' I quickly say, turning back to face Rick. 'Jack drove me back from Hayling Island and it was late so I said he could crash on the sofa. That's all. I swear, we didn't—'

'It's okay, Emma, you don't need to apologise. I told you yesterday that I don't want to get in the way if there's something going on between you and Jack. I get it; you've known him longer and I'm okay with it.'

'There's nothing going on between me and Jack, I swear. We're just friends.'

Rick looks away for the briefest moment, clearing his vision and fixing me with a stare. 'I just want to know I'm not wasting my time pursuing something with you. I like you, Emma. You're funny, smart, and more beautiful than you realise. I appreciate you might not be looking for a relationship, but I'd like the opportunity to get to know you better, and for you to know more about me. For context, I don't bring flowers and call by to every house on my beat, and quite frankly your neighbours are probably growing jealous of all the attention you're receiving.' His broad grin is back, and I can't help smiling back at him.

I'm not used to men falling at my feet, and am still using the flowers to hide my utter embarrassment. The truth is, I could see myself falling for a guy like Rick: he's kind, takes care of his family, and has a job that serves others. If Jack wasn't on the scene, I wouldn't think twice about seeing how things could develop with Rick, but life is never that easy, is it? I don't want to string Rick along if I'm always going to be wondering if I should have waited for Jack, but at the same time, Jack has told me not to wait, and to move on, so isn't that what I should do? What would Rachel tell me to do if she was here? I shudder as I picture *exactly* what she'd tell me to do.

'I think you're a nice guy, Rick, and I would like to get to know you better too,' I say, the words sticking in my throat. 'As I said, there's nothing between me and Jack – we're just friends.'

'So,' he begins, stretching the vowel out, 'dinner tonight?

Dorchester has some cracking restaurants. Italian, Indian, Thai? Whatever you fancy. I could pick you up after my shift, drive you to Mum's if that's still okay, and then on to dinner. I promise I'll have you home before midnight. What do you say?'

I hear Jack's words in my head: *If you like this Rick, then I think you should go for it.*

'Dinner sounds lovely, and yes, I'm happy to say hello to your mum and sign any other books that she wants.'

Rick looks like the cat that got the cream. 'Perfect. I'll meet you here at seven then, if that's okay? Gives me time to shower at the station before I come over.'

'Okay,' I say, and close the door as he moves away.

I let out a deep breath and return to the kitchen, hoping Jack didn't catch the end of our conversation, but unable to keep the spring out of my step.

I've barely started the kettle again when my phone is ringing on the table. As soon as I see Maddie's name on the screen, my pulse quickens at what this could mean. Answering the call, the trepidation clings to every sentence as I desperately try to sound casual.

'Hi, Maddie, how are you?'

'I just got to the office, Emma, and there's another A4 brown envelope here with your name on it. I'm certain it's the same handwriting on the front. Should I open it?'

The breath catches in my throat. 'No, just leave it as is. We're on our way.'

Chapter Thirty-Six

NOW

Blackfriars, London

As soon as I told Jack about the new envelope, he said we should leave straightaway, and we only stopped to grab a sandwich for breakfast at a petrol station when Jack needed to fill up. If we are to have any chance of catching the person sending these pictures to me, we need the evidence preserved. It's bad enough that a postman and Maddie will have handled the envelope, but by leaving it sealed, it may be possible for the flap of the envelope to be examined for DNA, assuming the sender licked it closed. At least if the envelope remains sealed, any fingerprints or DNA attached to the photograph itself should be preserved.

Jack hasn't mentioned Rick's appearance at my door, and I suppose if he meant what he said last night, then maybe he feels nothing needs to be said about it. I always knew that Mila would come first – as she rightly should – in his life, and actually, our working relationship will probably be stronger without the romantic element hanging over us like Damocles' sword.

The silence of the car journey gives me time to once again reflect on who is behind the sending of these photographs to me. My conversation with DC Knox in Manchester effectively rules out a member of Faye's family, and there is still no evidence to suggest that Faye and Cormack were taken by the same people, even if that is what the voice in the back of my head is screaming. And if it isn't Faye's family, the possibility that the pictures are from Cormack's family also feels unlikely. So who does that leave? The person who did take them? But why would he – and yes, I am assuming it's a *he* responsible – want to highlight what's been going on under everyone's noses? Is it for some kind of twisted fame like Tina Neville? If so, why target me and not just contact the police directly? It just doesn't add up in my head.

Could there be an unwitting witness out there who was somehow embroiled in these abductions and murders? Again, I'm not convinced. If I'd witnessed someone being killed and secretly buried, I'd go straight to the police, rather than anonymously sending cryptic messages to a writer who may or may not receive them. There's just too many elements of this that don't make sense, and it's giving me a headache. I crack the window on the car as we pass through Richmond and Kew, the Thames already snaking beside us, its mixture of pollution and hidden secrets as cloudy as my head.

If it isn't a perpetrator or a witness, then I'm at a loss. An amateur sleuth trying to flag these unconnected cases? A frustrated police officer finding no traction with their bosses? Usually I get a sixth sense about what's happening. If presented with enough facts, my brain is good at deductive reasoning, and that was how I saw through Arthur Turgood's lies when I first met and interviewed him. This was back when I only had Freddie's word, and at the time Turgood was arrogant enough to think I wouldn't keep digging for the truth. It was only when I found corroborative witnesses that he clammed up and refused to speak to me. It was the final nail in his coffin as far as I was concerned, but this time I have no such instinct as to who is responsible.

Once parked, we hurry along the road to Maddie's office, finding her in reception ready to sign us in through the security gate. Maddie's agency occupies half of floor 6 in this ten-storey building; the other floors are occupied by a variety of other small businesses – including two other literary agencies – who can't afford to let an entire building in London without support. Usually the lobby takes my breath away, but today the overhead lights reflecting off the shiny marble walls make me feel as small as a pea. I've always been in control of how I investigate a situation. Be it Freddie's story about St Francis, the Cassie Hilliard abduction, or even the Sally Curtis disappearance, it's always been me asking the questions and hunting for clues. This is different though; I feel like a puppet being made to dance a jig at someone else's whim.

She leads us through the barrier, up in the lift, and into her office, where she is careful to make sure the door is closed before removing the envelope from a locked drawer; it seems the importance of what is in her hands hasn't been lost on Maddie either.

Jack snaps on plastic gloves and delicately takes it from her, placing it into the evidence bag he brought with him from the boot of his car.

'Don't you want to know what's inside?' Maddie asks, ever

the curious creature.

I look at Jack, also somewhat surprised he is so prepared to accept that the envelope will contain the image of another missing child.

'It's safer to open it in protected surroundings,' he says, 'to prevent potential cross-contamination.'

Maddie bites down on her finger, pulling an awkward grimace that speaks volumes to me, even if it is somewhat lost on Jack.

'Maddie, what did you do?' I ask, reserving my judgement.

Her face almost folds in on itself as she shuffles awkwardly from foot to foot. 'Okay, listen, I didn't realise what I had at first. I'd just got in from my run and I fell into my chair as I always do, and started opening my post. I've been waiting for one of my other clients to forward me some work, and… I'm sorry, I opened it without even looking at who it was addressed to.'

Jack removes the envelope from the evidence bag. The slit in the top is more obvious now. The ceramic letter opener that was used for the deed shimmers on the desk.

Jack glowers but doesn't say anything, I guess realising that taking it to the lab for forensic examination is less pressing now. Tipping the envelope upside down, he catches the image as it slides through the paper lips. I'm relieved that he's the one who caught it as my palms are clammy in anticipation. I'm dreading the prospect that he's about to flip over an image of Anna, along with an address. I've already been through the shock of the prospect of her being dead, only to be corrected; I'm not ready to about turn again just yet.

I rest my forearm on the filing cabinet beside me, leaning into it for strength, as Jack flips the image over. For the briefest of seconds I see Anna's face staring back at me, and my legs almost give way, until I blink and realise that it isn't her. In fact, it isn't a picture of a child at all. Instead, what Jack appears to be holding is a black and white picture of three men sharing some kind of joke, judging by the open-mouthed grins.

Jack holds the image in one hand while examining the envelope for any other documents and, when finding none, returns the envelope to the evidence bag.

'Can you flick on the light?' he says to Maddie, who is closest to the switch of the desk lamp.

She obliges, and Jack holds the image beneath the glare, examining all the surfaces for signs for prints, but even I can see there aren't any. Whoever put the photograph in the envelope was careful not to reveal their identity. Does that suggest some wrongdoing, because they're worried about being caught? Should we be looking for a co-conspirator rather than an unwitting witness?

Jack flips to the reverse of the image, but again there is no obvious sign of fingerprints, though I'm no expert. What is noticeable is the lack of any dates or imprinted postcodes.

'Is this all that was in the envelope?' Jack asks Maddie, scrutinising the front image again.

'I swear. I opened the envelope and peered inside, and as soon as I saw the picture I checked the front of the envelope and stopped what I was doing. I didn't touch the picture. I phoned Emma straightaway and then locked it in that drawer. I'm sorry if I've ruined anything.'

Jack doesn't acknowledge the apology, instead straightening and holding up the picture for me to see. Now that it is straight and the desk lamp beam isn't reflecting from the surface, I can see the three men more clearly.

My brow furrows as I immediately recognise the figure on the far left of the image. 'That's Arthur Turgood,' I say.

Jack nods. 'Anyone else you recognise?'

I concentrate on the figure in the middle, and I'll admit there's something vaguely familiar about him, but I can't place where I've seen those capped teeth and bushy grey moustache before. I gulp when I study the third figure.

'Is that Peter Saltzing?'

'Looks like him,' Jack says, still looking at me rather than the image. He suddenly turns to Maddie. 'Would you mind leaving us to it for a minute?'

She doesn't argue, quickly standing and vacating her office, maybe less keen to hear the conversation, and still feeling guilty about jeopardising the evidence.

'Turgood looks younger than when I met him,' I say once she's left, daring to take a step closer to the picture. And certainly not as vulnerable as he made himself look in court.' I focus on Saltzing next. 'He looks just like he did in the newspaper cuttings we took from the vicarage yesterday, but this isn't news; we know he had dealings with the St Francis Home. Freddie confirmed as much last night. Why would this person send us this picture?'

Jack remains silent, allowing the connection to fire in my mind.

My eyes widen at the realisation. 'Are they suggesting Saltzing and Turgood were involved in the abductions?' A second connection fires. 'Or are they saying that Turgood and Saltzing had something to do with the murders? Cormack is potentially buried in Jean-Claude Ribery's grave, a service which Saltzing oversaw, but there's been nothing to link him with Pendark thus far.'

'But we know Turgood was at Pendark from what Freddie told us. Maybe all this picture is telling us is that Turgood was involved in what happened to Faye, and that Saltzing was complicit in Cormack's burial, but I think it's more than that. Do you recognise the man in the middle?'

I look at his moustache again, but shake my head. 'Should I? It's only when I look directly at Jack that I see the blood has drained from his face.

'Unless he has a twin brother, that's Sir Anthony Tomlinson, the former Commissioner of the Metropolitan Police. The same man my DCI has been teeing off with.'

The implication hits me like a steam train. 'Oh my God.'

Jack nods. 'I'd bet my house on it being him, but before we jump to conclusions, it's just a picture of three men laughing. Right? We don't know where it was taken, who by, or whether it's even genuine. There's so much people can do with photograph manipulation on apps and software these days.'

I know he's right to be cautious, but if I don't say it, nobody will. 'But what if it *is* genuine?'

'There could be any number of reasons the former commissioner would come into contact with two prominent figures, right? I mean, we don't know when the photograph was taken but all three look much younger, so we must be talking twenty to thirty years ago at best guess. Back then, Peter Saltzing was being celebrated for all his charitable work to support places like the St Francis Home, and there was no public outcry about Turgood and the home until you came along. It could be a perfectly innocent meeting – a fundraiser maybe, or a political event, I don't know. We need to tread *very* carefully, before we start accusing Sir Anthony Tomlinson of collusion with known predators.'

When I think back to Freddie's initial dealings with the police when he spoke about the abuse he suffered, and how no formal investigation into Turgood and the home ever materialised, this makes sense. I too know better than to muddy a person's name without definitive proof, but something in my head has finally clicked, and even if Jack isn't willing to say the words just yet, today's picture screams conspiracy.

I take a deep breath, and slowly exhale. 'Where do we go from here?'

Jack slides the picture back into the envelope and seals the evidence bag before snapping off his gloves. 'I don't know. We have to be careful but I'm not prepared to ignore it.'

'Can you take it to your boss at the NCA? If he knows Tomlinson maybe he can shed some light on why he might have been pictured with the others.'

Jack shakes his head. 'And what if Dainton is working with Tomlinson to influence the investigation? The reason I recognise Tomlinson is that Dainton has a photograph hanging on his wall from when the commissioner presented him with a bravery commendation. I'm not implying Dainton wouldn't take our questions seriously, but I'd rather we secure something more concrete before speaking to him.'

'We can't do this on our own, Jack, but if he *is* involved, how do we know who we can trust?'

'I know, I know,' he concedes, the blood only now just starting to return to his face. 'I'm not suggesting we go it alone. There is someone I think we should speak to. Someone I trust implicitly with this kind of information. Come on, if we leave now, we should be there within the hour.'

Chapter Thirty-Seven

THEN

Newbury, Berkshire

'So, what sorts of things are you into?' the old man asked, as he gently rocked Joanna on his knee. There was something familiar about the way he spoke, but based on a voice she'd heard on one of her mum's soap operas. Was it *Emmerdale* or *Coronation Street*? Certainly not local to her.

His thick white beard brushed against the top of her arm as he jostled her up and down much as her own grandfather had done with her when she was a toddler. Was this man someone's grandfather as well? The end of the cigar glowed orange with every intake, and although he seemed to be doing his best to blow the smoke away from her, the room was filling quickly with smoke and it was making her eyes water and throat burn.

She looked across the room where Precious was smiling and laughing with the man she was with, occasionally brushing his cheek with her hand or thumb in an affectionate way she'd seen her parents do when they thought she wasn't looking. At least *he* looked more normal. Less old and rugged than the man who was staring at Joanna, awaiting her answer. Precious glanced over and nodded encouragingly again, urging Joanna just to speak to him.

A bit of a chat counts for nothing, Precious had said.

'Do you like ponies?' he asked when she still hadn't responded. 'I keep horses at my stables. Such beautiful creatures, don't you think?'

'I-I-I like ponies,' Joanna replied, turning in to face him, mirroring Precious's posture and stroking his beard. It was like a wiry old brush her dad used to clean the griddle of the barbeque and she quickly withdrew her hand.

'You're very beautiful too,' he said next, leaning closer so that only she could hear.

She didn't know how to respond. 'Thank you,' she settled for.

'What's your name, lovely?'

'J-Jo,' she began, before stopping herself. 'Kylie. My name's Kylie.'

'That's a beautiful name. You look like a Kylie. Pretty little Kylie. Like the pop star. Do you want to know my name?'

She didn't care what his name was but nodded as enthusiastically as she could muster.

'I'm Bill. That's what my friends call me. You can call me Bill too, because we're friends now, aren't we?'

She looked back to Precious who was talking non-stop while her beguiled client listened, eyes wide and mouth shut. The room was uncomfortably warm, the wood crackling in the fireplace as it burned bright and hot.

'If you'd like, you could come and ride one of the horses at my stables. Would you like that, Kylie?'

Her mum had taken her and her sister to the beach to ride the donkeys there sometimes, and she'd always quite enjoyed it, but as much as she liked the idea of riding a horse, she didn't yet trust Bill.

'That's what friends do,' he continued. 'We look after our friends and do nice things for them. Would you like to come and visit my stables? They're not too far from here.'

A thought fired in the back of her head: if he was offering her a way out of this place, and could get her away from Grey and Mr Brown, wasn't that a chance worth taking? She didn't have her pot of savings, but if he could take her away she might be able to get a message to Precious, who could join them later and bring the money with her. If they could get away from Mr Brown and Grey, Joanna was certain they'd be able to start afresh on their own. Precious had certainly proved herself resourceful.

'Can we go now?' Joanna asked him.

'Now? Oh no, it's a bit late, sweetheart. No, not tonight, but if we *are* friends then I can definitely have a word with Mr Brown and see if you could come and stay at my farm for a bit. Would you like that? You'd be able to go riding every day, and it would just be the two of us. We could get to know each other better.'

In that moment, she saw through his lies, but nodded in compliance. He would tell her anything right now if it kept her from objecting to whatever he had on his mind. He rested a heavy, warm hand on her leg, and continued to bounce her jovially. Why were none of the other girls and boys complaining about this situation? She knew enough about the world to understand that old men didn't date or marry children. Precious had alluded to what would happen when the clients moved to different rooms, but had been adamant that she would keep Joanna safe. She didn't feel safe in this moment and desperately wanted to be anywhere but here.

A gong sounding from somewhere behind her made Joanna turn round. Mr Brown had returned to the room and was addressing his guests in an overly theatrical manner. 'Gentlemen, it is time for you to make your choices and to retire to more comfortable surroundings. Everything you have asked for has been provided in your allotted room and each has been soundproofed. If you require anything further, you are only to sound the bell in the room and we will accommodate as best we can.'

Excited chatter and murmuring grew across the room as the men helped their prizes down from their laps and escorted them one by one towards Mr Brown, who complimented them on their choices.

Bill lifted Joanna down and took her hand, walking her towards the front of the room. She searched frantically for Precious but it was so hard to see past the wide girths blocking her view. She didn't know exactly where they were going or what Bill had planned, but knew deep down it wasn't something she wanted. Precious was still talking to her client, and couldn't see Joanna's pleading eyes.

'And who have you chosen tonight, Bill?' Mr Brown's voice echoed above her head. 'Oh, I see you've picked our latest arrival Kylie. An excellent selection as always. Have fun.'

Bill began to move her past Mr Brown, who had already started speaking to the next client. Joanna tried to pull her hand free of Bill's grip but he was so strong that all she managed to do was slow them down. She tried digging her heels into the carpet but she wasn't used to walking in them properly, and went over on her ankle, yelping with pain. The noise caught the attention of all those still in the room, including Precious who rushed to her side.

'Please don't let him take me,' Joanna whispered urgently to her friend. 'I don't want to go with him.'

Precious looked up at the hand still clutching Joanna's wrist, only now realising what was going on. The venom filled her eyes and she leapt up, aiming her glare at Grey who was cowering just behind Mr Brown.

'What the hell, Grey? We had a deal! Kylie is off limits for tonight.'

The outburst had Mr Brown looking from Precious to Grey who was squirming, his mouth opening and closing but no words emerging.

'You said me and Kylie didn't have to go with anyone tonight,' Precious continued, making no effort to control her anger. 'She's only eleven, for heaven's sake!'

'What's going on here, Brown?' Bill spoke up, still holding onto Joanna's wrist. 'I thought you said this was okay?'

Mr Brown's cheeks reddened. 'It is okay, Bill. Just a *misunderstanding* here, I think. Come on, Kylie, on your feet, there's a good girl. Let's not disappoint Bill here.'

Precious folded her arms and glared at Mr Brown, finding an inner strength that Joanna could only envy. 'Over my dead body. We had a deal; she comes here tonight as a taster only. She's not going anywhere. And neither am I.'

Grey appeared from behind Mr Brown and stooped over to quietly address Precious. 'Stop playing silly beggars and get her on her feet, yeah? You're embarrassing Mr Brown in front of his friends.'

'I don't give a shit!' Precious snapped back. 'We had a deal! She isn't ready for all this. It was a mistake to bring her tonight.'

Grey looked down at Joanna, and she could see the longing in his eyes – stuck between a rock and a hard place.

'The deal's off. If Mr Brown says Kylie's available, then that's how it is. She goes with Bill, or there's going to be trouble for all of us. Listen, I'll make it up to both of you, okay? Double wage tonight if you stop all this nonsense and just go along with it. What do you say?'

For a moment Joanna thought Precious was actually considering the offer, but then she shook her head firmly. 'She's going nowhere with this… this filthy pervert.'

Bill discarded Joanna's wrist, his face a deep shade of beetroot, and waved a finger of warning in Mr Brown's face. 'Just what bloody shambles are you running here, Brown? Either control your girls or you and I are going to have problems with that planning application of yours. Am I clear?'

'I *will* handle this, Bill, and I'm sorry for the trouble. Can I suggest you make a different selection for tonight – on the house – and I'll make sure we don't have a repeat of this next time? I truly am sorry.'

Bill looked at the unchosen ones at the back of the room, before pointing for two to step forward for closer scrutiny. Joanna watched as he stalked around the two of them, and then back to her, clearly annoyed by the situation.

'Why don't you take both?' Mr Brown said, all smarmy smiles now. 'On the house. Consider it a gesture of my goodwill to redress the situation.'

Bill chewed hard on his cigar before nodding and clicking his fingers for the two girls – both younger than Precious, judging by their underdeveloped physiques – to follow him to his room.

The man whom Precious had been sat with had also selected an alternative girl, and with the room cleared, Mr Brown closed the doors before turning his attention back to the three of them.

'Bill's choices are coming out of your cut,' he growled at Grey. 'Never have I been so humiliated. And as for you,' he said, glowering and turning to face Precious before slapping her hard across the face, 'it seems someone is going to have to teach you some goddamned manners.'

The sound of the slap echoed off the walls of the room, but she remained on her feet, tears splashing against her cheeks and made no sound of protest.

Grey stooped and lifted Joanna, holding her firmly though she tried to kick and butt her way free. Her efforts were in vain and he carried her out of the room. She screamed for Precious, who nervously watched as Brown unfastened his belt and closed the door to block Joanna's view.

Chapter Thirty-Eight

NOW

Uxbridge, London

It feels so weird being back where it all began. Uxbridge Police Station hasn't changed much in the eight months since Jack and I last worked missing children cases. For all of our best intentions to reunite parents with their lost ones, Jemima Hooper was the only new victim we could tie to the videos found on Arthur Turgood's hard drive. Her body had been dumped in woods in Tamworth years earlier, so we didn't even manage to reunite her with her family. Instead we broke her parents' hearts by informing them of what she'd been subjected to after her abduction. Not exactly the worthy achievement we'd aimed for.

All that seems so long ago now though, and I think I'd sooner be back in that time than where we are now. Everything we've learned since we first stumbled upon Turgood's hard drive suggests there is a wider paedophile ring that has been taking these children and subjecting them to various horrors.

Aurélie Lebrun is another who still carries the scars of her time with such a monster, and she too has spoken of the parties that Freddie told us about. 'Party' feels like such an inappropriate word to describe an evening where dirty old men degrade and violate children; maybe 'cattle market' would be more appropriate, but then that would do a disservice to the agriculture industry. There are no words to properly describe what these people have done other than *vile* and *evil*, and even those don't feel adequate.

Jack takes a deep breath as he gets the words straight in his head, before knocking on the large ply door.

'Come in,' the voice booms from within the office, and Jack holds the door open for me to enter first and take one of the seats across from Detective Chief Superintendent Jagtar Rawani. His gaze remains fixed on the laptop screen before him, and it's only when Jack has closed the door and is seated beside me that he looks up to the two of us.

'Miss Hunter, Jack didn't tell me you were tagging along too. You look well.'

Although DCS Rawani can often cut an unassuming figure, I know he doesn't suffer fools lightly and that this comment is a formality rather than a genuine concern for my wellbeing. I could tell him of the challenging week I've had, but I already know that he has witnessed and experienced far worse situations in his twenty-plus years in uniform. The room is decidedly warm for the time of year, even though the only window is wide open.

'Thank you,' I reply. 'How are you?'

He narrows his eyes as his mind works a hundred calculations to determine the potential consequences of revealing anything meaningful about himself. 'Well.'

'And how is Mrs Rawani?' I don't know why I've asked that as I've never met the woman, and he's never spoken of her to me, but the picture of the two of them on their wedding day has pride of place on the corner of his desk.

'We are both well, thank you.' He turns to Jack, the limited pleasantries now complete as far as he is concerned. 'What is so urgent that I had to postpone lunch with the mayor?'

Jack shuffles uncomfortably in his chair, as if the cushion is packed with pins. 'Well, sir, I don't know quite where to begin.'

I cringe inwardly. It's not a good start. Rawani despises indirectness, and I can see we are already losing his attention.

'There's something I need to escalate,' Jack continues, still wriggling, 'and I didn't know who to speak to, or how to…'

Rawani's eyes have returned to the laptop screen and we are probably only seconds away from being ejected from the room.

'We've uncovered a sinister ring of paedophiles and we believe former Met Police Commissioner Anthony Tomlinson is involved,' I come out with hurriedly, refusing to meet Jack's disapproving glare.

Rawani slowly closes the laptop and looks straight at me. 'I'm sorry, but I'm going to need you to repeat that, Miss Hunter.'

'We – Jack and I – believe the ring of individuals who abduct children and force them into the sex industry *does* exist. It all ties back to the videos recovered from Arthur Turgood's hard drive following his arrest three years ago. You'll recall Jack discovered a video featuring my missing sister, and that we later also identified Jemima Hooper on a second video.'

Rawani makes no move to acknowledge what we have said, remaining emotionless behind the desk, but listening to every word. His navy turban is wound tightly, but despite the warmth of the room there isn't any sign of perspiration on his face.

'In the last week I have been sent photographs of two missing children – Faye McKenna and Cormack Fitzpatrick – who have been missing since 1998 and 1996 respectively. Faye's remains were recovered from the site that was the Pendark Film Studios and which is now under development, and we believe Cormack is buried in another man's grave in Hayling Island, Hampshire. Today I received a photograph of the two main suspects in those murders, laughing with the former Metropolitan Police Commissioner. Jack?'

Rawani's gaze moves from me to Jack, but still he doesn't speak.

Jack lifts the evidence bag onto the desk but keeps it sealed. 'She's right, sir. I have the photograph of Sir Anthony and the two suspects in here. For context, there is nothing within the photograph to imply that Sir Anthony has any awareness of who the two men are, or what they were involved in. Furthermore, Sir Anthony's name has not come up in our investigation at any point before today.'

Rawani is giving nothing away as to how he feels about this claim, and I sense he would be an astute poker player. 'I know you better than to assume you've jumped to such a conclusion based purely on his presence in this photograph.' He is looking straight at me when he says this.

'It's not so much him being in the photograph,' I begin, uncertain of quite how to describe the feeling in my gut. 'It's more about *who* sent the picture.'

He remains silent.

'The photograph of Faye McKenna arrived on Friday, right

after remains were discovered in a suitcase in Newbury. The picture of Cormack arrived yesterday and included the imprint of a postcode, which led us to Hayling Island, and a particular grave. So, two photographs, and two dead bodies—'

'*Potentially* two dead bodies,' Jack interjects. 'We don't know for certain that Cormack is buried in that grave. The bunch of flowers is hardly conclusive.'

I don't like that Jack is undermining our assertion that Tomlinson is involved; I'm sure Rawani is capable of debunking the theory without Jack's help. I try to ignore his doubts because I know he's only playing devil's advocate.

'We know that Turgood spent time at Pendark Film Studios from Freddie Mitchell's testimony, and we know that Peter Saltzing had dealings with Turgood at the St Francis Home from the newspaper cuttings we found, and he oversaw the burial of Jean-Claude Ribery in Hayling Island. Whoever sent the pictures of Faye and Cormack wants me to follow this road, and this latest photograph leads us to Tomlinson. I'm not saying it's enough to arrest him, nor to even present our findings to the squad that handles police corruption, but I do think it warrants further investigation.'

Rawani sits back in his chair, his eyes moving so quickly it's almost imperceptible. 'You have nothing else?'

I look to Jack, hoping he can talk in a language that will help Rawani understand that we both feel this is right in our guts, even if we have nothing tangible to support it, but he remains silent.

'An accusation like that, with nothing to support it, will mean dismissal, Jack, do you understand that? And for you, Miss Hunter, you'd probably spend the next decade in civil court for libel. The ramifications would be enormous.' He pauses again, before turning to Jack. 'Why did you bring this to me? Why not take it to your boss at the NCA? Harry Dainton is heading up your investigation, is he not?'

'He's good friends with Sir Anthony, sir. They were playing golf together only yesterday. I thought it best to wait until we have something more solid before speaking to him.'

Rawani doesn't look impressed. 'And what did you think I would do about it?'

Jack opens his mouth to speak before thinking better of it.

'We need help,' I speak up. 'This is bigger than Jack and me, but we don't know who to trust and how to approach something like this. We came to you because you aren't part of any boys' club or masonic lodge. You believe in doing things by the book, and I imagine you've seen enough examples of internal corruption to know the best path to steer us towards. We need someone we can trust.'

I don't think Rawani is one who bends to flattery, but I mean every word.

He stands and tucks the chair beneath his desk. 'I have another meeting across town that I need to attend. Tell me something: aside from this Faye McKenna's remains being discovered in Newbury, do you have anything else to link her to what was going on there at the site?'

Jack and I look at each other before simultaneously shrugging.

Rawani straightens his tie. 'If you could tie Faye and Cormack to the videos found on Turgood's drive, that would put you a step closer to linking their deaths to this potential ring or syndicate, or however you want to refer to it.'

'We could have the photos you were sent compared to the video footage,' Jack says to me.

Rawani picks up a briefcase from behind his desk. 'Do that and then meet me back here at one o'clock.'

He opens the door and holds it until we realise it is our cue to leave. Locking the door, Rawani moves around us without another word, and to any casual observer it would be as if he didn't even know we were here. Jack directs me along the narrow corridor before diving into a small kitchen room, closing the door behind him.

'Have you still got the images on your phone?'

I nod and unlock the screen to show him.

'Good. Can you forward those to me? We'll go to my office in Vauxhall and have the pictures checked against what was taken from the videos.'

'But won't that take days rather than hours?'

Jack shakes his head. 'The team examining the footage have captured cut-outs of every face for quicker comparison. They can now run any picture against the selection in a matter of minutes. We'll know one way or another before the end of today.'

Chapter Thirty-Nine

NOW

Uxbridge, London

'Why didn't you back me in there?' I ask Jack once we're in his car and underway.

He lowers the volume of the stereo. 'What do you mean?'

'With Rawani… I thought we were on the same page regarding Tomlinson's involvement, but as soon as we got in there, you started backtracking.'

'That's not what I was doing. I was being pragmatic and keeping my personal feelings out of it. You don't know the DCS like I do. He isn't one for gut instincts and sixth sense. For him, it's black or it's white, and there is no middle ground. If we actually had anything tantamount to evidence against Tomlinson, he would have sanctioned the arrest warrant himself.'

I lower my window for air. 'I wish you'd warned me that was the stance you were going to take. It felt like I'd imagined our discussion in Maddie's office.'

Out of the corner of my eye, I see his head turn towards me. 'I'm sorry if that's the way I made you feel; it certainly wasn't my intention.'

I keep my eyes fixed on the window so he won't see the tension in my face. 'So where do you really stand on the Tomlinson situation? Is he involved? What does *your* intuition tell you?'

Jack's head turns back to the road, but he is quiet for several seconds before replying. 'Ever since I read Freddie's story in *Monsters Under the Bed*, I've suspected collusion at some level. Those kinds of accusations levied at a children's home don't disappear without pressure from somewhere. It's not like it was in the 60s when enough money could silence even the loudest critic. Freddie's original claims were made in the 90s when the world was more switched on to the kind of abuses that could occur in certain areas of social care. For Freddie's and the other boys' claims not to be pursued would have taken a lot of effort. I suppose I figured at some point we would stumble across some relatively senior figure manipulating things behind the scenes. I hoped we wouldn't, and that I'd be mistaken, but it seems not. You want to know whether I think Tomlinson is guilty. My answer is that I can't say without evidence. If you're asking if I think he *could* be involved somehow, then absolutely.'

I try not to show my relief that Jack's thoughts mirror my own. I still remember some of the negative attention I received after *Monsters* was first published. Even now, the likes of Zoe Cavendish see me as someone trying to muddy the good name of law enforcement when it simply isn't the case. If there are a few bad apples, then I'm duty-bound to find and remove them wherever they are.

The offices of the National Crime Agency in Vauxhall are fancier than I was anticipating, with tall glass windows marking the public entrance and a taller red-brick building sprouting from the back, plus a secured gated entrance. Jack drops me by the entrance and tells me he'll come through and sign me in once he's parked his car. He appears at the door a few minutes later and after explaining who I am to the officer on the front desk, I'm given a visitor's lanyard and allowed through.

The freshly painted walls and open-plan office space make it feel more like a contact centre than a centre investigating some of the most serious and violent crimes in the country.

'The team dealing with missing persons overall is based in Hook in Hampshire,' Jack explains as we take the lift up to the fourth floor. 'I have a video call with them most mornings to review progress in the investigation. The videos retrieved from Turgood's hard drive are here, but as I explained, they have been carefully reviewed and individual faces of the victims have been captured to allow for facial recognition. It's been painstakingly slow but the database is virtually complete, and once it is we should be able to run the faces of any missing children against the database and find matches.'

My phone vibrates as I receive a text message from Rick asking if I've decided where we should go for dinner tonight. It had totally slipped my mind and I don't now know whether I'll be back in Weymouth by seven. I don't want to mess him about, but I know he'll see me cancelling the date as exactly that.

'Trouble?' Jack asks, clearly noticing my furrowed brow.

'No, nothing to worry about,' I reply, quickly typing a response that I'll let him know later.

The lift doors part and we exit into another open-plan office, but this time with dividers separating some of the desks. There are only a handful of people on the floor and Jack nods at one or two as we arrive at his desk on the far side of the room. A photograph of Mila has been stuck to the bottom of his monitor with Sellotape.

'Emma Hunter, this is Jasminda Kaur, one of the smartest women I've ever met, and this is Geoff Macaulay who is the man who helped…' He pauses, choosing his words carefully. 'Geoff was the one who found your sister's face on the video.'

I shake both their hands in acknowledgement, but neither stand, quickly returning their attention to their monitors. If they've recognised me neither lets on, and it's a relief.

'Actually, Geoff,' Jack continues, 'Emma has a couple of faces she'd like running against the database you developed. We believe the pictures were taken a couple of years after the two went missing so facially there would be a better chance of finding a match. I've emailed them to the team account, if you could check for us?'

Geoff nods without speaking.

'The reason we've not yet had much success with matching faces with missing children so far is either the angle of the captured frame won't allow for comparison, or the face is older than what we hold on file for the missing child,' Jack explains. 'We're experimenting with manually aging the photos we do have to see if better comparisons can be made.'

'Found them,' Geoff says, eyes still fixed to his screen.

'What? Already?' I ask, surprised at the speed with which the match was made.

'The girl is an 86.5 per cent match to one of the extracted

frames, and there is a 64.9 per cent match to the lad. Not perfect, but see for yourself.'

Jack and I move round behind him and stare at the screen. Sure enough, the still frame shows a girl pressed up against a wall who does resemble the headshot I was sent. The frame of Cormack is less obvious, though the dark ginger hair in the frame looks to be the same tone as that of the missing child poster I found online.

I move away from the screen as the enormity of the discovery sinks in. Faye and Cormack *were* at Pendark. It isn't a huge surprise about Faye, given her remains were discovered in the suitcase there, but it ties Cormack to her, and that in turn potentially ties Saltzing to Pendark. And it possibly ties them both to my sister and Freddie.

'Great, thanks, Geoff,' I hear Jack say, before joining me back at his desk. 'You look like you've seen a ghost. Are you okay?'

I'm far from okay, but I can't bring myself to answer that question, as I'm hit with a wave of emotion. I'm grateful when Jack catches me and I bury my head in his shoulder.

DCS Rawani is waiting in his office when we return and I'm surprised to find he has printed off images of Arthur Turgood and Peter Saltzing and stuck them to the notice board out of sight of the door. He is standing beside the notice board studying further printed pages in his hands.

'Good, you're back. I trust, by your faces, you found a match?'

'Not close enough to say categorically it's them,' Jack confirms, 'but close enough that it's worth pursuing.'

'How close is enough, Jack?'

'86 and 65 respectively. That's a better start than we had when we were reviewing Jemima Hooper's case.'

Rawani narrows his eyes. 'Very well, that is what you are to report back to DCI Dainton. File a report on the photographs that Miss Hunter received, but for now do not mention the picture received today. I note you've sealed it in an evidence bag, presumably because you were planning to have it forensically examined? I would urge you against such a measure, as we don't want others to know the former commissioner is under investigation.'

I can't help smiling through my fatigue at the mention of *we*.

'For now, re-investigate the disappearances of Faye McKenna and Cormack Fitzpatrick as you did with Jemima Hooper with Tomlinson always in the back of your mind, but never mentioned in public. As soon as anyone gets a sniff that we are actively pursuing the former commissioner, we will come under huge scrutiny. For the time being we need to keep those dogs at bay.'

Jack is nodding along, jotting notes as Rawani continues to suggest directions the investigation can take.

'And that brings me back to you, Miss Hunter. Are you prepared to make a formal statement to Jack about how you came to receive the pictures of Faye and Cormack, but leaving out reference to the latest photograph?' He narrows his eyes, awaiting my response.

He is asking me to lie in a statement. No, okay, it's not exactly lying, but he wants me to omit part of the truth, and now that he's asking, I don't know how I feel about that. Jack says he trusts DCS Rawani, and until this point I have had no reason to doubt his credentials. However, what happens if we're wrong about him and his offer of help is solely to take control of the investigation and bury any reference to Tomlinson? My omission would make me complicit in such an act, and that's not something I'm prepared to do.

'Miss Hunter?' Rawani presses when I haven't responded. 'I understand your reluctance and I believe you are right to have reservations. To that end, I would also like you to make a second statement in the presence of Jack and myself, where you *do* share what was received today. That way, each of us can hold a copy of that statement offline, so that if firm links to Tomlinson are discovered, it can be resurrected as required. Would you be in agreement with that approach?'

'Absolutely.' I beam, grateful that he doesn't resent my reticence.

'Good, then I suggest we do that next, and then you can be on your way, Miss Hunter. Might I also suggest you use your journalistic instinct to make discreet enquiries into Tomlinson's background? It would certainly put a protective barrier around Jack and me – like tackling the problem from opposite ends and hoping to meet somewhere in the middle.'

'Sounds like a plan,' I concur.

'And you really have no idea who is sending you these pictures?'

'None whatsoever.'

Chapter Forty

THEN

Basingstoke, Hampshire

The caravan was warm and musty as Joanna sat, head buried in her hands, awaiting the return of Precious. She'd cried all the way home until the tears had run dry, and as much as she wanted to make Grey feel guilty for his part in their separation, her eyes remained dry. He hadn't left her since they'd returned, maybe still conscious of her escape attempt last year. He needn't have worried; it was black as death outside and it had started raining when they'd arrived back, and she wasn't stupid enough to run off in such conditions. Not again. The pitter-patter on the roof confirmed it was raining hard outside now.

'You want something to drink?' Grey asked now, watching her from his seat across the small room.

She raised her head and shook it.

'Sure? I make a mean hot chocolate. You should try it.'

She shook her head again; she had no appetite for

something hot and sweet. The alcohol she'd consumed at the party hadn't settled well with the wine they'd drunk before they left and she couldn't tell if it was that or the frantic ball of worry in her gut that was making her feel so nauseous. She hadn't eaten anything since lunch, but her appetite was long gone.

Precious had warned her what would happen if they ever crossed Mr Brown, and Joanna had seen the look of pure hatred in his eyes as he'd removed his belt and closed that door. He was going to make her suffer, and it was all Joanna's fault. Had she not kicked up a fuss and gone with Bill and his bushy beard, they wouldn't be in this situation now. In fact, they would probably have finished their assignments and be on the way back with handfuls of cash each. Instead, she was trapped here with only the lascivious letch Grey for company.

She started as Grey slapped his hands on his thighs and stood. 'Well, I'm going to fix myself a drink while we wait.' He opened the fridge and peered around inside, then slammed it shut with dissatisfaction. 'What happened to that wine I bought you two? You can't have drunk it all already. Have you got any other booze in here?'

'No,' Joanna replied quietly.

Grey sighed, settling for filling the kettle from the tap and putting it on to boil. He looked so unkempt: his suit jacket hanging from the chair was creased, his shirt only half tucked in, and his tie pulled into a tight ball of a knot. He was a far cry from the man she'd met at the newsagent's eighteen months before – a lifetime ago. Precious had warned her at the party that she should consign that part of her life to the history books, and in a way she'd already started packing it away. She couldn't remember the last time she'd thought about her mum and dad. Presumably they were out there somewhere, though she couldn't be sure if they'd still be looking for her. Grey had told her that her parents had given her to them, and if that was the case they'd have no reason to look.

'Ha!' Grey exclaimed, pointing a finger in the air and moving across to his jacket on the chair with a gleeful grin. Reaching inside the jacket, he extracted a metal hip flask, unscrewing the lid and taking a swig. He lowered the canister and offered it to her, but she shook her head.

'You don't need to be scared,' he told her, moving across to the table and dropping onto the cushioned seat beside her. 'It's only a drop of scotch. I won't tell if you don't.' He pushed the flask towards her again but she pushed his hand back.

The pungent aroma caught in her throat, causing her to dry retch.

'Suit yourself,' he admonished, taking another swig for himself. 'S'pose it's not to everyone's taste. What sort of stuff do you like then? You like sweet wine, right? I'm sure Precious doesn't drink it all on her own, right?'

In any *normal* situation, asking an eleven-year-old what her favourite alcoholic beverage was would be a weird question, but not here.

'When's Precious going to be back?' she asked, deliberately fluttering her eyelashes as she did.

He looked away when she caught him looking at her. 'I told you, I don't know. All I was told was to bring you back and wait with you here until Mr Brown returned. That's what I'm doing.'

'But when will they be back?'

'How long's a piece of string?'

She considered him: the scar on his forehead that broke one

of his eyebrows in two, the scar tissue stopping the hair follicles from growing. She'd been so terrified of him that night in the woods, but that fear had diluted since she'd experienced just how terrifying Mr Brown was by comparison. What was it Precious said about him? My enemy's enemy is my friend, or something like that.

'You're scared of Mr Brown too, aren't you?' she said, reaching out and gently resting her hand on his.

His head snapped round at the comment as if he was planning to bite her head off, but instead he looked at her hand and then into her eyes. 'We could get out of here, you know.'

The lust she'd seen so many times in the photo studio was there again, constricting the veins beside his eyes and dilating the pupils. She began to withdraw her hand, realising her plan to sweet talk the information out of him had been misjudged, but he caught her fingers and gently pulled her hand towards his lips, kissing it.

'I'm not a bad man. You understand that, don't you? I'm not like Mr Brown. I care for you girls.' Lust dissipated into trepidation. 'I *care* for you, Kylie. You know that, don't you? You're special to me. The way I feel about you...' He chuckled to himself. 'I know how ridiculous it must sound, but I've never felt this way about anyone before.'

His confidence grew and he shuffled round so that he was facing her and could hold both of her hands. 'What if we left this place now? Together. You and me. I can't believe I'm even suggesting this, yet somehow I know you won't laugh in my face. I'm in love with you, Kylie. There, I've said it now and I can't take it back. I love you, Kylie! I am *in* love with you, Kylie. That's why I didn't want any of those other men to be with you tonight. That's why I've kept you from attending those bloody parties for so long. You don't have to say you love me, but I think if you got to know me – away from this place – then you'd see I'm not as bad as you might think now. I'm not the most handsome guy, but you could do a lot worse.'

Her head was spinning. She had not foreseen this turn of events.

'We could go now, somewhere they'd never find us. Somewhere we could just be alone. We could go to South America; they'd never look for us there. What do you think? Nobody would judge us there either. I know you're still developing, and I promise I won't touch you until the time is right and when *you're* ready. Please, Kylie, just say the word and we can go right now, before Mr Brown gets back. What do you say? Will you give me the chance to love you as you deserve to be loved?'

She had no intention of going anywhere with him, and she couldn't leave Precious behind to face Mr Brown's wrath alone. He would be angry if Grey took her away, and he would only have Precious to take it out on. Precious had already suffered because of her, and she wasn't prepared to repeat the mistake. She was about to tell him as much when they heard the squeaky brakes of a car pulling up outside.

Grey dropped her hands like they were diseased and hurried to the door, peering out before quietly cursing and hiding the hip flask back in his jacket and retaking his place on the chair, as if the last five minutes hadn't happened. His cheeks were flushed and his hairline bore the sheen of perspiration.

'Not a word about what we discussed,' he said in a loud whisper moments before the door opened and Mr Brown hurried in out of the torrential rain.

He pulled the door closed behind him and locked it. There was no sign of Precious. Joanna could only hope she was still in the car and would be brought in shortly.

Mr Brown saw her staring at the door and launched towards her, dragging her out from behind the table by her hair. She yelped and screamed and tried to prise his hand from her hair, but his grip was strong and his pull tight.

'You belong to me,' he said evenly, almost lifting her from the floor. 'When I tell you to go and screw a client, you *will* fucking go and screw that client. Am I clear? Do you realise how much you cost me tonight?'

Tears had found their way to her eyes once more and she continued to claw at his hand without success. 'Let go of me,' she spat. 'I won't do what you tell me. You're just a brute and a bully.'

He slapped her hard across the face with his free hand but held her tight, which kept her upright. Her cheek burned with the pain. He slapped her again in the exact same place and the anger erupted from her gut. She scratched her acrylic nails down the side of his face, drawing blood. He immediately released her hair and she toppled to the floor, breaking her fall with her hands and immediately diving away from his lunge.

'Oh, there's nothing I like more than a girl who thinks she's got a bit of fight in her. I broke that out of that black bitch and it'll be fun to break it out of you too.'

He lunged again but she shuffled her feet out of his grasp. She was now on the linoleum of the kitchen but that meant she was heading towards a dead end. But if she could just slip into the bedroom, she could barricade the door until she thought of a better means of escape. Scrambling over the floor, she'd almost made it to the next strip of carpet when she felt the warmth of his hand on her ankle, dragging her back towards his menacing sneer. It was the same look he'd worn when he'd closed the door on him and Precious earlier.

'Leave her alone,' she heard Grey say, but out of sight.

'You stay out of this,' Mr Brown barked back. 'If you kept better order around here I wouldn't need to dole out the punishments.'

Grey came into view and she saw him push a hand into Mr Brown's shoulder, causing him to release her ankle.

'Oh, you want a piece of the action, do you?' Mr Brown sneered, before a fist flew out and connected with the side of Grey's head.

Grey stumbled, crashing into the crockery and cutlery on the draining board, sending it hurtling to the hard floor, narrowly avoiding Joanna's feet as she scurried out of the way. Grey straightened himself before lunging back at Mr Brown, driving a shoulder into his gut and forcing Mr Brown to take several corrective steps backwards. Mr Brown drove an elbow into Grey's back and her knight dropped to his knees, but he wasn't beaten yet, coming back with an uppercut to Mr Brown's chin, before having his legs kicked out from him. Grey fell to his knees and Mr Brown took advantage, delivering blow after blow to his face, blood splashing across the cupboards, tiles, and floor.

Joanna didn't want to watch the two of them any longer and saw her opportunity to make it to the bedroom and barricade the door, but as she pressed her palms into the linoleum, she felt something sharp catch her skin and saw that the blade of the chopping knife had drawn blood. She stopped and looked back to where Grey's face was rapidly swelling under the force of Mr Brown's punches. Without a second's thought for her own safety, she grabbed the knife's handle, and charged towards the two of them, aiming for Mr Brown's chest. But he saw her coming and took a single step back, swivelling Grey in the process, and Joanna's momentum was too great to stop. The knife cut through Grey's crumpled and bloody shirt like it wasn't even there.

He grimaced and blood spurted from the wound as he crumpled to the floor, clutching at the area where only the handle remained visible.

Joanna stared open-mouthed at what she had done, but couldn't move to do anything to help him. Shock shut down her brain and she stood as still as a statue while the blood quickly spread over the rest of Grey's creased shirt, swallowing the stains caused by his bloody nose and lips.

'Oh, fucking brilliant!' Mr Brown shouted at her. 'Look what you've bloody well done now!'

Grey spluttered on the floor as his breaths came quickly, but they started to slow until they stopped altogether, leaving him staring ashen-faced and wide-eyed at Joanna.

She still couldn't move and made no effort to fight Mr Brown as he picked her up and carried her out through the rain, forcing her into the boot of his car. 'I should have buried you with that black bitch but I can't afford to lose any more money tonight.'

She stared at him from the rough surface of the boot liner, paralysed by fear.

'You've cost me far too much already,' he growled, 'and it's about time you started earning some money. So you're going to go away for a while, Kylie, somewhere you can't cause me any more trouble. And I know just the man who'll pay good money for a virgin like you.'

Chapter Forty-One

NOW

Weymouth, Dorset

I'm absolutely exhausted as the train door whooshes and opens and I step down onto the platform, leaving only a scattering of passengers who will continue their journey on to Devon. I don't envy them. All I want to do is get home, shower, and rest. I received a follow-up message from Rick while I was on the train, telling me he's reserved tables at the Italian, Thai, and Indian restaurants that he suggested earlier, and all I have to do is tell him which to cancel. I certainly have to give him credit for enthusiasm and perseverance.

It has been a long time since anyone showed such interest in me, aside from Maddie, but her interest is usually a show to allow her to check on how I'm progressing on my latest manuscript. After the week I've had, maybe there is more benefit to putting it all out of my head for a couple of hours. They say a change is as good as a rest and, frankly, if I sit on my tod at home, I will spend all night going over everything again.

I reread Rick's message and reply to tell him I'm in the mood for a chicken madras and a garlic naan. A bubble of excitement ripples up from my gut. If Rachel were here, she'd tell me to forget about Jack and see where things could go with Rick, and I'm prepared to accept the advice of the imaginary version of my voice of reason in lieu of the real thing. It's just gone six, so I should just about have enough time to get ready before he calls for me.

DCS Rawani and Jack were certainly thorough with the taking of my statements and printed copies of both are safely secured in the satchel on my back. The second statement will remain locked in Rawani's desk until such time as we need to use it. Jack has agreed to keep hold of the picture of Tomlinson with Turgood and Saltzburg as we all agreed it was too risky to have it tested forensically. Jack has already checked it for prints and has deduced that the envelope was pre-glued, so there would have been no reason for the sender to lick the flap. The chance of recovering DNA from the photograph or envelope is slim, and doesn't outweigh the danger of Tomlinson's face being recognised and word spreading. Rawani is right: we need to keep this off the books until we have more evidence pointing either towards or against Tomlinson's involvement. As Jack rightly claimed, the photograph could be perfectly innocent, and sent by someone trying to deflect suspicion from themselves.

The sky overhead is thick with fluffy white and light grey clouds, the beach is deserted save for the occasional jogger or dog walker, and the only sound in the air is the call of the seagulls welcoming me home. I wouldn't change it for anything! Don't get me wrong, there's nothing I love more than paddling my feet as I walk along the beach with the heat of the sun on my face, but there is something so tranquil about my town during the winter. In a world so busy and loud, this is a little piece of paradise.

I have to double-take when I see two bright suitcases – one hot pink, and the other sky blue – stacked up beside my front door.

'There she is!' Rachel exclaims, throwing her arms into the air and hurrying across the road before wrapping them around me. 'I was about to send out a search party!'

'Rach? What are you doing here? I thought you were still in Spain?'

She kisses my cheek and I can't get over the giddiness of her smile.

'We literally got back at lunchtime and I told Daniella that we have to come straight here and tell you our news.'

I spot Daniella waving nervously from the edge of the pavement, as if she's reluctant to intrude on our embrace.

'News?' I ask.

'I will tell you inside. Come on, let's go.'

Rachel links her arm through mine and drags me across the pavement, stopping only so I can greet Daniella, before she is thrusting me up the steps and to my door.

'I did give you a spare key for a reason,' I say as I open the door.

She grabs the handle of the pink case and pulls it inside. 'Yeah, I know, but that's at home and we came straight from the airport.'

I help Daniella with her suitcase and can't imagine what she is making of my humble abode. She is a model used to the glitz and glamour of five-star hotels, where champagne is on tap and dinner comes in those tiny bite-size portions. She must feel like Alice tumbling down the rabbit hole.

We park the cases in the hallway and squeeze through to the kitchen, and I immediately fill the kettle. 'Your postcard only arrived this morning,' I say, pointing to where it's stuck to the fridge door with a magnet.

She turns and looks at where I'm pointing. 'See, that's what I've been saying for years! I wrote that on about day three of our trip and I almost beat it home.' She turns back and I can see that her frustration at the poor delivery time hasn't affected her excitable mood.

'So how was the holiday? Sorry, Daniella, I know it was work for you.'

Daniella joins Rachel at the breakfast bar. 'It was really nice.' Her Italian accent is as strong as ever. 'How have you been?'

I open my mouth to offer my usual 'I'm fine,' before closing it again. 'I want to hear whatever your news is.'

Rachel's smile widens as she looks into Daniella's eyes and they clasp hands. 'Shall we tell her together?'

'No, you tell her,' Daniella replies, her cheeks darkening a fraction.

Rachel turns back to look at me and I can genuinely say I've never seen her looking so happy, and tears start to haze my vision. She takes a deep breath. 'Well… while we were away, Daniella asked me to marry her, and I said yes.'

If Daniella wasn't holding onto Rachel's hand, I dare say she would have torn round the room like a rapidly deflating balloon. She thrusts her left hand out, and I see the sparkling shimmer of the gem on her ring finger.

I throw my hands up and my mouth hangs open. There are so many words I want to share: to tell her how happy I am for her; how happy I am that she's found someone who can make her this happy; how it's the best news I've heard in a long time. The words remain in my head as they vie for attention, and instead I waddle over to the two of them and pull them both into the biggest hug I've ever given anyone. I can feel the tears blotting on my cheeks, but I don't care. I love this woman more than any other friend, and my heart is fit to burst for the two of them.

I break away and kiss them both on their cheeks, still unable to put my emotions into coherent words. 'You'll have to tell me all about the proposal,' I manage to blubber.

Rachel is tearing up too. 'I knew you'd be as excited as us.' A frown threatens to sully the atmosphere. 'Oh shoot! I meant to pick up some champagne on our way over and I forg—'

'I'll go buy some,' Daniella says forthrightly. 'You two have a lot to catch up on. Emma, is there a shop nearby?'

'There's a grocery shop on the corner, but I'm not sure if they'll do champagne. If you head into the town, there's a Tesco Express a little way along. You might have better luck there.'

They kiss and Daniella takes her leave.

'I can't believe my best friend is getting married,' I say when we're alone.

'I know, right? I always thought I'd become one of those cat-loving spinsters, but when she asked, I couldn't think of anything I wanted more. When we broke up after that row with my parents… it was a really tough time for me and I don't know if I would have got through it without you there to support me.'

'I really didn't do a lot,' I counter.

'Yes, you did, Em. You were there for me and you didn't pass judgement when I was becoming obsessed with her social media feed, and on those nights when I probably should have laid off the wine. You were there to hear me sounding off, but you allowed me to mourn the most serious relationship in my life. And then when she came back and wanted to get back together, you didn't discourage me. You've been so loyal while I've been coming to terms with my sexuality, and I'm a better person because you are in my life.' She takes another deep breath. 'Which is why I'm desperately hoping you'll agree to be my maid of honour?'

Fresh tears erupt as I nod frantically. 'Oh gosh, I'd be so honoured.'

'You'll do it?'

'In a heartbeat, Rach. It means the world to me that you asked.'

We share another hug and my heart truly feels close to bursting. This was just the news I needed today, and having my best friend back is a bonus I wasn't expecting.

'There's something else I need to tell you…' she says conspiratorially. 'Before Daniella gets back.'

'If you tell me you're also pregnant, I think my head will explode.'

She laughs awkwardly. 'No, not that.' She takes my hands in hers and fixes me with a hard stare. 'Daniella isn't the only reason I went to Barcelona.'

My brow furrows. 'I don't understand.'

She leads me to the table and makes me sit while she drags over a second chair to sit before me. 'Before we went, I was doing some digging of my own. After what happened with

Aurélie Lebrun, it got me thinking. She was abducted while on holiday in the UK and held here, but what about those British children who go missing abroad? Do they remain abroad, or are any of them trafficked back to the UK, and vice versa?' She breaks off for a minute, summoning the strength to continue. 'I heard a rumour about a British girl seen in Girona, a town about an hour north of Barcelona. My source saw a picture of Anna and claimed it was the same girl. This would have been a couple of years after her disappearance. I know I probably should have told you about it, but you've been through so much recently that I didn't want to send you down another garden path.'

The breath catches in my throat.

'So I decided I would go and do some digging on your behalf, but it didn't lead to anything. I managed to find a kind of commune which was raided by the Spanish police a few years ago, in which a number of underage children – boys and girls – were discovered. I don't know if you remember, but it was quite a coup at the time and all the children who had run away or been abducted were reunited with their families. I spoke to one of the detectives who worked on the case but he said he didn't see anyone matching Anna's description, and the lead has run cold. I'm so sorry.'

In the years since Anna disappeared, the prospect that she was sold to someone overseas has crossed my mind, but there's never been any evidence to support such a theory, and so I haven't pursued it with any gusto. I do recall the police raid in Spain that Rachel is referring to, though I didn't realise what part of Spain it occurred in. This second revelation has certainly dampened the mood.

'Please don't tell Daniella that's what I was doing; she says

I'm a workaholic and I promised her I would relax when she was working so she doesn't know I caught the bus to Girona and I'd prefer it stay that way.'

'Of course.' I nod. 'Thank you for sacrificing your pool time to look for Anna... Sorry, I don't know what else to say.'

'You don't have to say anything. I just wish it could have been better news.' She releases my hands and sits back. 'So, what's been going on with you while I've been away? Seen much of Jack?'

I'm about to tell her about my date with Rick when my phone rings and I see Pam Ratchett's name on the screen. A sense of dread claws its way across my torso.

'Hi, Pam, is everything okay?'

'Yes, Emma, I'm ringing with good news for a change. You said you wanted to be notified when your mum was next having a good day. She's just woken from her nap and she's asking for you directly. I appreciate it's short notice, but if you're close by do you think you could come up here?'

I picture Rick's face when he reads a message from me asking for a raincheck, but what choice do I have? She's my mum, and she needs me more.

Chapter Forty-Two

NOW

Weymouth, Dorset

Rick said he understands my need to see Mum, but I could hear the hurt in his voice when I phoned to explain that I needed to postpone our date. He told me not to worry and that he could easily switch the reservation to tomorrow, but it hasn't helped alleviate my guilt. Here's this guy desperate to impress me and I seemingly keep finding excuses to keep him at a distance. Maybe I'm just not the loving kind; or maybe – like Jack – I'm not ready to welcome love into my life while all this is hanging over me.

Rachel and Daniella debunked to the nearest hotel with a vacancy and I've agreed to meet up with them after my visit to the home, if time allows, or for brunch tomorrow otherwise. I do so desperately want to celebrate their engagement but I'm sure they can find plenty of other things to do without me crashing their celebration. I've never so much as been a bridesmaid, so I will have to read up on what is expected of the bride's maid of honour. They haven't set a date yet, so I have plenty of time to educate myself and it will serve as a welcome distraction from everything else.

These thoughts play in my mind as I make the journey to the home on foot once again. It's only when I see the old building and the wrought-iron gates at the top of the road that I start to feel positive about the journey. Pam was adamant that Mum is in a much better place today and I don't know how many more days like this the future has in store, so I need to grasp it with all my might.

Part of me is tempted to video the visit for posterity, but I think it would make Mum feel weird having a camera pointed at her. She was never much one for posing when I was growing up; in fact, we weren't much of a family for photographs at all. There are two albums in her room at the home, and from what I can tell she and Dad rarely took more than a couple of pictures of us as a family when we did go on holiday. After Anna's disappearance we barely left Portland, so the few photographs there are of me between ages seven and my graduation day were taken by me and my friends.

Visiting hours at the home are usually restricted to between meal times so that the nurses can maintain a routine with the residents. I'm assuming Pam's invitation so late in the afternoon is an exception to the rule. I explain why I'm there as I sign in, and the bored-looking girl behind the desk tells me Mum is eating supper in her room and is expecting me. She's less sullen than she was on Sunday and there is no sign of a sudoku book this time. I thank her and hurry along the corridor, knock twice, and open the door to Mum's room.

She is sitting at the small round table, eagerly eating sausages, mash, and gravy. She leaps up with excitement as she sees me enter and shuffles over, putting her hands on my upper arms.

'Ah, there you are, Emma. I had hoped to have finished supper before you arrived, but I still have a few mouthfuls left. Would you like a cup of tea or coffee? I can ask one of the nurses to bring you a drink.'

This is the most coherent and welcoming I've seen her in I don't know how long. Even before the specialist suggested the round-the-clock care offered by the home, I can't remember when she seemed so pleased to see me. If I could bottle a moment, this would be it.

'Tea would be lovely, Mum, thanks.'

She leans in conspiratorially and nudges me with her elbow. 'I can ask if there's any bangers and mash going spare too, if you fancy?' She adds a wink at the end.

'That's very kind,' I say with a smile, 'but just the tea will be fine.'

She ushers me to sit in the remaining chair at the table then scurries to the door, opens it, and attracts a passing nurse's attention, before returning. 'Do you mind if I finish? I'd hate for it to get cold.'

'No, please finish your dinner. I don't want to intrude.'

She picks up her knife and fork. 'Why don't you tell me what's been going on in your life while I eat? Have you got any new books due out soon? Pam was telling me you're quite the success story these days.'

I don't know how to answer that. Usually when I'm here she doesn't even recognise me, let alone recall my writing career. I try to tell her about some of the success, but it always feels like it falls on deaf ears, and I don't like to boast.

'Well, I don't know where to begin. The hardback version of

Isolated came out recently, and I was signing copies of it at the Waterstones in town on Sunday. My next book is waiting to be reviewed by my agent and then it'll be sent to my publishers, and is shelved for release before the end of the year. I'm keeping busy in between times, helping the police with cases involving missing children and we've had a couple of big successes, but I'm not allowed to share too much about all that as it's top secret.'

I could easily tell her about Faye and Cormack and Tomlinson's involvement as she'll probably forget most of it by the time she wakes in the morning, but I don't want to spoil her positive mood by bringing Anna to the forefront of her mind. I know I'm being selfish, but I don't remember a time when it was just me and Mum, without the spectre of Anna looming over us.

'My agent Maddie is confident of selling the media rights to a television company who are interested in adapting my next book into a series. That's what happened with my first book, and the company we worked with did a great job by all accounts.'

She opens her eyes wider as she chews on a slice of sausage. 'They're turning one of your books into a television series? When's that going to be on then? And will it be BBC or ITV?'

'It was released a year ago on a digital streaming channel, Mum, so you probably wouldn't get to see it in here, as I don't think they have access.'

'Oh, I see. Well, do you think you could get hold of a copy for me to watch? I'd like that.'

I blink back the sting behind my eyes. To be honest, I'm pretty sure she wouldn't enjoy the subject matter of Freddie's troubled past, but it means the world to me that she wants to watch it because of my involvement.

'Sure, I'll see if I can find it for you,' I say smiling. 'How are your sausages?'

'They're herby, which I'm not a fan of, but passable with the gravy on. The mash isn't as lumpy as I'd like. Your grandma used to make the best mashed potato. She wouldn't overmash it, and then she'd put it in the oven with lashings of butter and cheese until it formed a hardened crust. I don't think she'd have cared much for this, but beggars can't be choosers and I shouldn't turn my nose up at food cooked for me.'

A knock at the door means the tea has arrived. I collect the tray from the nurse at the door and set it down in the narrow gap on the table before pouring us both a cup from the pot. Mum finishes her meal and we stack the plate on the tray and just sit there while I tell her more about my adventures in publishing. She listens to what I have to say and asks interested questions from time to time. Before I know it, an hour has passed, her plate is collected, and two bowls of rice pudding are brought through.

'Pam said you might be hungry,' the young nurse explains as she hands them over, and I don't hesitate to tuck into it.

'There was a little girl went missing locally, wasn't there?' Mum says when she's finished her pudding. 'I read about it in the newspaper. Did they call you in to help with that?'

'Do you mean Jo-Jo Neville?' I ask with a hint of trepidation, worrying that her good day is deteriorating and she's now talking about Anna.

'That's right. They said her mother hid her away or something. Did you hear about it?'

I nod. 'I had nothing to do with her being found though.

Poor girl. I don't know how her mum could have concocted such a sinister plan for media exposure.'

'The story reminded me of… Anna. I'm certain she would have been found quickly if she'd disappeared today.'

I don't have the heart to tell her that just as many children disappear without trace in current times despite the onslaught of camera surveillance and social media. Although I didn't want to mention Anna specifically, now that she has raised it there's no hiding.

'I'm still searching for her, Mum. It's become something of an obsession for me. I won't stop looking until I do find out what happened, and where she ended up.'

'You need to move on with your life, Emma. How old are you now?'

'Twenty-eight, Mum.'

'Well, there you go. I was married and your father and I were trying to get pregnant by the time I was your age. It took longer than either of us imagined, mind you, and if you take after me, you really should start trying soon. Are you seeing anyone at the moment?'

I know she means well, and I don't want to allow her outdated viewpoint to spoil what has been my best visit to see her. 'I've got plenty of time to start a family *if* I decide that's what I want. I'm not sure what I want yet.'

'Well, I think you'd make a fantastic mum, my darling. Don't wait too long and regret not taking action. There, that's all I'm going to say on the matter. You're a grown woman, and you don't need to pay attention to a silly old fusspot like me.'

'Thank you, Mum.'

'You certainly couldn't do any worse than that woman who

hid her child and claimed foul play. What did you say her name was again?'

'Who? Tina?

'No, the daughter.

'Oh, Jo-Jo – well, short for Joanna.'

Her eyes glaze over and she looks out of her window into the darkness. 'It's funny, your sister never used to like that name either.'

I frown. 'What name, Mum?'

'Joanna. That's what we christened her with, but she hated it, which is why we always referred to her as Anna instead. Do you remember? You couldn't say Joanna when you first started to talk, because the J-sound was too difficult, so you always used to call her Anna. It just kind of stuck from there.'

She had always been Anna as far as I was concerned, and I wonder what else Mum has hidden away in those memory banks. Alas, she is yawning and time is drawing on. I don't want to force her to relive that horrific day again, not now. Hopefully we'll be blessed with at least one more day like this, but for now I just hold her close, and cherish my mum.

Chapter Forty-Three

THEN

Dover, Kent

With a deep breath, the young woman hoisted herself onto the brown wheelie bin, uncertain it would support her weight and size, and was relieved when it didn't topple over. She'd waited across the street until she saw him leave, but had waited an extra ten minutes in case he returned unexpectedly, but now that the coast was clear she was free to make her move.

The air was damp from the earlier downpour, but there was a crispness to the wind, suggesting that the bad weather would pass. The gap between the bin and the flagpole protruding from the wall looked far greater now than when she'd planned how she would enter the property from the safety of her car.

Her next move was simple: vault from the bin to the flagpole, using her momentum to swing her legs up until they reached the veranda above the bay window, and then she would scramble up to the balcony and be at the window he'd left open despite the uncertain weather. Well, the theory was simple. What it didn't allow for was the prospect that the flagpole wouldn't support her weight, that the pole itself would be slippery from the rain, and that the veranda was only made of thin slate tiles.

She didn't have time to debate the move any longer. Get in and out was what she'd promised herself when she'd finally found his home. Almost twenty years since he'd sold her overseas and left her alone to face hell on earth. It wasn't about revenge, rather… redemption. She would tear down their organisation brick by brick if necessary, and that meant starting at the top.

She slowly shuffled her feet to the edge of the bin. From here she could almost reach out and touch the flagpole, but it would take a leap of faith to make it. If she failed and missed, she would have to delay for another day, but she didn't want to run the risk that he would disappear again. She'd been so close to catching up with him in Girona, only for him to slip through her fingers. She couldn't afford such a slip-up again. Back then she'd phoned the local *federales* to hit the commune, but he must have been tipped off. That was why she hadn't dialled 999 this time. She wouldn't repeat her mistake; she would go it alone.

With a deep breath, she threw herself forwards, arms flailing in the air as her hands wrestled for the white pole. But she needn't have worried, as she felt the cool, wet metal beneath her palms, and swiftly coiled her fingers into a grip while her legs flew beneath her and cracked tiles as her soles dug into the uncertain surface. Tentatively poised between pole and veranda, she took a second breath, pushing against the pole and into a standing position, able to grip the metal frame of the balcony for support. A second tile cracked beneath her feet and it was all the motivation she needed to pull herself up the metal frame and over the top, crashing to the wooden floor with a thump and a huge sigh of relief. She remained still for a couple of seconds, composing herself, before looking back over the balcony, searching for curtain-twitchers. She was relieved when nobody in the private cul-de-sac appeared to have noticed her vault. Fate, it would seem, was on her side.

Pressing herself against the rain-covered window frame, she reached her arm through the small window, crooking her elbow and twisting until her fingers made contact with the tiny key in the handle of the main pane. Twisting, she gently eased the handle up, and prised the window open. There was no sound of movement inside, nor any alarm ringing either; it almost felt too easy, but she was in no position to question it.

Poking a foot through the window, she hopped over the frame and crouched down in the large office. A wide oak desk to the right of the window held a monitor, desktop computer, keyboard, mouse, and printer. Beside the desk stood three tall grey metal filing cabinets, and beside them a bookcase containing a variety of literary fiction, autobiographies of sportsmen, and an alphabetised encyclopaedia collection. Across the room there were framed pictures of him and presumably his wife – memories from holidays abroad and pictures of him hobnobbing with a cast of once-famous celebrities. To an untrained eye, Mr Brown's office was the picture of respectability. Of course, look a little closer at some of those framed pictures and it was easy to identify several Operation Yewtree suspects.

Bypassing the computer, she pulled on the handle of the first filing cabinet, unsurprised to find it locked. Same result with the remaining drawers on the other two cabinets. This might have fazed her once upon a time, but the internet truly was a wonderful thing. Reaching into the pocket of her jet-black jeans, she withdrew the small nail clipper, and pulled out the metal emery board. Pushing this into the lock of the first cabinet, she gently wiggled it as she'd seen in the online video, before turning and springing the lock.

Pocketing the device, she pulled open the top drawer and scanned through the dividers, reading name after name. Reaching the end of the dividers, she closed the drawer, and moved on to the next one, paying closer attention to C, until she found what she was looking for. Extracting the divider, she moved onto the next drawer, until again she found what she was looking for. Tucking the dividers under her arm, she studied the remaining drawers, uncertain what she would find, until she reached the final drawer of the third cabinet. This one was different to the rest, but it soon became clear as she withdrew a divider with a name she didn't recognise.

'Don't move,' a gravelly voice sounded over her shoulder.

She froze, sliding the third folder under her arm with the others.

'I don't know what you're doing in my house,' the voice spoke again, 'but you've made a huge mistake in coming here. On your feet now.'

She pushed the drawer closed and stood, keeping her back to him and the hood of her jacket pulled over her head. He wouldn't be stupid enough to phone the police, she was pretty sure, but that didn't mean he would just let her go. She'd anticipated this possibility, reached into the pocket of her jacket, and gripped the handle of the small blade.

'Who the hell are you anyway?' he said.

She counted to five, slowly spinning on her heel and withdrawing the knife in one motion.

He was older than she remembered. Still portly, his hair was much thinner and whiter.

'First rule of combat is never bring a knife to a gunfight,' he sneered, cocking the pistol and gesturing for her to discard the knife.

She remained resolute in her stance; she'd come too far to give in so easily.

'Come on, we both know I could shoot before you get anywhere near me with that thing. Pull down that hood. Let me get a look at you.'

She didn't move until he retrained his weapon. She doubted he'd have the courage to shoot her here in his office, not with his wife due back from her trip to the hair salon, and the mess it would entail. More likely he'd make her go outside first, though she doubted he'd have it in him to pull the trigger himself.

Slowly raising her free hand, she pulled the hood from her pixie-cut brown locks. A slight hint of recognition took over his face, as if her features were familiar but he couldn't place why or where he'd seen them before.

'I know you, don't I?' he asked, still staring into her eyes.

She didn't answer, trying to calculate if she could throw the knife before he cracked off a shot. Anything could happen, but she wasn't trained in the art of knife throwing, and she could just as easily strike the wall as the soft tissue of his neck.

'You might as well throw that thing away,' he sneered again. 'We both know you don't have the balls to actually use it. No pun intended.' He chuckled at his own lame joke.

She considered her surroundings. He was blocking the

doorway, which meant she wouldn't be able to get past him and downstairs to the front door. She'd left the window open, but he was bound to fire before she'd got within spitting distance of it. Even if she ran zigzags and threw herself through the open frame, the balcony was quite narrow, and she'd just as likely miss it and hurtle head-first down to the ground below.

She brought her gaze back to him and tightened her grip on the blade. 'I've killed with a knife before and I'm not scared to do it again.'

His expression changed as the pieces slotted into place behind his eyes. 'Kylie,' he snorted. 'I always wondered whether our paths would cross again. My, my, you've grown a lot since I last saw you. How long's it been?'

'Not long enough,' she scowled.

'And what's all this? You thought you'd kill me in revenge for what happened to you?'

'Cut off the snake's head and it can no longer cause harm.'

'Oh, and you think I'm the top of the chain? More fool you. I was merely a pawn in a much larger game.'

'You're lying.'

'Am I? Kill me then, and watch someone else take my place.'

She couldn't tell if he was bluffing, but as she thought back to that night at the party, when all those other children appeared from nowhere, was it possible she'd given him far more credit than he deserved?

'I have to admit it has crossed my mind to wonder whatever became of you. I assumed you'd have been disposed of when you'd stopped serving your purpose, but then those that choose to join the cause earn themselves a reprieve.'

She closed her eyes as the memory of those she'd helped coerce flooded her mind. So many faces, too many names to recall, and yet she could remember every single one, and she would do what she could to seek their absolution.

'Grey was another who found a way to outlast his youthful appeal. And if you think that your ending his life puts me on any kind of edge, forget about it. We both know you didn't mean to kill him. And unless I'm very much mistaken, his dying breaths probably still haunt your dreams. I can practically read it in your face. You're not going to stab me, so stop wasting time.'

She allowed the knife to drop from her fingers. What other choice did she have?

'Good girl. I'm pleased to see you've finally learned compliance.' He moved forwards, swallowing the distance between them and snatched the folders from beneath her arm. 'What exactly were you looking to achieve by taking these? Nobody cares about missing children. They're yesterday's news stories. There's far too much going on in the world. I bet you can't even remember your own family, and I doubt they remember you.'

He'd lowered his guard coming so close and she quickly thrust her hands towards the weapon, hoping to take him by surprise, but he pulled his arm away before she had a chance and used his shoulder to spin her into the desk and onto her knees. She was about to try again but he quickly retrained his sights on her temple, and the fight left her.

'Pitiful child. I never did understand why Grey became so obsessed with you. Maybe you reminded him of his own daughter. I can only assume that's why he spent so much time ogling those photographs. I warned him not to mix business with pleasure, but he couldn't see the dangers.'

He dropped the folders on the desk near her face and a small gust of air fluffed her fringe.

She looked back at him, suddenly doubting her own belief that he wouldn't kill her here. But something else had now contorted his features.

'I suppose there's only one way for me to find out what the appeal was.' He kept the gun pointed at her, and used his other hand to work his belt free, before unfastening his trousers. 'You want to live, you know what to do.'

She could see the colourful pattern of his boxer shorts poking through the zip of the trousers and her stomach turned.

'Do it, or I kill you now,' he threatened, pressing the cold barrel under her chin and pointing her face up towards him. 'It isn't like you haven't done it a hundred times before. Probably more.'

She swallowed hard and slowly moved her hands upwards, willing herself to put her fingers anywhere near his crotch.

'That's it,' he scoffed. 'Old habits die hard.'

She threw her head backwards, cracking the base of her skull on the edge of the desk but ignoring the searing pain and at the same time she grabbed the barrel of the gun and pushed it towards his body, just as his finger tensed. The explosion was deafening, so close to her right ear, and she wanted to retch as the warm liquid splashed against her cheeks and closed eyelids, but it was over in a second.

He fell backwards, writhing in pain, the gun abandoned, clutching his groin as though he might be able to keep everything attached by sheer will.

'You bitch! You fucking bitch!' he was screaming, but the cries were muffled.

Pushing herself away from him and the desk, she picked up the three folders, and backed out of the room, keeping her eyes on Mr Brown to ensure he didn't reach for the gun again, but there was no danger of that. Scooping up the blade from the carpet's edge, she zipped it back into her coat, and continued backwards out of the room and down the stairs, wiping the blood from her face with the sleeve of her jacket. Her eyes didn't leave the upstairs until she felt the handle of the front door protruding into her lower back, and only then did she turn and pull open the door.

Her exit from the property was less careful than her arrival. Tearing down the paved driveway, she darted through the gates, across the street, and into her waiting car. Dropping the folders onto the passenger seat, she started the engine and hauled out of there.

She finally stopped when she was a good five miles away, and it was while in the car park of Dover train station that her breathing finally returned to a more regular rhythm.

She could have remained at the house and waited for the police to arrive so that she could explain exactly who Mr Brown was and why she'd broken into his home, but she wasn't ready to go on the record about her own misdemeanours yet. She also could have picked up the gun and finished him off, but she liked the idea that his wife would return home and find him bleeding, and leave him to explain why.

She lifted the top folder and pulled out the picture of Faye McKenna – or Precious, as she had known her. The fire at Pendark last year was bound to uncover her remains eventually, but without help the police would be unlikely to connect her death with the man responsible. Her only hope was a gentle push in the right direction, but who could she trust?

Opening the glovebox, she extracted the book she'd found on the shelf in the library. Here was a woman writer who did seem to care about the plight of others, and if the detective skills she'd demonstrated in the book were anything to go by, she might just be able to unpick the conspiracy. If Mr Brown was right then she had more work to do if she was to find the head of the organisation.

Writing Faye's name on the photograph, she slipped it into one of the prepared brown paper envelopes she'd brought with her. Then, putting the copy of *Ransomed* back into the glove box, she exited the car in search of a post box.

THE END

Emma Hunter will return in *Repressed*...

Acknowledgments

I always find writing acknowledgements in a book challenging, because I'm always terrified that I'll end up inadvertently omitting a key collaborator, and just waffling. But here goes.

For once I'm going to start by acknowledging my personal support network whose love and support enables me to keep writing. What is any writer without the support of a loving spouse? My brilliant wife Hannah keeps all the 'behind the scenes' stuff of my life in order and our children's lives would be far duller if I was left in sole charge. They are my reason for getting up and soldiering on every day, and I want them to know how much I love them all.

I'd like to thank my parents, Ann and Nick, and parents-in-law, Marina and Robert, for all they do for us as a family. Thank you as ever to my best friend, Dr Parashar Ramanuj, who never shies away from the awkward medical questions I ask him. Thank you to Alex Shaw and Paul Grzegorzek – authors and dear friends – who are happy to listen to me moan and whinge about the pitfalls of the publishing industry, offering words of encouragement along the way.

And thanks must also go to YOU for buying and reading *Discarded*. You are my motivation for waking up ridiculously early to write every day, and why every free moment is spent devising plot twists. I feel truly honoured to call myself a writer, and it thrills me to know that other people are being entertained by the weird and wonderful visions my imagination creates. I love getting lost in my imagination and the more people who read and enjoy my stories, the more I can do it.

I want to finish by thanking every member of the One More Chapter team who've played some part in the production of this book. I'm lucky to have an editor like Bethan Morgan who 'gets' Emma and her close friends, and is always there to fine tune character voice and to point out when one strays into another. I'm always nervous when I'm waiting for Bethan's first reaction to the latest manuscript, as I'm always thinking: is this going to be the one she doesn't like? Thankfully, four books in and she's loved every one more than the last. The only question that remains is will this continue to be her response with the final two (keeping my fingers crossed).

Thanks to Lucy Bennett for her work in producing the series' covers; to Tony Russell, whose copyediting is always relatively painless; and to Lydia Mason, who kindly completed the proofread to pull out those all embarrassing spelling mistakes. Finally, no book release is complete without the fervent effort of the publicity team, so big thanks to Melanie Price and Claire Fenby for all they've done to raise awareness of the series and encourage new readers to pick up the books.

I started writing *Discarded* in June 2020, back when we'd

already survived one lockdown and were being encouraged to try and get back to some semblance of normality. I found it odd writing about characters who didn't have to socially distance, and could hug one another when the mood struck. I've been asked several times why I've made no reference to the global pandemic in my writing, and to be honest it's because I want this series to be a means of escape for readers. Who really wants to be reminded of all the sacrifice we've all endured these last eighteen months? I certainly don't, and if you're reading this years from now and the world has returned to normality, I hope you're finding your place in it.

I'd love to know what you thought about *Discarded*, and whether you spotted the twist that it was Anna who started Emma on the quest to find Faye and Cormack? I am active on Facebook, Twitter, and Instagram, so please do stop by with any messages, observations, or questions. Hearing from readers of my books truly brightens my days and encourages me to keep writing, so don't be a stranger. I promise I *will* respond to every message and comment.

Newport Community
Learning & Libraries

One More Chapter is an
award-winning global
division of HarperCollins.

Sign up to our newsletter to get our
latest eBook deals and stay up to date
with our weekly Book Club!
Subscribe here.

Meet the team at
www.onemorechapter.com

Follow us!

 @OneMoreChapter_

 @OneMoreChapter

 @onemorechapterhc

Do you write unputdownable fiction?
We love to hear from new voices.
Find out how to submit your novel at
www.onemorechapter.com/submissions